Fractures

Running On Empty

- BOOK THREE -

M. R. Field

FRACTURES
© 2016 M. R. Field
All Rights Reserved.

ISBN-10: 0-646-96139-X
ISBN-13: 978-0-646-96139-2

Edited by Lauren McKellar
          http://mcstellarediting.blogspot.com.au

Proofread by Faye Gemmellaro and Eva LeNoir

Formatted by Max Effect
          www.formaxeffect.com

WHAT SOME BLOGGERS ARE SAYING ABOUT

M R Field:

"M.R.Field creates a romantic masterpiece, and it reminds us of the chivalry that still exists somewhere."

- Komal Chandwani, The Library Whisp

M R Field is one of those rare stand out authors who writes amazing unique books that have you hooked from the first page. Grab your oxygen mask because you won't be coming up for air!

– Lisa Sleiman, The Literary Gossip

"Everything M R Field writes is eloquent and emotive. Every word she writes drags you into her world and captures your attention until you've run out of words to read, leaving you begging for more"

- Bexxy, Desperately Seeking HEA's Book Blog

Note For The Reader

This book is set in Australia and has been written using UK English and contains euphemisms and slang words that form part of the Australian spoken word, which is the basis of this book's writing style.

Please remember, that the words are not misspelled, they are slang terms and form part of the everyday, Australian lifestyle.

If you would like further explanation, or to discuss the translation or meaning of a particular word, please do not hesitate to contact the author – contact details have been provided, for your convenience, at the end of this book.

Dedication

To my beautiful nieces and nephew,

Always strive to be the best that you can be. You're pretty awesome already, so it won't take you long to get there.

I love you.
Love, Zia xxoo

One

"Know that I fought, Trinity, with every part of me, I fought."
Love, M

TRINITY
Autumn, 2007

The soft wind kisses my tear-stained cheeks as I watch in hopeless silence as the mahogany wooden coffin lowers into the deep, dark hole. The purple ribbons that lace through the steel handles catch flickers of sunlight as the funeral staff lower the coffin down slowly. With each movement, my heart beats erratically against my chest. My eyes linger on the sprigs of lavender, yellow sunflowers, and red gerberas that sit on top of the dark wood. Flowers that often filled our house with their sweet scent are now a bitter reminder of what our house will no longer be. The ribbons lower as I clutch my mother's memorial booklet to my chest, wanting to reach out and touch the casket just one last time.

My mother hated being in cramped places. My chest seizes in panic, only to release a harsh breath that thunders in my chest as the tears continue to fall. *She's so cramped in there. Is she cold? Uncomfortable?* My father stands by my side, his arms draped tightly around my shoulders as his pain-filled sobs thrash against me. His voice, tinged with agony, cries out for his wife. Lifting the booklet, I stare at the photo taken during our last family trip together. Before our world turned to shit. Her windswept hair lay across her brow, and her deep blue eyes stared back into the camera as her wide smile tore through me, fracturing my thoughts.

"Another photo?" She giggles at my father. "Don't you have enough, Felix? Take a photo of that tree or something. Now, that is beauty. Nature at its best."

"Never, Harmony," he replies. "Now, sit there and give me that smile, darl."

"It'll cost you a kiss." She laughs.

"Eww, guys. Your only child is standing right here."

"What's your point?" My dad quirks his eyebrow at me. "You do realise, you got here somehow." He winks at my mother, moving closer to her to steal a quick peck. I shake my head. Gross.

"Can't wait for you to go crazy and gooey over a guy, baby girl." She giggles, her lips barely apart from his.

"No way." I cross my arms. "Now, can you take your damn picture?"

"Yes, ma'am! That guy will have to be able to deal with her feisty attitude too." My dad raises the camera to his eyes as I raise my eyebrow at him, unimpressed. Whatever. Click.

That smile that stared back at me from the shiny booklet was all I needed on a bad day. After I struggled to get my designs to fruition, that smile made me believe I was worth something and could conquer anything. That smile brought warmth into a dark room. Now, that smile was becoming a memory. The face that remained was now descending into the cold, hard earth. The flowers are no longer visible, and I reach out into the crisp air. *She's too far away from me.*

"No," I sob, as the ribbon continues to winch her down. Breaking free of my dad's grasp, I step forward to peer over the edge of the grave. Reaching its final destination, her coffin halts against the dirt.

"She'll freeze down there," I cry. I point to the casket. "Dad, she needs her afghan. Did you put it with her, or her scented candles? The ones for her headaches …" The soft lyrics of Eva Cassidy's "What a Wonderful

World" float through the air as I struggle to stay standing. This was not a wonderful world. Far fucking from it. My mother's favourite song, taunting me with every beat of my broken heart.

My father's musky scent lingers behind me as his hands grip my shoulder.

"Baby girl." His voice cracks, as he pulls me into his chest. "She's gone."

"But, I wasn't here ..." I sob, the guilt building up in my throat. "I never got to say goodbye. Or tell her I loved her one last time. She didn't hear me while I stood near her."

"She knew," he sniffs, his arm trembling across my front.

"I was too late. I'll never forgive myself," I whisper. Around us, the congregation moves to throw petals into the grave. The pastor holds the basket out to me and I gently reach forward and take a petal, my eyes filling with tears once again. My father loosens his arm from my front and moves to grab his own. I step closer to the mouth of the grave and raise the petal to my lips. *I'm so, so sorry, Mum. I'm a selfish bitch and you deserved better.* I clench my eyes shut for a moment and plead for forgiveness before my trembling arm lifts and the petal falls from my shaky fingertips. It lands against the cold, hard wood, and the moment of finality hits me like a baton to my chest. I wheeze and clutch my side, my legs bending, unable to take my weight as I collapse against the mound of dirt, my knees scraping against it. The pain tears across my skin, but I don't care. Nothing is as painful as staring into my mother's grave. I tremble, not feeling the cold but the despair that rips at my insides.

She is gone.

I wasted her last moments.

I will never forgive myself.

I'm a fucking coward.

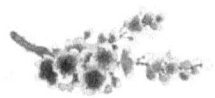

The mattress rustles beneath my thighs as I clutch the stiff cream paper. With tremulous hands, I run my finger across my endearment, "baby girl." With a deep breath, I unfold the crisp letter and begin to read.

My baby girl,

Oh, how much I would give to be sitting next to you right now. I know you're hurting, my love; I can't tell you how much it pains me, knowing that you are reading this letter. Leaving you with this breaks my heart. How does a person even begin? If I could, I'd write you a million letters, so you'd have one every day. But I can't. I barely have the strength to write this one.

Know that I fought, Trinity—with every part of me, I fought. Sadly, my life on this earth took a turn that I didn't expect. So, if my destiny is to be robbed from watching you grow and be ...

A lone tear falls onto the page and splashes, stunning me for a moment. I snap my eyes shut and tightly grasp the crinkled paper, too pained to continue reading. Shallow breaths move up and down my chest rapidly, my heart beating to the sting of each word.

I can't read this.

If I read this, it means she's *really* gone. This is all I have left.

My shoulders shudder as I cry out, my fingers curling further into the paper. I open my eyes and begin frantically folding the letter closed. Running my finger across the page, I yearn for another moment with her. A sign of warmth to ease my cold heart. *Send me a sign. Please, God, let my mother send me a sign. What the hell do I do now?*

I glance up, and my reflection in my freestanding mirror stares back at me. My blonde hair is a frazzled mess, and I'm wearing a black knee-length dress that contrasts against my pale white skin. There's a tear in my stockings from when I stumbled at the gravesite, too shaken to watch the petals falling on top of my mother's coffin. *She's in that wooden box ... alone. She's all alone ... She will suffocate ... It's cold ... She needs me. She needs her candles, anything.*

I blink as the trails of mascara stain my cheeks, while blue eyes filled with torment stare back at me. My soul feels drenched in misery, and I ache for my broken heart to break entirely, to take me with her.

I want my mum back. *Please, God. Let me be with my mum. I'll do anything.*

A soft knock behind me sounds, and I turn to find Theo standing by the door, holding his sketchpad. His green eyes stare at me as his lips press together in a grimace.

"Hey." I lick my dry, cracked lips. His shoulder pushes against the frame as he moves forward, his worried eyes running from my tear-stained face to my cut knee through my stockings. His long black hair drapes across his face, but his eyes are never hidden from me.

"Hey." His deep voice is a caress to my ears as he moves closer.

My eyes drop to my lap, to the folded letter, and I bite my lip to stop the tears that threaten to fall. Taking a deep breath, I tilt my head when his hand cups my cheek and my body leans into his touch. We were close once, and my body craves his caress to be the balm for my aching heart. I miss him.

We linger in this moment, his touch calming me yet ripping me at the same time.

"I'm so sorry, firecracker," he whispers as his thumb moves across my jaw. I sniff and nod, too determined to hold onto his touch as some means of selfish torture. *I don't deserve to be comforted today, especially after I was so mean to him.*

His hand glides to my cheek and I move with it, losing balance for a moment before I right myself on my bed's edge. Theo's broad back is turned as he walks out to the hall and into the bathroom, leaving his sketchpad by my feet. Small tinkling of the water pipes is heard as he runs the tap.

Wordlessly, he returns with a wet face-washer in his hand and lowers to the ground at my feet. He gently places the cloth against my knee, wiping the caked blood away.

"You'll need to disinfect this, but it will do for now." His eyes raise momentarily to mine. All I can do is nod.

"I didn't think you'd come today," I said, afraid of my own voice. He stops and stares back at me, his brow rising slightly.

"Why wouldn't I?"

"Because I ..." I swallow the guilt that lies at the back of my throat. "Because I ... kept her illness from you for ages."

"I don't think now is the right time to talk about that." His jaw clenches as he bundles the washcloth in his fist before turning to toss it in the wash basket. I look away quickly, running my thumbs over my letter again, my eyes too ashamed to meet his. I didn't tell him about her illness because I was jealous of his girlfriend, a fact that causes my stomach to tighten. My insides jolt in consecutive blows.

"I'm sorry." My lip trembles. "All I can tell you is that I'm sorry."

Theo bends to the side to retrieve his sketchpad before standing to turn and sit by me. We sit shoulder to shoulder, but the gulf that lies between us feels oceans apart. He rests the pad against his thighs and opens the black cover to pull out a piece of paper.

"I made you something." The sheet glides across the booklet.

My breath seizes. An image of my mother so vivid, stares back at me. I reach out and run my finger ever-so-gently along the contours of my mother's face. He has captured her sitting in her hammock with a book in her hand, smiling down at the pages. Her sunburnt orange scarf is tied around her head as if she's some Arabian princess, while her slender arm rests across her abdomen. The book is raised close to her face as her eyes stare at it in wonder. The colours, the shading, all bring this moment to life. I stare at both curves of her shoulders, the smoothness of her neck, and I gaze, transfixed, as I lose myself in the beauty of her image. The skin at the back of my neck prickles as the realness of the picture surrounds me. I can *feel* her.

"Oh my God," I whisper, tears rolling down my cheeks as I marvel at the intricate detail he's created. I glance closer and see the title across the spine of the book, *Pride and Prejudice*, and I chuckle. "When did you do this?" I ask, raising my eyes to his.

"Easter weekend. I came and visited her and couldn't help it—I just wanted to capture the moment."

Guilt tightens my heart. My eyes sting with envy. *I was supposed to come home that weekend.* But I'd been afraid to see her. I was afraid that I'd see her illness. Instead, I'd missed this. I missed her vibrancy.

"Thank you." My lips tremble. "I should've been here but I was …"

"Shush." Theo reaches around my shoulders and pulls me flush against him. "No more punishing yourself."

I clutch his shirt and sob, aching for the moments I've lost with her and grateful that he is here all the same. Even though I hid her condition from him, he still managed to find out about it and be there for her. I rub my chest against his and listen to his heart palpitating. *Maybe this is the sign.* I wonder.

Moving back slightly from Theo, I gaze into his caring face. The face of someone that I had shared a deep friendship with, one that I selfishly pushed aside out of jealousy. *Over a girlfriend. How fucking childish.* But now, we are here, together, and for a moment I want to feel again. I want to feel anything but sorrow.

I shift slightly and move closer to him, watching his eyes as my face moves nearer to his. I stare at the lips that had been my first kiss, my first love before I pushed him away, and I want to feel that moment again. To take away the hurt and make me believe that this moment is right where I should be, as screwed up as it sounds.

"Theo," I whisper.

An intense look comes over his face. I lean forward and just as our lips are about to touch, Theo jolts and moves back, knocking his sketchpad from his lap.

"We can't," he mutters, removing his eyes from me. "It wouldn't be right, today."

I shake my head, a hot blush rising rapidly across my cheeks as I stare down at the floor, too embarrassed to move. *What the fuck was I thinking? I'm a selfish bitch. Again.*

"Yeah, yeah, you're right." I bite my lip and focus on the papers and photos that fell onto the carpet. My eyes narrow down at the photo that lies on top of my foot. I reach down, grab it, and to my abject horror, see a very naked Claire, who *had* been Theo's girlfriend for two years, staring back at me. The same girl who *had* caused the rift between us, who *had* taken Theo away from me. The one who I could never live up to.

"What the fuck is this?" I screech, shaking the image in the air.

His long fingers yank the photo from my grasp. "It was taken for my life-drawing class. Claire now models in it." His cheeks stain with a red tinge, but I don't care that he's embarrassed.

"You carry naked photos of your fucking ex-girlfriend with you? On my mother's funeral day? What the fuck is wrong with you!"

"It fell out. This is my sketchpad I use at uni; we take the night course together. It wasn't supposed to be seen. I was finishing the sketch this morning."

My blood boils as I leap from the bed and glare at him. "Get the fuck out," I roar, pointing to my door. "Get the fuck out of my house, and take the bitch with you!"

"Trinity!" My father storms into my room, breaking through my rampage. "What on earth is going on?"

"I want to be left alone!" I cry, the mortification of it all suffocating me.

"Trin, it's not what you think—"

"Never again," I seethe. "You will never make me feel like this stupid jealous idiot again," I vow.

I stretch over to my bed and grab the sketch of my mother. With a furious growl, I crumple the paper in my shaking hand and tear it in half, the rage multiplying as my fingers continue to tear it into strips. I throw the strips into Theo's face and sneer. "Did I stutter? I said, get the fuck out of my room!"

He stands there, speechless, his eyes boring into mine with the same intensity as my own, the torn pieces of paper floating down between us, collecting all the shards of my shattered heart along the way.

Winter, 2012

The morning light flickers across my eyelids as my arms reach out to stretch above my head. My fingers touch an unfamiliar metal frame and freeze. That is definitely not my bed.

I open my eyes and stare at the white ceiling where the single light bulb flickers in the quiet room like an eerie art house film. *What the fuck did I do last night?*

A sharp pain in my temple shakes me, and I curse myself for drinking too much. I hold onto the metal bar while I gingerly bend my arms a fraction to turn my head and peer through the gap to my side. *I am not alone.* My stomach drops, as I taste bile at the back of my throat.

A broad back faces me, sleeping soundly. With each breath, the ink across the back of his shoulders rises and falls, with the script "makin' waves" scrawled across it. I roll my eyes and wince at the shame it causes. *Oh, him.* Underneath it, another tattoo of a surfboard moves with each breath. His messy, wavy blond hair touches the base of his neck. His thick arm lies down at his side, and as my eyes continue to adjust to the bright light in the room, the sheet has fallen down past his waistline to reveal his very naked behind. Why did I pick the surfer loser? It wasn't as though I could have fucked some intelligence into him.

Nothing. I feel nothing. I can't even remember his name.

The cool air brushes across my naked skin as I sit up slowly to try and stop him from waking. I drape my legs over the side of the mattress and scan the floor for any signs of my clothes. A red stiletto lays beside the bed. As I lean forward and grab it, I see my underwear under the bed's frame. Abandoning my shoe for a moment, I pick up my underwear and quickly wiggle the panties up my legs. *Now that the business is covered, I can concentrate.*

I stand gradually and shuffle across the carpet, noticing no ache between my legs. *So last night was uneventful.*

My clothing lies scattered across the bedroom floor. Being the stealthy ninja I am, I find my dress and bra in quick succession. I thread my arms through the loops of the red lace and stop. The side strap is torn away from the back strap, leaving a large hole. *Arsehole!* This was one of my best bras!

Pinning the back hooks together, and ignoring the chill of regret that prickles against the skin at my back, I slip my feet though the neck of my dress and pull it up my torso, shimmying into the smooth fabric. I had made this dress quickly, and at the time was delighted that it had turned out well. The black satin holds a slight ruby shimmer that catches under the flickering light. Last night, I had felt empowered and sexy. Now, in the cold, harsh light of day, I feel like a cheap imitation of a whore.

My thick jacket lies on the floor by my feet and I quickly put it on, buttoning over the remains of last night. I bend down and collect my abandoned clutch in one hand, quickly checking its contents, and then thread the loops of my stilettos with the other. Looking over my shoulder one more time, I check that the sleeping giant is still passed out. His chest heaves evenly in soft snores as I begin tiptoeing out, mindful not to step on any objects that litter the floor. It is like a fucking sex-toy landmine. There is shit everywhere.

Running on the tips of my toes out his bedroom door, I race towards my freedom only to be stopped short. *Where the freaking hell am I?* Looking around the room, my lip curls, and I flick my labret in annoyance at the state of the kitchen. The white bench tops no longer look *white*. Almost every dish that could have lived in the cupboards seems to wreak germ-infestations in a dirty stupor. I wrinkle my nose as the pungent smell of God-knows-what suddenly hits me. *And I let that festering slob touch me. One bath of bleach, coming right up.*

Despite the mess and the need to swallow my bile, the microwave grabs my attention as it sits to the side. Lo and behold, a few opened letters sit scattered across the counter top. I spot my mystery man's address and retreat back to the front door, unlocking it and slipping out quietly. The bitter chill bites against my cheekbones as my shivering fingers clasp around the phone in my clutch. Looking down at it, I count my lucky stars that I still have some battery left. I quickly dial and order a taxi.

As the minutes tick by, the moments from last night begin to replay in my mind like a bitter and dirty B-grade film. *Dancing, laughing and twirling in the arms of the giant as I continue to drink.* Another way to chase away the loneliness of my heart. With my warehouse recently open, I had been celebrating solo. *My mother would be so sad about what I was doing to myself right now.* I am going to have a launch party in the next few months, but right now the old familiar ache I feel for not having my mother resurfaces. *Again.*

The ride in the taxi only compounds the ache. Paying the driver quickly, I hustle up my front walkway and jam the key into the lock. I push through the doors with the steadily growing need to get to the back of the shop. Punching the security code into the panel, I race through the stacked boxes and mannequins that line the wooden floor. The open space of the showroom begins to suffocate me as I continue to duck and weave through the obstacles.

Reaching the back office, my clutch lands on top of my messy desk, and I ignore the contents that roll out from it and onto the floor. My feet continue to propel me forward until I am face to face with the gleaming, pale green metal case of my mother's sewing machine. Unfastening the metal clasps, I slowly place it by my feet, stand straight, and stare at it. My eager fingers brush across the cold metal, and my accelerated heart begins to slow its pace.

The sharp intake of my breaths eases as I continue to run my fingers along the top of the machine, remembering, *remembering.* The long strokes soothe the ache as I focus on the *now* in order to survive. Like a flamed arrow, grief punctures all that it passes. It nips. It tears. It bleeds. I want to be rid of this ache I feel. I want to feel something else. To remember without the pain crippling me. But the guilt tethers itself, reminding me what I have done. What I failed to do.

My eyes lower to the side of the table, where a misshapen pincushion that has seen better days faces me. The weathered edges of the faded red cupcake, now lopsided, momentarily distract me. I straighten it, only for it to topple over like it always does. *"See?"* he says, *"This sewing caper isn't too bad. I can make you cupcakes!"*

"Looks more like a tomato," I reply, delighted when his brows rise in shock.

"No way, Firecracker! It's perfect."

"Stick to drawing or playing the piano. Leave 'this sewing caper' to me."

I squeeze the ball and the sharp pierce of a needle stings my thumb, drawing me back to reality. I suck my thumb gently as my thoughts continue to swirl and the green eyes of my best friend appear in my mind. The man I've lost my way from, and am probably never going to find my way back to.

Two

The panel shows a dark cloud looming. No cover is nearby. "He will always find me."
TTE

THEO
Present day

I push open the heavy wooden doors, and the sharp smell of burnt wood assaults my nostrils. I have an appointment at The Emerald Vixen with the owner, my friend Robbie, who hired me to help restore it after a fire caused significant damage a few months ago. Jerry, that psychotic bastard.

The creak of the hinges sound as I shove the door wider, the gleam of the mirrors across the far wall reflecting against the smooth surfaces of the floor.

The establishment is separated into two sections—the club itself, and to the side where I now stand, a studio that Robbie's sister, Trice, uses for rehearsals with the rest of the girls, or for her own personal dance classes.

As I step farther into Trice's dance studio, the pristine room gives an illusion that all is perfect, unlike the burnt wreckage that lies in the adjacent room. Each step I take in Robbie's club plunges the stench of smoke into my senses, and I clutch my fists in anger. If the smell weren't so pungent, you would never know that my high school friend and her baby almost died in that room.

The door to the club opens and Robbie walks in, his phone against his ear. He sees me and waves with his free hand, walking closer. The door shuts behind him with a loud thud, secluding us away from what I imagine is pretty heavy damage.

"No, babe, it's fine." He shakes his head as he gets closer. "Just text me what you want for dinner and I'll get it ... Of course I don't mind. Gotta keep my *farfalla* happy."

I tuck the satchel under my arm and busy myself looking at my reflection in the dance mirrors. My hair is ruffled by my helmet, so I run my fingers through it, but since it's short, it doesn't make much of a difference. Spikey weird guy it is.

"Hey." Robbie moves in front of me, his phone tucked away as his hand is now outstretched towards me. "Thanks for coming."

We shake hands, and his grip is firm but friendly.

"No problem." I tilt my chin to the room. "Doesn't look like there's any damage in here."

Robbie's brow furrows as he looks around. "Yeah, the bastard was good enough to spare this," he jokes sardonically, turning to walk to the door to take us back towards the club.

"How you going with it all?" I follow.

"It's pretty fucked, but the sooner this shit is sorted, the sooner we can begin forgetting that fucker." He grips the handle before turning to look over his shoulder at me. "Hazel still wakes screaming sometimes, clutching her stomach." He breathes out deeply, "You know how many times I've had to show her Gian in his cot so she can settle?" Robbie's head shakes, his mouth tightening. "Just erase him."

My pulse quickens in sympathetic rage. I wish I could make that prick disappear into air.

Just a few months ago, Hazel's psychotic ex decided to douse petrol around her legs after tying her and her mother to chairs, with every intent to end their lives. Poor Hazel sat terrified, her son still in her womb, alarmingly *too* still as her burning contractions tore through her. I will never forget Robbie's face as he recounted the hell that she went through. She thought their baby had died and had to sit there watching the petrol drip onto her legs.

I suck back a breath to calm my raging thoughts as I follow Robbie through the door. The scent of the burnt floorboards smashes into my face like a blunt plank of wood. My eyes sting as the reek of destruction fills me with absolute fury. I designed this place when Robbie first moved back from the mines. I fucking spent hours with Robbie making his dream come true, and some jerk decided that a match and some fuel could take it all away.

"It's fucked, isn't it?" Robbie's boot kicks against the burnt floorboards. "He didn't get the whole room, but he burnt out the heart of it."

My eyes travel to the side where the burnt-out stage stands, dishevelled. The back walls behind the stage still have traces from the licks of the flames. I step closer, my shoes scraping against the debris, taking in the stage itself, which is a complete disaster. Luckily the piano wasn't there, but still, only a fool would think its salvation could bring any relief. Walking closer, I see the floor itself has been cleared, but a stream of blue and white police tape that originally surrounded the stage hangs loosely across the stairs.

I roll my shirt up to my elbows, my tattooed forearms contrasting against the stark white shirt. The plus side of working out of the office for certain jobs is that I can loosen up a little. Now, looking around the room, I need a little bit of tension released, so I don't make a special trip to jail and hunt down the prick responsible.

I'd imagined that I'd see the burnt furniture and tossed parts of tables and chairs everywhere. But I don't. Instead, I see an empty room that held a dream, smothered in ash.

I am going to restore The Emerald Vixen to what it was. I am going to erase that fucker alright. When Hazel returns, her memories will only be from before that incident. I hope.

I run my eyes along the darkened surfaces; it's all a blunt reminder of what could have been lost.

Robbie stands facing the stage with his arms crossed in front of his chest, staring at the ruins and the floor itself, the broken scorched floorboards.

"I worked my arse off for this," he mutters. "I wanted it perfect for her. It was all part of my plan to woo her. Get her to finally give a schmuck like me a chance." His arm releases as he gestures to the side of the stage. "She was tied there." His mouth tightens. "That rope was so tight across her belly, I thought he was trying to saw through our child."

"Oh man." I frown, shaking my head. "I can't even imagine going through that."

"It was hell," he growls. "He was planning on lighting it up like Satan's playground, too. I finally got my girl, but he was a second away from taking her away from me."

"Bloody hell," I mutter, gripping the sketchpad in my hand. "Let's erase this prick."

"Make it like it was, but add in a few new things if you want." He turns to face me. "Do what you can to make my *farfalla* sleep well tonight."

I nod and flick open the cover of the pad to find scribbles of my latest comic that I was going to work on properly later this evening. I'm almost tempted to add the bastard in the next panel I draw, having him pushed off a cliff into the fiery pits of hell. Instead, I refuse to immortalise the motherfucker. I'll erase that bastard alright.

With renewed determination, I flick to a new page and begin to sketch a basic outline to make this cabaret even better. I'll have this club so perfect that he will not be worthy of a presence here. He'll be vapour. Robbie's dream is about to be resurrected and fuck, am I going to enjoy bringing it back to him. This dream is worth it.

For the past few months, I've been chasing after my dream. A dream that has claws. A dream that holds silent tears. A dream that melts under my fingertips and against my binds.

Trinity. The only woman I can love and hate in one breath. Who caught my attention from the moment I met her.

"Your eyes are green! I'm Trinity. Not Tricia."

All I can do is smile. Her vibrancy knocks the wind out of me. "Theo."

*"Nice to meet you. If this class sucks, there's a fire escape over there."
She tilts her head towards the corner of the room. "I heard the canteen
has Mars Bars."*

With her, I wasn't expected to always be my best, unlike what my
father expected.

For years, Trinity and I had been caught in a power-play—one
moment we were best friends, the next enemies, too immature to act
rationally, and too stubborn to relent. Since our teenage years, she was
the core of my happiness. Being close to her was enough. As a teenager,
I lived in an emotional cage that stemmed from my father's upbringing,
imprisoned by my own insecurity or naïve stupidity. Dating my best
friend was a dream I wanted but could never have. I'd already lost so
much, and the thought of losing her as well ... it was not something I
could risk. We'd shared a moment once, but it was more frightening
than the destruction that had been going on in my home life at the time.
Our friendship was everything.

Now, as adults, twisted by the need to be near each other but too
willful to admit it, we are caught in a web of fear and denial. Sure, it
might seem easy to date, but neither of us has the courage to broach
that subject. If we make it real, it is just as easy to lose it all. Instead, it's
easier to hide behind the smokescreen and under the sheets.

Our connection simmers between us. We cling to and thrive on the
seductive torture. For years, we've been caught up in an evocative
dance, our friendship being the common thread that holds us together.
Our emotions are too volatile. A side look, a slight touch of the hand—all
minor gestures that have led up to the moment we are now in. A
complete clusterfuck.

I watched her for years, throwing herself at guy after guy while I sat
on the sidelines. I needed to let her be her; I needed her to break free
from the wall she kept up to hide from me. When you've spent ten years
in verbal foreplay, slowly getting closer and closer to each other, it is
only a matter of time before you walk away or you jump. When that

moment struck again a few months ago, there was no way I was going to let her try to ignore it.

The war that we had been raging eclipsed once we touched. When I finally won her body over, I knew it would consume me. It is only a matter of time before my firecracker unleashes her final blow and decimates me. I am going to have a lot of fun with her before she tries to do that. All is fair in sex and war. Game. On.

For the past few months, she has been the addiction that roars through my veins. We've chosen not to speak while we let our bodies do the talking in a constant lusty haze. Our emotions are still soaring, but that wall remains. My constant need to wear her down, to get her to admit her feelings for me, is waning. But the smell of her, the taste of her, is something that I can't let go of. She is my emancipation.

I turn around the room and focus on the parts that need renovating. Scribbling furiously, I want every idea that gathers to imprint permanently. Robbie looks at the page and smiles faintly before leaving me to sketch a little more, while I continue to stand. I have too much burning energy to try and find a seat. The original concept for his bar, The Emerald Vixen, got me on my boss's radar, and I want to stay there. Being a recent graduate, I am still learning the ropes, but I am dedicated and disciplined. Growing up in a household ruled under an iron fist left little room for straying. Or putting in a lacklustre effort.

But my future has still been tainted by the strict musings of my father. The compulsion to be perfect in my industry runs through me like a hungry lion. Nothing is ever represented half done. The lines and etchings of the sketches are exactly how I want them. No room to fall short. I had been disciplined to be that way. Even after stepping out of my childhood home all those years ago, Ko's teachings are still embedded in my everyday facet of being an architect. Except my tattoos. If anything, the colour I had tattooed was my true way of rebelling from him. His shame was my redemption. To push this depth onto my skin so that nothing of myself is hidden like it had been when I was a child. My skin is my soul's canvas.

My phone buzzes in my pocket. I close my sketchpad while moving my other hand to retrieve it. In some uncanny coincidence, my father's name blinks up at me. The black cloud that never seems to leave. Even though he is my burden, as I look around the burnt bar I think at least he would never try to have me killed or ruin my life, like Hazel's mother and ex-lover had. Nope. At least I could be grateful for that.

My thumb hovers over the screen until I press *end*—again. What had my mother seen in him? I barely remember her, yet her betrayal untethers me to him. The dead can't speak. I'm sure, though, if my mother had her chance, she would tell me to answer the missed calls left by him. That his recent persistence is one of concern. But I have nothing to say to the man who I have barely spoken to for ten years. If I could ask her one question, it would be to hopefully shed some light on what the fuck I am supposed to do about him now, without hitting the *answer* button.

I look up and see Robbie staring back at me.

"You look like you could use a drink." He gestures to the back of the room.

"Or ten." I tuck the notepad under my arm. "But since I'm due back at the office soon, I'll take that drink on opening night."

"Deal." Robbie winks, and I try to ignore the weight in my pocket from my father's phone call.

Click.

Click-click.

Click.

I stiffen in my seat next to my fellow workmates, flattening my feet to the ground as I stare across the oak table at my boss, Cole. He leans back in his reclining chair, rocking slightly as he thumbs the pen poised in hand. *Click-click.* With one knee bent across his other leg, he reclines farther as he circles the pen in the air in front of him while looking at the brief laid out. I'm surprised the orange fluorescent ankle strap he wears to protect his trousers while he rides to work isn't fastened around his leg.

My fingers tighten around the fine liner pen that rests on top of my notepad. A sketch of an angry figurehead is in the corner, lurking inside a black panel I drew, now competing for thought space in my mind. Maybe I should add my boss in my next addition—one where that pen explodes once it's pressed. *Kaboom!* Where did he explode? Over there! New scene.

But I never draw pantomimes. Far from it. More like art imitating life.

Most of what he's talked about quickly turns to vapour as the incessant clicking resumes. *New client with a mega-dollar project. Eager to begin. World-renowned reputation.* The incessant clicking continues, and my jaw clenches as each sound reminds me too abrasively of the regimented childhood I experienced. *"Each note will be practised to perfection, Theo." My father's thick Japanese accent fills the silent room, as he watches the placement of my hands along the keys. "Perfection is paramount." The hands of the grandfather clock that stands by the piano tick away each gruelling moment. "You cannot succeed without perfection."*

I clear my throat to dispel the memories from lingering further. *Click. Click.* That fucking pen. *What is it with my father being in my head today?*

The desire to ram that pen down Cole's throat is short-lived, as his bent leg finally drops to the floor and he leans forward to press his feeble marker against the paper.

"Our new clients have heard great things about us. Seems they took a liking to our recent subdivision project along the Docklands."

This isn't new news to me. Ever since the launch of the sky-rises, our company has been jacked up with new projects. Seems our new apartments are a significant advancement over the dreary-looking flats that face the Yarra. Our boss is still living in the midst of that success. "Now, these investors have approached us in the hopes of revamping the old area by the gardens. Many potential firms fought tooth and nail to get these guys. The fact that they ignored them and came directly to us just goes to show that the quality of our projects is second to none. The call-out by investors has been a great endorsement of our designs. We didn't win them over for nothing, lads. We have a great pedigree of talent right here, gentlemen."

A faint yawn is heard next to me and I turn my face slightly to Letty, our secretary, who looks bored while her long fingernails tap on her keyboard. No doubt she is probably secretly messaging her sister in Toronto while listening to the usual bragging. Most days Cole seems to forget that she is the only woman in the room. *Again.*

Letty and I make eye contact as her gaze then flicks over to Cole for a moment in disapproval, her lips pressing together. She looks down at my sketch of a black cloud looming and raises her eyebrow at me. She is one of the few who know about my drawing. I nod in recognition of our boss's brush over her before a sharp tap on the table catches my attention. I turn my head back to find Cole staring back at us. Letty continues to type on her tablet, her fingers tapping quickly, no doubt recounting being glared at. Cole raises his eyebrow for a moment as his eyes move from Letty to me before he breaks eye contact and juts his chin out towards the papers in front of him.

Reaching for the leaflet, I focus on the sheet in my hand without looking back at Cole. Taking note of the client's name in the top corner, I freeze in my seat. Macaro. Fuck, these guys are loaded. Opportunists. They were the ones who bought half of the northern suburbs and now are coming back to the central business district. Ruthless businessmen with their eyes on the prize. Who could blame them? They were all about new infrastructures, shopping centres, and businesses popping up left, right, and centre.

I stare at the shelves behind Cole and focus briefly on the folders where most of the previous designs are stored. Fresh new designs that are striking to the consumers. Dynamic and bold. I want in on that project. I could revamp those gardens and make them mine.

"Steve, Brad, and Nige, I need you to read over the request, and we'll meet here in an hour to begin planning."

I freeze. *What?*

Cole stands, quickly adjusts his suit jacket and grabs his pen and unread folio from the desk. "Theo."

I stare back at him in confusion.

"Follow me. Grab your jacket—we're going to grab a coffee."

Oh shit. I turn sharply, quickly double-checking that my shirtsleeves are rolled down to cover my tatted arms before grabbing the jacket that I had draped on the chair earlier. As I weave my arms quickly through the sleeves, my gut clenches. I don't have a good feeling about this.

Tucking the chair under the table, I turn to find the other guys at their individual desks, already planning their next project. Nige looks up at me and nods before bending his head back down to his desk. Lucky bastard.

"Leticia," Cole calls over his shoulder to summon Letty. She rises from her seat and glares back at him.

"It's Letty—you should know that by now," she responds through gritted teeth. My tension unfurls as I bite into my cheek to stop from smiling at Cole stumbling over her name again. *No clue, man.*

Cole tucks the pen into his top pocket as he points to his office in the far corner, ignoring her. "Hold any calls until we come back."

He turns, walking towards the door. Letty presses her lips together, and I shrug in disbelief. *One day she's going to stick her boot up his arse.*

His hard footsteps thud across the carpeted floors as we make our way to the elevators. I move my hands to my pockets to hide the clenching of my fists. Not being put on that team isn't good.

As we walk briskly down the hallway, my mind automatically narrows to our last group project. Stills of the designs begin to flick in succession through my mind as I check and recheck the sketches I made. Was my design too vague? Not edgy enough? Am I too rigid?

We reach the elevator and I stare down at my shoes, momentarily dreading not being more "carefree" with my work approach. Maybe I need to involve myself in the Friday beer raffle or something. Or maybe, just maybe let myself go like I do in TTE. *I wonder what my boss would think of his employee living an alternative life?*

As the steel doors open, we step in quietly, and all the while I stare at the room lights above. "Be sure to remind me to get the quote from Leticia on the Nico project sorted when we get back to the office."

"Sure."

The elevator pings and we step out into the foyer, Cole walking briskly towards the front doors. He tilts his head towards the café across the street and I follow him quickly, eager to get this over with. Gesturing to the empty chair out front, I take a seat while he sits opposite me. I sit still as a waitress takes our order, wondering when the guillotine will drop.

"So, Theo." Cole reaches into his jacket and retrieves his phone. He glances down at the screen while swiping his finger across it. "I know we could have had this chat in my office, but a coffee was calling me." He chuckles, seemingly oblivious to my discomfort. "Right, so, you've been with our firm for almost two years. You came to us as a fresh-faced lad on work placement who was keen to get started."

I swallow and nod, trying to control my nerves.

"You haven't stopped since we hired you permanently, either," he continues.

I remain sitting in limbo as the waitress arrives with our coffees, but I'm too wired to reach out for mine. Cole takes a moment to sip his coffee before slowly replacing the cup. I focus my attention on the watch that appears from his cuff as he sits for a moment, turning his phone in a circle with his other hand on the table top.

The seconds continue to tick by until Cole clears his throat. He taps the screen on his phone to illuminate a picture of a large, dark room. Pointing to it, he finally continues, "Take a look at these pictures I was sent by a client."

I reach forward and grab the phone, focusing on the unknown building shown on the screen. For a moment it reminds me of Trinity's warehouse but unfurnished and bare.

"Looks like a warehouse," I add stupidly.

"It sure is, but the client is hoping that it will be much more."

I nod, still confused as to where this is going. I feel my hands tighten, so I reach for my coffee to keep my stiff fingers occupied and controlled. Taking a sip, I stare at the image and flick to the next, trying to make out the location better. It has tall dark walls with high windows and a staircase in the left corner leading up to a second level. It looks like many pre-existing warehouses that are around North Melbourne.

"Well, our client recently purchased this site to build another of his award-winning restaurants, but this time with a different motive—to revamp the vibe a bit." Reaching out, Cole swipes the screen to the next image of the building's front, where an old heavily graffitied garage door and a worn front door do little to solve what Cole is going on about. "What would you do with this front, Theo? How would you make customers want to enter the front doors and dine here?"

I frown at the image for a moment and respond. "Rip out the doors and run three rows of square-edged double-glazed windows above them." Pointing from one edge of the image to the other side, I add, "They'd run from here to here. Underneath, where the doors are, I'd replace them with three double-thick oak-edged doors with large windows." Moving closer, I circle my finger around the front and continue, "You could easily open them all up for entertaining if need be, or just enjoy the natural light streaming through."

I glance up to find Cole smiling at me while he drinks from his cup. I place his phone back onto the table and sit back.

"Great answer." He reaches out for his phone and taps on the screen a few more times. "I can see why he wanted you for this."

I stiffen in my seat as I lean forward in confusion. "I'm sorry, what do you mean?"

"Well, Theo, I know my company hasn't been established as long as others, however, we've managed to secure a solid reputation. Having said that, I've been speaking to a new client who not only believes that his business will be in the right hands with us, but he's also specifically asked for *you* to be the head designer on this project."

"What?" My mouth falls open in disbelief. "You sure?"

"Absolutely. He is incredibly keen to make a start. He expressed an admiration for the minor projects that you've run so far, and thought you were the eyes needed to revamp this."

"What ideas has he had to transform this place?" My heart races as the excitement begins to build. It's not a high-rise building, but a restaurant that can garner a hot reputation can also get more clients.

"A restaurant, similar to what existed in the area years ago, but bigger and with a stage and a salsa dance floor. He wants to get in touch with his Spanish roots. Seems he's been here most of his life and is feeling nostalgic. He wants a lively atmosphere."

Too easy. I designed a cabaret establishment; this will be just as invigorating.

"Looks like I'm getting into a niche market for club designing," I chuckle.

"Indeed," Cole responds, tucking his phone away and reaching into his pocket. "Leticia will email further details but in the meantime"—he pulls a business card out of his pocket—"here are his details. He is eager to begin discussions and from your initial thought just then, I think you'll get along just fine."

I smile and nod, reaching for the card. "Thanks so mu—" I begin, but freeze mid-sentence. The name that stares back at me is the same name that changed my life ten years ago. The name that erupted my identity and made me forge a new existence. *Ricardo Arce—Entrepreneur and Award-Winning Restaurant Owner.*

Ricardo Arce from Arce's Enterprises, the ruthless businessman who stopped at nothing until he achieved success and all the accolades. Even if that included seducing my mother while she was happily married, leaving my father to bear the brunt of the betrayal while Ricardo never even tried to get to know me. It was all to protect his reputation. Why else would he wait sixteen years to approach my father and finally meet me, his bastard son?

Now, this arsehole wants to work with me. My jaw clenches as I press my thumb into the card.

"Everything okay?" Cole asks, staring at my thumb.

"Yep, sure. I'll get onto it right away."

He nods and stands. I shove the card into my pocket and grind my teeth together. *What the fuck is he trying to do?*

I shake my head and rise, following Cole back to the office. My shoulders stiffen as the thought of the email that no doubt is waiting for me creates a brick of lead so heavy on my chest that I want to pass out.

As we enter the quiet office, I make my way to my desk, my feet dragging across the carpeted floor in resistance. I have no choice. I'm about to work with my *real* father.

There I was thinking I was getting a demotion or fired. In some ways, I wish that were the case.

Three

"When you choose to live by a dream, know that one day you'll wake up. Be prepared for that."
Love, M

TRINITY

"**Hey little ninja,**" Trice whispers, as she bends forward to kiss the forehead of her sleeping nephew in Hazel's arms. Gian has been home from the hospital almost one week and has settled in really well. According to Hazel, he is still a sleeping possum, but we know that isn't going to last much longer. After the fire at the club, which caused Hazel to go into labour almost a month early, we were given the biggest fright of our lives. Luckily, though, our little man came out roaring to begin life, and that shitty moment hasn't been mentioned since—and that worries me. Our gal is holding out on Trice and I, and it needs to stop.

Hazel shifts in her armchair, adjusting the pillow that sits under her elbow. Her eyes never leave Gian as he continues to sleep peacefully in her arms.

"Do you want me to take him, hon?" I offer, stretching out my arms. "Aunt Trin is happy for a cuddle If you'd like to go nap or something."

Haze glances up at me and smiles. "No, thanks sweets. I'm enjoying watching my little man. I don't think I'm ready to let go just yet. Even

Robbie has to wrestle me for him." She clears her throat, and although she means to be playful, I know she is anything but. Her tight smile is a clue to that. After knowing Hazel for more than ten years, I know that smile is bullshit. That fire scared the living fuck out of her, and it still affects her just as it affects all of us.

"Haze, if you want to talk about it ..." I start, but her shoulders stiffen.

"No." Her voice cuts through the air like a blade. "I don't want to give that arsehole any further mention. He almost killed Gian and me. He destroyed Robbie's business. He and my mother can go burn for all I care."

"Okay." I hold my hands up in surrender. "But know that when you're ready, I have a punching bag in my warehouse that you're welcome to. I can probably source a couple of voodoo dolls, too. Just say the word, and we can make him a eunuch."

Trice snickers next to me as the tension releases from Hazel's shoulders.

"Thank you, Trin." Haze's voice drops to a soft whisper. "I know I need to talk about it, but right now, what's in my arms is the only thing keeping me from losing my mind about that day." A lone tear cascades down her face, and I bend down to the floor by her knees.

"He's pretty special." I reach out and place my hand against his shoulder. "I am sensing that he's going to have all of us wrapped around his little finger once he starts moving around."

"Definitely," Trice adds, grabbing her phone to take a photo. She turns and faces the screen towards her to take an awkward selfie of the three of us.

"Oh!" I giggle. "She's capturing a moment. Smile biatches." I rise slowly to avoid waking Gian and move to the couch next to Hazel's chair.

"So, whose arse am I going to put in lace and silk now that the group is on hold? You girls were my saving grace from the bridezillas." For months I have designed some kick-arse outfits for both Haze and Trice for their Emerald Vixen cabaret group as a side project. It has spurred my creativity, and I love the naughty edge to it. Don't get me wrong—

my designs are pretty fucking epic for my bridal range, and even my formal gowns are to die for. But it is worth stepping out and doing something a little quirkier once in a while.

I enjoy being busy, but my spare time was often spent with Theo. The non-boyfriend. I could perhaps put him into some lace outfit to fill the void from the group, but I doubt he'd let me try. After all, we spent a lot of time tearing clothes off rather than putting them back on. Hence, the power of the vagina.

"Well, at least Alex won't threaten to cover me up in overalls or something." Trice rolls her eyes as she sits next to me. "Can't get over how protective he was. How did Robbie not lose his mind at you, Haze?"

"I think he just liked the idea that at the end of the night I was all his and that he could show me how much he liked the costume. Boy," she breathes, "he knew how to show me."

Trice scrunches her nose and visibly shudders. "Do not ask me why I wanted to know that about my brother."

"Yeah, well, you won't have to worry about wearing your soundproof headphones. That won't be happening for a while. Unless they block out Gian." Haze frowns as she strokes his face gently. "I really hope he isn't keeping you guys awake. We can't really control it."

Trice moves across me to touch Hazel's arm. "Never, honey. Even if he screamed the house down, I'd happily take him to cuddle to sleep. Know that, okay? It's us who might get under your feet. We don't want to disrupt the little *famiglia*."

"I love having you guys with us." Haze's lip trembles.

Trice straightens, but not before I move closer to Haze. "Hey, what's going on? Are you okay?" I ask.

Hazel sniffs as she draws Gian tighter to her for a moment. "I'm fine. Just a little overwhelmed. At the hospital we had so many nurses around us, and coming home almost feels like a big test. I know I have you gals, but I'm scared I'll fail. Look at where I've come from—the biggest dysfunctional family. My poor son is barely a month old and already I'm worried I'm screwing up somehow."

Just as I am about to reach for her, the front door opens, and heavy footsteps sound across the polished floorboards.

"Hey, how's my *Farfalla* and little man doin'...?" Robbie's boisterous voice halts as he freezes in the doorway to the lounge. He stares intently at Hazel. "Babe, what's wrong?" His voice instantly softens.

"I'm just being emotional." She bends her head, trying to hide the tears that stream down her face.

Robbie walks quickly to the front of the lounge and drops to her knees. "Now, tell me what's wrong, so I can make it go away." His voice is like a warm caress, and I watch Hazel's bottom lip tremble.

"I'm just worried that I'm going to screw up," she sobs, her eyes filling with tears. "I keep thinking my family has ruined me."

Robbie places his hand onto her knee and leans closer to her. "Those fuckwits didn't know perfection while it was staring in their faces. They didn't know the beauty that they created. The kindness and caring nature of the most captivating woman I've ever met was wasted on them." His knees shift to the floor so he can rise closer to Hazel's face. "But I know what they've missed. I see the beauty and the love you show Gian. They will never take that from you. In less than a month, you have shown yourself to be a better parent than those fuckwits ever were."

"You're the best parent too, *Tesoro*." She sniffs.

"Only because I have you to guide me." He pushes off the ground to kiss Haze on the forehead. "They're fuckwits." He sighs. "They had no fucking idea."

"*Tesoro*." She giggles. "You can't swear in front of Gian."

Robbie leans back and raises one eyebrow at her. A little smirk appears across his lips. "He's heard worse, but I'll tone it down."

"Love you." She smiles up at him.

"Love you, *Farfalla*."

The way they look at each other chips a little at the ice around my heart.

"Okay guys, I'm happy being a zia and all, but the feels here are making me think you're about to make another baby." Trice squirms next to me, her mouth in a fake grimace as her eyes twinkle with mischief.

"Well, Alex will be home soon," Robbie throws back at her. "Maybe you should make Gian a playmate."

Trice rolls her eyes and pokes me in the ribs. "I think there's more chance that Trin will do that before us. Kids freak Alex out."

I tap the couch end next to me and rise abruptly out of my chair. "On that note, my ovaries thank you for your pimping, but sadly my endometriosis is declining that move." My uterus is on protest, and only surgery is going to help give me a chance to become a mum—if I ever want to be. Funny how the one thing a woman's body is meant to be able to do, mine has decided it will play Russian Roulette with in a combat warzone. *I'm surprised they are still intact after the cramps they gave me earlier this month.* Plus, the surgery that I am going to have in a few months is going to give me the big clean-out. Not looking forward to that.

Gesturing to the door, I step away from the couch. "I'm going to go see how many grey hairs appear through my blue hair after my bridezilla appointment."

"Is your arm different?" Robbie asks, staring at my latest tattoo.

"Sure is." I paste a grin on my face, pointing to my forearm. I trace my fingers from the cherry blossoms under it until I circle the purple edging of the mandala that sits above them. "It's a symbol for creativity and harmony." I feel the vibe change slightly in the room, but I power on. *No pity today.*

"It's beautiful." Trice rises up from the couch and walks over to me and touches it. "It almost makes me want to get another tatt done."

"Yeah, I haven't had a chance to go sky-diving lately, so this can be my kick." It is common knowledge that I like my thrills, but a certain someone is taking up my time.

Turning towards Hazel, I kiss my fingertips and gently touch Gian's cheek. "See you, little cutie. You keep growing up so fast."

"Give him six months and he'll be taller than you, pixie," Robbie laughs. I glare at him before giving him the bird, while mouthing, *"fuck you."* Blowing a kiss to the girls, I turn and give an exaggerated wave as I stroll towards the door.

"Hey Trin," Robbie calls out to me. I look over my shoulder to see him massaging Haze's shoulders. "Thanks for looking after my girl, here with Trice."

"No probs. She was my girl first, buddy. You remember that. You know how us country gals like to roll. Yeehah." I wink and walk to the front door, the giggling of my friends following me out.

Watching Robbie with Hazel made my heart clench in a good way. Someday, I want that. I want a guy to stare at me like I am his everything and have nothing stand in our way. No ugly past. A baby? I ache for the possibility. But after my recent check-up, it's clear that my ovaries have other ideas, leaving my chances slim to none.

I shrug as I step out into the street. I am used to heartache. This will be something else I'll have to learn to hide. I am the master of disguise, after all.

Four

The panel shows the man staring, facing away from the black cloud.
"You will not rule me," he snarls.
"I already do," The cloud responds.
TTE

THEO

My white-knuckled thumb presses against my index finger as I stare at my laptop. The bright glow from the screen stings my eyes as the sole email that I've left unchecked for a week stares back at me. I bet that prick has activated his read receipt on it.

Cole had asked me earlier today if a meeting had finally been set up for the restaurant, as my excuses of, "Mr. Arce has been busy," were starting to look suspicious. Submitting the designs back to Robbie for his club didn't take too long, so now I am trying to look busy. People still bug me.

With a sigh, I let my fingers drift over the touchpad. Here goes nothing. With a single tap, the email opens in front of me.

Theo,

I would like to arrange a meeting to discuss our newest project with you. Please email me directly to organise a time. Our company is eager to work with you. I look forward to hearing from you soon.

Ricardo

Of course he would want to meet up with me. After all, he's already requested I be the sole person he works with. My finger clicks on the reply button before I can tear apart his email further.

Mr. Arce,

Cole notified me about your interest in our company. Due to the magnitude of your project, may I suggest one of our senior partners to assist you in developing your restaurant? You will find their knowledge and experience superior to mine. May I also suggest you contact Cole with an alternative?

Regards,

Theo Eien

I smile as I hit send and lean back to stretch in my desk chair. Two of the guys in my office chose to sit on physio balls to be more ergonomic, but I needed the stability. It was also satisfying to rub it in occasionally how easy it was for me to move around on my seat, while they were working on their abs—abs that seemed no different than six months ago, due to their pie addictions.

My smile is abruptly halted as the sharp ping of an email notification sounds. Leaning forward, I hastily press the mute button to avoid accidentally interrupting my workers again, considering we are often emailed dozens of times a day.

Ricardo Arce flashes in the address heading. What CEO has time to reply so swiftly to emails? Why isn't his secretary filtering them?

Clicking on the tab, his short email appears.

Theo,

This is non-negotiable. Your efforts in recent projects have caught our eye. Either I work directly with you, or we take our business elsewhere. I would hate for Cole to lose such a profitable venture over a minor misunderstanding. It would be very disappointing to tarnish the reputation of the company that he works tirelessly to uphold.

Our meeting will be scheduled for Friday. I will CC Cole on an additional email so he is aware of our movements. See to it that you will be there. I look forward to working with you.

Ricardo

My blood simmers below the surface. Schooling my features so as not to raise concern, I lift my hand and slowly close my laptop. No negating my skills—this was just another ploy to speak to me. It took him sixteen years to give a shit, and after he rocked the only world I knew, I ignored him. All I knew after my father had admitted about this jerk was that he took advantage of my mother. Then, surprise! Me. To say that it fucked with my head was an understatement. Now, ten years later, he is back to rupture what stability I recreated. Not a chance. I already had a father, and he was shit. I didn't need another one. Real or not.

Looking at the wall clock, I see it reads close to five o'clock. I reach below my desk for my rucksack and helmet, and I stand.

The nature of our occupation means that time spent at a desk is flexible. So despite never before leaving or wasting work time, I try not to let any guilt set in. I need to hop on my Ducati and feel the wind whip by.

Waving a quick goodbye to my colleagues, I make my way to the unisex bathroom to change into my leathers and get out on the road. A quick ride is what I need, and while the traffic is going to be a nightmare, I am determined not to let that add to the bullshit that swirls in my mind.

Tightening my thighs against the seat, I whirl down the narrow city streets, dodging the busy areas, gripping the throttle, eager to distance myself from my desk. The vibrations of my bike thunder beneath me, my body naturally veering me towards the quiet, familiar café in North Melbourne. A new wave of determination takes hold, and I'm eager to unleash some of this tension as I ride there.

Parking my bike, I switch the engine off before flinging my leg over my seat onto the curb. Unfastening my helmet and hooking it under my arm, I run my fingers through my hair to smooth it out.

The busy chatter of patrons fills the small café as I stroll inside. Light polished floorboards and sky blue walls with framed travel pics work to ease the manic of the heavily wanted waiters as they shuffle past the tables. This café may be small, but it is never dull.

I scan the room quickly and find Elly behind the bar, loading coffee cups above the coffee machine. Our eyes meet as I head towards her, and a big smile spreads across her face.

"Hey!" She grins as the cups clink against each other. "What brings you to this neck of the woods? I thought we were meeting on Wednesday?"

I perch on a wooden stool and gesture to the cup in her hand. "Fill that. Make it strong, with one sugar."

She flicks her wrist to spin the cup in her hands, catching it easily. "On it." She fills the portal-filter and shoves it up into the machine, fastening it. Pressing a button, she rests her hand on the bench as a smile deepens on her face. "We are more similar than you think."

She clicks her tongue to the roof of her mouth to turn back to the coffee. Grabbing the milk jug from the fridge underneath, she eases it under the nozzle. The steam of the machine whistles as she froths the milk while using her other hand to tap the cup lightly against the bench. Pouring the milk into my cup, she sits it in front of me.

"Thanks." I smile as I take a sip. A good coffee and a ride is exactly what I needed.

"So, judging from the clock up there, you either have a client in the area or you're ditching work."

I place the cup down and turn it between my hands. "I need you to get Ricardo off my back," I huff as I clutch my cup. "He's now trying to get me to work with him."

"Would it be so bad?" she asks, her eyes shooting to the side and back. "Maybe, it's what you both need."

"Nope. What for? Too little, too late."

"If you didn't find him, you would have never met me, Theo. He only wants to get to know you."

"I know that. But I don't understand after twenty-six years, why now?"

"Because you're my son," a heavily Spanish-accented voice mutters as I stiffen in my seat.

"Nice to see the CEO of his own company out for a leisurely stroll," I add sarcastically, swirling the contents of my coffee around in my cup.

"Por favor. This is the only way that I could get close to you, Theo. By setting up these meetings. The only way."

I turn my eyes towards the man who never existed until I was sixteen. "Has it ever occurred to you that maybe it's not what I want? You want to get close to me?" I point to my chest. "No, thanks. I already have a father, and he was pretty crap." Picking up my cup, I sling back the last of my hot coffee before returning it to the table top. "See you, Elly. Catch you next Friday. I know you make the best coffee in town, but everything tastes bitter when he's around."

I rise from my seat and adjust my jacket to keep my hands busy. While walking past the man who had abandoned my mother whilst she was pregnant, I can't help but say, "I guess I'll see you next Tuesday for our appointment. Mr. Arce."

"I'll create another hundred restaurants if it means working with you, Theo. I will do it." His thick accent is unwavering, but I ignore his plea.

"Better get my passport renewed then," I grumble. "A secluded island far from here is looking pretty damn good." My jaw tightens as I pick up speed and march out the door.

"Twenty-six years," I mutter to no one and myself. "A bit too fucking late."

My mother raised me in a loveless marriage until she died, leaving me abandoned with a heartless man who I'd thought was my father. I spent forever never being good enough, and now this jerk wants a part of my life. How long will that last? Until his next fancy project? What the hell would anyone want with me? I'm nobody.

My hands twitch as I move them to my side. I need to feel. My skin seems tight as I fumble with my helmet, slamming it onto my head. I need the one person who makes me feel something. Like I matter. I barely sense the vibrations from the bike as I zoom the short distance to her warehouse. I need her, *now*. I fucking hope she's ready.

Five

"A girl can never have too many pairs of heels. Make sure at least one pair is pointy as you never know what you'll want to use them for."
Love, M

TRINITY

I rinse my coffee cup in my office sink and wish for the hundredth time that I had put a shot of scotch in it. *This bitch better be normal today. Please, for the love of all that is holy, make her be normal, or I'm gonna—*

"Hello? HELLO?" Virginia's ear-piercing shriek sounds from out front.

I place my cup gently on the bench top, trying desperately not to chuck it into the sink. It is, after all, my Wonder Woman one, complete with a cape, and if this bitch makes me crack it, I'm not gonna be happy.

"Coming," I call out, my voice laced with fake energy. I flick my hair up in a messy bun and jam a pen in it for later. Pushing the loose strands behind my ears, I wish for a moment that they were Medusa's serpents so I could sick them on her. I reapply my lip gloss and check my eyeliner. Turning sharply, I push my shoulders back and start thinking of ten bald men to calm me down before walking out into the showroom.

I stop abruptly as my nostrils threaten to explode. A wave of nauseating perfume hits me in the face and I stand stunned, wondering what superpower she has to project her perfume across a warehouse floor and into my freaking nostrils. My hand rises to my face and I try, really try, not to swipe the perfume away, but I can't. My hand starts to fan as I crave clear and unpolluted shitty-perfume-free air.

I make my way over to Virginia, who has taken to the mannequins that I have on display on the other side of the room. Her bridesmaids, Leah, Sky, and Eloise, stand by her, admiring my designs.

This month's designs are under the theme of "Desire is Futile." I've used my black mannequins to contrast with the red and purple dresses that they're wearing. I used a red nylon chiffon for a mini skirt that has ribbon lines down it. With French-cut red hot-pants underneath, the focus automatically goes to the sexy behind. I've sewn a tight triangle lace bra that is both sexy and cute, but, being my cheeky self, I strapped a thick chunky red belt around the neck.

The other mannequins wear tight-fitting purple satin pants with purple lace bras to match the other mannequin. This time around, I used silver suspenders that match the silver back pocket edges that I made across the back. Normally I have more designs, but lately my inspirations haven't been so forthcoming.

"Ladies," I greet as I reach them.

Eloise turns and gives me a cheeky grin as she tilts her head towards the red mannequin. "Should I be calling you *mistress*?"

I throw my head back and laugh. "Not today. That's only on Friday and Sundays." I wiggle my eyebrows at her. *She isn't too far from the truth.*

"Right, so like, have you got something to show me today?" Virginia snips, making Queen Bitch eyes to Eloise before flipping her hair over her shoulder. *Ugh.*

"Yes, Ginny, I certainly do!" I smile as she flinches at my nickname for her. I try most times to call her something different from her name, and the temptation to call her Vagina is always at the front of my mind. But, I'm not that cruel ... well not today, anyway. I step to the side and gesture for them to walk to the other part of the warehouse, where I've already moved the bride's dress to the dressing room.

The girls begin to walk over, but not before I can have some more fun. "I hope you took the time to shave, hon, as it would be super awkward if your jungle legs were on display while we dressed you."

Virginia's shoulders stiffen mid stride, but surprisingly, she keeps on walking. Hmm. For the past six months, it's been a love/hate relationship between us. As in, she tries to give me horrible ideas that I change constantly. It is a wonder she hasn't tried to request to have angel hair weaved through her veil—she is that demanding.

Anyone who knows me knows that I do not stand for any shit. If need be, I tell her to shut her mouth when she is being a super bitch to her bridesmaids, and I make sure that she is going to look amazing on her big day. I am proud of my designs and don't need some stuck-up bitch to be rude and spiteful to her girls or me. I don't need to prove myself. Even if I do give Madam Vag the shits, she is going to look fabulous while I do it.

I draw the dressing-room curtain back and point to the chairs to the side of the waiting area that I organised earlier. I gesture for the girls to take a seat while Virginia and I step into the room. She stands for a moment with her handbag, and I roll my eyes, pointing to the stool in the corner. "Put it there, princess. It won't run away."

She huffs and stomps towards the chair, hesitating before placing her bag there like it was a porcelain doll.

"I'm half expecting you to give it a pat or something," I mumble as I begin to lower the mock-up from the hanger.

I've sewn together a muslin mock-up. Due to the nature of the low-cut front, I've used strips to link the front together so her "girls" aren't on show for us. Only a third of the hand-beaded overlay is completed; the pieces are kept in my workroom, but Miss Fussy Pants has kept a close eye on the intricate detail I've interwoven through the satin. Which I'm sure she'll ask to see again, today.

I hold the dress open for her to step into, turning my head slowly so she is a little hidden from my view. Once she has stepped into it, I move the fabric up her body and hold it for a moment with one hand while I bring the back straps up to fasten securely with the pre-existing pins across each shoulder. The final design will have an open back with lace and beaded overlay at the sides, but for now she has the main material. I pin the base at her spine, folding the material to bring it closer to her waistline.

"Now, remember, this isn't as glamorous as your real dress. This is to see the seams and adjust where we need to. Got it?"

"Yes, fine," she barks. "Just hurry up; I can feel pins in my side."

I'm half tempted to make a few more prick her, but I draw the curtain open and lift the back to help her shuffle out of the dressing room instead. We move over the step that she'll perch on while the girls are sitting near, which she steps on too quickly. As she faces the wide gold-trimmed mirrors, I release the hem to allow it to fall gracefully at the back.

I glance in the mirror. The grimace that lines Virginia's lips hightlights her irritation as she squints at the fabric. I move to adjust her left side, but movement from her right catches me off-guard. Her right knee shifts back and forth under the fabric, a nervous twitch I've noticed in our private discussions about her ideas. It is usually a warning that she is about to explode.

"Honey." I soften my voice to gather her attention. "I want you to stand very still for me. I need to make a few adjustments."

Her eyes widen as she nods in silence.

I move to the stool nearby to gather a couple of pins and put them through my belt. I'd love to have a pin-cushion holder attached to it, but I know I'd bend or something and get pricked a zillion times at once. I quickly bring in the edging along the side of her skirt, drawing the material in at her waist, pinning it securely. Stepping to the front, I grab a few more pins from my belt and then blow on my hands quickly before using my fingertips to adjust the front V of her dress. Releasing one side of the strip, I pin the loosened side and then unpin the strip completely, pleased with the result. *The girls are still safe.* I continue adjusting and pinning the fabric until I'm happy with the outcome.

Stepping back, I wait for her to explode, ready to try to pacify her.

Her eyes are wide as she stares up and down the gown. From the front, thin straps begin at the shoulders and then thicken gradually in a semi-Grecian look as they plunge into a V between her breasts. The muslin rests tightly against her narrow hips until it flows down in an A-line skirt.

"Remember, along here"—I point to her stomach—"and here"—I move my hand down her body—"we have those sections to add with the beading and ruffled edge strips."

"It's so fucking plain," she whines. "It looks shit."

I take a deep breath before repeating myself. "We still have to add the extras to your dress. It will not be plain. If anything, you'll be a Grecian sex bomb. Just trust me."

"How can I trust this?" She swipes her hand at the skirt. "I can't see what the hell you're trying to do."

That's because you're a vapid bitch who needs me to draw it in fucking crayons for you to see.

"Virginia, you need to use your imagination." Leah leans forward in her seat, her eyebrows drawing together.

Skye rises from her seat and stands in front of Virginia. "You're going to look amazing. Just wait until you see this in the material." She scans her phone, then brings it up to Virginia's face. "Remember the beading? It's going to look fantastic. Like, totally hot." She lowers the phone for me to glimpse a photo I had sent to Virginia of the beaded section.

"Well, I'm sure those will cover this shit." Virginia flicks the material again and shrieks. "Ouch! A pin got me."

Hello, Karma. Thanks for stopping by.

"Well, that's what you get for being mean to the material." I can't help but smile. "Let's get you out of this so I can make a start on the 'non-shit' part, hey?" I tap her arm and gesture for her to follow me to the dressing room, not helping with the back of her dress. *Fuck her. She can handle that by herself.*

She stomps to the dressing room, and I take pride in watching the grimace that lines her face as a few pins poke her. *That's what you get for rushing and not being careful.*

Afterwards, as the girls gather at the door to leave, Eloise steps closer to me and squeezes my hand.

"Don't let her get to you," she whispers. "We're on the home stretch. Five months to go."

"Yeah, thank fuck for that," I murmur.

"Let's do coffee sometime," she adds. "I like your style."

"You know where I work. Happy to."

They make their way out, farewelling me, while Virginia reaches into her bag to grab her sunglasses. Pushing them onto her face, her lip curls as she turns towards the street, ignoring me.

"See you later, Virganina!" I can't help but call out. So much for not calling her the V word.

Strolling back towards my office, I raise my arms to stretch the tension out of my shoulders. Moving them as if I'm climbing an imaginary ladder, I move my hips in sync, enjoying the fluidity in my joints.

The front door to the warehouse suddenly slams, causing me to jump, my hands landing on my chest. I turn quickly to see Theo strolling over to me, a hard look on his face. His broad shoulders move with determination as his fisted hands hang by his sides. His nostrils flare as he gets closer to me, his deep green eyes watching me intently.

"Hey." I wave. "What's up? Looks like someone pissed in your cornflakes."

"Back room," he seethes. "No talking. I want you on your desk. Take off your skirt."

"Um, hello to you," I say sarcastically, as I put my hand on my hip. "What has gotten into you?"

He walks until he is a step away from my face. Grabbing my hips, he moves me into his hard body. Even with my wedges, I'm not even up to his shoulder.

His breathing deepens as he moves his lips an inch away from mine. "I said ..." His hard voice stills me. "Get to your desk and take your skirt off. I want to eat you. Now."

My pulse quickens as a deep throb pulses between my thighs,

causing me to rub them together.

His eyes drop to my thighs and his face softens slightly. A wicked smile appears across his lips. "My firecracker wants that."

He brushes his lips against my cheek. I have a feeling he's about to make me want it badly.

Six

"The panel shows the man, staring at her from a distance. Wanting. Waiting. Imprisoned by the pain of never being seen."
TTE

THEO

Get **her to the back room.**
Get her there now.
My pulse quickens as I curve the base of my palms into her hips to start moving her backwards to her office. She stumbles slightly as her hands grip my upper arms.

The rage that fills my veins continues to flow through me. Wayward thoughts of my encounter with Ricardo's pass through my mind. "Because you're my son ... get close to you ... I'll create another hundred restaurants if it means working with you, Theo. I will do it ... the only way." I continue to move us as his voice tries to trespass into this moment. I need her. I need her to stop my brain.

"I presume you locked the door after you tried to slam it off its hinges?" Her husky voice tears through and centres me.

I stare down at her, watching her every move as I lead her along the polished floorboards, moving stealthily in a seductive sway. *Fuck. Everything she does is sexy. Even walking backwards.*

"Of course I did." I squeeze her hips to move her faster. "Though I wouldn't care if anyone walked in."

Her breath hitches as I glance right into her blue eyes, a faint blush appearing across her cheeks. *Yes, she remembers that night too.*

Her footsteps pick up momentum, and she sidesteps her front counter and shuffles into the back room. The crisp *swish* of fabric passes our feet as we stumble farther into the colourful space. Mannequins with half-pinned get-ups and countertops with measuring tapes, sketchbooks, and pencils surround us. Her talent is etched across every surface. I could have taken her upstairs to her room, but my parched tongue craves her taste to burn through me. To settle me. To prove that not all my life is shit.

Her lower back halts against her main drawing desk, causing a wisp of air to curl under it and flick a sketch up like a wave until it sails to the other side and onto the floor.

"Hey!" Trin grumbles. "That's my latest sketch. You better pick that up."

"Later," I growl, moving my lips closer to her face. "I'm busy." And with that, I grip her hips tighter to hoist her onto the desk. She squeals, her eyes lighting up with excitement. Her hands move quickly up my forearms, but I release my own grip to catch her fingers before they move any higher. "Hands on the desk. Now. If you move them I will stop."

A cheeky smile appears across her red glossy lips. "Um, it's not like you're doing anything at the moment, so I thought I'd take the reins a bit. You know, get to the good stuff. Seeing as you like to head there usually."

A chuckle abruptly passes my lips, releasing the tension in my shoulders. As my muscles marginally relax, my anger changes into fevered desire. I want to tear each wisp of clothing off her and tie her to this fucking desk. *I'll know next time to bring my satin ribbon.*

"Hands. Desk. Right now."

She raises her hands by her sides, a foot above the desk and smiles at me, casting me a wink as she moves her palms slowly to the sides of the mahogany surface. I lower to my knees, shifting her legs onto my thighs.

Without breaking eye contact, my fingers crawl up the pleats of her skirt until I find the edge of her boy-leg underwear. My fingertips curl into the waistband, moving it slowly down her thighs. I grin as her hips rise off the desk, her Black Widow underwear shimmying down her legs. Her teeth bite deeper into her lip, and I struggle not to stand and replace those teeth with my own. She shifts a little to allow the smooth fabric to glide off her feet.

"Good, honey." I lean closer to whisper my lips against the edge of her pussy, a mere breath away from tasting paradise. "Hold on tight."

My lips touch the edge of her pussy. Her chest rises with every touch of my mouth. Her lips pucker, desperate for a kiss. But I stay down. Her eyes narrow at me in frustration. We haven't kissed since we were sixteen. *Our kisses are for another day. One day.*

I shake my head at her, grip her knees firmly, and open her legs wide. Sinking between her legs, I watch her. I watch her chest rise in anticipation. I watch her bite her lower lip. I watch her frustrated eyes darken with want. *I could watch her all day.*

I stare at her in silence, watching her chest continue to rise and fall rapidly, and I linger in her sultry wave of desire. If I lean closer, I will smell what I do to her. I will see what my touches and looks make her feel.

In this instant, her need for me is real. Her need for me is the palpable link that ties us together. Like a thread, it is only a matter of time before it snaps. The resulting carnage would be irreparable, our time together so fractured that none of my actions or pleading would draw her to me again. But I'd rather suffer through a thousand moments of watching her than never having her at all.

I turn from her gaze and move closer, abruptly flicking up the skirt onto her narrow hips. My breath sharpens as her arousal reaches me. My finger glides down her, relishing in the feel of her smooth, soft skin. *I have barely touched her, and now I'm calmer.* I trace her lips, up and down, quickly discovering her edges, feeling her desire coat my restless fingers. I need to taste her.

Leaning forward, I look up from her swollen cunt to her darkened eyes and wait for her to make the next move. I know she wants me, but that tiny nod, the movement showing she is barely holding on while her fingers dig into the impenetrable surface of the desk, spurs me on. Our eyes hold as her tongue moves under her teeth to trace her swollen lip. I raise one eyebrow and smirk, waiting for her command. With a deep breath she pants, "Yes," and I burn for her. *My girl has been patient, so the reward now will be sweeter.*

I smile before I take my first lick into Eden. I groan as her taste coats my tongue, calming my senses. *This. This is what stills the anger that soars through my veins.* I continue to feast on her, moving my hands to grip her hips closer to me, increasing each lick to get her nearer to coating my tongue. My lips narrow down on her swollen clit, and I suck it sharply as her pussy quivers against my feverish mouth. Her breaths quicken as I feel the tell-tale sounds of her approaching orgasm. My fingers move in under my mouth, pushing into her in a steady rhythm against my hungry tongue. Her walls tighten against me as her head tilts back, and the desk creaks under her grip, gasping into the open air. I lick her slowly through her release, clutching her thigh to my cheek as I take in that last tremor.

"Fuck," she gasps, her back falling to the bench top. Her legs shake against my face, so I lean back to hold both sides of her legs with my arms. I watch her for a moment, her chest rising and her arm thrown over her face in tired ecstasy. I could stand and crawl along this desktop and lie beside her—but we don't do that. My chest tightens. We will never do that. Unless I can break her down. I need to. We have the destructive force that could tear us apart. But within the wreckage lies beauty for reformation and rebirth. For a new us.

She sits up slowly, her top hanging over her shoulder, revealing the red cherry blossoms underneath. Her skin is a tapestry of art—how she lives her life, like her workroom that is filled with vibrant materials. All around us is a whirlwind of colour, and I gaze at her body, wanting to see the colour that covers her skin blending into mine.

"So, you gonna tell me why I'm gonna have fingerprints in my hips?" *Fuck. I must've done that on the way in, while dragging her to the back.*

My hands slide to her hip, lifting her off her desk to stand in front of me. She flinches in my grip. "And on my arse?"

My jaw clenches for a moment. I want to tell her, but I can't. I've spent so long with my thoughts, it's hard to share them. It's hard to share that my identity is a lie. I've spent so many years hiding that my disguise has moulded into my skin. It's a part of me. From the moment I wake, it consumes me.

I look at my hands and see faint smudges of black lead. Miraculously, I've left no stains across her pale and red skin. Only traces of my fingertips bruising across her body remain.

"I can still taste you; don't sour that for me," I mutter, rising from my seat. Her tussled hair falls to the side of her face, causing me to lose my breath for a moment. There's not a day that goes past when her beauty doesn't stun me.

I bend down, retrieve the sketch that fell, and hand it to her.

She stares at me, studying my face. The sketch is quickly thrown onto the table before her eyes return to mine. She tilts her head to the side and stands with her hand on her hip. "You looked like hell when you stormed in here. What's up with that?"

"Nothing. Maybe I just want to fuck."

She flinches as her eyes narrow at me. "Well, we aren't 'fucking.' " Her fingers gesture as she steps closer to me. "Are you okay?"

"I'm fine." I breathe out slowly. Now that arsehole has me taking this out on her.

"Theo ..." Her voice lowers.

I sigh and shake my head, weaving my fingers into the back of my hair. "I wouldn't know where to start, and I don't want to talk about it. Can we drop it? Please?"

Why does my life always do this to me? I'm exhausted, and it's only early afternoon. Without wanting to, my sister's voice drifts back into my mind ...

"He only wants to get to know you."

A small hand flicks in front of me.

"Earth to Theo."

I blink as the blue tips of Trinity's hair shuffle in front of me. "Sorry." I shake my head. "Got a lot on my mind."

"Theo, the offer still stands ... if you ..."

I untuck my hands from my hair and grab her small face. "Please." My voice lowers as her face fits perfectly in my grasp. "I can't go there; there's just so much bullshit that I don't know where to begin." Reluctantly, I release her face and point to the sketch on the table. "Looks like that sketch is unfinished. I'll leave you to it."

She blinks up at me and nods. Silence is her response. I run my tongue along the inside of my cheek in frustration at my past, stopping myself before I open my soul to the memories that I've long held at bay. I tuck my hands into my suit pockets and walk out of her warehouse, back into the afternoon sun.

So much for coming here to clear my mind. Now it's running on maximum capacity. My past was catching up with me.

Seven

"Being an adult will send challenges your way. Best to have a heady supply of chocolate to see you through them."
Love, M

TRINITY

"**W**hat are you making, Mum?" *I sit eagerly on the stool by the kitchen bench, watching my mother stir a double boiler pot on the stove.*

"Some lavender melts." She wipes her hand on her apron while her spare hand stirs, then turns to look over at me. Smiling, she winks at me. "They're great for stress."

"Are you stressed, Mum?" I shift on my seat, eager to watch her.

"No, baby girl. But you are. You haven't learnt to let go yet. Now, wake up and get a move on and get right onto that."

A soft breeze tickles my cheek as my dream fades away. I open my eyes slowly to find myself in my bedroom with the unlit lavender candle sitting on my bedside table. I sniff, wanting to embrace its scent, hoping that my dream can return.

Disappointment shrouds me as the sincerity of the moment in my dream unravels like a worn-out thread. Seven years ago we lost her, and still I can't seem to let her go. How old is too old to be missing your mum? For Dad, being alone in that big house with those memories would have to be akin to torture. I run a hand across my mandala and take a deep breath, release, and tell myself to get on with my day. Maybe I need to get Trice to start up her Saturday morning yoga sessions again, or just use it as an excuse to wear yoga pants.

I kick off the sheets and decide that even though it's the end of the week, I'm not going to end it being a Debbie Downer. Fuck that. Once again, I'm awake at the crack of dawn. I need a juice and to get to *Vagina's* wedding dress.

I stroll across to my chest of drawers and get a pair of comfy tailored cargos and a funky black top with a red lightning bolt down the middle. Grabbing my underwear and bra, I make my way to my bathroom, eager to get all soaped up. I know that being at work, I should dress more business-like; however, I like being a bit funky.

I lathered up the long strands and wondered for the zillionth time how I had let my hair grow so long. It was down to my bra strap; it hadn't been that way since I was a kid. When it was shorter, I could work a funky colour into the ends for a retro look, but now I just played with bright colours. It took too long to get the funk back into it. If I could call electric blue normal. Still, maybe I was up for a change. Out with the old and in with the new.

At least I knew that there were some personal adjustments I needed to make, starting with having a firm discussion with my vagina over missing Theo. I was sick of going to sleep and almost reaching for my phone. We were friends who chatted regularly, but after last week's Tongue of Destiny encounter, he had gone incognito. All that was left were the bruises that had faded gradually from my skin.

Every time a motorbike zoomed past outside, my heart raced. Ain't that just the shit. So much for no-strings sex. Well, I'd thought it was no strings. Did we even have that conversation all those months ago? Seems that my vagina made up its own mind. It wants more. But it isn't just that; I want to hang out more like we used to. I'm drawn to him, and I wish I could stop it.

I rinse and get out of the shower, dressing quickly and applying some thick eyeliner. It isn't until nine that I open my doors, but I can make a start of the wedding dress or at least have a few drawings up for potential future clients. As I walk across the landing towards the kitchen, my footsteps thud across the floorboards. I run my fingers along the banister and, before I can stop myself, Theo's solid chest comes into my mind. *What a night that was all those months ago.* Naturally, not only my mind but also other areas are remembering him. Dammit. I'll message him soon. This radio silence is bullshit.

I grabbed the fruit out of the fridge for my morning smoothie, then I retrieve my oats from the pantry. Growing up with a super healthy family made it hard to start the day with a "cheater's breakfast" as my father would say. Lunch and dinner and all that time in between, I wasn't so strong. A girl can only do what a girl can do.

Blitzing the fruit together, I pour it into my cup and take it and my oatmeal over to my round table. When I had decorated the top section of this space, I'd wanted to use all of it whilst maintaining a comfy feeling. The view through the back window onto the next selection of warehouses isn't really therapeutic, but my seashell blinds are.

I pull the notepad that permanently sits on my table closer as I start to jot down my list for the day.

1. Work on satin mock-up for Miss V (gina)
2. Begin second mock-up for bridesmaids
3. Double-check orders and plan for next appointments
4. Stock up on red material for Valentine's Day
5. Stop obsessing over the non-boyfriend.

That isn't too hard. As I crunch my breakfast, I begin to draw a few ideas for the next theme for the mannequins. I love the quirky momentum they create and how I can capture an audience with their dynamic. Being able to house my art just rocks.

As the edge of the pen brushes across the page, my hand takes me to a new idea. *Reminiscing.* Memories, fond memories, weave into the edge of the skirt. Embers from burnt-out candles frame the hem as I flick up the edges of the flames with the pencil's lead, like heated waves.

Before too long, the page is filled with three high-waisted skirts that each represent a period of my life. I sit back in my chair and stare at the drawings, taking in the moments with a bittersweet sense of nostalgia. How the customers who stroll through my shop don't think I belong in an institution, with all my wacky bits, is beyond me. I doubt any of them have ever seen a shop like mine that has elegance on one side with all the bridal and formal gowns, and another side that prompts the reaction of, "What is that? The thing that I can't stop looking at and need to go and take a sticky nose at?" Yeah, that would be my brain, coaxing you to the dark side.

Satisfied with my next side project, I wash my dishes and head downstairs. The soft glow of the morning sun beams through the transparent curtains that line the front window. I rarely ever close the thick blinds, as I love watching the moonlight serenade my mannequins at night. Leaning on the bannister and staring down into the moonlit room always takes my breath away.

As I walk across the creaky floor, my phone sounds in my pocket with "Material Girl" by Madonna. I chuckle for a moment before I see "Daddy-O" on the screen. Answering, I smile as I raise it to my cheek.

"Yo! Daddy-O!" I singsong.

"Hey baby girl." He laughs. "You're spritely, as per usual."

"Only way to be."

"Busy day ahead?"

"Hoping so. I have to check the orders I've done, plus plan out my next appointments. It's the end of the week, but Valentine's Day is around the corner, so I'll be getting a few bites for chicks who make an effort. Gotta stock up on the red."

"And the sonnets," he adds. "Just have a few pre-made ones for the no-hopers."

"Sounds good." I grin, enjoying his carefree tone. These past few months, he has been sounding a lot more upbeat than he used to. I shuffle the dresses along the rails.

Dad's throat clears before I hear, "So, baby girl …" He pauses as I move to the other rail. "I was wondering when you could next visit home?"

My hand grips the rail as my feet plant to the floor. *I'm not good at home trips.*

"Trinity? You there?"

"Ah, yeah." My tongue thickens like concrete in my mouth. "I'm not sure; I'm just really busy with things."

"I understand." His voice softens, losing its bubbly gait.

"Almost two years I've been open here, so I try to keep the momentum up so no one forgets me." I attempt to lighten the sudden change in the air. I tighten my thumb across the rail to centre myself.

"I understand, especially with ... our tough economy at the moment," he stammers, "but I really need to discuss a few things. Especially ...," he pauses, and I hold my breath, "the house."

The house?

"What do you mean?" My heart thuds. "What's going on?"

"Look, I'd rather talk to you about this face to face ..."

I swallow, not liking where this conversation is going. "You're selling our house? What about Mum's things? What about all the memories we have there? You can't fucking do that!" I screech down the phone.

"Trinity!" my father's voice barrels through the phone. "Calm. Down. Now. This is why I need you to come home. It's not what you think." His voice lowers slightly as he exhales sharply. "Just come home, soon. Okay? I promise you, all will be fine."

"Okay ..." I concede. "I'll fly up next weekend."

My dad's breath catches on the other end of the line. "You're going to come *home*?" Scepticism is laid thick in his tone, but he's right. Getting me to travel home usually takes a lot of coaxing, layered with guilt. Each time I visit the house it feels empty, while his loneliness coats me like a thick blanket.

"Yes," I sigh. "I'll fly home. I'll book flights this afternoon."

"Thank you, baby girl. Let me know when you arrive, and I'll pick you up."

"Sure, Daddy-O. I'll text you later."

"Bye, honey."

"Bye, Dad." I lower my phone from my ear and hang up, taking a moment to close my eyes. I breathe in deeply to calm my nerves. The thought of visiting my childhood home spikes a surge of anxiety. That wooden box still hides in my closet. I need chocolate. Stat. And Vodka. Lots of and lots of vodka. Is eight a.m. too early for a shot?

I arrange the hangers evenly along all the rails before retreating to the back of the room to work on the second mock-up of Vag's dress. The morning drags like a snail's arse, as I cut through the satin and wait for the time for the doors to open. I could open the doors early, but my head isn't ready for it. That call is running on a loop in my mind.

I line up the sections of material to start recreating the dress, and take a moment to clear my head, before I stuff up this mock-up. Running my fingers along the edges of the satin, my eyes travel to my desk where my single sketches sit for further fixing. The sketch that Theo saw lies against my stacked pile.

Walking over to it, I pick it up. It's of a simple but elegant knee-length dress, strapless, with a sweetheart front and rogued side. I don't have the boobs to prop it up if I made it for me, unless I use chicken fillets or something. I would change the original colour I sketched from blue to a deep purple when I finally did decide to make it. I just need a muse to create this for. It needs something a bit more, but I can't put my finger on it. As Theo suggested, it is unfinished, and even after all the time I spent working on it after he left, he is right.

Sigh.

It seems that the men in my life are clouding my thoughts at the moment.

"Yoo-hooo!"

I hear the call while bent in the middle rack of the bridal dresses.

One is caught on the window's ledge, which a customer must have accidentally pushed, and I am attempting to swipe it back without the lace catching on the edge.

"I'll be with you in a tick," I say as I lift the lace gently back. Shuffling backwards first through the dresses, I tilt to the side towards the voices to find Eloise, and a younger Eloise clone next to her with black-rimmed glasses.

"Hey!" I smile as I stroll over to them.

Eloise stands there with a white box in her hand wearing a cute yellow summery dress, while her sister is in jeans and a *Star Wars* T-shirt.

"I thought that dress had almost dragged you to the other side. All I could see was your shoe." Eloise winks at me as I get closer.

"Being short has its limitations, but I was able to escape its clutches through my ninja-tastic skills." I tilt my chin to her sister. "Who's the clone?"

Eloise laughs as she grabs her sister's shoulder with her free hand and rubs it affectionately. "This *clone* is my sister, Anastasia."

"Greetings." I put my hand out for her to shake. Though it's obvious that she's younger than I am, she's at least a foot taller than me, like her sister. "Do I call you Ana?"

She reaches for my hand and shudders. "No, just Anastasia." Her hand grips mine as she says, "I don't like nicknames."

I smile as her green eyes look at me and then cast away quickly. "Well, you have a beautiful name. No reason to shorten it, really," I add, and Anastasia looks back at me with a small smile on her face.

"So ..." Eloise holds out a box in front of her. "I brought you something. It's kinda an apology gift."

"What do you mean?" My hands gather the box from her. "You don't have anything to apologise for. Not that I know of, anyway."

"It's my sorry-my-friend-was-such-a-bitch-while-you-dress-fitted-her present."

My fingers tighten on the box as a laugh escapes my lips. "No bloody way!" I shriek. "I'm pretty mean to her."

"She is horrible, every time."

"But I constantly stir shit up."

"She deserves it—trust me." Her eyebrow raises as she lifts her chin in the direction of

the box. "C'mon. Open it."

I shake my head, flip open the cardboard lid, and begin giggling as I stare into the box.

Inside are five cupcakes that each have a word iced on them, reading 'Vagina-is her-real name.'

"It totally is," I agree. "C'mon ladies." I walk over to the back table to put the cakes down. "I have delicious hot chocolate that will go great with these. Stay here for a tic and I'll grab some for us while you keep an eye on the door."

We spend the next half hour talking and munching on the delicious cupcakes, the conversation flowing freely. I watch Eloise's sister sit nervously in her seat, her eyes trained on my arm. She adjusted her glasses in a nervous twitch, and after a few moments of unexpected silence, Eloise rubs her sister's shoulder as her eyes flick over to me.

"Ask her," she says softly. "Trust me, you won't regret it."

"Honey, you can ask whatever it is." Pointing to my arm, I add, "They weren't too painful, if that's what you're wondering."

"Oh, no," she looks down at the floor, her face reddening. "I like them, though. I just wanted to ask you if you could make me my formal dress." She bites her lip, her eyes returning to mine, a soft blush gracing her soft cheeks.

"Absolutely. Only because you love *Star Wars*. Otherwise, it wouldn't happen."

She chuckles as her shoulders loosen.

"So, when is it, and do you have any ideas?"

"Not until October, but I want to be ready." She adds, "I'm in my last year of school and don't want to wait until the last minute. I have a lot of studying to do, and I need to make sure that it's ..."

Eloise reaches forward and puts her arm around her sister's shoulders. "This is our little stress head," she says tenderly as she holds her. "She likes to plan things and is meticulous to a T. But the times we come in here, I've told her that school doesn't exist. Just enjoying the moment."

"Exactly," I add. Standing up, I point over to the racks. "Let's go see if I have something already, or we can sketch out some ideas."

The girls agree and stroll over to the dresses. I take this moment to watch Anastasia to get an idea of her body shape. Tall, long legs, and a curvy waist. She reminds me of Hazel in her curves, but her long black hair is tied up in a high ponytail. I love her geeky look—if only I could inject a bit of sass into her.

Her fingers flick through the rails as a customer enters the warehouse. I excuse myself and assist her in general enquiries about my dress-making as the girls move along the rails. Before long, I've scored another potential client, and I head over to Eloise once the customer has gone.

"Anything here?" Eloise points to the three long dresses that have been put together at the end of the stack. Two are black and the other is grey. Anastasia stands next to Eloise, her head tipping to the side to look at them more.

Before her sister even tries them on, I know they won't suit her. I hold up the first black dress and gesture for Anastasia to walk over to me. "Tell me what you like about this one, honey."

"It's long and pretty."

Pointing to the others, I ask, "And those?"

"They're long and pretty too."

"So, you want a long dress?" I coax, holding the dress I have in front of her body and running my eyes up and down her physique.

"Yeah." She looks to the ground. "I don't really like my legs."

"She has great legs, too," her sister chides, crossing her arms in front of her. "I think these dresses are pretty, but they aren't you."

"I agree," I add, noticing Anastasia's shoulders tense. "But tell me more about why you don't like your legs, and we can go from there."

"Um, it's just that ... they look funny."

I pull the dress back towards me so I have a clear view of her.

"What's so funny about them? They look pretty good to me."

"The girls at school said I have giraffe legs."

The coat hanger in my hand bends as my fingers threaten to snap it. "Say what?"

"Um, that's why I don't like short dresses. The girls said ..."

"Oh, fuck no." I turn and hang the dress before I throw it across the room. "You mean, you don't like your legs because a pack of mean bitches said—"

"They're my friends, they're just ..."

"A pack of mean whores," I growl. "No friend would say that to you. I've known you half an hour, and even in jeans I can tell you're beautiful."

"Thank you!" Eloise claps, and she stares at the ceiling for a moment. "Finally! Someone else besides family sees what we do."

"I don't like this." Anastasia steps back, avoiding my eyes as she stares at her sister. "You said I could find and choose something that *I* want."

"Honey." I step forward. "I want you to leave my store in a few months with a dress that says how beautiful you are and that is worthy of you. I know I made these"—I gesture with my thumb over my shoulder—"but please, can you trust me? I just want you to try on a few short ones, and I'll let you try some long ones, too. I want you to see what I see."

She adjusts her glasses quickly and sighs. "Okay, but I probably won't like the short ones. Just saying."

"Why? Did you forget to whipper snipper the legs today?" Eloise chuckles as her sister wiggles her nose in disgust.

"Ew, gross."

"Well then." I turn and pluck two short dresses from the rack. "Hold these for me, while I grab some more." Pointing to the back, I indicate. "There, up the back to the right are the changing rooms. Off you go."

"These my size?" she asks disbelievingly.

"Yep. Now go. I want to see you look fab-ulous."

Her ponytail swishes as she walks across the floor to the back. When there's enough distance between us, I turn to Eloise and demand, "You. Spill, now. What is with her?"

She shrugs and steps closer to me while keeping an eye on the back of the warehouse. "Her friends are passive aggressive and put her down all the time. She hides a lot in the library to study as they antagonize her."

"Tell her to find new friends."

"It's not that simple, unfortunately. She's shy, and they play on that."

"They're not friends—they're bullies. Does she have anyone else?"

"She chats to her lab partner a bit. He's sporty though, so he's usually out on field trips. They give her shit about him, too. I just can't wait until this year is over and she goes to university and breaks the ties with them."

"You need to get her to break those ties, now. That girl is sweet and gorgeous. Jealousy is misery's best friend." I grab another long dress and start walking over to the room. If there is something to get my blood boiling, it's bullies. Fuck this shit.

As we step closer, Anastasia steps out with the first black dress, which clings to her curves in the wrong places.

"Sorry, honey. Take it off and try the next one." I reach into the dressing room and pluck the other two dresses she had off the hooks. "These will do the same. Try on this long dress if you *must* have a long one, and then I want you to try on these two."

She stares at me dumbly, as I clap my hands together.

"Chop, chop, let's get you hot." I gently grab her arm and walk her into the changing room. "Trust me," I say softly.

As the dresses change over the next twenty minutes, it becomes loud and clear how gorgeous Eloise's sister is and how absolutely fucking clueless she is to it. When she eventually tries on the knee-length fuchsia dress and steps outside for us to see, my breath catches. Not because of how beautiful she is or how loudly Eloise is cheering (and she is pretty vocal), but because I have just found my muse for the sketch on my desk.

"Wait here for a sec." I scurry away to my workshop, narrowly avoiding slipping on the polished floor. I reach my desk and snap up the sketch and a pencil, and race back into the changing room. The front door opens as another lady comes in, and I quickly yell, "Be with you in a second! Please feel free to take a look around," as I run like a loon back to Anastasia.

She stands there with clasped hands in front of her, biting her lip. Even in this dress she's stunning, but I know I can do better.

I look her up and down and shake my head. "Those bitches," I mutter under my breath. "Your legs are hot. Woman, if you don't want them, I'll have them, and I'll take your boobs, too. Sound good?"

She stands and flinches at my comment, before a small smile crosses her red lips. No makeup, no pretence—this girl is gorgeous. "Um, thanks?"

I point to the mirror. "I don't see a giraffe anywhere. Look closely. Do you?"

She stares at the mirror silently and gazes at her legs.

I walk up behind her and link my arm through hers, personal space be damned. "Really look at yourself. I want you to empty your mind and tell me if you see what they see."

She takes a moment before her soft voice, barely above a whisper, says, "No."

I squeeze her arm with mine and nod. "You look amazing, but honey, I have something in my hand that I think will be even better." Raising the sketch up to her with my other arm, I continue. "I spent this week trying to work out what I needed to make it right, but what I realised it needed was you." I turn the sketch towards her. "What do you think?"

Her fingers instantly reach for the sketch as she breathes, "I love it." Looking at me, she asks softly, "Can you make this?"

"Oh honey,"—I flick my hand back and forth—"I can create anything, provided my muse is in my mind. What do you think of a deep purple?"

"It's my favourite colour." Her eyes light up.

"Fabulous." I look over to Eloise, who stands to the side with tears in her eyes. I raise my eyebrow at her in concern. She mouths *thank you*, and I shrug like it was nothing. After watching my best friend Trice deal with bullshit bullies in high school, there's nothing I hate more. "Okay, gorgeous gal, get dressed and we can make some adjustments to this sketch. I'm just going to see to this customer. I'll be back in a second."

I walk past Eloise and wink at her as I stroll out into the warehouse. A tall blonde woman stands with another shorter brunette by the bridal gowns. I smile, ready to launch into my greeting as I get closer.

My steps sound along the floor, alerting them to my presence and causing them to both turn. I am about to greet them when my eyes lock on the blonde, and I falter momentarily. Her eyes widen in recognition as she goes to greet me, but I shake my head, clenching my jaw.

Standing before me is one of the girls who victimised and terrorised my Trice for all those years. One who watched her group's ringleader carve into my friend's wrist with a Stanley knife.

"Brit," I seethe, my fists clenching at my side. "Mind telling me, what the fuck you're doing in my store?"

Her eyes widen in surprise in my stance.

"I, um ... heard you had your ... own bridal ... store," she stammers, her pink-glossed lips trembling. I put my hand on my hip and narrow my eyes at her.

"Well, aren't you fucking clever. Didn't answer my question, though. What the fuck are you doing here?" Her hand moves along her Gucci bag strap as she steps closer to me. I can't help but feel that she's testing the waters. *Step closer; see what I'll do.*

"I'd like you to design and make my wedding dress."

My jaw drops.

"Your wedding dress?"

"Yes," she whispers.

Reluctantly, my mind takes an automatic trip down memory lane and back to high school. Despite her and her minion's pathetic apologies, after watching their ringleader bully Trice, they had engraved their names on my shit list. The scar that Trice has is now covered in a symbolic tattoo for her and Alex. Another way of saying *fuck you, bullies.*

I point to the door.

"Fuck off. No way. No how." I snarl, her features flinching in shock, as she steps back. *Unbelievable.* "You may have forgotten what you and your whore friends did, but I haven't." Her shoulders slump as she turns quickly and walks out the door.

Yeah, bitch. Good to see you're still gutless. You better leave. Right the fuck now.

Eight

The fractured tree trunk stands with a beating heart inside, bursting through the wooden stems. The man holds a tattered white flag in his hands.
The gutter that lines the panel lies heavily scripted with, "Take a chance. Be the better man. Before you're trapped forever."
TTE

THEO

Straightening my tie, I enter the open door to the empty warehouse and shake my head. Why am I worried about how I look? It's not like he's going to fire me.

I am due for another tatt appointment for the next stage of my back. I bet that would make him reconsider seeing me. Fancy his son having arms full of ink; it probably would disgrace him as much as it does Ko.

The strong aroma of coffee fills my nostrils as I step across the wooden floors. I clasp my satchel at my side, eager to get this over and done with. Hopefully one of his underlings will be here to filter any discourse, but I doubt it.

Being summoned has left a sour taste in my mouth, yet as I step into the foyer area my senses become alert. I don't see him. Looking around the empty room, my designer instincts begin to simmer. Working with an empty warehouse lures me like putty in my hands. Looking around and not seeing anyone is strange, but while the room is quiet, my senses begin to kick in. From the high-end windows up the back, to the exposed beams in the ceiling, ideas begin to churn rapidly and my stomach quivers in anticipation. Despite having to work with my *father*, I can't help the excitement that comes with creating something new. Leaving your own mark and creating a piece of immortality is the icing on this shitty cake.

I walk farther into the warehouse and continue to look around. Without waiting, I open my satchel and reach for my sketchbook, fine liner, and measuring tape. Flicking open my book, I draw a faint line to represent the border of the room and begin making little marks along the edges for the current room features. Eager to map it out, I make side notes for potential posts to add in the construction. The internal battle of getting the measurements down whilst holding back the ideas makes my fingers tremble slightly. An hour passes, and I sketch more characteristics of the walls and floors, the location of windows and columns.

I tuck the pen behind my ear and stow the notebook under my arm as I walk to the closest wall with my measuring tape pulled. I hear a deep cough behind me.

"It's great to see you have a strong work ethic," Ricardo states, as he steps closer to me.

I hold the tape mid-air and turn to him with a stoic expression on my face. Definitely no plebs sent out here today. "Is that your form of sarcasm, as this is our first meeting? Nice to see *your* strong work ethic of being"—I pull out my phone for a moment to check the time—"an hour and a half late." I click my tongue against the roof of my mouth in disapproval as I watch his passive face break out into a grin.

"On the contrary. I am merely observing how you are working today." His thick accent rumbles. I was used to Japanese accents from back home, but his Spanish one unnerves me.

"Good excuse. And I was almost thinking you leaving this place open and unattended wasn't weird at all," I add sarcastically as I wave to the tape in my hand, eager to get on with the job. "Back to it, I guess."

Just as I'm about to turn, he holds up both hands, and my eyes lock on the coffee cups he holds. "Elly prepared these. She knows what you liked, so I hope you don't mind. It is, after all, our first meeting, and what day would it be without a good coffee?"

Fuck. Here I am, trying to get on with it, and he brings me coffee. His kindness is something I don't expect. I already know refusing it will result in a barrage of text messages from my sister.

Sighing, I walk begrudgingly towards him and extend my hand for a cup. He smiles and hands me mine, then gestures to the sketchbook under my arm. "What are you doing?"

"I'm taking notes of the room before we discuss the plan. It's so I can ..." I pause and look at him, quizzing. *Why is he here?* He should know this part is about the preliminary meet, unless ...

"I'm here to work and spend time with you, Theo. I can see your confusion. I normally have my foremen in charge of projects see to the arrangements, but in this case, I've made an exception."

The tape whirls shut in my hand as I process his statement. "So, you'll be here ...?"

"At every meeting while I try to drop in weekly to see how it's coming along."

"But, I won't be here. I'll be at the office."

"No," he pauses. "I have requested that we have weekly meetings here to discuss the project."

"To spy on me?" I straighten, my fingers tightening around the coffee cup.

His heavy accent softens as he continues, "No, to work *with* you."

"What if you hate my ideas?"

"Está bien. Then we can modify them."

I take a sip of coffee as I watch his face study mine. As a child, I had been told that my deep green eyes came from a great grandfather on my mother's side, and I was too naïve to not believe it. My mother was half Japanese and half Australian. Subconsciously, I spent my youth with my hair covering my face as my shyness limited my social contact. I hated when people stared. But now, staring at Ricardo, my very own green eyes bore into mine. It is no wonder my father hated me so much. I was a constant reminder of a lie. One that I had innocently tried to mask.

"Did you know my father? Before I came to find you?" I blurt out and cringe, shaking my head in frustration.

"No. We only met when you were a teenager. I have spoken to him on the phone once, though," he responds instantly. "After you visited me for the first time." His shoulders straighten for the verbal battle that he is obviously expecting.

That time I visited him, or stormed in on him, really, I had met my siblings, and the rage I felt towards him dissipated as soon as I was confronted with sisters that I had known nothing about. My internet stalking had been limited to him only. But when I saw my sisters standing there, the connection had been instant. Elly's embrace had been so strong, it was a wonder I didn't lose a rib. My father had never done that.

But I don't retaliate. I don't need to be reminded about him. I wonder for a moment what my *oba-chan* would say if she knew I was standing here with my real father.

Blinking away the thought, I lift my coffee cup in a mock salute. "Let's get this show on the road, shall we?" I swing a large gulp back and head to the other side of the room. Resting my cup along the protruding edge of the bar, I unbutton my shirt and roll my sleeves up. No use having any pretences here; if he wants to get to know me, he can get to know the real me. Piece by motherfucking piece.

My phone buzzes in my pocket, and I bring it out quickly to see a text from Trinity. I've hidden from her this week to meet the other part of my life that she is yet to know about. The other part that I use to bring out the anguish and the hurt that I conceal and turn them into something poetic and meaningful. To bring meaning to it, in some sort of weird and fucked up way. It is also a good excuse to unleash my dark and twisted side onto the coloured pages and create my own world within a fantasy that no one can touch. The world of TTE.

Each month, I release another graphic novel that follows the lives of my two central characters. Ryder, my agent is persistent in making sure that I'm releasing monthly. He was intrigued by my narrative and it spurred me on. After leaving Trinity so abruptly, I'd buried myself so deeply into my drawings, capturing moments where if she looked closely enough, she'd see a story about the forgiveness that I hoped she would give me one day. Our real-life story is tragic enough, but on the pages in my novel, I can restore us. I can tie her to me indefinitely. It's our little piece of immortality that will hopefully bring us closer ... when I eventually have the balls to tell her about it. Rather than hide behind my sketches when life gets too hard.

Last month's submission has just been printed and shipped to the stockists. One in particular, I have a view of from my office window across the laneway.

Swiping across the screen, I read her message with a smile. Despite me being a moody arsehole, she wants to talk to me.

> **Trin:** Hey.

> **Me:** Hey.

> **Trin:** So, did the recent southern action cause your fingers to drop off?

> **Me:** Nope, my fingers are working just fine.

> **Trin:** No sprains?

> **Me:** No. Should they be sore?

> **Trin:** Just looking for a reason as to why you haven't called me.

> **Me:** You haven't called me.

> **Trin:** No, dude. You left in your man PMS. You had to call me. That's how we roll.

Me: Oh, I know how we roll. ;)

Trin: Ugh. Haven't heard from you all week. That's like a decade in our terms. You over your man rags or whatever was bothering you?

Me: I'm getting there.

Trin: Typical man response. I'm looking for my friend, Theo. If you see him, tell him I wanna hit the flicks sometime. His shout for being a douche.

Trust Trin to go straight to the ultra-familiar. But I'm not ready to bow down yet.

Me: Did you miss me?

Trin: Where are you?

Typical of Trin to avoid emotion, too.

Me: On a worksite at the moment.

Trin: Oh. So, you want to go to the movies tonight? I've been cooped up all week.

An idea strikes me as I begin typing.

Me: I have a better idea. I'll swing by this afternoon when work finishes. We'll take a ride on the wild side.

Trin: Typical male who wants to go there. We can't do that this week.

Me: No, firecracker. Wear jeans and a long sleeved T-shirt. That's all.

Trin: Neat-o. I'll dig out my Bananarama tee.

I smile as I type:

Me: I'll find my Hanson one.

Trin: Fuck off you will. See you tonight.

Me: Bye-bye.

Tucking my phone away, I chuckle. Feels like a week since I've done so.

Since our tryst began, she has softened slightly, while still keeping me at an emotional distance. We have a long and jagged history that neither one of us want to talk about. If she ever severed our ties, I fear she will dissolve me.

I pick up my coffee and take a sip, chuckling at her brevity. Trin is never one to back down from an argument if she can see herself winning it. Getting my attention is obviously what she had set out to do.

I place the coffee down and tuck my sketchpad back into my bag. Grabbing my camera, I turn it on and take the lens cap off to try and capture the room while the light is good. Raising it to my eyes, I snap a couple of shots, complete with Ricardo standing in the middle, observing me. His charcoal grey tailored suit sits crispy pressed against his solid chest. Even through the lens he is intimidating. His two-toned grey hair is brushed back, leaving only a few strands to fall over his forehead. His beard is kept short, and his expression is hard. Apart from our eyes, I cannot see anything that ties us together.

I continue to take photos of the room, moving quickly to capture the different angles. We are yet to discuss the actual construction, but seeing an opportunity to put a little distance between us, I take it. As the photos fill the memory card, one thought strikes me about this place.

The floor is solid and methodical ... if that's even possible. I tap my feet against the wooden floorboards for a moment and nod.

"I noticed the noise too." Ricardo breaks into my thoughts. "When I first inspected this place, my feet sounded like tap shoes. It was distracting at first, until the feature of my restaurant came to me." Holding his coffee in one hand and using his free hand to press against his abdomen, he takes a few steps back and forth. "This floor was made for the salsa." He stops suddenly and readjusts his jacket to smooth it down, like he never just danced for me.

"Nice moves, Sinatra."

"When this place is done, it will be reinventing what music and dance is all about in my family."

I nod and face the front to take more pictures.

"You're part of that too, Theo," he adds.

I roll my eyes and take a few steps to the main doors. I have a father already; I don't need another one. Elly's face flashes before my eyes, and a stab of guilt pierces me.

"I'm just going to finish the photos for the room so I can then work on the dimensions. I can email you the plan I make this afternoon of the room itself and the capacity you have to work with ..." The more distance I can put between us, the better I will be. I look over my shoulder as I gesture to the front door, eager to get back to the office.

He reaches into his breast pocket and retrieves his phone. "Let me check when I can schedule our next appointment."

Let's hope it's in another week or more.

"Right, tomorrow at nine a.m. Is that suitable? I'll have your safety vest and hard hat ready as it's going to be an active site."

The surprise obviously shows on my face, as his eyes twinkle as they meet mine. I nod, perplexed at his genuine desire to spend time with me.

"I will schedule that time for the rest of the week so we can make solid progress, okay?"

"I'll run that by Cole, I need to postpone all further meetings until I have a draft. I can set up a meeting to confirm ..."

"No need," Ricardo interjects. "He is aware that I will be working extensively with you. Come with what you have planned."

My jaw locks. Any semblance of control that I thought I had in this situation begins to slip from my fingertips. "I don't think we need daily appointments for this project. It's going to be time-consuming and ..."

"Theo." His voice raises slightly to cut me off. "If you think after all these years I'm not going to finally get to know you, you're mistaken. I lived with the guilt of not doing anything sooner."

My heartbeat thuds profoundly in my chest. My breaths escalate as I try to calm the anger that builds within me.

"How about we don't fucking talk about that?" I seethe through clenched teeth.

"Why not?" He waves his hand in the air. An inscrutable expression lies across his face. *Is he trying to piss me off? I'm not in the mood for this shit. Ever.* "We can get it all out in the open and move forward."

I feel like banging my head against the wall. "Not today, not ever. Got it?"

I turn and face him, head-on. The harsh methodical piano chords of a ring tone that I hate hearing sounds from my pocket. I deliberately set it for Ko, and each time it pissed me off. I sigh in frustration as my fist clenches around my side, holding the phone in my pocket. *What the fuck? Did he have beat your son while he's down intuition? Could all the "fathers" in my life currently just FUCK RIGHT OFF?*

The chords cease to annoy me as the room silences.

"Who was that?" Ricardo gestures to my phone, his brows tightening in concern.

"My *father*." I release my pocket and shake my head, turning away from him. "I'm not in the mood to hear what a disappointment I am today, thanks. Maybe tomorrow." Adjusting the strap on my shoulder, I point to the door. "I'm going to the office; I'll have the area plan mapped out by this afternoon."

"What song was that?" he asks.

"It's Rachmaninoff's *Piano Concerto #3*." My throat dries and I look down at my shoes as I remember. "I started piano lessons when I was three, and that was the song that tortured me in its forty-five-minute glory. It also led to me smashing a $15,000 piano." I run my tongue along the front of my teeth in hopes of stopping my lips from disclosing any more.

"Theo ..." His feet move closer to me, but I hold my hand up to halt him getting farther.

"And, that would be enough storytelling for the day. I'll see you here tomorrow."

"Theo," he calls out to me as I grab onto the doorframe. I look over my shoulder at him as he adds, "I won't ask about him again, until you want to talk about it."

I nod and head out the door. That was a discussion I hoped we'd never have.

After spending the entire afternoon in the office fighting with the designer software,

I manage to get the basic floor plan done with the features of the warehouse. The base outline is ready to start adding our ideas to. Now, as I send it to the printer, the reality of the project strikes me. I am going to be working with my *real* father. Part of me wants to do a mediocre job so he won't want to spend time with me, but the other part, the pathetic child that wants to please, resurfaces. Entrapped in a never-ending self-depreciating cycle, I scold myself for being so weak. In front of me, I've unconsciously lined my pens in order of length. Another fallback from being part of such a strict household. My fingers begin to curl and press into my palms.

I stand, walk over to the printer, and retrieve the plan. Gazing at the lines, I double-check the observations I made until my eyes blur with fatigue. Blinking, I look through the window as I step closer to the glass surface to cast my eyes down into the busy laneway that separates our steel tower from the rusty bricks that lined the building next door. A small line of eager patrons has formed outside the ice cream parlour; the shop's business never seemed to dwindle during summer.

The dark doorway to the comic book store beside it sways with the excitement of patrons coming up and down the stairs. I turn my head to look at the clock on the wall and smile. While my new comic is off being printed, my recent comic has just been released. The seesaw of stress in comic book author life. Expel it all out only to have it launched back at you. Turning back to the window, the gelati line progressively moves and I wonder if I should make the effort to go down there for a break.

A shimmer of bright blue captures my attention as Trinity's sleek body comes into view from the road. I quickly retrieve my phone and take a photo, taking care to focus it on her directly. I'll need it for my next edition. I watch her strut as she confidently strolls down the road, oblivious to the half-dozen guys and a few girls who are surreptitiously checking her out.

She reaches the comic book store's front and eagerly jogs out of sight down the stairs. My pulse quickens at the thought of her grabbing the latest edition. Will she discover my other identity? Or do I need to be making things clearer to her? Tonight, when she's on the back of my bike, I'm going to find out.

Nine

"Don't let your stubbornness hold you back. Forgive. Love. Live."
Love, M

TRINITY

My precious.
No, step back.
You can't touch it.

The amused clerk stares at me, stupefied.

"What?" I ask, clutching the plastic-covered goods. I'm only hugging a magazine. What's wrong with that? Pressing my thumb and index finger together, I feel the thickness of the comic. Is it thicker, this edition? I glance down at the glossy contents, trying in vain to guess the page number. Does she finally see him?! Oh my God! He can't be captured! My excitement flares until the clerk's eyes clash with mine.

"Haven't you worked out internet shopping yet? You can order it online and have it delivered to your front door, you know." He hands me the receipt for my precious purchase, but I can't move. His sheer stupidity has me frozen to the ground.

I stare at him. Right at him. Why was he discouraging customers from coming in?

Can I poke him on the forehead to check for any sign of life in there? Check that he isn't a damn fool?

I snap out of my trance and snatch the receipt out of his villainous fingers.

"And you fucking work here," I mutter in disgust. "The whole purpose of coming in here is to immerse myself in the vibe. The unity of like-minded people in one place. You clearly do not have the said vibe to be standing behind that desk." I stand on my tiptoes and look over the desktop at him. "You're not even dressed like you belong here. Where are your Docs? Where's the metal in your face? Where's the chain to your wallet? You're wearing ordinary jeans … did you lose your way from the GAP?"

He leans forward and stares down at my outfit, paying significant attention to the cherry blossom tattoo that crawls over my shoulder. Stare at my boobs, buddy, and my shoe goes up your arse.

"Did a Smurf attach itself to your head?"

I touch my tongue to my labret and run a hand quickly through the loose ends of my bun, unweaving it to form a ponytail. "Well, there was a Smurf orgy, actually. They all got excited and left a mess." His face stills as he stares at me. "Yeah, I know, I took it too far. But, you have to admit, you kinda don't fit in here if you can't take on the weirdos." I chuckle as I bring the comic closer to me.

"I get off in fifteen if you want to hit a pub and yell at me some more." He winks, leaning his elbows on the desk. "We can see how weird this conversation can really get."

My chin flinches in surprise. He's cute. I'll give him that. He has short blond hair and blue eyes, but that familiar feeling of interest doesn't come. No accelerated heartbeat, or pulse—nothing.

A year ago, I might've said yes, the quick thrill of want overriding anything else. The need to escape my clouded thoughts had been easily fixed with a cheap screw. So why not now? 'Cause I had a boyfriend? We weren't even classified that.

I consider my response for a moment longer, not realising that I've kept him waiting until he clears his throat.

"So, I take it that's a no, then?" He tilts his head, leaning closer to me, but I take a step back. His cuteness does not lure me in. He chuckles and winks. But, again, nothing. No twitching—nothing igniting between my legs. I honestly think my vagina is on a hiatus or holidaying in the Bahamas. All the while it sunbakes, waiting for Theo. We need to sort our shit out.

"Sorry. I'm not able to," I say, clutching the mag to my chest. "But … um, thanks?"

"You're asking a question?"

"It's not every day you get a backhanded compliment after being accused of a Smurf invasion."

He smiles and points to the magazine that I grip at my chest. "Off you go on your special adventure with that." He gestures as the magazine crinkles slightly between my protective fingers. "Try to avoid any Smurfs on your way home."

I release the magazine in one hand and point up towards my left. "I think once you're up those stairs, the GAP is that way."

Turning before he replies, I make my way through the shelves to the stairs. The low lighting contrasts against the stark colours of the magazines that I pass, and I love it.

Once a month, this place is my destination. I even deliberately leave the last appointment blank on release days so I can come to visit.

I climb the steps and eagerly make my way up the narrow one-way street to the tram stop. The shop lies hidden between an ice cream shop and an alleyway, one that I decide to turn down to take a shortcut. Behind me, a steel skyscraper faces my back, looking onto the shops where the comic store is. Each time I walk down the alley, I get a weird sense that something strange lurks in that building. But I can't put my finger on it.

As my feet travel down the crowded café-filled alleyway, I take a moment to people-watch as I walk. The brusque nature of the waiters hurrying from table to table as impatient patrons snap their fingers has me thanking my lucky stars that I'm not a part of the hospitality industry. If a customer snapped their fingers at me in my store, they would probably be told where to shove those snappy hands.

A blonde by the side catches my attention, and for a moment, I think it's Brit. I blink and shudder, shaking my shoulders to get rid of the thought. After she came in last time, it left a bad taste in my mouth. High school might've been a few years ago, but I remember what bitch looks like. Me, fucking me, designing her wedding dress. You can't be a fucking bullying whore to my best friend and expect me to forget. No fucking way. I would line her dress with arsenic and see how she likes that.

My steps continue as I eliminate that serpent from my mind. Aside from the hustle, I love the eclectic Melbournian way of life. I could wear my Marvel pyjamas down here and no one would think it was strange. As I surreptitiously note the shoes of some of the women at the tables, I mentally catalogue where to find them online and skip a little in my step. I have a new magazine in my hand and hopefully in a week or two, some new shoes on my feet.

The edge of the worn alleyway approaches as cars and trams on the road trundle along past. Posters line the brick walls, advertising bands and comedians, until one about the recent Comic Con convention catches my eye. I had gone with Robbie's friend Ty and Maxi from Hazel's band, who both were keen comic book fans.

I stop for a moment and stare at the jagged edging of the lettering on the poster. I had gone there with keen enthusiasm, hoping to catch a glimpse of the secretive TTE writer, whose magazine I clutched in my hand. I wanted him to be there to finally put a face to the name, but he hadn't come. According to the geek grapevine, he wants to remain anonymous. His magazine has been a hot commodity for the last three years, and his identity is still unknown. He is male and lives in Melbourne. That is it. The dude could've worn a mask or something, or at least spoken somehow so on lonely nights I could give myself a soundtrack to masturbate to. It's funny that I'd fantasise about a person who I'd never seen, but comic book guy never stood a chance.

I sigh and begin walking over to the tram stop. Reaching into my satchel, I check my phone for the time and find I have just forty minutes until Theo will be at my place. My other hand is itching to open the magazine, but I need more than forty minutes for that. I want to see what the characters are up to this edition without rushing it. This is my guilty pleasure, and I want to relish every second of it. I love reading romance, angst, and mind-fuckery. This comic by TTE has it all.

I arrive home and rush through the warehouse to dash up the stairs. I wasn't joking when I said I'd dig out my Bananarama T-shirt. I may be a kick-arse designer and comic book freak but 80s rock and 90s pop are also loves of mine. Slipping into my skinny jeans, I wiggle into my shirt and have a giggle at the "I'm your Venus" on the front. Trice and I used to sing this as, "I'm your penis, your vagina." I stare at the bright neon pink lettering, thinking that I should've ironed on an arrow pointing down to my own Venus.

I slide my feet into my cherry Docs and grab my satchel. Although it is summer, typical Melbournian weather doesn't mean it will be hot. A cool change for the evening has already begun, so riding wherever Theo wants to is going to be great.

I jog towards the steps, flicking lights off as I go. Despite my parents being environmentally conscious about everything when I was a kid, I somehow managed to be a power sucker. I flick the last switch near the landing as a faint memory of my mother grips me.

"Be careful you don't strain your fingers, flicking all those switches, honey." Her smile fills my thoughts as I thump down the stairs, pushing the memory back with each step. A lump forms at the back of my throat as the guilt threatens to undo me. I could've had more memories if I weren't so fucking selfish. I'd have more memories that I wouldn't hide from or push away.

My dreams knew when to trap me. They always knew when my mind was unguarded.

I reach the last step and turn my head towards the back, double checking that all the lights are off. The front door opens, and my hand grips the railing as my foot swings back and forth in front of me. If I fall on my face, it might knock some sense into me as the dirty thoughts have arrived.

Holy shit.

Theo is in leather.

And tight jeans. Not boy-band tight, but nice.

His hair is brushed back as he strides towards me, and I try in vain not to check him out, but my eyes fail me. His black boots stride over the floorboards, and he holds a helmet in each hand. His leather jacket is open at the collar, which gives me a glimpse of the dragon head that I know covers his shoulder, ending just under his collarbone. He looks hot. Enough to make me crave him.

Our arrangement is complicated. We started in a mad rush of long-awaited passion but have yet to give ourselves a label. I couldn't admit to being anything more than sexy-time buddies. Being more to him means the chance of one day meaning nothing to him when this all eventually implodes.

"Hey." He reaches me and holds out a helmet. "For you."

A warmth begins to tickle my lower stomach. If only I'd sewn that arrow on my shirt pointing down to my nether region--by the way my pulse is ricocheting, I could imagine that my pheromones have now carved one onto my skin. Yes, Theo, I want to attack you. Screw the helmet and the bike, I can think of other things I would rather ride.

I shake my lusty thoughts away. He has been distant lately, and we don't need this. The leather is causing my inner hussy to go nuclear, and we have barely spoken. Another chat about boundaries to my vajay-jay is seriously needed.

Dammit. Can't a girl catch a break? I reach for the helmet, and his strong cologne warms me. Clutching the helmet between my fingers, I step down to the floor, grab his zip, and pull it up. Tapping his shoulder, I step past him and head towards the front door, putting distance between us and my bed.

"So, where are we going?" I ask, swinging the helmet in my hand, my footsteps springing into a near skip, my eagerness as flippant as a child's. The spur of adrenaline begins to curl within my fingertips, channelling my lust for him to change into a hunger for speed.

His solid steps shuffle suddenly as he races past me. We both laugh as our old teenage selves make a run for the front door. Moments like these remind me of when we'd hang out by the river near Trice's house and muck around. We were so young then, and had no weight of the world on our shoulders. Now, it seems we both carry enough weight to cement the planet.

Theo charges through the door as my other hand reaches into my satchel to get the keys. As the door closes behind me, I notice Theo's helmet is already on as he sits on top of his Ducati, starting it up. I lock the door and follow suit by putting my helmet on and climbing on behind him. I wrap my arms around him and press against his back. The vibrations feather through me as feelings of excitement stir again in my lower belly, and I run my tongue along the inside of my mouth. I want to hold him like this all the time. It is hard to keep the friend line when all I want to do is rip that leather off his hot body.

He pulls from the curb, and the thunder of the exhaust roars to life. We glide through the streets of North Melbourne as my arms tighten around his waist. The buildings whirl by as we weave in and out of traffic. As the tyres reach the freeway, Theo revs the bike even more. The wind continues to blow against the sides of our bodies, and I rest my head against his back, with the hustle of traffic gliding along with us. A while later, we turn off the freeway, and I look up to see a sign to Dandenong Ranges.

A short time later we ride up the mountainside itself, winding through the roads. I close my eyes for a moment as the curve of the mountain begins to make me feel ill. After growing up in a flat-arse town, where the only elevation was a two-storey building, windy roads are quick to make me upchuck. I take deep breaths to help the sickness calm down a bit.

"Almost there," Theo yells against the wind, and I nod against his back. I clench my eyes shut for another moment, and the bike begins to decelerate. I sigh in relief and rub my helmet against his back.

I brave the moment, open my eyes, and find us driving up slowly into a car park lined with small hedges. A sign reading, "Sky High Mount Dandenong" lines the rotund wooden building in the distance.

Theo parks the bike, and I flick my leg over and climb down. I loosen my helmet and then take it off, my eager lungs embracing the clean, fresh air. As I face towards the city, Theo stands next to me and takes his helmet off. He locks both in his carriage and walks towards the fence line where several telescopes are mounted. Peering into one, he glances around before he steps back for me to have a look.

The view is incredible and picturesque. It's still light; however, looking down into the city is still breathtaking. As I continue to scope the city, I hear Theo clear his throat behind me and mutter, "This is where I can breathe when I want to forget."

My head moves back instantly as the need to hold him overwhelms me. There are many moments in my life that I wish I could forget, while others tragically hold onto me. Looking at Theo's sad face now makes me feel like all my troubles are insignificant in some way. We are just two broken shards that don't seem to want to cooperate to repair.

I peer over the length into the ranges and take a deep breath. Turning my gaze to him, I ask, "Hey, wanna go base jumping? We could try to hire some packs and launch. Perfect way to erase your mind."

A small smile touches his lips as he leans forward and looks down. "Sure." The smooth tone of his voice shivers across my skin. "It would feel liberating until"—raising his hand, he points it down over the ledge—"until you hit that tree and that tree … oh! And that tree over there."

"But you wouldn't be thinking about your problems, now would you?" I wink, as he shakes his head at me.

"True. I'd just have new ones. Some that would require plaster and intense physiotherapy."

"Oh, imagine if you got a splinter in a really unfortunate place?" I tease.

He turns to me and leans in, his smile widening to show me his straight teeth. "Don't you have a nurse's costume somewhere?"

Oh boy. His green eyes stare into mine, and heat climbs up my neck. I swallow my lust down for a moment, because really, climbing him at a tourist attraction is not the plan. In fact, I had been going to attempt not climbing him at all until he turned up looking like a biker's dream. I pause to answer for a moment and then draw the tip of my tongue across the bottom of my lip. Who am I kidding? If you want to play, I'll play.

"Yeah." I flick my labret and watch his eyes follow the trail of my tongue. "I have two, actually."

He raises his eyebrow as I turn my shoulder and move around him. "But I'm hungry, and I've heard they do awesome dessert here. So, get a move on, Lone Ranger. I have a crème brûlée to demolish, and it ain't gonna eat itself."

Ten

"The panel shows the woman in the embrace of another man. The man stands, with the heart in his chest beginning to shatter."
TTE

THEO

"**N**ice work, Theo," Trin mutters through a mouthful of prawns, as she twirls her fork in her linguini. "This is super yummy."

I smile at her and bite into my steak, enjoying the chargrilled taste. The clear windows to our side us a great view of the city below as the sun begins to set. I slice through another piece of meat as a wet fleck brushes my cheek. I pause and raise my hand to wipe at it, and as I draw back, Trin's cream sauce covers my fingertips. My eyes move to her face, where her big doe eyes stare back at me in shock, the remnants of pasta hanging from her cream-lined lip.

"Sorry," she mumbles as the cream drips onto her chin. Mirth fills her eyes as her gaze trails over my cheek, her jaw working slowly to finish her mouthful. "What?" she quips as I continue to stare at her.

"Just making sure your mouth is empty in case you cough on me."

She narrows her eyes and tilts her head. "Whatever. I'm not that much of a klutz." I raise my eyebrow at her. "Okay, maybe a little."

"Considering all the crazy shit you've done, it's a miracle you're still alive."

"Don't knock it till you try it, dude. I still have to jump out of a plane."

I sit back in confusion, surveying her face. "I thought you already did that?"

"Nope." She shakes her head, looking down into her pasta as she twirls her fork. "I jumped out of an air balloon. There was a deal on, so I picked that."

"With a parachute, of course," I add.

"Of course, you idiot. But there are some people who have done it without it and have someone catch them." She pulls her fork up towards her mouth, her eyes twinkling at me. "Now, *that* would be a fucking adrenaline rush."

"Don't even fucking think about it," I warn. "Dudes who do that are unhinged as shit."

She chews slowly, studying my face for a moment before raising her left hand to wiggle her fingers in front of her. "Don't stress, Nancy boy, as if I'd trust these pixie fingers to be caught by some goof."

"Plus, you're a control freak," I add, enjoying when she stiffens in her seat. She's anything but in control. Especially around me. Well, in some areas that is.

She loosens her shoulders and pokes her tongue out at me for a moment, and I laugh.

"Look how well-behaved you are in public," I taunt. She lowers her fork to the side of the plate and folds her arms in front of her.

"Is that a challenge?" Her eyebrows dance at me.

I don't know what it is about her that has me wanting more. Always more. Yet, when I reach out to her, her walls go up. Sexually, we're explosive, but emotionally, we remain impenetrable. Too caught in our past to confront it. But I want more. If I have to tear her walls down, I'll do it. Brick by brick. I rub my thumb across my chin and study her for a moment. All the things I'd like to do to her ... It has been almost a month since I've been inside of her. My pants tighten at the thought. An idea strikes me as I tap my finger against my chin. "Plane is higher than the air balloon. You still want to do it?"

Her eyes widen in excitement as she wiggles on her chair. "Fuck yes!" she squeals.

A gasp is heard from the neighbouring table. I glance over to the couple and wince. Trin ignores their discomfort and rocks more excitedly in her seat. *Can I jump out of a plane?* Probably not. But I'm sure this fiery little fairy could convince me to go through anything if she tried, just by breathing.

I lean forward to tell her my idea, but the stark piano chords sound from my pocket. Almost instantly, our moment has vanished and is replaced with discontent. My body stiffens, my skin tightens, and the need to throw my phone takes over. I pull the phone slightly out of my jacket pocket behind my chair and flick the mute switch.

"Who's that?" Trin asks, leaning forward.

I sigh. We were having just what I needed and that prick had to ruin it all. "My father."

"Oh." She frowns. "How is Obi-One-Cunt-Obi going?" she asks, lifting her wine glass to her lips. "Still pleasant? Has he learnt to shit a skittle rainbow yet?"

The tightening of my shoulders dissipates. The anger that carries along my shoulders evaporates into thin air.

"Not sure I'd want to see that," I admit, shuddering at the thought.

Trin licks her bottom lip and smiles before taking a small sip. She knows of the home life I had, and in an embarrassing way, was often some of the cause behind it. *"You still waste your time with that* busu?" he'd said once, when I left to go to university. He was never happy with my friendship with her. In his eyes, she distracted me from my role of pianist prodigy.

"I'm sure I'm still one of his favourite people." She looks down at my bare forearms under the hem of my T-shirt. "He must love the ink. Especially the dragon." Her voice oozes with sarcasm.

My lips twitch as I look down at the scales on my right arm. I run my finger along the blue ink that I remember having to specially order. Six months to have it done, and worth every scrape across my skin and incessant buzz of the tattoo machine.

"He hasn't seen any of my ink, actually," I tell her honestly, my finger tracing the scales that coil into the inner side of my forearm.

Her small hand reaches over and stops my hand in its tracks. "Really?" Her bubbly voice lowers to just above a whisper.

I raise my eyes to her face and grimace. "Haven't seen him since after your mother's funeral."

"Oh." She presses her lips together.

"Yeah, well ... we had a disagreement just before I left to come back."

"Far out, Theo. It must've been huge. I know we've ..." She stops, realising the time when that happened. When she pushed me out of her life. Taking a moment, she sighs before continuing, "I knew things were tense, but I didn't realise. I can't think about that day without wanting to cry. You and I were ..."

Ripping each other's heads off? Sparring daily?

Her hand squeezes my arm as she discloses, "I feel like a shithead friend for not knowing about that argument. I just figured you guys were distant as he was an arsehole."

I shrug and shift back in my seat. Her hand slips from my arm as I distance myself. The pain my father causes is all too familiar. He is the point of the dagger that scratches at my skin, cutting it deeper and deeper. Five years ago, Trin had kicked me out of her life, but I'd worked my way back in. Fuck, did I work for it. Without restraint, memories of that disagreement reappear, like an old wound that won't heal.

I pull my closed suitcase down from my bed to stand beside it and take a quick inventory of my room. The sheets and bedspread sit neatly folded at the end of my bed, as they do each time I visit, while blank walls stare back at me. No traces of my teenage years are left. No sign that anyone lives here. A hotel would feel more like home. My drawings, sketches, and random band posters have all been taken to university, where I have made my dorm room my own. Ever since my grandparents died a few years ago, I have been dodging through time, waiting for the day when I would be old enough to never return. Both their deaths had been a shock, occurring only a couple of months apart. I can honestly say I think my grandmother, Oba-chan, died of a broken heart. There is no reason to come back here again. I first came back for Trinity, to remember her mother. But never again will I step foot into this room.

I roll the case out of my room and into the lounge. My father stands by the mantelpiece, waiting. The back corner of the room is now bare from where the piano used to be—a reminder of my family's betrayal of my true father's identity and the hollow life that I led as a result. I roll the case to a stop beside me and wait for him to speak. Our relationship may rest in Shitsville, but the politeness that's been ingrained in me is difficult to wash away.

He turns and looks down at my suitcase without any expression lining his face. "You have everything?"

"Yes."

He nods quickly as I reach for the handle of my suitcase.

"I will call you when I arrive there."

"You have all your books?" he asks, clearly thinking that I'm still a child. "You must study daily, although I do not believe that you need a lot of time to do it for your course."

I fight the urge to roll my eyes. Architecture is not on his list of "approved" courses. Six months into it, and so far I am loving it.

I'm not going to stand around for any more lectures. He lost that privilege when he tried to fuck up my life two years ago. He can't expect me to be kind to him, when all I got was a hollow pseudo father who lied to me and chose to make me feel insignificant. I will never forgive him for keeping my identity from me.

"Okay, so if that's all, I'll go, as the road ahead is a big trip." I turn and begin to roll my suitcase towards the back door when his voice tears through the room.

"You still waste your time with that busu?"

My feet freeze to the floor as I stiffen my shoulders.

"She is nothing. You cannot be friends with her. Her trash will stain you."

My hand tightens on the handle as I refuse to look at him. "Why is she trash? Because her parents were happy?"

"They were low-class," he sneers, his feet shuffling along the carpet behind me.

"We fucking buried her mother today, you disrespectful prick." Fuming, I turn around to face him. His face is set in anger, but I know it isn't half as angry as my own. Stepping towards him, I let go of the suitcase handle. "They worked hard and were happy. They loved their daughter."

"Love does not equal success. Dedication and discipline amount to it."

"What is the point of this, old man? Has this house made you more hollow than you

already were?" My tongue loosens. "I was dedicated and disciplined, and what did that achieve?"

"Watch your tone," he scolds. "You will be successful, even if the profession is menial.

Your little drawings might actually become something. She will amount to nothing. Just like her mother."

Not even the anger I felt on the day that I found out he wasn't my real father enraged me like he did in that moment. My fist curls voluntarily, and in a split second, it tears through the air like an electric wire and smashes into his cheek. He stumbles back, his hand gripping his face as I point at him.

"You gave up the right to tell me how to behave when I found out my life was a fucking lie." Tapping my finger against my chest, I thump against it in anger. "If you had told me earlier, maybe I could have understood why I was such a burden to you. My mother's actions were not mine. I was innocent, and you took it out on me."

He grunts in response before I turn and march away, slapping my hand around the suitcase handle as I pull it quickly with me towards the back door. I smack my hand against the screen door as I push through the frame.

Pausing for a moment, I look back at him as he stares at me, waiting for me to deliver my final blow. "She was more of a mother to me than you were ever a father. She taught me love, compassion, and everything that you failed to teach. Her words were not hollow. They were filled with life.

Life that her daughter, Trinity, carries with her every day. You will never speak ill of either of them again. In fact, don't speak to me at all."

By the time I arrive at my dorm, Trinity's voicemail has picked up each of the six times I've called. My jaw clenches in frustration as I pace the floor of my room, desperate to reach the one person left in my life who means something.

I fetch the sketchpad from my desk and begin to draw a story that has been unfurling in my mind. As the ink moves into shapes and edges, I begin the process of apologizing for the bullshit of my past whilst begging for her to forgive me. Each scene is a canvas so filled with hope. With every painful thought I launch across the page, I hope to bring her back to me. Back before his poison wrecked me.

As each scene forms, I moronically chuckle, thinking of how my father would react to me "drawing." I continue to draw in spite of him. To set myself free. As I fill the page, an image of a fierce dragon conjures itself in my mind, and I move the pen from the page to my forearm. The dragon awakens at the fire and passion I pour into it, igniting a breath of life.

All the while, I wait for my father to call. To make me apologise for being the disrespectful son.

He doesn't.

No contact.

Until this month. Five years. Five fucking years, and now what?

I blink as a small set of flicking fingers clicks in front of my face. Trin's luminous eyes stare at me in concern as I shake the last part of that memory away.

"Sorry," I smile. "Talking about dear old father tends to have me taking a nap."

Her hand opens as she taps my cheek. "Sure, sunshine. I call bullshit. I'm heading home next weekend to visit my dad if you want to join me—no pressure, though. Booked my flights so I don't have to sit in a car for a day wondering why the same type of fucking tree keeps passing by. Now, for the sake of not talking about that piece of work, let's discuss more important matter—like dessert. Mmm crème brûlée."

Picking up the dessert menu from the side of the table, she turns it over in her small hand to read from it.

"Sure." I grin, leaning forward. "I wouldn't mind something sweet. But I can think of something else I'd rather have for dessert that's not on the menu."

Her eyes stop reading as they flash at me in excitement.

"Nutella pizza from in town," I suggest, watching closely as the excitement in her eyes dulls for a moment before she smiles.

"Sounds better than crème brûlée."

"Eaten from on top of your body," I taunt, standing up to retrieve my jacket. Her arms straighten in front of her as she lets the menu fall onto the table.

"Please," she scoffs, standing to get her bag. Walking around to face me, she leans up to whisper in my ear, "I have the three-kilo bucket of Nutella in my pantry. We don't need the pizza." Her hand taps my hip as she sashays towards the cashier. I follow her as she leans up on the counter to order our bill I missed her too much these few weeks. This is what we are. Effortless. How it should be.

I walk behind her at the counter and whisper, "Maybe next time, but we're not going to your place tonight."

A grin lines her lips as I step to the side of her. "No Nutella makes for an unhappy camper." Her head tilts to the side as she taps the bench top. I put my hand on top of hers and shake my head.

"I'll pay." I gently push her hand to the side, she narrows her eyes at me. "You can do the next time." She huffs and rolls her eyes. She knows that I won't let her do that either.

Once the bill is paid, we move to the entrance where we are farewelled by a waitress.

"So nice to see a young and in-love couple these days." The manager smiles as we pass her.

Trinity stiffens beside me, as she quickly corrects her, "No, sorry. We're just friends. Really good friends."

Yeah, I think as the rock of disappointment sinks in the pit of my stomach. *Friends who fuck.*

I clutch Trinity's hand and walk her swiftly out the door and into the cool night air. The tension between us begins to rise as I march towards my bike. *Just friends.* My mind repeats the words over and over. I know that's what we're meant to be, but surely she can *feel* there is something more? How can she not when everyone can see it?

Unlocking the helmets from the caddy, I toss one to Trinity before slamming mine on. *Calm down, dickhead. You're acting out like a toddler.*

"Ok-ay," she muses. "In a rush, I see. The Nutella will still be there when we get back."

Screw the Nutella. If I have to fuck the friends out of her, I will.

She flicks her tongue across her labret quickly, and my pulse quickens. Her eyes twinkle in mischief as I track every movement of those lips. A sensation jostles in my stomach as she continues the assault, running the tip of her tongue slowly along her bottom lip, sending a jolt straight to my groin. I know how good her tongue feels along my cock. I have felt that tongue trace almost every crevice of my body bar my lips. I stop watching her tongue and look to my boots for a moment as the excitement turns to a pang of unease, as it does every time we're together. Our lips never meet. Not from Trin's lack of trying. Instead, my stubborn self regresses back to that time when we were sixteen.

I blink that memory away, eager to get her to my place and in my bed. She is just as beautiful bound to a bed as she is free. The thought of her nails tearing along my spine almost tempts me to break every road rule to get home, but I won't—just. Instead, I begin to plan. I want precision and control while savouring each moment. The short distance apart from her is enough to have me kicking myself for being so foolish. It's time to show Trinity that this is not just a friendship. It's a necessity. We belong together.

I lift my leg over the bike and crank the ignition, tilting my head to motion for her to get on. Time to ride, in more ways than one.

Eleven

"Your tough exterior, isn't always going to protect that fragile heart of yours. Tread carefully."

Love, M

TRINITY

The bike roars beneath us. My pulse accelerates with every twist of the throttle. The wind cools against my skin under the edge of my helmet as we ride along the freeway, whizzing past the traffic that shadows us.

Theo takes me along the streets, determined to reach his place sooner rather than later. The tightening of my arms around his waist causes him to shift beneath my grip, his abs tightening. He's on a mission, and so help us, move, traffic, fucking move. *Hurry, Theo.*

We arrive finally at the entrance to his apartment. He bought this building two years ago and has busted his arse to rebuild it. From outside, the worn bricks give it that dirty, edgy feeling. Inside, it is an artist's dream.

He clicks the remote button on his keychain, and the corrugated-iron roller door begins to rise. He decided to leave the original door and attach it to a metal frame to complement the outer structure. As the door rises, I feel him straighten, and my grip naturally tightens, eager to hold on to him. I know he's just as excited as I am. He rolls his bike into the foyer, across the original concrete floor that existed here. Low-beam lights surround our feet so as not to show the outside world what inside looks like. I remember him explaining how the lights worked a while back, but my mind didn't give two shits about that right now.

As the door closes, the internal sensors flick on, flooding the bottom floor of the building with light. I dismount and unbuckle my helmet, and Theo climbs off after me. Our helmets are haphazardly thrown on the floor. His hand cuts through the tension-filled air to find my own, pulling me along the polished concrete floors of his lounge. He marches over to the left where the steel staircase is, the one that I deliberately asked him to copy for my own warehouse. I have memories from that staircase and banister. Good, hot, memories.

The polished floor has flecks of blues and reds that blast through it as we hurry up the stairs. Our heavy breathing is the only internal noise that I hear while trams outside trundle past. His hand tightens in mine as the last few steps are taken onto the top landing. My heart thumps with each stride. We swing a hard right past the study and bathroom and head into his bedroom. Theo lets go of my hand to suddenly block me from walking in any farther. His hard body turns in front of me, and my face flushes in anticipation. His strong hands reach forward and lift my bag over my shoulder and toss it at my feet. He raises his hands to grasp my shoulders to face him.

"Do you want to play?" Theo squeezes my shoulders slightly.

I feel a small tickle in my abdomen. I bite my lip as my eyes follow his forearms down to his shoulders and chest. A small smirk lines his perfect lips. Those lips that I yearn to kiss, but I know he'll reject me should I try.

"Do I have a choice?" I tilt my head, raising my eyebrow in a silent challenge.

"Always." His dark green eyes bore into mine, and I know that he could tie me naked to a moving bus and I'd be fine with it. I have already discovered that his Boy Scout knots for the bind and grind are pretty fucking spectacular.

"Then ...—I focus on his stare—"... you know I wanna play."

I turn my head towards his hand on my shoulder and brush my lips across his thumb. His breath hitches like I knew it would. If he moves his thumb to my pulse, he'd know I was feeling the same anticipation. My heart pounds for his next move.

"Hard or soft?" His thumb rubs across my collarbone and my nipples ache, wanting his hand to go lower.

"I get a choice?" I push my chest out slowly, hoping to drop a hint.

"Just one." He rubs both hands over my chest and stops just below my breasts before curving around them, leaving me to ache for him more. His hands drop to my hips, squeezing them before pulling my body flush against his.

"Surprise me." I rub my crotch against his before his hands go behind me to cup under my arse and lift me up against his hips. Wrapping my arms around his neck, I squeal, feeling the moment sizzle between us before his playing really starts. In just a few quick strides, he puts me down at the foot of his bed and sits on the edge of it. My feet totter for a moment before I regain my balance.

"Strip." His voice deepens as he leans back, running both hands down his thighs to rest them on his knees.

I play coy for a moment by reaching for the hem of my shirt and, as my hand tilts to drag it up my body, I release my fingers to bring them up to the side of my face and retrieve my earring. *I know he'll pay me back for teasing him, and leaving my shirt on, but it'll be so worth it.* I tilt my head to the other side and collect the other one before sashaying over to his bedside table. They chink against the wooden top as I reach down and pull open his "fun times" drawer before strolling back to stand in front of him. I want him to know that I'm all in. Now, it's up to him to decide.

"I don't believe I asked you to move or touch that." His head tilts back towards the drawer as he intensely stares at me.

I giggle before letting my fingers pull the soft material of my shirt up my body and over my head. I twirl it into the air before flinging it on the armchair in the corner.

"I just wanted to make sure that you've got your game face ready to go," I quip, unclicking my bra as I run my finger along the edge of the black lace. I fling it over to the side as his stern face watches my cheekiness. I kick off my shoes and flick them across the room while my hand unclips the top button of my pants. I shimmy my jeans down my legs, and am about to slide my undies down when his deep voice punctures the air.

"They stay on."

Standing in front of him, I cross my arms in front of my crotch, my feet jittery on the spot. Moments pass where he blatantly stares at me. I feel his gaze roll across my skin in a seductive caress that makes my knees wobble. Theo stands and takes a step closer to me, his eyes continuing to roam my body. Moving to my side and bending, I feel his warm breath against my shoulder. I continue to face forward as he steps behind me, out of sight. I know his eyes are trailing up the curves of my back, down past my black boy shorts to my ankles and back up to my neck. Each gaze causes a prickle to rush across my back, causing my hips to sway slightly.

"Stand still." He lowers his voice, and my thighs quiver. I clench my hands to quiet the rush that fills my blood, to try subdue my desire for him to touch me.

His face reaches the side of my cheek as he whispers in my ear, "Easy, firecracker. We've only just started." My cheek leans towards the sound of his voice while his lips move to the edge of my ear. "I have plans for you yet."

I swallow and close my eyes, using the sound of his breathing to mirror my own. I rub my thighs together and feel the dampness between them. His body is a hairsbreadth from mine. The heat from his chest transfers to my back as he moves his torso down the edge of my hip until his knees hit the floor by my feet.

"Keep your eyes closed," Theo orders while his fingers whisper between my ankles, slowly pushing my feet apart more. He turns his hands completely around to cup my lower calves while pressing his thumb to the base of my leg. His fingers extend and straighten on my calves as he moves them up the backs of my legs, gently yet ever-so-slowly. A slight tickle from his fingertips lingers against the edge of my skin, causing my hip to tighten and curve outwards.

Theo continues to run his fingers up my leg slowly as I feel them turn until they reach under the hem of my underwear. The cotton of his shirt brushes against the backs of my thighs while he rests his thumb under the elastic and squeezes under my bottom. I want him to tuck his thumb under the cotton and rub against my wet clit, but his hands remain against my skin. Unmoving. My core clenches involuntarily, knowing full well the power that his fingers will have once they're inside me.

"I was going to make you come on my bed, but after that little dance right there, I've changed my mind." He shifts behind me and releases the grip on my calves to run his hands down my legs, sending more shivers to my feet. Theo's hot breath whispers against my calf, and he runs his lips against my feverish flesh, causing my toes to curl. My fingers press into my palms as I try to rein in the uncontrollable urge to lift my feet off the ground. His palms recommence gliding up my legs while his soft lips trail after them. By the time he reaches my underwear, I'm soaked and panting for his touch. Theo moves his hands to my hips to tighten his grip, holding me upright. He breathes sharply between the juncture of my thighs, and I arch my back towards him and gasp loudly, the slap of his breath a direct hit on my already quivering nerves.

He chuckles against my skin, causing my legs to open slightly, wanting those lips closer to my aching clit. His thumbs trace along the underside of my buttocks, curving below to move between my legs. The damp cotton of my underwear is shifted inwards while he tucks both thumbs beneath me, running them along the edges of my pussy. His hands turn inwards and out, tracing along the edge as I internally beg for him to tear my undies off and plunge his fingers inside me.

Instead, I stand, restless, while his fingers continue to torment me, moving closer to my opening before moving away to trace along my crevices. My buttocks clench, the heat of his breath against the back of my thigh charges against my trembling skin with each wet stroke of his tongue. Theo runs his lips in a seductive kiss as his tongue flicks alongside my flesh. His lips move closer to the apex of my thighs, his breath leading the way to my swollen core that hungers for his fingers to finally touch it. I feel his tongue dart out to trace my underwear, and I lean into his touch.

His thumbs then shift to move to my core. Fucking finally! He traces my cunt. He weaves his hand across my clit, bunching my underwear to the centre to dip inside me. His arms push my legs farther apart as he dips his face deep into me, his tongue leading to lap at my aching core as I tilt my head back and moan loudly through each stroke. My legs tremble as I struggle to stand, swaying on the edge of my feet, my pussy tightening against his assault.

He feasts on me like a starved animal, his thumbs pressing in and out of me in a frenzied dance. I feel my pussy begin to throb, as I'm close. So close. He sucks on my lips hard before withdrawing, his fingers grasping the sides of my underwear to wrench the material down my legs. I growl in frustration as he stands and pushes me forward stopping us by the edge of his bed, his heat at my back. His hand grips my right hip, pulling me towards him. His teeth nip at my neck as he asks, "You want me, firecracker?"

"Yes, yes, please."

"You ready for me, firecracker?" He nips against my earlobe again, and I shiver. My shoulders are stiff from aching for him.

"Yes! For fuck's sake, just fuck me already!"

He chuckles and steps back, grasping my hip in his right hand and pushing me forward to lean against the edge of his bed. "Because you asked nicely."

He grasps my hip in one hand, and his other lowers his zip as he positions my pussy in front of him. Grabbing my hair, he pulls it back towards him, thrusting his hard cock inside me. I clutch the bedspread in front of me, crying out loud as he continues to rock into me, one thrust after another. I feel him plunge into my body's edge, the piercing in his cock rubbing against my walls as each stroke renders me speechless. I clench him while he thrusts, our pants the only noise heard in the room until his hand tightens on my hip and he roars, "This cunt is mine."

He thrusts as I tilt back into him, my hips jacking forward with him eager to reach my orgasm.

He slaps the side of my arse as he yells, "Isn't it?"

"Yes," I gasp, clutching the edge of the bedspread as I feel my orgasm approaching.

"Hold it," he orders, powering through my body as his fingers dig into my side. The heat begins to rise farther within me as his unrelenting thrusts take over. "Now, come now, honey." His voice stutters, and on command, I catapult into euphoria, my core clenching and throbbing as I moan through each stroke to release. His movements slow gradually as he groans, filling me.

Theo releases me and runs his hands along my back, rubbing me up and down. My legs give out, falling forward, and I allow the bed to catch me as his length slips out of me.

"My intentions were to do that slowly." His voice is coarse, and he coughs to clear his throat. "But while turning you on, and making you want me, it made me crazy too."

I giggle into the bedspread, lying my face to the side, watching him. "You couldn't even get naked, you horn dog."

He frowns slightly, as he rubs his hands against his thighs. "I honestly couldn't hold back. Fuck, you deserve better than that."

"You were quite the animal, Theo." I wiggle my eyebrows at him. "Lucky I like your animalistic side."

He smiles shyly, bitting his bottom lip. "You love it." The bed shifts as he climbs next to me, rubbing my back some more. "But honestly, around you, I can't seem to keep that animal in line."

"Don't even think about trying," I mumble, my eyes droopy until I feel *him* between my legs.

My body stiffens as I slide back, clench my thighs, and do the quick bolt to his bathroom. I hate this part. Despite us having our safe sex talk to go bare, it doesn't diminish the sense of *bleh* afterwards. I didn't like sticky thighs.

I quickly clean up and race back to his room, the chilly air tickling against my flushed skin. Theo stands by the bed, fully dressed. The only thing out of place is his tousled hair.

"You're quite distracting when you're naked," he muses as he gazes at my naked torso. "Any thoughts I had just turned to mush." His brows tighten for a moment and, his mouth opens to speak, but he shakes his head.

I scoot towards the pile of clothes thrown haphazardly around the place and begin dressing. Part of me wants him to continue what he was saying, but the chicken shit in me can't bear it. As I lift my bra from the floor, I look over to him and catch his eyes lingering on my hips. They trail up to my breasts before lifting to mine. His expression darkens, but I hold my hand up to halt those thoughts. *I guess he didn't want to talk after all.*

"Uh-uh, buddy. I have a ton of work to do tomorrow and appointments all day." I point to my hip. "This already feels tender, so I don't need you to add to it. I have stairs to walk up, for shit's sake."

Theo stands for a moment before he blinks, clearly enjoying the moment of my semi-naked torso. I quickly finish dressing and grab my bag by the door. "Let's go," I yell over my shoulder, dashing down the stairs. We don't do sleepovers, and while the moment isn't awkward, I want it to stay this way. The same pang of longing throbs in my chest, but I ignore it. Strolling along the landing, I pass his study, look in for a moment, and halt as the edge of a red drawing evokes a vague sense of familiarity.

Before I can look further, Theo's arm wraps around my shoulder, steering me away and down the stairs. Odd. I shrug and follow him down, enjoying this moment and wondering when I am going to have the lady balls to tackle an even bigger subject. *Us.*

Twelve

The panel displays a female character holding the sun in her hands, while he stands in the dark.

TTE

THEO

The small tip of the pen scratches against the sketchpad as I arch over the drawing to get the angle just right. I trace on top of the grey lead, taking my time to add the symmetry needed for the scene. Tilting my head to the side, I glance over to the desk lamp and move my hand to adjust it. The light overhead is adequate, but on dark nights with weary eyes, I need the extra light to seal my thoughts onto the canvas.

The figure that stands in the middle of the sketch is the one that takes the most time for me to draw. Each time I draw her, I feel a sense of connection to her as I unfold each thought into the story. As I trace her jawline, I have to hold myself back from making her identical ... to Trinity. I leave subtle hints each time, but I can only drop so many breadcrumbs until she discovers finally it's me who has her greedily awaiting the next novel. I don't want to spring it on her. I want her to discover it organically. Rather than slapping it down in front of her.

I make each page gutter perfect for the scenes that take place, being sure that each pencilled sketch has a maximum effect once it's coloured.

I work down towards her chest, using my memory to capture the long-sleeved shirt from last week. Instead of the actual naming of the band, I draw silhouettes of the band members' sides to distract from the original shirt she wore. For my own personal benefit, I increase the frizz in their hair to stand out more.

Trinity. I could spend hours staring at her and remember each detail a month later. She has a way of working into my mind so deeply that she now infiltrates almost every facet of my life.

I readjust the page slightly, to continue with the secondary characters. Our story is the basis of my novel, *Shatter Till I Fall*. When you grow up in a household where your mind is pushed but your words are meaningless, you learn to channel your emotions in another way. The pages in front of me can't hold back or trap silence. They scream with emotion and intent. Just as I want them to do. Of a woman who even though she has a companion so close to her side she could touch him, barely notices he's there. Instead, he stands trapped beside her, watching as every moment she lives digs into the cavity of his chest.

I play dirty in my novel. I know that Trinity is a believer in her "happily ever afters," even if she boasts that she thinks they are bullshit. I know the books that are stacked on her bookshelves all give her closure to a world where she thinks love is bound to a contract that will most definitely fail. What she hadn't banked on was me. TTE is my way of saying that she can fight love all she wants, but it is me who will show her that it isn't bullshit. TTE stands for us. It stands for our journey to hopefully get to where we should've been years ago. Trinity. Theo. Eternal. Our trifecta.

While I was at university, I had seen a few advertisements for a publishing competition to enter the "first chapter" of your graphic novel. It was the day after Harmony's funeral. Not only was I wrestling with the sadness of having lost the closest mother figure I had besides my grandmother, but Trinity's anger over that stupid fucking photo was also tearing me apart.

Claire, my only ex-girlfriend, was both my mistake and my escape. I had chosen to date her to distance myself from Trinity. She fell in love with me, but I never returned it. Instead, I used her to protect myself against the one thing that mattered to me. The one thing I couldn't afford to lose when the shit hit the fan in my household. We broke up when she realised that she could never get close to me, and I stupidly remained friends with her not realising that she would try to cling onto me. She even followed me to the same university in a desperate plea to convince me that we could be together. When she volunteered as a life model for one of our joint classes, I still felt nothing. When she was naked on stage, having her photo taken, I felt nothing. The disappointment on her face was evident. The photo itself was just a reference, purely to get as close to detail as possible for my subject. I barely felt anything when we had fucked throughout our relationship. Emotionally, I was empty.

That day, Trin's distraught face after seeing that photo, made me feel like shit. It made me ache for her. Her pain was my pain, and although we were caught up in a vicious circle of hurt, all I ever wanted was to be there for her. She is the only girl I've ever cared for, the only one I've loved and been hell-bent on winning back.

I poured myself into the pages of the cartoon—I sacrificed the remainder of what was left of me, and engraved it into a story of longing and hope. All these emotions were thrown onto the page in a vortex of colour and anguish. Two figures who represented us, who captured the essence of who we were.

After I submitted the first chapter to ComicWorld, it caught the eye of my editor, Tamara, who demanded the first edition in a fortnight. I was excited and made it happen. She then handballed it to my publisher. Ten novels later, the rest is history. Now the focus is the story of Adam and Mila, names that at the time meant nothing to me as I frantically chose them, but now worked for my fans.

Adam and Mila's story was simple—the poor schmuck Adam, hopelessly in love with Mila, the girl who never noticed him. If I could draw him in transparent ink, it would be perfect. Whilst they undergo their adventures together in life, a looming black cloud lurks at the edges of the panels, a constant threat to smother Adam in his last-ditch efforts to win Mila over. She's oblivious to the signs he throws at her, and he holds onto the hope that she will one day see him. But not everything is what it seems. Sometimes, those who wait on the sidelines get tired of waiting. Barely existing as they hold on by a thread.

As pathetic as that plot sounds, it works. It seemed that my misery makes for excellent sales … and commercial merchandise. It still floors me that I have a mug with the same tree of life that Adam and Mila always began and ended their adventure at, with the title *Shatter Till I Fall*, in front of it. Mine is hidden in one of my top kitchen cupboards.

Once the ink is dry, I check the final panel and gently erase out the pencil from my original sketch under the pen. Blowing the shavings away, I place it face down on the pages that are already completed. Reaching out to the side, I slide my rolling chair over to the right and open the lid to the scanner that is connected to my laptop. Grabbing a specialised wipe for it, I make sure to clean the entire glass to rid it of any possible smudges. The next part is just as important as my actual drawings.

Once the scanner is turned on, I lay the first page down to scan while accessing the Illustrator program on my laptop. For precaution, I cover the scanner in a black towel and begin to scan the pages individually. As the tunes of the Red Hot Chili Peppers sound in the background, my earlier fatigue begins to evaporate. Seeing the panels on the screen is always exhilarating. Bringing them to life with colour and extra details kick-starts the adrenaline in my veins. Before the characters were flat, but now, with the extra shading, filters, and backgrounds, I make it fucking phenomenal. Adding the blue tips to Mila's hair, I smile as her face likens to Trinity's even more while still holding a sense of ambiguity.

Tapping my foot on the carpet, I continue to add the fillers while humming along to the music. My editor has suggested I get in tune to the digital world by using the latest stylus touch screen, but I can't yet. For me, the tactile feel of the pencil is reminiscent of when I first met Trinity in our junior art class. I can't just throw that away, all for the sake of moving with the times. I need to get her my way.

As I make the finishing touches on the last page, my eyes are drawn to the bottom left panel. My chest flickers in hope as, within the crevice of the border, the single word "only" lays written neatly in the left corner. My final plan to have her notice all of me.

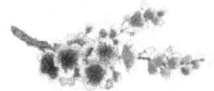

The drone of the jet engines whirls beside Trin and I as the plane cuts through the clouds effortlessly. I rub my hands on the armrest, eager for this tin can to land. Riding through chaotic traffic never worries me, but being in something I cannot control, does. Not to mention that my nerves are on high alert. In less than forty minutes, we'll both be home, and I will be visiting my father, all the while hoping that whatever the hell he wants can be said in a few minutes so I can go back to Trin.

"Oh, is someone scared of the itty-bitty plane?" Trinity croons as she stares down at my hand. I follow her gaze and instantly untighten my white knuckles from the armrest to move them to my leg.

"Yeah, yeah." I nudge her with my shoulder. "Not all of us can be tough as you, firecracker."

She smiles as she points towards the window. "We're fine up here—nothing to worry about. I was going to ask you to be my trusty sidekick in my next adventure, but I think I'll have to look at other applicants."

"You know this flying pencil is made from aluminium. The same shit you cover your roast with while it cooks in the oven."

"A ..." Her finger rises in the air. "As *if* I know how to cook a roast." She raises a second finger, and continues, "And B, there are other materials used in making planes. Like titanium."

"Oh." I raise my voice slightly. "Well, aren't we clever." I tap her on the head like she's a little girl, and she snaps her teeth at me.

"Watch it, smartarse. Or we can go skydiving now." She gestures to the cabin door, and I chuckle.

"Not today. I just washed my hair this morning," I deadpan.

"If you're chicken shit inside this plane, how are you going to cope when we jump out of the air balloon?"

I straighten, turning to face her. "I never said—"

"*Au contraire, monsieur,* I believe you did. You might just need to double up on the incontinence undies … for those embarrassing moments."

"Oh, someone is a shit stirrer today." I lean forward until my nose is almost against hers. "Mock me all you want, because for every gag I can tease you right back."

A slow smile moves her painted lips as she raises her eyebrow in challenge. "Promises, promises," she whispers close to my face.

"Always," I respond before glancing down at the bag by her feet. The corner of my latest novel sticks out and my gut clenches. I return my eyes to hers, but she doesn't notice my panic. Instead, bending down, she pulls the novel out and places it on her lap.

"Have I told you this month's dilemma?" she asks excitedly. She runs her hands along the cover, and her knees wobble slightly.

"Yeah, you did … on the phone, remember? When you ordered me to book the same flight as you."

"I did not order you, fool. Just politely encouraged you. There's a difference."

"You mean the, 'just fucking book the nine a.m. before they're all sold out, idiot' was just positive reinforcement? Bonus." I reach forward and grab the novel from her lap and flick through the pages.

"Gently." Her hands move up to guard around the magazine.

"I know." I smile, a sense of pride filling my chest. To know that she is enamoured with my novel makes it all worthwhile. All I have to do now is get her to be enamoured with *me*. She begins to prattle on the latest episode, and I stop flicking to watch her. Trin's eyes brighten whenever she's excited, and as she recaps the scene, I can't help but remember how I deliberately got her to read it in the first place.

Trin has read my collection of comic books and graphic novels, right from when we were teenagers. Rather than suggest reading this one, after I first released it, I fanned out a normal selection of novels, and simply tucked my first edition within them on my coffee table. Hook, line, and sinker. The only thing I hated was her paying for it. If I got her a subscription, she'd completely flip, even if it were a birthday gift. Yes, I paid for our dinners, but she'd lose her mind if I spent any more money on her. I found many different ways of paying it back to her. Especially through orgasms.

In my warehouse, my shelves are full of magazines and art books for drawing techniques. Trin has stood by those shelves and never recognised the signs. She's only seen me as being arty. My subtle hints might need to be turned up a bit. If only I had the courage to just tell her.

I interrupt her mid-whine over Mila being so damn blind and tell her of one of my plans. I can't hold it in any longer.

"I'm adding to my back tattoo next week."

She jolts back in surprise and grins wide, her eyes sparking with mirth. "Oh, what are you doing? Filling the tree?"

"Yep. Going to bunk up my trunk," I joke, "and thicken the branches."

"How many sessions until it's done?" She shifts in her seat, her thumb pressing into my novel.

"Four more."

"Oh, so how's your spine?" Her eyes twinkle knowingly.

I shudder. "Hurts like a bitch. Got a bit to do, but this time it's more on the roots. I have to build myself up to that pain again." The memory of my last session causes me to grimace. I am now a "seasoned" tattoo victim, despite the scratching and the third-degree burn sensations that I grit my teeth through, but I am not looking forward to having the last part of my lower spine done.

"Yeah." She sighs. "My back hurt like shit, but the reward of having it is worth it."

My eyes travel over Trin's bare shoulders, where her tank top rides low on her back while she sits forward. The cherry blossoms along her shoulder and the tree on her back reminded me of my oba-chan. In her home, she loved to display traditional artwork. My particular favourite were the two vases she had, one with a cherry blossom tree, and the other with a Geisha looking down at her kimono robe with the branches of blossoms along the hem. When she wasn't slaving away at her restaurant before she retired, Oba-chan taught me folklore whilst she baked my favourite dishes.

At times like this, I try not to dwell on missing my grandmother. I know she loved me, and I adored her, but the tension that my father caused that kept me suspended in a whirlpool of angst ruined the last few years I had with her. It has taken all my power to hold the bitterness at bay. Acting distant has worked better for me. Until this weekend. I turn from staring at Trinity's back and focus on the now rather than the later.

My identity is askew, caught in between two cultures, one which is all that I know, that I thought was all me. The other, which I presumed would be so foreign to me, is now felt beneath my skin. It's a lingering presence that I can't deny. The instant connection I felt with Elly when she charged into my life was proof of that, not to mention the rest of the family that she steamrolled through as well.

The thump of the plane wheels suddenly on the tarmac jerks me out of my daydream. As we glide along the runway, my stomach tightens while the stiffness in my joints increases. I barely register the plane halting and our movements to dismount the plane as my nerves begin to spike. The stress must show on my face as I walk along the tarmac, and Trin grabs my arm and squeezes it.

"Hey." Her grip tightens. "Dad and I can stay in the driveway while you go into your house, if you want?"

I shake my head. "No, I need to do this. Your house isn't far if I have to walk there. I'll be alright."

"You sure?" she asks as we step through the revolving door.

"I have to be," I reply sullenly, keeping my eyes focused ahead. I don't want to see her pity. It will weaken me. Heaven knows I need all the help I can get.

Forty minutes later, I knock on the front door as the reflection of Felix and Trinity in his car shimmers against the side windowpane.

Shuffled footsteps sound against the carpet that I remember is inside, and the door slowly opens to reveal my father, Ko. He stares at me for a moment, clutching the doorframe as though I'm an apparition. I guess after being ignored for so long, I'd wonder if I were real, too. He still looks the same, with only a few wrinkles here and there.

"Theo." His jaw twitches as he nods. Clearing his throat, he steps to the side to allow me to enter, the tension thick in the air.

I turn to look over my shoulder and wave to Felix, and my eyes dart quickly over to Trin, who is leaning forward, ready to jump out if I need her to. I'm glad I've left my bag with her and won't be staying long. I give her a thumbs up and wink before turning around, exhaling to expel any excess nerves. Time to get whatever this is over with.

Thirteen

"When are you going to forgive yourself, baby girl?"
Love, M

TRINITY

"I can't let him go in there alone." I grip the dashboard as Theo enters his old home. "His father will eat him alive."

"Baby girl, you have to let him go. He's a grown man; I'm sure he can handle it."

"How about we go to a café around the corner? I can message him and tell him that I'll S.O.S. him in ten minutes or so? I could make up that I was getting attacked by a wild gorilla or something."

My dad chuckles beside me as he puts the car into reverse. "Considering we are a good five-hour drive from a zoo where there are gorillas, I think you'll be safe."

"Ugh." I slouch back into my seat. "This sucks."

"Sorry to be the fun police, but let's head home and wait for him to contact us if he needs to."

"Okay, Mr. Word of Reason. But I'd happily go for a chocolate thickshake before that anyway."

"And a choc chip cookie?" My father smiles knowingly. When I was a kid, we spent most Friday nights after his work finished going into town and having a thickshake and cookie. We continued it into my teens.

I nod and straighten in my seat. "Sold. Take me to the goodies, Daddy-O."

He shakes his head and puts the car into reverse, leaving me to watch Theo's house, slightly less heavy hearted than I was a few moments ago. *I hope he's alright in there.*

As we drive away, I face forward and watch the same streets that I passed as a kid, marvelling at the subtle changes to houses and buildings. Even though change is inevitable in these country towns, it's still warming to see a couple of places maintain their original charm.

My abdomen clenches as a cramp weaves through me. I wrap my arm around my stomach in effort to calm it. *Yep, that time is approaching again. The dreaded painful hurricane.* Next week, I will be wondering what type of demon has infiltrated my body while trying to break out of my vagina. If being a girl during this time of the month isn't bad enough, the crippling pains from my endometriosis have me curled into a ball of hurt. And if my recent appointment with my gynaecologist was anything to go by (as in, from shit to hell), it seems this pain is a lovely reminder of my window of conceiving getting smaller and smaller. Every time a pain seizes me feels like a brutal reminder that my odds of achieving motherhood someday are most likely nil.

I breathe in and out slowly, conscious of my father next to me. Talk of pains can sometimes send him into over-protective mode. And after watching my mother die of ovarian cancer, any talk of the nether region sends him into high alert. If he knew when I saw my specialist, I was sure he'd fly down to make sure that the tests were clear. As much as it sucks that being a mum might not be in the cards for me, I'm lucky that it's nothing worse.

We pull into the café Bica, and I smile. The cramp lessens as I move apprehensively back in my seat. My dad parks the car by the fence near the jacaranda tree that instantly makes me wants to turn my hair a shade of purple. The blooms are a bright purple-blue, and I love how at home these trees make me feel. We step out as a gentle breeze sends some blooms floating down onto the bonnet.

"It's lucky your hair is that shade of blue; otherwise, I wouldn't be able to spot you," my dad jokes as he closes his door.

"Hardy har-har." I scrunch my face up and wiggle my finger at him. "Keep one eye open while you sleep, old man, or you may find the same shade in your hair in the morning … you know, the four wisps of it."

"It wouldn't surprise me in the slightest if you tried," he adds, as we walk side by side to the café. As we reach the entrance, he grabs my arm and looks directly at me. "Are you okay?" His eyes travel to my stomach and back to my face. Concern lines his brow as wrinkles that I hadn't noticed last time appear.

"Yes, it's just normal 'women's things.' " I pat his arm as his mouth tightens. "I promise, I'm okay. If anything, be grateful my trip was this weekend and not the next—you'd need to fill both your fridges with chocolate and stock up on rom-com DVDs."

Instantly, his mouth loosens, and he sighs in relief. Wordlessly, he opens the door and we make our way past the cake cabinet to the far corner, closest to the couches. Being the au fait café enthusiasts that we are (not really, but we pretend) taught us that we can people-watch better if we sit at our regular table. Facing the windows. Eyes on the prize.

"I'll just run up and order." Dad motions with his thumb to the front counter. "The usual?"

"Yep. Don't hold back on the choc chips or the full cream. None of that half cow crap." I nod as he strolls over.

Reaching into my bag, I retrieve my phone and check for messages. Nothing. I quickly open a new text and write to Theo.

> **Me:** If you need an S.O.S, I can come and sing ABBA outside your front door. Just give me a text.

I hold the phone in my palm and wait. Nothing. I place it on the table, and my dad returns soon after. Glancing at my phone, his brow raises. I had forgotten how much he hates phones at the table. The schoolgirl in me wants to reach up and grab it, but I can't miss a text from Theo.

"Sorry," I quickly explain. "I just sent a message to Theo. Can I just leave it there, just in case?"

He frowns but quickly gives in. "Okay, but what did you say to him?"

"I asked if he wanted an S.O.S. Offered to sing ABBA if needed."

My dad clutches his chest in fake surprise. "What?" he gasps. "He does know that you can't sing? Is he prepared to retrieve all the lost dogs that go bolting out of the neighbouring yards in fear?"

"I'm not that bad," I argue.

"No, you're worse."

"Dad ..." I warn.

"No, honey. We can't have you singing. Maybe you could mime or something. I'll just turn the car stereo up loud. It would help humanity." He squeezes his shirt more, and I stare at him for a moment. *He sure is chipper this morning.*

"Someone is a bit cheery today." I tap my phone as I stare at him. He wiggles his eyebrows as the waitress nears.

A soft wave of relief flutters over me. For a long time, I've kept phone calls short with him, as I couldn't handle his melancholy. I know that it is mostly on me to accept the blame for what I missed, but the grief from losing my mother still compounds into my basic thoughts sometimes. Seeing Dad crack a joke is both a blessing and a curse. I want him to be happy; I know that mum would want that also. It's another thing that makes me miss her so much. *Yet, I wasted our last time. Will she ever forgive me for ...?*

"I have a chocolate thickshake and skinny latte?" The waitress leans forward, and I straighten in my chair. She attempts to slide the latte to me, but I halt her by rotating my fingers in the air.

"Just swap them, please." I smile, while she frowns. "I have a sweet tooth," I inanely add, watching her slide her eyes quickly over me, probably wondering how many reps I would do tonight. None, lady. None. Another waitress walks over with our cookies, and I'm grateful that this one doesn't have Judgy McJudgy pants on.

That is the thing about small country towns. I don't miss the way people judge you. This city may be small, but it has more hairdressers and gyms per person than Melbourne. I am surprised the stench of fake tan isn't smelt in the room.

I look down at my dad's piece of fruitcake and cringe. Old habits die hard. "Geez, Dad. You couldn't have ordered something that was covered in chocolate? I just got the *fatty fatty boombah* look from that waitress."

"No, firecracker. She was just looking for the invisible barrel for where you store it all."

Being small usually means that I am at the butt end of jokes, but in my body, I could eat what I wanted, when I wanted, and not gain weight. Take that! Arsehole. The drawback is I am petite and have small boobs. I throw enough sass, though, to be almost mistaken for an emo-looking teenager. I take a sip of my thickshake and enjoy the rich chocolaty taste.

Laughter from a nearby table initiates fond memories of being here with Dad as each memory slips into focus. Us, laughing over stupid things or people. Watching couples and adlibbing their conversations (mostly with accents) while trying not to stare at weirdly dressed residential freaks. Great times. It was also a place for us to talk about the serious times the world had hurt us and let us down. When Mum's diagnosis ripped our lives apart, we came here in the comfort of the café after leaving many hospital visits, to have our moment to curse the world and call it an arsehole. My eyes travel to the couple over the other side and automatically, it makes me miss Theo.

"So," Dad interrupts my perusal of the touchy-feely couple in the corner who haven't realised that people can see under table tops. *Perverts.* "What's going on between you and Theo?"

"What?" *Is he psychic?* I grab the cookie from the plate, avoiding his eyes. I flip it over in my hand, counting the choc chips.

"Your old man isn't blind. So, what's going on?" He leans forward until his presence fills the space in front of me. *It's too intense for café hour.* I slump in my seat before sliding my eyes to him.

"We're friends, Dad."

"And the rest," he adds. "You dating?"

"It's complicated ... We're just enjoying the moment, I guess."

"Back in my day," he starts, and I bite into my cookie to avoid rolling my eyes, "we courted a girl."

"Dad ..." I groan. "Not the birds and the bees talk, seriously."

"Let me finish." He takes a sip of his coffee before continuing, moving his face back avoid steaming up his glasses. "I know you want to have fun, but why not have both?"

My face heats, and he smiles at me.

"Don't tell me my shy little flower is uncomfortable with this discussion?" He points to my face.

"Just cut out the sex talk, Dad. I'm a bit old for it. Should've had that a long time ago ..." *Maybe when I lost it in the back seat of a dickhead's car at a bonfire party. The day after I found out mum had cancer.*

"You might be too old for that talk, but you're not too old to talk about love."

I freeze in my seat as my hand shoots up in front of me. "Whoa!" I wave my hand quickly from side to side. "Now, where the hell did that come from? You can't just throw that word out there like that. Give me a heart attack."

"I find it very hard to believe that you're only friends."

I lower my hands as I glance down at my phone.

"Stop checking your phone. He'll call when he's ready,"

"I know, just ..."

"It's complicated?" Dad asks, raising his eyebrow at me.

"Yeah." *How can I possibly explain it to my dad when I can barely understand it myself?*

Since leaving the café, the conversation has turned down to a murmur between us. We arrive in the driveway of our old weatherboard home, and the nerves that I thought were controlled begin to swirl in my stomach. Five years later and I still feel what I did then. I stare at my lounge room window, and I can see our friends and family in there, sipping cups of tea while I struggled to stand. To breathe.

My car door opens, and Dad stands outside, holding my bag. His mouth twitches as he struggles to hold his emotions back. I close my eyes for a moment to push out the pain that continues to strike me like a shard across my chest. I puff out a breath quickly to flush out the nerves. *I can do this.* Opening my eyes, I unclick my seatbelt and climb out of the car. I have returned home on a few occasions, and I felt the sting that held me down each time. This time, it feels worse.

We walk along the paved path as Dad's hands shake the keys next to me. My bag brushes along my leg, and I control each exhale from my trembling lips. *Get your shit together.*

He fumbles a little, before sliding the key into the lock, then unlocking and pushing open the door. Our silence continues as we enter the lounge, and he drops my bag onto the floor.

"Trin, it's okay." His lowered voice fills the sadness in the room.

"I know," I whisper. "I just wish I wasn't such a mess in here still, you know?"

He steps closer to me and squeezes my shoulder. "We all have to face these battles head on. You've just learnt to fight them on your own. When you haven't needed to." He tilts his chin to the couch. "Come on. I need to talk to you about a few things. Let's get this over with so we can enjoy the rest of the weekend." I flinch under his fingertips, but he holds me still for a moment. "Come on, firecracker. It all will be okay."

I nod and walk over to our plush couch.

Growing up, my parents were really alternative. Taking a seat in the crushed red velour is a reminder of that. I run my eyes along the far side of the room, where the fireplace is. The mantelpiece holds many family memories. Mum's smiling face tears at my heart as she clings to me in one of the photos. That day, we had been to the beach at Apollo Bay, and it was freezing. I can remember her warm skin cocooning my shivery frame, protecting me against the harsh winds that flew our hair across our cheeks. From the smiles on our faces, you wouldn't know that I had slipped on a rock two minutes before or scrunched my face as the accidental taste of salt water. We'd laughed in that moment, enjoying the trepidation of any wave coming to push us over. The thrill of the unknown held us in its jubilant mercy. It was a photo of pure joy. If I thought about it more, I'd smell the sweetness of the berries of her shampoo. Everything that was her.

Swallowing the lump that gathers in my throat, I peruse the remaining photos. One more recent one sees me standing in front of my warehouse, jumping in the air with a champagne bottle in my hand. My legs are bent, and my back is arching. I look like a goofball, but it helps to soften the lump that falls in the pit of my stomach.

"Trinity." My dad's voice beckons me to turn to him.

"Okay, whatever it is, hit me with it."

Facing me, he rests a hand on my leg. "I've been thinking lately about what I want to do in life. I've got my long-service leave coming up again, so I'm going to be taking on some new things and making some changes." The lump begins to roll into my stomach. I feel my house is going to be slipping away from me, but I can't hold onto it anymore. My dad's happiness has to come first now.

"Of course. You should think about you, Dad. I hate that you're in this house all by yourself, miserable. You need to get out more."

"Trin." His hand taps my knee. "I've got a few big changes that I need to tell you about."

I squirm on the couch cushions and wait patiently.

"For starters, I'd like to get back into painting."

"That's great, Dad! I'd love to see you pick up a brush again. It's been ages."

"But in order for me to do that, I'd like to create a workroom. The garage isn't where I want to sit and paint. I need great light and comfort and ..."

"So, you're going to build an extension?"

"Not exactly." He pushes his square glasses up on his nose before returning his hand to my leg. "I was hoping to do some internal remodelling. Maybe change your old room into my new art studio."

My head jolts as I blink in surprise. "But that's my room," I say, feebly.

"Baby girl, this will always be your house, but since you have your new place, I was hoping to do a few things for *me*."

"I know, I know. I'm just being silly." Irrationally, I begin to tense up. My dad is right. This *is* his house, yet why do I feel a sense of abandonment? Surely moving my old things shouldn't be too hard. And then I remember what lies in my bedroom.

"There's something else I'm going to do." His hand moves from my leg to the back of his neck as he begins to rub it, his brow creasing in concern.

"What?" I turn, eager to hear him and block out the thoughts that just overtook me.

"I'm going on a few cruises in a month. Through Europe, the Caribbean, and hopefully flying

back this way to do some trekking through Asia."

"Wow, Dad!" I shrill. "That's awesome! Of course you should go. Can I fit in your suitcase?"

"Ah ..." He clears his throat as his hand holds the back of his neck. "I already have someone coming with me."

"Oh, nice. Is it Brett from work?"

"No, honey. It's Samantha."

"Who's that?" My voice quietens.

"She is a friend from work."

My heart thuds in my chest. "Is she a girlfriend?"

His hand squeezes my leg, and I wait. "We have been seeing each other, but taking things slow."

I swallow the emotion that I know I shouldn't feel. "Oh." I nod, biting my bottom lip. *It's been five years; I can't expect him to be alone forever.*

"She's not your mother, nor is she a replacement. Your mother and I spoke of the future, Trinity." He brushes my hair away from my face, and I lower my gaze. *I wasn't there to hear what she wanted. I was too busy trying to pretend she wasn't fading away.*

120

"I missed so much. I don't have anything to ..."

"Trinity, it's time."

My eyes rise to his. "For what?"

"You need to forgive yourself."

My spine stiffens as I slide back across the couch away from him. "I can't. I don't want to talk about it. I'm fine."

"Trinity, how do you expect anyone to remain close to you when all you do is shroud yourself in grief and pretence? Do your best friends know how much you hide from them?"

"Don't try to get into my head. You will never understand."

"You wonder why I was miserable on the phone? Because my only daughter couldn't stop blaming herself for something that was out of her control. Instead, she'd rather live a life punishing herself."

"BECAUSE I DESERVE IT!" I jump off the couch, the guilt crawling across my skin like a disease. "I feel how I should be feeling. You think I've forgotten that day? There's no way I can, and no way I should."

"I remember that day too, Trinity. Not once have I ever, ever made you feel accountable. I knew you would do that all on your own when you should never have had to." He pushes both hands behind his head and sighs. "You need to forgive yourself. Be happy. Be with Theo and have a future."

His words trigger a lightning bolt shooting into my spine, causing me to wince in pain.

"I kept her illness from him ...," my voice cracks, "... as I was a jealous bitch when he started dating Claire. I will never hurt him like that again, by punishing him. He deserves someone better than me. My feelings are irrelevant. I'm irrelevant." Slamming my hand against the wall, I yell, "How can I expect him to forgive me? I will never deserve a second chance, and you're a fuckwit if you think I do." I turn and rush to the mantelpiece, and snatch the photo of mum and I on the beach. I bolt down the corridor, clutching the frame to my chest, my cheeks stained with endless tears. I barrel through my door and slam it shut, locking it behind me.

Throwing myself onto the bed, I wail on top of the covers as the misery takes over. Turning the frame over in my hands, I stare at the photo as the grief strikes me once more. *I miss you, Mum. Help me. I don't know what to do anymore. How could I snap at my father like that?*

As the tears continue to roll, I ignore the constant knocking at my door. Instead, I push the frame to the side of me and clutch my pillow, burying my face in the pool of tears that begin to leak every painful memory.

Fourteen

The man stands within the panel, his clenched fists at his sides as the cloud looms closer to him. "When will you ever learn?"
TTE

THEO

I slip my shoes off in the foyer and look down to find the last pair of slippers I wore in this house on the shelf to the left. I still for a moment, surprised that my father kept them after all these years.

Shifting my shoes to that shelf, I grab my slippers and place them in front of my feet, sliding into them. The shuffling of my father's footsteps echoes along the hall as I follow him silently down the passage towards the living room.

As a child, I never wore proper shoes in the house. Even visitors had token slippers to wear. If I wore other shoes, it would be to stir up the wrath of my oba-chan. She could wield a Frisbee like a ninja and whack it against my back for showing disrespect. The one time I rebelled by wearing my sneakers, she managed to clip me at the back of the head with a shoe from the distance of two rooms away. She might've been a daughter of a Samurai from the precision of her moves.

Maintaining my family's native traditions was as important to them as it was necessary for my father. At the restaurant, my grandparents were one thing. My Japanese grandparents cooked Chinese for the country folk who, sadly, wouldn't have known the difference between cultures. In this case, ignorance hadn't been bliss; it had been fucking insulting. If they had tasted some of my oba-chan's Kombu soups, maybe they would have appreciated them more. Sadly, they just wanted their Number 13 with fried rice.

However, as time progressed, my grandparents modified their ways to blend with the Australian lifestyle --to a point. Importing furniture was expensive, so a part of who they were was sacrificed due to financial constraints. Some tokens were slowly shipped over, but mostly large parts of their furniture were bought here. They didn't sleep on the traditional tatami mats that I saw in photos or in the movies on the floor; instead, they compromised with lush mattresses for their ailing joints.

The Batsudan, however, was something that they didn't compromise on. As I enter the living room, the sweet scent of incense lures me to look over towards the family shrine. The dark wooden cabinet with opened folded doors sits at the back of the room. Inside, it holds a Buddha statue, whilst the candles that sit at the edge of the cabinet cast a soft glow against the gold carvings that line the wooden sides. The names of our family ancestors are carved there, and I can see small offerings of fruit and tea my father has put there on the Tamadana in front of it.

This cabinet is meant to remember the ancestors and family members that passed before us and, traditionally, it was meant to be passed to the first grandson of every family—me. Sadly, after the painful discovery of my real ancestry, I was never going to have this. Being distant from my father didn't mean that I was closed off to what I had grown up in. There were some binds that I couldn't break. A link to my grandparents was one of them.

When he revealed the secret of me being his *ainoko*—a half- breed—his shame was paramount. I was a son that was never his. I was a reminder of my mother's infidelity. The only woman he ever loved, who'd deceived him. The woman I was never allowed to speak of and whose betrayal had put me in an emotional impasse with my father.

My eyes move to the far end of the room, where a new small dining setting fills the space where the piano used to be. I had spent hours upon hours there. The piano my father worked hard to get, and that in an instant was smashed to smithereens by my hands and a handmade bat. Shame surrounds me as I remember how violently I attacked it all those years ago. As shit as it was to discover the lies from my past, I destroyed something that had always been a part of me. Even if it hurt to play. It was the only way I knew how to make Ko take a vested interest in me.

Ironically, I used the bat he had made so that we could blend in. As my mother's infidelity was revealed and my emotions torn up, I'd taken to that piano in the same way he'd controlled my entire life. I'd taken to smashing away the hurt from my youth. The broken anguish for a mother, whose memory was taken away from my childhood. How could I feel for her, when I was never given the chance to? Being told that her infidelity led to his poor treatment of me became my rage. In that instant, he became a spectator. Afterwards, I'd stepped over the broken pieces, vowing never to play the piano again.

A cold sense of dread layers my shoulders, and I roll them back to shake the memory away. Behaving that way in front of the Batsudan is one of the most disrespectful things I could have ever done. It is the equivalent of behaving badly on an altar or shitting on the carpet.

Ko clears his throat, and I turn to face him. *Do I call him Father? Dad?* I've never called him that. He stands to the side of the Batsudan, the smoke from his cigarette floating up beside him as he shuffles on his feet slightly. The photos of me as a child no longer sit across the wooden edge of the mantelpiece. They, too, became casualties that day.

The tension thickens as the silence continues to permeate the room. There is nothing in this room to connect it to me. To my pseudo identity.

I fold my arms across my chest, not wanting to appear intimidated or frightened when every cell in my body tells me to leave this house and close the door behind me. I can't be made to feel like I did all those years ago. I am not afraid. I am not the angry teenager they left here. I will wait for him to speak and show him that, despite my loathing and my ineptitude, when it comes to staying away forever, manners are still ingrained in me. I will not be made a fool of now. Like the imaginary bad children, he would compare me to when I got things wrong. The taunts, the criticisms ... no. I will not dishonour my grandparents as much I would like to dishonour *him.*

He takes another drag of his cigarette and squints as the end of the butt cinders. Blowing out the puff of smoke, his hand rises to the ashtray as his fingers twist the butt out.

"Theo." He puffs the remaining smoke through his lips. "Come, sit. I will bring us some tea." He gestures to the couch that separates us.

My feet remain planted. The couch is for comfort, and I don't want to be too close to him. I tilt my head towards the new table and say, "I'd prefer the window. It would be a shame to waste that new *setting.*"

He bristles from my tone, but quickly moves towards the kitchen's entrance as I move the chair back and take a seat. He returns soon after carrying a tray with a teapot and two traditional teacups, and then sits across from me. As he pours our tea, I can't help but compare him to my *oji-chan.* He was my distinguished grandfather who held himself well. His broad chest would puff out as he vividly told stories, his hands poignantly building tension. It was not common to experience this as he was not naturally warm in nature, but we valued each other. He was quite unlike my father, who preferred the passive-aggressive treatment to going for Father of the Year.

I prefer the civil approach as opposed to affection. I don't want the hugs and kisses. But like fuck am I going to be made to feel worthless again.

The warmth from the cup that I rotated between my fingertips did little to calm the chilled nerves that shivered below the surface.

"You've been well?" Ko asks, taking a sip of his tea before calmly placing it down on the table's surface.

"Yes." I nod, also placing my cup down to stop my fidgeting. Another ingrained habit from when I was a child. "Busy, but well. You?"

"Fine." He lifts his cup to sip his tea again. I awkwardly mimic his actions by raising my cup to sip my tea, ignoring the silence as the awkward tension continues to simmer. *I feel trapped in a prison of robotic servitude. What is it about this house?*

I take a moment and stare at him. The edge of his dark hairline is now grey, and he has more wrinkles around the edges of his eyes than he had seven years ago. Age has been kind to him, even if the lines make his grimaces more defined. A faint twitch of his right eye catches my attention for a moment before he turns his face away to blink quickly, his mouth flinching. He stiffens in his seat—anymore, and I wonder if his back will snap. I pick up my cup to drain it and almost chuckle at the thought. Almost. As riveting as this is, I'd rather be back with Trinity than sit in silence. I miss the peace that her noise gives me.

"Theo." He sighs as he clasps his hands together in front of him at the table. "Thank you for coming to visit me. I have thought about what I would say to you many times, when you would finally return home."

My pulse begins to quicken at the change in the air.

He presses his lips together before he continues, "There were so many times that I wanted to talk to you, but I knew you would not answer me."

What the hell did he expect? I push my shoulders back to sit straighter, taller.

"I have many things to talk about. To tell you."

"I'm here now. What is it that you want to say?" I gesture with my hand for him to go on.

"To be honest, I don't know where to start. There is a long history that you aren't aware of. It is my fault. All of it. That day when I told you ...," he clears his throat, "... that you weren't my son, I didn't stop to think."

My skin tightens from that memory. I stand from my seat abruptly, my father flinching in the process. I am too close to him. I don't want to be reminded of that day. I thought he had other things to talk about. Not this.

"I don't want to talk about it," My voice weakens and I clear my throat. I shake my head and curse myself for looking so vulnerable, hoping my chest doesn't cave in.

"There are many things that we must discuss," he presses, his tone heightening as a tinge of desperation lingers across his voice.

"Why? It was eight years ago. You should have told me twenty-four years ago. Instead of conditioning me to feel nothing for my mother. To only learn of her betrayal because you met Ricardo when I was sixteen. Him demanding to meet me was no reason for you to wait so long! Not now. Just be done with it." My hand swipes out in front of me to cut him off.

"No, Theo!" His hand thumps on top of the table, shaking the teacups. "No!"

"What?" I lean towards him, staring him down, disregarding every oath of respect I was ever taught. "You want another piano? Is that it? I'll buy one for you." I flick my hand in the air. "I'll buy a grand if it means you'll stop talking, right now!" I grind my teeth before I snarl, "You want me to call Amaya a whore? Is that it? You want me to be angry for what she did to you?"

"You must hear me out." His jaw trembles slightly. "You must."

I stand transfixed for a moment. These past few minutes have shown more emotion from my father than I've seen in years combined.

I sigh. My shoulders slump in defeat. Shaking my head, I relent. *It can't be that much worse than what he laid out on me all those years ago* ... surely.

"Just say your piece and be done with it." I thump the table for him to continue. "Get it over with."

He folds his hands together and leans forward slightly. "You know, I never wanted to love you," he tells me solemnly as I feel the weight on my chest tightening like a punch to the heart. Hearing what I always suspected he felt didn't make me want to fist-pump the air with *"I told you so!"*

"Well, you didn't have to." I try to keep my voice calm. "It was obvious."

He stares in front of him, his eyes lingering on the cherry blossom vase my oba-chan used to have in her house.

"I thought I was enough."

"What?" My brow creases in confusion. "For who?"

"Your *mother*. I hoped that I was all Amaya needed. But I was wrong."

"Because of me?"

"Before she betrayed me in order to get *you*."

I should walk away. Walk out and never come back. But I can't. I need to know. Part of me wants to hear exactly why I was never enough. Why Ricardo made an appearance to come and help ruin my life.

"You never told me what happened. You only told me I wasn't your son."

He closes his eyes for a moment and sighs. Shaking his head, his eyes open as he begins to tell me about my past. The past that I only heard snippets about, hints fed to me in daily whispers of being an *ainoko,* a half cast. The past that shook the foundations of the only life I'd ever known. "We married young and tried to have children for a few years. As time progressed, we had a feeling that something was wrong. Amaya went through all sorts of tests. As it turns out, the problem was with *me.* I was infertile."

He sits back in his chair as he unclasps his hands to press them into the table top before continuing. "After the initial shock, I thought that was it. It was enough. But I underestimated Amaya. Her hope for a child continued to burn. She wanted to adopt, but I forbade it. We were not in a financial position to afford it at the time. She began to resent me. I could see the love that she held in her eyes for me slowly dwindling. Months flew past, and the distance began to increase. She was travelling more and more for work, and spending time with brokers in Melbourne and Sydney rather than spending time here with me, where she belonged. Instead, she was trying to build our portfolio and increase our finances."

He looks out the window briefly while I shift in my seat, to resume, "I was still not interested in extending our family. I no longer wanted children. They served no purpose for me."

"What purpose could they serve?" I asked incredulously.

"I didn't need them. She was all I needed." He shakes his head and sighs. "Amaya began going to Melbourne frequently. It was one of the only times when she looked content. Relieved. A few months later, she confessed that she was pregnant."

"Did she ask for a divorce?"

"No." He grunted. "Shockingly, she threw her arms around me and said that she had 'fixed' us. That the affair she'd had finally gave her what she always wanted. She felt no connection to him and that the real father didn't even know. She threw our marriage in jeopardy all for being a mother." He shifts in his seat and frowns. "I couldn't stand her touching me. I stepped away from her and asked her to terminate it. Told her that she'd dishonoured me. But she refused. Instead, she made me choose her and you, or nothing. I was too proud to walk away. If I was not man enough to keep my wife with me, what did that make me? I chose her when she never chose me."

"Is this the part where I pat you on the shoulder and say, 'there, there'?" I snigger. "Where I tell you I'm sorry that my mother lied and betrayed you to get me? I refuse to be made to feel guilty for the actions of my mother who wanted a child. I was never at fault."

"No. But her actions were. She was not honourable."

"No, she was not honourable." I take a deep breath and it all begins to make sense to me. A sense of protection for a mother who fought to have me, despite her ill choices. "Yet, she was. To me. To the dream of having me. She fought for me." I clench my fists as I'm torn about wanting to defend my mother even though she had an affair.

"Even after you were born, it was still not enough. I was criticised for not bonding with you, for not playing with you. I was not making us a family." He huffs as he shifts in his seat. "One night, we fought and it escalated so badly that she threatened to leave with you. I held open the door and told her to go."

My mother died when I was young, and the memories I have of her are a haze. I can barely remember her voice or even how she smelled. Nothing of hers was kept in the house. Not even photos. Only the ghost of her remained, and I could see how that tormented my father while I was growing up. But in this moment, I feel a connection to her. A strong link, tying us together. The protection she cast upon me to get me in the first place is an indestructible force.

"She left in a haze while you were asleep, saying she needed to go for a drive. Before leaving, she stared me square in the face and told me that the next day she would leave with you and I would never see you again. That she would go to Melbourne to see if Ricardo Arce would be the man that I never was, taunting me with that man who had robbed me of my wife all those years before. She could no longer stand to see *my* face. I was the man she used to love, who refused to give her the one thing she wanted. She stormed out, and later that night, we lost her." He stands from his seat and keeps one hand resting on the table top as we make eye contact. "I was trapped. Made to look after a son who I never wanted. A boy who was a constant reminder of what I couldn't give to the woman I love—a failure. I was never enough for your mother."

"So a kid was enough to emasculate you? I was a child! You expected to drill regimented rules into my life and then tell me I wasn't even yours? You waited sixteen years to tell me that I had another father."

"Who never knew you existed. He deserved to know. I couldn't deal with the burden anymore, Theo. I had to tell him."

"I'm a fucking burden now?" I seethe, watching his mouth twitch. "Oh, this is just getting better and better." I step closer to him until I can see the redness in his eyes. "I don't want to know anymore. You have said *enough*."

"He deserved to know. I went to him and he demanded to get to know you. I couldn't have you never knowing ... especially after—"

"Enough." I hold my hand up. "Not. A. Word."

I turn and stare at the two vases on shelf near the table. One has a geisha made up of cherry blossoms in blue, red and ivory. *Trinity would love to see that.* The other depicts the face of geisha on an ivory vase. I pluck them from the shelf and call over my shoulder, "I don't want any of the things in my old room. But I want these." I reach forward and grab the alligator onyx ashtray that reminded me of my *oji-chan*. "And this. These are all I want."

"You deserved to know your real father." His voice wavers.

"Yeah." I turn towards the hallway, refusing to look at him. "Thanks for that. Now, he's infiltrated my life with building projects. Because one arsehole wasn't enough in my life, I had to get given another one."

I begin to walk briskly, but the tips of the slippers almost trip me up. Flicking them off my feet, I leave them on the carpet and pick up speed with my steps.

"THEO!" Ko bellows, shuffling in the lounge behind me. "I forbade him to see you before you finished high school. I had worked hard to get you to the top, and I wasn't going to let some distraction get in the way."

"You took away my identity as a child and swapped it into what you wanted. You have some nerve, you bitter old man."

"But I gave you his address; I needed you two to meet. I needed to make sure that you would be okay."

I continue to walk. I need to see Trin. I need to get the fuck out of here.

"I have Parkinson's disease." The words gush out, and my feet stop abruptly. "The doctor told me ten years ago, and I didn't know how to tell you."

His tremors ... moving slowly ...

"It's going to rob me of my life, Theo. My brain is going to be imprisoned by a useless body. I didn't want you to be alone after everything."

I shake my head. *Why can't there be a clean break where we both walk away from this?*

"What do you expect me to do about this?"

"I'm sorry. I just need you to know that. I should've never let discretions with your mother affect the love I have for you."

"Now you tell me? Really? I'm an adult now; I needed to hear that ten years ago when I thought all I was to you was a pianist, not a son. The burden who displeased you. Who was cut off from knowing his mother's family and even knowing his real father. Now you make me feel like shit when all I want to do is leave."

"I've failed again." His voice trembles behind me.

I turn and stare him square in the eye. Clasping the sleeve of my long-sleeved shirt, I begin to roll it up to the elbow and watch his eyes widen at the ink that lines my forearms. I move my hand to the other sleeve and slide the fabric up, revealing more ink.

"This dragon"—I point to my right forearm—"is what I got when I turned eighteen. I didn't have the guidance I wanted from you, but this?" I tap my arm. "It's my protector. When you dished your shit out to me and watched my world detonate, you told me no real son of yours would be so weak to take the news so poorly. In my sadness, you chose to take the liberty of shattering me even more. I didn't need you anymore."

"People will think you're a *yakuza*," his shakes his fist in disgust.

"A gangster?" I shake my head. "You have to be full Japanese to be that, and we know after our rendition of *This is your Life* that I'm definitely not."

I wish I could unburden myself from all of this shit. I slide my feet into my sneakers as Ko's voice whispers, "Please forgive me, Theo."

I turn to look over at him, and my chest tightens as I watch tears cascade down his cheeks. "I may not be your son by *blood*"—the cadence of my voice lowers—"but I will honour my ancestors. Even if they weren't mine in the first place. Forgiveness must be earned. You should know that."

I open the door and stomp through, tucking both vases under my arm to slam it behind me. Reaching into my pocket, I grab my phone and see the text that Trin sent. The tension in my shoulders loosens. Only she has the power to strengthen me—the only face I want to see. Notions of her singing, though, aren't as cheerful as they seem. Cats and dogs fighting hold a more melodic tune. I opt out of the text for the time being as another idea comes to mind. I quickly scan my contact list. Tapping my phone against the contact, I put it to my ear and wait.

"Theo!" Jason calls down the phone. "Long time no hear. How's things?"

"Good. I'm in town. You wouldn't happen to have a tattoo slot free would you? I know it's Saturday and all ..."

"As a matter of fact, this afternoon has been a bit slow, but drop in as

I'm not booked for another hour. The drunk eighteen-year-olds tend to take up my Saturdays, but today is a bit light. They must be sketching their butterflies and dolphins."

"Excellent. I'll see you soon." I pick up pace as I head for the main street. The script that circles in my head becomes more vivid and calming.

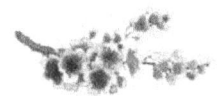

Afterwards, my back stings like I have sun-baked for twelve hours. When my shoulders move, the burn intensifies. But it is worth it. I pay Jason and shake his hand, a new sense of hope beginning to rise. I am done feeling like the victim. I have a reason in front of me that gives me hope. Trinity. Like my mother, I know what it feels like to want something so badly. To risk it all for a dream. I'm ready.

As I step out of the tattoo shop, my phone rings in my pocket. I shuffle the vases under my free arm and retrieve it with my other hand.

Reaching down, Trin's number flashes on my screen. *Ask and you shall receive.* Grinning, I brush my thumb across the green button and bring it to my ear. "Hey—"

"Theo." A deep male voice cuts me off.

"Felix?" I ask.

"Yeah. Trinity is in a bad way. Are you finished with your father? I need you to help her."

"Yes. I'm done? What happened?" My hand grips the phone, and I don't care if I crack the screen.

"I'll explain when I see you. Tell me where you are. I'll come and get you."

"No need." I pick up my feet and begin moving faster. "I'm about ten minutes away. I was in town. Tell her I'm on my way."

"I don't think she'd hear me through her wails." His voice breaks. "Hurry, Theo. My baby girl needs you."

I tuck my phone away and grip a vase in each hand, shooting through town, remembering all the shortcuts on my way to Trin's house. Could this day get any more fucked up?

It doesn't matter.

My girl needs me.

That is all that matters right now.

Hold on, firecracker. I'm coming.

Fifteen

"I forgive you."
Love, M

TRINITY

Uncontrollable pain.
My stomach hurts.
My legs hurt.
My head hurts.
My heart hurts.

Wave after wave, the hurt continues to wash over me, through me, around me, like a tidal that has clipped me off my feet. I clutch the corner of my pillow as my knees curl higher against my stomach. I can't breathe. I can't think. I can barely exist.

What the hell did I say to my dad? I am the last person to have any right to throw insults. I'm a selfish fucking bitch.

Oh God.

My memories of her and us are so scared and pure that I still struggle with letting her go. I hadn't wanted to leave for university the year after she was diagnosed, but she'd been stubborn. Holding her hand in mine as the tears rolled down my face and onto my acceptance letter, she'd told me, *"Live your life, Trinity. I want to know about all your adventures. I'll be fine."*

But she wasn't. Before I moved away at the end of my final year, she tried to hide most of it—the excess tubes of toothpaste to keep her mouth clean, the nausea, the scarves, the secret bouts of crying in her bedroom when she'd thought I was sleeping in ... all to evade the big "C" from taking over our lives. So while she tried to hide it, I played on the façade. It had been easier to pretend that everything was okay.

When her beautiful lush golden hair had first fallen out in clumps, I lost my shit. Even after it had grown back, I couldn't take the new dull brown hair that peaked through the silk scarves she wore on her head. Her running shoes were replaced with slippers and her satin dresses turned into robes over her pyjamas, all showcasing what was underneath. While one hand had carried the truth, the other concealed it with disguises, all as a tapestry of guilt that wrapped itself around her failing state, closing them all in.

So, I'd hidden. I'd gone to university, studied, and partied like a mad woman, making infrequent trips home. The doctors had only given her a year or two at best, but my imagination coaxed me into believing that it wasn't going to happen to us. It wouldn't happen to me.

We spoke almost every day. Through text or emails, brief or long, I carried my mother through what I was doing. I narrated the life of her only child as I flitted through uni life, sampling all that it gave to me.

The times I'd spent visiting, she carried on just like her name, Harmony. Being as harmonious as possible. As I'd aged, we'd meshed our roles of mother and daughter into a close bond as friends. While I'd sketched designs, she would scold me if I wasn't letting myself be seen. *"Never conform,"* she'd tell me. *"Instead, let the part that makes you alive fly."* For the assignments where I was restricted to traditional styles, I gritted my teeth and bore it. When the task gave us free rein, I took it and flew. Just as my mum had wanted.

But it had only been a matter of time before the peaceful façade had erupted. As her health had deteriorated so did my ... morals. I'd drowned myself in alcohol and men, looking for something to keep my mind from connecting to the moment. I'd dragged the girls to clubs and danced until my feet ached. Drank until my brain switched off and held the tug-of-war friendship with Theo, as I couldn't handle him not being there. I let my jealously over his relationship with Claire, override my need for his friendship. For his comfort.

As her hospital stays had grown longer, I'd pushed myself harder in the cycle of denial. The week before she died, I made a special trip to visit her, and she looked better than my dad had told me on the phone. She'd sat in bed and beamed at me as we'd talked, and my heart had hoped her smiles wouldn't be the last ones. They couldn't be. Surely. Such a foolish, fucking naïve idiot I was.

On her final day, I'd been the one who ignored Dad's plea to come home. I couldn't believe that she was worse. How could she be, when we had spoken on the phone the day before? He was obviously being paranoid. No one tells you how when death approaches, a person can have a slight second wind about them. A soft glow that glimmers with hope until their candle fades.

So, I'd taken to the dance floor and wrapped myself around a stranger. Our sweaty limbs had rubbed against each other's and I'd tried to get closer. Deeper. As the strobe lights had flashed with the music, I'd been lost and empty. While we kissed I fought away the voice of my father, telling myself that tomorrow, everything would be alright.

Until a hand had clasped my shoulder and pulled me away from the stranger in my arms. The dark brown sleeve turning me towards its body as the lights beamed towards the heavy chest that rose and fell in exertion. *Theo.* Without a word, he pulled me from the dance floor and led me to gather my coat and bag, and, in silence, we'd gone into his car for what was to be a six-hour journey.

As the alcohol had swirled in my stomach, I remember asking him to pull over several times to purge it. Still, no words had been spoken. It wasn't until we were parked in the hospital car park that he'd uttered the words, "I'm sorry, Trin. I tried to get us here as fast as I could."

Then, my world exploded. I'd thrown open the door and run to the entrance, bashing my fists against the closed glass doors that were locked afterhours. In a haze, I vaguely remember Theo holding my elbow and bringing me to another entrance in emergency, where we were rushed through doors and long corridors. Each felt like a rabbit warren with no escape.

The faded green door had been ajar, and I'd pushed it open to see soft light from within. My dad had sat with his head forward on a bed, his hands clasped around my mother's. My eyes had roamed instantly up to her face, her skin soft under the glow from the side lamp. My chest had ached and I'd rushed forward to the bed, my dad's body rising from the seat.

"Oh Trin," he'd wept. "Oh, baby ... she's gone."

"No!" I'd screamed, my hands frantically moving to her hands, arms, up her shoulders to her neck. "She can't be." Stroking her face, I'd sobbed, "Please wake up, Mum. Please, please wake up. Open your eyes for me. Let me see your eyes. I need you to wake up!" My thumb had stroked her cheek as the tears had streamed down my face, the heat rising in my skin and the cries continuing to wrack at my chest. "I di-didn't think," I'd stammered. "I tho-thought she would b-b-be okay."

Dad's arm had wrapped around my shoulder and pulled me back to lean against his chest. "Oh, Trinity." He'd wept. "What are we going to do?"

I'd broken out of his embrace and dived forward, needing to feel her hands. To check in my despair for any sign of movement. I had been gutless, selfish and horrid. She'd looked so tiny on the bed. I hadn't been able to bear watching the cancer chew her up and spit her out like some ragdoll, and I hadn't been there when she'd needed me the most.

"I should've been here. Oh my God, I should've been HERE!" The weight of my body shifted as my legs had struggled to stay upright.

Two strong arms had wrapped themselves around me, and I felt Theo's mouth against my ear. "I've got you."

"I never got to say goodbye." My voice had broken.

The loud thumping on the door shakes me from my thoughts. Clenching the pillow, I clutch it in my fist as I turn only my head to the door.

"Please," I beg. "I just want to be alone. I'm sorry for what I said, but I can't—"

"Trin, it's me." Theo's loud voice reverberates on the other side of the door. "Let me in or I'll break down the door."

I sit up slowly, my sobs still breaking through my chest. I breathe in small spurts, and turn my legs to the side until my feet plant on the floor. My forehead pounds, and it feels as if it's going to explode.

"Trinity." Theo's voice softens slightly. "Baby, let me in."

My ears prick at his endearment while my body raises off the bed. In a flash, I am unlocking my bedroom door and then Theo is there. In an instant, I'm in his arms; my sobs escalate, and the cries pass my lips.

"Shhh," he coos in my ear as his arm rubs my back up and down. "I'm here—it's all going to be alright."

I wrap my arms around him and hold on. He moves me back and we walk awkwardly in this embrace until we reach the bed. He shifts me to sit us next to each other, my head now resting on his shoulder, and he continues to hold me close.

I take big breaths to control the crying. Tremors rock my shoulders as the grip around his back intensifies. I close my eyes and focus on the sound of his own breathing, and I feel his neck is hot against the back of my head. I lick my lips and taste the salt of my shame.

"Have you be-en runn-ing?" I murmur through puffs of air.

"I was in town and ran straight over. Your father called me."

"Oh God." My nose wrinkles. "I was so disrespectful before. If you had heard me ... I was a fucking bitch." I sniff as my nose congests. "The things I said ... I've never spoken to him like that. I'm so ashamed."

"He wasn't angry; he was worried. He's waiting in the kitchen for us. He could never be angry at you."

"Thanks." I smile timidly, my cheeks stinging slightly from the salty tear streaks. I hate feeling pathetic, but I am rocking that look today—pathetic, selfish, and useless. Yet Theo's embrace is restoring the warmth into my broken body. His hand brushes the side of my face and I lean into it, savouring his tenderness. We stare at each other, not saying anything but saying everything at the same time. My eyes linger on his mouth, and I run my tongue along my bottom lip, wetting the dryness away.

My stomach tightens. Will he kiss me?

His face draws closer, but his lips don't pass across my own. Instead, his forehead presses gently against mine. I close my eyes as allow the ache of my body to leave me.

We're forehead to forehead, breathing each other in. His chest rises and falls, and my hand reaches out and holds the side of his arm, bringing him closer.

"Trin." His deep voice is like a warm chocolate. "With everything that has gone on in our lives, you are the only constant I have."

"In what way?" I ask, nuzzling closer, needing the connection with him to anchor me.

"That no matter how shit, confused, angry or weak I feel, I have you to guide me." He leans back and I can see his eyes. "Let me be that constant for you."

My stomach melts like warm honey. I'm not going to wait any longer. I can't. I want this more than anything.

I raise my hands up to cup his face and smile. I lean forward and rub my nose across his, back and forth, as soft butterflies tickle my insides. "You already are. Even though I know I don't deserve you."

"You're right." His nose moves against mine as my heart thuds. "You deserve better."

"Oh!" I lean back and stare at the ceiling, moving my hand to my hip in indignation. "Well, aren't we just a bunch of sorry fools!"

He throws his head back and laughs, and instantly I wonder why the hell we've been dancing around one another for so long. I can't wait anymore. I can see from how he looks at me that he can't either.

My ankle shifts as it nudges something under my bed. My eyes widen as I remember what lies under there, breaking the tension that tethers Theo and I. My body flicks up in fear as my foot moves away, afraid to touch it.

Theo frowns in confusion as he leans to the side to see why I'm turning on the freak. "Did something bite you?" he says, as he peers at the floor by my feet and then looks back at me.

I shake my head. I turn to the other side and run my fingers along the edges of my bedspread and pinching overlap until I make peaks, even though I preferred where my hands were a few moments ago. Anything to keep me distracted.

Some people are scared about monsters under their beds. They hold their feet in under their sheets so as not to be bitten when they cover their tiny bodies in bedding so besides their head, no flesh will show. They clench the top sheet between their fingers, holding it up to their chins so tightly that not even a crow bar could extract the white-knuckled fingers that clasp it for dear life.

Me? The monster lurking under my bed is in the shape of a brown box. I am scared of the box under my bed containing the frayed-edged papers as another assortment of guilt is enclosed inside. My terror lay in that box. Within it are several handwritten letters, all folded up and lovingly tucked into envelopes, ready for me to read. Messages from Mum to me. Her last wishes, thoughts, and desires. All of what I haven't been able to bring myself to read.

With every beat of my heart, I long for her to be alive. I've convinced myself that reading those letters will be the final goodbye. The goodbye I robbed her of while I was a tart on a sticky dance floor. In my mind, I need to suffer and be punished. If I open those letters, then it means that she is really gone. All she will be is mist and she will gradually fade. I feel like my heart lies with that box, crushed between the pages of words too precious to hear and too sacred to disturb.

Theo moves beside me and before I know it, a very dusty brown box is placed on my lap.

I stiffen like my body has been thrown a fireball. I'm about to toss it across the room when I consider what lays inside.

"It's letters addressed to me ... by my mother," I say softly. My hand begins to wipe away the dust from the top of the box as I hold it with my other hand.

"Have you read them?" Theo places his hand on my knee, and I realise that it's been trembling.

"No. I only read a little of one letter the day of her funeral, but I can't bring myself to do it." He squeezes my knee and I continue, "I didn't say goodbye to her. Or kiss her and tell her that I loved her while she could still understand me. Now? They're empty words that are carried off by the wind. She can't hear me."

"You should read them. You need to."

"But I don't deserve to," I whisper.

"We all make mistakes. But it's the lessons we learn ..."

"Please don't quote a self-help novel. I can't deal with that crap right now."

His thumb traces my knee as he reaches forward to grab the box. "Well, we can burn them then. If you're not going to read them, might as well ..."

"NO!" I shriek as I grab the box from him and hold it close to my chest. "Never."

"Good. Then we'll take it back with us, and you can read them when you're ready."

"Wait! What?" I hold it closer to my front.

"No more regrets. You need to begin to live properly. You're not yourself fully. But we can get back there."

"But the letters will hurt." My lip trembles.

"Sometimes a little pain is what we need to grow," he reasons.

"I don't have the strength to cope. Don't you remember that day? I was reading that letter, and you and I ..."

"Yes, I do. But still, you need to move forward."

"It was a shitty day. I swear it must be this room. The funeral and then when we were sixteen and in this room, and you jumped ten feet in disgust after you barged in here and kissed me."

"Trinity," Theo lays his hand on top of mine as it rests on the box. He sighs and takes a moment to respond, rolling his bottom lip between his teeth. "There's so much you don't know." Taking a moment, he frowns before staring at me straight on, leaving me wounded. Breathless. Desperate. "That was the worst day of my fucking life."

Like a punch to the heart, I suddenly feel alone.

My Theo.

Probably not mine after all.

Sixteen

The woman and man stand in the panel, facing each other in front of the broken tree. The heat within the pulsing heart beats as he holds her face in his hands.

TTE

THEO

"It's not what you think," I add hastily. "I have so much to tell you."

I watch her startled expression, her eyes widening as they fill with fear. I curl her fingers beneath mine into her letterbox. If I don't act soon, I know she'll start to build that fortress again to protect herself and shut me out. No more distance. *Not after today, you won't be keeping me out. You're mine now. Destiny would not have the two of us here in this room to fuck with us yet again. Surely.*

Trin stiffens her shoulders, and shuffles back along the edge of the bed, her hand attempting to move from mine it, but I tighten my grip. "No, Trin. Please listen."

Glancing at the box, I move my hand to the lid and remember the last time I was here. Sometimes, the ugliest moments are the ones that we need to work out before we can move forward. Trin is long overdue for explanations, no matter how much they make my stomach churn like a meat grinder.

"You know"—I tap my finger on the box lid—"the last time I was here, you had a letter in your hand and you were a mess."

"I remember," she whispers.

"You still need to finish it," I add tenderly,

"I know ..." Her voice breaks.

"Another time, when we were in here ..."

"You kissed me and lost your shit," she interrupts, slipping her hand from mine and moving back, leaving a gulf between us.

"We don't have a lot of good memories in this room," I add, trying to work out how the hell to fix the hole that I'm digging myself into. To make everything finally right.

"You mean, when we kissed like animals and you jumped back at least a foot? Way to ruin my first kiss, by the way." Anger simmers around her like tension-filled waves.

"Okay," I raise my hand, standing from the bed to step away as the stress of that moment comes lurking again. My hand curls into my hair at the front of my head, but it's too short to pull. *Old habits die hard.* Years spent hiding behind my fringe, and now I almost need it. My fingers flex as I try to keep busy. "I just spent time with Ko cementing the bullshit that I learnt a long time ago. Not only was I reminded how desolate my home life was, but in actual fact, I was reminded I was never really meant to be part of it. It made me hide from you, from my friends, and even from myself. That day that you're remembering, when I came here ..." I shake my shoulders to relieve the tension that builds across my back, "... was the day that I found out that my father, Ko, wasn't my real father."

"What?" Trin's back straightens as she moves the box from her lap to her bed. She leans forward to stand, but I hold my hand out to stop her.

"No, let me say what I need to say." I pace, worried that I'll jam up and not continue, but the friction of the moment pushes me to go ahead. "You *know* what my household was like." I flick my hand in front of me. "I didn't have parents like yours, who were normal. Instead, I had strict grandparents who tried to give affection, but couldn't, and one parent who was more a boss than a father. That day ..." I stop as I turn to face her, "... I had just finished my last piano exam for the semester, and my fingers were tense from playing *Rachmaninoff Piano Concerto #3*. I had stuffed up the final movement in the finale. Much to my father's dismay," I spat. "We stood afterwards in the lounge area, where he proceeded to tell me what a failure I was that the *toccata climax* was dismal in its intended effect and didn't receive a perfect score." My mouth tightens as memories of the hand cramps from that time resurface. "I don't remember school or the things I did during that time, except practicing that song. The movements ran through my head on repeat—a never-ending torment. When I was home, I practiced. At school, I used my free time to march across the two campuses to use the piano room *with special permission my father had organised*," I hissed. "I thought about that fucking song until my ears bled."

"I don't understand why he took it so seriously?" Trin gently prods, folding her leg to sit it underneath her.

"He was disappointed in me. What better way of letting me really feel that hole of disappointment than by telling me that any son of *his* wouldn't make mistakes." I stare at the carpet and close my eyes for a moment. "After he scolded me and dropped that bombshell, everything else imploded." Holding my hand in front of me, I began to tick off the memories. "I could break it down, and it still wouldn't make it better. My mother wanted kids, and he didn't. My mother had an affair." My finger ticks off my thumb. "Today, I learned my father found out about her affair and was too proud to make her leave as he loved her ... until he wasn't. Then she died in a car accident after they fought. Back then I was angry, because I'd been lied to; today I'm livid as he neglected to tell me the whole truth all those years ago." Raising my next finger, I continue, "My *real* father didn't know I existed until Ko contacted him. Apparently, the guilt was too hard to bear. Looking after someone who was a constant reminder of his failings in his marriage. It wasn't enough that he had to make life hard—he had to just keep adding to the mix."

"Theo ..." Trin begins, but I'm on a roll, and my tongue continues to lather the words that tumble out of my mouth.

"Back then, my real father actually wanted to meet me and get to know me. But Ko forbade it."

"Why didn't your real father at least try? Why wouldn't Ko let him?"

"He did try, but he was told to keep a distance to not fuck with my schooling. Can you believe that? I thought at first Ko wanted me to suffer just like he had. Once I moved to Melbourne for university, I stalked Ricardo online and went to his office. The day I stormed in, I not only marched in on him, but my siblings. They looked so similar to me. I hadn't felt that familiar to anyone ever. Not even my mother, from the little memories I have of her. So aside from Ko burning almost all her pictures and any sources of memory of her except the photo I had kept on my bedside table, he had to take the only thing that was real to me—an actual father. For all those years."

"Oh, Theo." Trin's voice wavers as she stares up at me. "What a shitty way to tell you, especially since you have a family you didn't know about."

"I couldn't take it," my lips twitch, my feet picking up to pace again. "So I picked up the handmade cricket bat that the man who I'd grown up thinking was my father had made and took out all the bullshit he had fed me and turned it into shatters. His worthless half-cast son was a tyrant. If he had mentioned me having sisters, I would have lost my shit on the whole house." I stop just in front of Trin as my chest heaves. "I left his house, needing to be anywhere else. I came running to you, as you're all I've ever had that feels like *home*. Someone who understands that I am weird, or need time to adjust. You just get me."

A small wounded smile breaks across her lips. "You came in like a hurricane," she sighs.

She's right. I'd flown past her parents in distress and charged into Trin's room, finding her on the floor, sorting out her latest art sketches. I'd thrown myself down at her feet, and before she could ask me what was up, I'd pulled her to me and kissed her.

"I felt like my lips were on fire." I reach for her face and rub my thumb across her cheek. "I never felt so alive as I did when I kissed you—until the fear crept in. After learning about my mother, Ko, and my real father, I couldn't handle it. I thought after all this fucked up mess

147

that the one thing that was always constant, was always there, was you—and you were too important to lose."

"How do you know you would've lost me?" She leans into my touch.

"I couldn't risk it. I was more frightened of losing you than anything else. I was scared shitless." I look away, dropping my hand, almost too ashamed to admit the next part. "So I threw myself at Claire when I got back to school. I needed someone who was *disposable*. Who I could leave without any hard feelings."

Trin snorts as my eyes flick back to her. "*Hard* was probably what you were testing out while with her." She smiles, but I know that smile is bullshit. Her eyes can't hide the jealous fire that rages within. "It made me a fool, too. I hid my mother's illness from you for a few months. That was uncalled for."

"We both fucked up. I was a naïve idiot, you were hurting on so many levels, and to top it off, when she hid those stupid naked photos in my folio to entice me to take her back, I never could. There was so much history between us. So much left unsaid. She wasn't you. But she made a good point of knowing how to keep us apart."

"She sabotaged us, without even knowing it," Trin concedes. "Those photos tore a hole in my heart, Theo. Seeing naked photos of someone you were intimate with is every girl's nightmare. I felt I could never compete with her."

"You don't need to. You surpass anything and everything about her."

"No, I don't," she snaps, startling me. "You *kissed* her"—her nose wrinkles in disgust—"repeatedly."

"I don't know how to explain it without sounding like a dick. Kissing you the day of the funeral, somehow meshed together with all the bad shit that circulated in my head. I felt like I was tainted, and if I kissed you, I would ruin everything once again. My mind has a fucked up way of making me panic."

"Ugh," she groans. "So I have cursed lips. Great." Her sarcasm stings as I try to muster the last ounce of courage for what I want to say and do. "I don't think I can handle talking about this shit anymore."

But I can't leave it there. "There's more." She flinches, but I continue

148

"My real father has been making random appearances in my life since I was eighteen. He's the wealthy businessman who owns Arce's Enterprises, and he has decided that the best way to get to know me is to ambush my career and make me design things for him." I blow a breath out before continuing. "I've met his family in parts now, too. It seems that they want to get to know me as well."

"Whoa." Her eyes widen. "Things are a bit of a mess for you at the moment, then?"

I sit down beside her on her bed and grab both of her hands in mine, curling them between my fingers. "In some areas, but there's some that I want to fix. But out of all this bullshit, there are things that I marvel at. My mother *wanted me.* Yes, she betrayed her husband, but it was all to have a child. That speaks volumes of her love for me and that striving for what you hold most dear is worth all the shit in between. I have sisters who want to know me and a father who I can't work out, but I now know what it feels like to be determined. I know, this time, I'm not going to lose. I want to take a chance."

We lean forward, and our foreheads touch. Her warmth bleeds into mine stronger than before. *Take a chance on us,* my mind begs. *Say yes.* My lips tremble as we breathe in each other. Every breath lingers between the divide of us.

"I'm scared." Her fingers grip mine.

"Say you'll give us a chance."

"What if we stuff up? What if we end up really hating each other?"

I tilt my head back to watch her blue eyes blink away tears that threaten to fall. "For starters, that could never happen. Wherever this journey takes us, you are always a part of me."

"Was that written on a Hallmark card somewhere? Because it's kinda cheesy." She smiles shyly.

"No, this is all me." I move my hands to both sides of her face. "I meant every word, like I mean this."

Before she can respond, my lips touch hers and strike the dormant match. But this time, I don't feel afraid. As my lips caress hers, the fire ignites and rises within me while our tongues fight the dance of a hundred warriors. We have fought to be in this moment. I can't get enough of her as my touch roams her body, dodging her own desperate hands, and they wander in the same need as me. She is mine. As our lips continue to devour each other, I grip her close to me, not wanting to break contact. She is the resin that casts my fractured soul, fusing it together. Finally.

Part of me wants to tell her that she should already know where my feelings lie. That they are scattered within the coloured pages of my comic that she loves so much. But, even in a moment like this, while I'm so desperate to remember every detail of her face to sketch later—I can't. This moment is far too precious to be captured in print. It's ours, and ours alone. I know I need to tell her, but now isn't the time. Besides, I want to give my characters the perfect journey and do right by her.

"Theo," she breathes against my lips, her chest rising rapidly as her pants turn me on. "I want this." She pecks my lips. "I want us." She kisses me again. "I want to take a chance." Her hand rubs down my back, and the burn causes my spine to curve slightly. "What's wrong?" Her heated gaze stares at me, a mixture of lust and confusion.

"I got more artwork done today after I saw Ko."

She smiles in glee, lifting the edge of my shirt, but I stop her.

"I'll show you later." I wiggle my eyebrows at her as she flicks my shoulder with her hand.

"I'll hold you to that. But for now, if my senses aren't wrong, I think my dad is cooking something, and I'm starved."

"Well, let's get you fed, then."

"I have an apology to make to him, too," she adds, biting her lip.

"He'll forgive you for whatever it was."

"I was rude to him about having a female friend. He should be meeting people. He shouldn't be alone. He's been so miserable on the phone."

"Then I bet you'll find that he'll forgive you."

Trin leans forward and wraps her arms around me ,muttering against my lips, "Still don't think I deserve you."

"I know. Like I said, you deserve better," I remind her, rubbing my nose against hers.

"Oh shut it, princess." I feel her smile against mine before she presses her lips harder and kisses me. We shift on the bed as the kiss unfolds, but the edge of the box beside my hip pokes me.

I break away, scrunching my hand in her hair to hold myself back. "I faced my demons today." I look at her deep blue eyes and tread carefully. "Are you ready to face yours?"

Her eyes lower to my hip as her face pales. "I've been so scared of that box." An uncomfortable chuckle passes her lips. "I thought I could hide it under the bed and it wouldn't come out to scare me. I guess I was wrong."

I straighten the box and move it closer to her. "I am here, if you want to do this. If you want to be alone, I can be just outside that door, and you can call out—"

"Stop!" she cries as she clutches the box. "I just need a moment to grow my lady balls. You're not moving. I can do this. I need to." Her chest rises dramatically, and she flicks her labret with her tongue. This would be the worst time to tell her that I want to lick it.

The dust from the cover unsettles as she opens the lid to reveal a box lined with letter after letter, all tucked away neatly.

"Wow." My eyes linger on the multi-coloured envelopes. Even now, Harmony still has a way to bring colour to our world.

"Dad told me that she'd written all these letters for special moments for me. I can't imagine which ones she wrote as this box is chock-a-block full."

"She wanted you to live a full life, firecracker." I rub her knee in support. My brave temptress is about to make me even more proud of her.

"God, I'm scared," Trin mumbles, as her fingers slide up the envelopes. She reaches the end and draws out the first. A soft sigh leaves her lips as she utters, "This is the one I started and never finished." Her eyes well with tears as she breathes out slowly. "Her goodbye letter."

"Take your time. I'm right here."

"If I pass out, catch me, okay?" she pleads.

"You won't, but I'll catch you either way."

"I'm going to be such a mess. Bet my face puffs up like a pufferfish." She chuckles half-heartedly.

I stroke her face to centre her. "There is beauty in pain. I see beauty through that pain that shines through you. Give me your fire, your anger—give it all to me. You're allowed to grieve. You're allowed to feel. Let me see you. All of you."

Unfolding the letter from the envelope, she shuffles on the spot until she's comfortable. She flicks her eyes up to mine. I nod, and she lowers her gaze to begin reading.

My baby girl,

Oh, how much I would give to be sitting next to you right now. I know you're hurting, my love; I can't tell you how much it pains me, knowing that you are reading this letter. Leaving you with this breaks my heart. How does a person even begin? If I could, I'd write you a million letters, so you'd have one every day. But I can't. I barely have the strength to write this one.

Know that I fought, Trinity, with every part of me, I fought. Sadly, my plans on this earth took a turn that I didn't expect. So, if my destiny is to be robbed from watching you grow and be the woman you are born to be, know that I am with you in spirit. Every step of the way. I want you to grow into the woman you were born to become—strong, determined, fearless, and loved. I want you to soar, my darling. I want you to never be afraid.

Choose a life full of colour, and never ever hold onto regret. Life is far too short. If I can't hold your hand along the way, remember that all you have to do is have a beating heart, as that's where I'll be. Beating alongside you. Taking each step with you as you live your life.

I love you. Past the stars, the love-heart-shaped ones, and all the mushy stuff in between.

Mum

"Oh my God." She hiccups, and streams of tears cascade down her face. "I can't believe she wrote our saying." Her voice breaks.

"Which one?" I stroke her face, a sense of pride fiercely resurfacing. I brush the tears away, marvelling at the strength she has, knowing that's a part of why I've always been drawn to her.

"Past the stars, the love-heart-shaped one ... we used to make up many other ones, like rainbow stars and unicorn stars ... Sometimes saying good night took a long time while my creative mind tried to think of more ways to say that I loved her." She reaches for the envelope as her mouth opens. "Look at this!" Her eyes brighten. She plucks out some coloured shapes from inside. She holds one out to me, and it's a heart with stars drawn all over it.

"That is so your mum." I chuckle.

"God, I loved her." Her voice wavers.

"You still do." I pull her into my embrace.

"Yeah, I do," she says into my chest as her arms wrap around me tightly.

"Was it worse than the time you tried to cut my hair and we used your mother's good scissors?" I ask slowly, my fingers caressing along her spine.

She sniggers as I continue to draw. "Yes."

We still haven't moved from her bed, but her nerves about speaking to Felix have resurfaced.

"Worse than when you told that teacher to stop staring up girls' skirts at school?"

"Oh my God, yes!"

"Or the time you stuck your finger up at that kid at the football game?"

"He was antagonising me, as my team was losing. I haven't been back since."

"Or the time you went to that bonfire and I found you in the back of that truck—"

She flinches and sits back. "Oh no." She glares at me. "We do not talk about that night. I gave up my V-card, and it was the worst night ever. He was a fucking jack hammer."

"You were determined to prove a point though."

"I didn't even know you were there!" She smacks my chest.

"I was near the portable toilets. I thought someone was strangling a feral possum." I smile, leaning forward slightly, while tickling her chin as she glares at me.

"I thought you were asking me about my worst tattoo pain," she accuses.

"Of course we were! You steered off course, as per usual."

"Did not!"

"There's my girl." I laugh.

"Not if you keep pissing me off!" She threatens as she wiggles out of my arms. "Damn it! Now, I'm going to speak to dad just to get you to stop embarrassing me! C'mon, Dad will be waiting." By now, the earlier tears have dried up and have been replaced with eyes of mirth. Wicked Trinity has resurfaced.

We move from her room, and before I can grab her hand, her feet pick up speed as she blazes down the corridor towards the kitchen. Felix is standing by the hotplate cooking as Trin rushes up to hug him from behind.

"I'm so sorry Daddy-O," she mumbles against his back. "I was being a shithead."

Felix raises his arm for her to slide under as he continues to cook. "It's fine, my little one. I think you've got too much going on in your head sometimes. Time to let all that negative energy go."

"Yeah, you're right. I think I'm going to start reading her letters …"

I stand back and watch them talking, marvelling at their bond. I've never known a parent to hug me like that. Sure, my grandmother had some fondness for me, but she was still slightly detached. When I'd first started visiting Trin, her mother, Harmony, would always give me warm hugs, even if my body responded like a 100-year-old corpse and refused to move. I'm sure she probably thought I was a freak for the first few years. I see a lot of warmth in Trin from her, and that makes me smile.

"So, have you two sorted that stuff out yet? Because if you haven't, the bedroom is that way ..." Felix's voice breaks into my thoughts.

"DAD!" Trinity yells, stepping out from under his arm to shake a finger at him. "Far out, you're embarrassing."

"Thought my little girl didn't get embarrassed," he quips.

"Thought my dad wasn't such a sex fiend," she fires back.

"I wasn't meaning sex. Just thought you could talk about it." He gestures with his spatula at her. "Now I think you've ruined my appetite."

"Good!" Trin huffs as she walks over to my side to nudge me with her hip. Hoisting a thumb in Felix's direction, she scoffs, "Can you believe this guy?"

"He's just looking out for his baby girl." I run my finger down her cheek.

"Not a real couple, my arse," Felix mumbles loudly from the stove.

"That's enough out of you," Trin scolds, as she tries but fails to hide a smile.

I pull her close to me and whisper in her hair, "Even he knew what our future was meant to be."

She wraps her arm around me, and I kiss her forehead. "I have a feeling that so did Mum." She sighs.

There's no more hiding. This is us, and we are going to make this work, even if it is the last thing I do. TTE can wait just a little longer to be revealed, if Adam and Mila let me.

Seventeen

"Relationships aren't all chocolates and daisies. It would be boring if they were."
Love, Mum.

TRINITY
Three months later

"I still can't believe I'm engaged," Hazel gushes as the phone nestles between my ear and shoulder, while I scamper around the shop, tidying up. It is approaching the end of the day, and I need to sort things out so my weekend is mostly unfettered to spend with Theo. That is, until I see the girls. I've been coaxed into movies and wine. It is a mini celebration for our girl's engagement, too. Initially, Trice wanted to do a yoga session to help me unwind. Apparently, I'd looked stressed the last time she'd seen me. I hadn't been stressed—I'd been caught off-guard while Theo hid in my workroom with his pants around his ankles, and I had a throbbing clit. Since then, I had invested in a bell on the door that jingled when a customer came in, or when Theo had unexpectedly, dropped in too.

We struggle to keep our hands off each other. It was like a lid had been lifted and we had taken flight. Ironically, my laparoscopy procedure is scheduled in a fortnight. It is meant to help alleviate my symptoms and potentially help me to have a baby one day, despite my doctor saying my chances are low, but it also means no sex whatsoever for four weeks. Bedrest with no sex. What the fuck is this type of hell? My vagina is going to chuck a tantrum. On top of that, Hazel and Trice are going to sell rack-only dresses, not bridal, while I mope around upstairs, as I'm not allowed to work. Technically, recovery is meant to be a fortnight, but there is nothing that will keep me in bed for that long, unless it is Theo's tongue. Dammit.

Tonight, it is going to be a girls' night to catch up on all things girlie.

"You're a lucky gal," I coo, picking up scraps of material from my desk while using my foot to slide the cotton to the side to tidy up at closure. The amount of loose cotton that wisps along my floorboards is astonishing. I could vacuum twice a day and still find cotton.

"You know, I've waited for him since I was sixteen. If I wasn't holding Gian in my arms, I'd think this was all a dream." She sighs

"Not a dream, sweet cakes. But a pretty wicked reality."

On cue, Gian's gurgle sounds through the phone. "I bet he's pretty excited too—he's going to need a suit and Aunty Trin-ka-belle can make him into a little prince. Just for Mummy's fairy-tale. He'll rock a bow-tie too."

"Aw, Trin. You're going to make me cry. I'm even more sensitive these days, now that we have this little guy around. I freaking cried at a home loan commercial on TV the other day. All those happy families ... the father swinging his child in the air ... the dog running across the backyard ..." She sniffs. "I broke down like a loon. It was the piano playing in the background."

"Ugh," I groan. "I hate that sentimental piano. I don't cry at films, but Disney has it covered, always making my eyes leak. Bastards." She sniffles again, so I quickly try to change the subject. "So, are you thinking about wedding stuff yet? We can go through some things tonight, if you like."

"Bits and pieces. I have a few ideas written down, but I'd love it if you could make my dress for me? If you have time, that is. Obviously, I'd pay you and— "

"Hazel," I cut in. "Of course, I'll do it and any bridesmaids' dresses too. Just let me know when it'll be and, even if I have a dozen other orders booked in, I'll give up sleep to make yours, okay?"

"Thanks, honey."

"I'll even use the best taffeta and make the shoulder pads touch the sky!" My voice pitches in excitement as I tease her. "But you need to have at least eighty buttons down the back. A girl mustn't be too excited to give up her virtue."

"That is so 80s." Her husky voice laughs in my ear. "You're an idiot,"

"I'll make it raunchy underneath so Robbie can be rewarded for the mammoth button trail." I run a finger down my leg. "I should do the opposite for Trice's dress. Make it provocative, as I know Alex will freak, and give her nanna knickers to wear underneath."

"Imagine!" Haze chuckles. "He'd go nuts!"

"He'd chase her down the aisle with a trench coat to cover her up!"

"She'd flip out."

"Ten bucks says she'd knee him in the balls before trying to jump him for being so protective."

"I won't take that bet, as it's a guaranteed win!" She shrieks, and Gian squeals in my ear. "Ouch! Gian just pulled my earring. See? Even Gian knows it's highway robbery to bet against that."

"Yikes. He's not wrong." I straighten my unused sketchpads from today and grab a spray bottle to use when wiping down the tables. "I better go, babe. See you tonight."

The spray sprouts from the bottle and covers the table, and I grab the cloth from the other bench to wipe it.

"Absolutely. And when you have a chance, design something really raunchy. Let's tease Trice and watch Alex's face light up. Bye."

"You evil, sweet woman. No wonder we're friends. I'm going to smut it up, big time. Later alligator."

She laughs and hangs up. I chuckle and decide on creating a few mock sketches on the tram later. All is fair in love and war, after all.

I slide my phone into the pocket of my cardigan and continue to wipe the tables down. Keeping an eye over my shoulder, I double-check for customers and then turn back to clean like a mad woman. I still have a few hours to go, but I want my workstations to look orderly, especially as patrons can see back here when they are at the counter. I chuckle and shake my head at these observations. Three months ago, I couldn't have given a shit what someone thought, but since being with Theo, I now want to feel better, do better, and be better.

I toss the cloth on to the side bench and put the bottle into the cleaning bucket. I glance at the rack in the corner. A few half-finished garments hang there, and a swell of excitement whirls in my stomach. Last month, Hazel had decided to go back on stage, so after I measured her up, I began to tinker with a few ideas for her and the girls. Even Trice has stopped by, eager to get started. Whichever one I don't end up using is going to become one of my display themed mannequins.

I've contemplated having a new theme of "rebirth" to capture the angst and tension of returning to the stage for the girls after Hazel's ordeal. My themes since are a far cry from what they used to be. The edginess has gone. *Far out. Even those mannequins have dulled down since Theo and I started properly dating. Some are even—dare I say?—romantic.* Now, a punch-drunk-love vibe naturally appears on the mannequins. Tim Burton would be horrified. I'd like to think that my designs have the capabilities to feature in one of his blockbusters, if I turn up the crazy a notch. Maybe I could line the wrists of the mannequins in blue ribbons to replicate what Theo did to mine last night. Sigh. That presentation dinner for his work was a bit dull, but at least the tie he wore to it was put to good use afterwards on his bed. Even if it came out worse for wear. Poor tie. Rest in peace, buddy. That bed was not letting you go.

As I turn to the front, my phone chimes, and I reach into my pocket to get it, muttering, "I bet that's Hazel with an actual idea for her dress, and she's too impatient to tell me tonight."

My stomach flutters when I see Theo's name, and I can't help but swipe along the screen to access my message as quickly as possible. Yep. I'm a sap.

Theo: Hey.

Me: Hey.

Theo: What are you up to?

Me: Working hard to make a living.

Theo: Through the shelter and the rain?

Me: Dude. Do not start quoting Cold Chisel to me. I'd think we were at bar night at uni or something.

Theo: Well, I'm being a working class man. I'm around the corner at my project with Daddy-O. Want me to bring you lunch when I have my break soon?

Me: Sure, I'll eat anything.

Theo: I know what I wouldn't mind eating
Me: Oh no, buddy. I need to get the shop sorted so you can enjoy a buffet this weekend.

Theo: Sounds delicious.

Me: How's Daddy-O today?

For the last couple of months, Theo's relationship with his father has developed in a positive way. He isn't really talking to Ko much, but that isn't anything new. He doesn't plan to keep in a lot of contact, and for him, I think it's better this way. I am yet to meet the illustrious Ricardo, with his ten-cups-of-coffee-a-day drinking habit, and his fondness for Theo's ideas. It isn't because I don't want to meet him, but rather while Theo gets to know him and gradually spend more time with him, I want it to be without me, so their relationship can develop without any more interruptions. It would be unfair to come between them. He has gained a pretty full-on family with little sisters who like to badger him to come over for dinner. He's offered to introduce me, but I am going to wait until the restaurant is finished. That way, I can see the dream that his father wanted to create by the hands of his long-lost son. That will be a pretty epic introduction.

> **Theo:** Giving me a history lesson on wine. Apparently one of the walls is going to be full of bottles. Like some sort of freaky wine rack with ladders. Walls aren't fixed yet, so it's all just dust and scaffolds.

> **Me:** Sounds weird, but I like it.

> **Theo:** Thought you would. See you soon.

> **Me:** Sure. I'm closing up at four. Gotta go into the city. TTE DAY!

> **Theo:** No prob. I'll sweeten you up before then.

> **Me:** Yay! You should be happy, seeing as you don't buy your own copy and just read mine!

> **Theo:** Oi! That's cheeky. Might have to put you over my knee for that.

> **Me:** Oh, I double dare you. See you then. :)

> **Theo:** Challenge accepted. Bye, firecracker.

I smile as I slide my phone into the pocket of my jeans and walk to the mirror near the front. While I had been home, I found some clothing of Mum's that now took residence in my wardrobe. All part of the healing process and allowing me to remember her like she would have wanted. Adjusting her white peasant top to sit off my shoulders, I turn to check that it sits properly. The long sleeves are transparent, while the chiffon ruffles at the front narrow in on my waist. My cherry blossoms weave over my skin, and the faint signs of my mandalas can be made out beneath the flowy material. My petite frame probably looks swallowed up amongst the soft material, but I love the breezy and carefree feeling it gives me. Plus, it makes me feel closer to her, somehow. I have pinned my hair up in a messy topknot with tendrils that fall to the side of my face. I also stick a red fake Dahlia at the side of the knot. My lips are coloured in a deep red to match. I can't pull off the rockabilly look like Hazel with her fiery red locks, by my newly red tips that poke out of my messy hair make me feel very fiery and feminine.

"Always be yourself," she had written in one of her letters I'd recently read. *"If you can't be her, then you're denying the world of something wonderful."*

I am slowly going through the box, making sure to leave most of the letters, but reading the ones she would've wanted me to read up until this point. Each is individually labelled for events or moments in my life. My university graduation, starting my own business—both were letters that I shed many happy tears over, despite the ache in my heart. As I'd clenched the letters to my chest afterward, the warm comfort of Theo's embrace centred me. I'd been a fool for pushing him away all those years. So much time wasted that thankfully we are both now making up for.

I curl a tendril around my finger to bring some curl to it, but it still looks a bit messy. Just how Theo likes it. I smile. If I didn't want to leave right on four this afternoon, I would coax him to take me upstairs and smudge this lipstick while I left it in certain places on him. We were close to covering every surface on this warehouse, bar the front windows.

Reaching the counter, I position the vases at either end Theo had given them to me after we returned from our trip back home. He told me the geisha one symbolized the artist in me, as geishas are known for their intelligence and creativity, while I know the cherry blossom one is for my arm tatts, and they symbolize hope, humility, and optimism. Having them on my desk brings a calmness to the area that I really like. Even more so now, as I had a bouquet of red gerberas and sunflowers delivered to fill them. Just like my mother would have done.

Bending down to the front counter, I press the volume higher on my iPod dock as the tune of Colbie Caillat's "Fallin' for you" fills the warehouse floor. Humming along, I sway over to the side racks to tidy the rails while also taking note of what I have and what I need. Since knee-length dresses are the rage these days, many sketches of them line the pages of my notepads. As I adjust one of my A-lines to face towards the front, the jingle of the bell rings against the front door.

"Good afternoon, I'll be with you in a minute," I say, as I straighten the other dresses. The sharp clacking of heels sounds and for a moment, I panic that Bridezilla has unexpectedly dropped in, knowing that her wedding is only just over a month away. Her "surprise" visits often make me want to jam a pin in her side. The handwoven beading I finished and had sewn onto her dress was spectacular, even though she tried to find a fault with it.

Shaking my head in agitation, I turn my face towards the sound to find Brit, the bystanding bully, marching towards me with a stern frown on her face.

Before she reaches me, I roll my eyes before turning back to the dresses to avoid looking at her. "The last time I saw you, I told you to fuck off."

"You hardly let me speak," she huffs as her feet stop nearby.

"Do I need to? Honestly, you can't be that dense."

"If you could just let me ..." she begins, but I shake my head at her and soldier on.

"Whatever you're selling, I don't want it ..."

"I'm not selling, I'm hoping to buy ... from you," her voice pleads, the words rushing out like water from an unsealed tap. "Like, I mentioned last time. I'm getting married. I want you to make my wedding dress."

My hand grips the rail for a moment before I lean back to face her, wondering if she's gone mad. Again.

"What makes you think that I'd change my mind from last time? What could possibly possess me to want to do that?" *Bloody hell. I'd take another fitting with Bridezilla over this bitch.*

"You're one of the best, who's making a name for herself. I've heard great things, and seeing as I'm a paying customer, I didn't think it would be such a big deal." Her head tilts to the side as she rests her hand on her hip. *The hell? Is that what she thinks?*

"So, my cheerful disposition from our last conversation didn't raise any doubt?" I raise my eyebrow, "You ran out of here like your arse was on fire."

"I wanted to give you time," she rubs her lips together. "Maybe, give you a chance to think about how good my order would be for your business."

"Oh, no, my dear." I flick my tongue against the roof of my mouth to tut at her. "If you are so well-researched, you would have discovered that I have a waiting list, and I specialise in certain fields. One is bridal, the other formal. If you also had fun chasing my name on Mr. Google, you'd find that I also specialise in not dealing with pretentious bitches, as I can say *no*."

"This is hardly high school." She holds her palm up to turn around and gaze at my warehouse. "We're not in the playground, and here we can conduct ourselves like adults. Surely, as a female entrepreneur, you can conduct business appropriately."

"I think you'll find that many female entrepreneurs wouldn't be so quick to bow down and conform. We take risks, we work our arses off, and we have the right to pick and choose depending on what we see fit in respect to our business. Now, are we having a business meeting or something? I honestly don't want to waste my fucking time any further with you."

"You can't be serious—"

"Normally, I wouldn't feel this way, if an honest, kind customer came in. I'd give them careful consideration. But make no mistake—I don't forget, Brit. What you girls did to my bestie in high school was beyond psychotic. You are lucky I don't throw you out on your"—I lower my gaze to her chest—"newly made fun bags. Though you'd probably bounce straight back up from the size of those monsters."

"I don't know how many times I can say I'm sorry." She adjusts her cardigan to cover her chest. "It was such a long time ago." She sighs. "I honestly thought we'd moved past that. I've apologised to her. I thought that was enough. I even stopped being friends with Stacey and Kristen."

"Well some of us don't give two shits what you want or what you ended up doing. You were just as much the bully. Your wants and desires are not welcome in my shop." I gesture with my hand in front of me toward the door. "Honestly, my previous, 'fuck off' still stands. Watching your ring leader torment an innocent girl and do nothing makes you just as guilty."

"Don't you think I know that?" Her foot stomps loudly onto my hardwood floor.

"Well, I'm glad you've realised, but I still can't do it."

"Please, Trin," she begs, as both her hands meet at her throat to plead. "I volunteer for Prider's Estate. I help run benefit dinners for women's shelters. I honestly have changed. I know I was a fool for participating rather than stopping it back then, and I regret it all. I work with my fiancé in his organisation to help others."

"Isn't Prider's Estate a bunch of Stepford Wives who have more money than sense, trying to help the homeless while they wear their posh leather gloves? Heaven forbid, you may touch something you don't like!"

"No, it's about a bunch of people who have the means to make a difference." Her eyes narrow at me. "That day in the lab, when Stacey hurt Trin, I learnt that I was in the wrong. I was a weak, pathetic bystander. Now, I work with all cases. I'm not just in that group; I'm a social worker."

I blink in shock as her words take me aback. Part of me is grateful that she's stepped away from that psycho bitch she was in high school, but the other is so fiercely tethered to loyalty for Trice that I can't see past what those bullies caused.

"It would mean a lot to me if you made my wedding dress, Trinity." Brit's soft voice breaks my reprieve. "My dear friend Virginia has been raving about your work with her. I know she has excellent taste, and—"

I snort loudly, as Brit's shoulders startle. "Virginia? My bridezilla sent you to *me* to make your dress, when all she does in our sessions is point out my faults?" I chuckle. "Priceless. This little chat is getting better and better. Look, I just can't help you. My loyalty lies with my friend Trice." I take a step towards her. "Even after all these years, I can still *see* the blood dripping from her wrist"—I point down my left wrist, where the scar lies on Trice—"and her heartbroken face when she realised Alex, her long-time crush, was dating her *enemy* and *bully* Stacey." Brit's face falls in recognition. "So, please. Save the sanctimonious bullshit. My business, my rules."

She nods in defeat as my chest tightens uncomfortably.

"I can give you another designer or two who will be perfect for you. Please. I'm not going to yell or bitch at you to get you out. I can give you the details and ask you to please leave."

"Here I was thinking you had grown up," she mutters.

Oh, no. She fucking didn't go there. "Here I was thinking you actually *did* change," I throw back at her. Straightening my shoulders, I lean closer. "So, tell me. Does your fiancé know?"

She flinches, and I smile knowingly. *Gotcha.* Like that, an idea strikes me. "Okay, here's the deal. If you tell your fiancé about what a lying, bullying bitch you were in high school, I'll make your dress."

"That's unfair!" she cries, her eyes widening in anger. "But I volunteer and help others! I was *only* a bystander."

"Like that fucking matters. You obviously have not learnt your lesson then, despite whining to me over and over." She cringes as I continue "You are equally to blame if you allow your friends to hurt others. Even if you were *only* a bystander."

"He'll never forgive me," she whispers, "He thinks the world of me and is so proud of how much I do for the company already. This would ruin us." Her lips tremble as her eyes fill with tears. "Why are you being so mean? Are you deliberately trying to get revenge on me?"

"No." I shake my head. "But something so pivotal from our lives is not something that can be easily washed away, like the blood from Trice's wrist."

Her head jerks from my painful reminder. Part of me wants to relent, but I can't. The bloodstained bandage from that day still occasionally makes its presence vivid in my mind.

"I just can't, Brit." Pointing to the door, I add, "Now, please leave. If you want those numbers for other consultants, I'll give them to Virginia when I see her later this week."

Brit pulls the strap of her bag across her shoulder and her tear-filled gaze stares back at me. "Keep those contacts. I'll sort it out myself. You know, you're not so perfect yourself," she hisses.

"Never said I was." I glare back at her.

"I remember what a bitch you were to Theo in high school. He followed you like a puppy and you trod all over him. You two were thick as thieves, and then you were the mega bitch in senior year."

My back stiffens as the pounding of my heart increases and sounds within my eardrums in an angry rhythm. I cross my arms in front of me. *I need to keep them that way, before I box this bitch out the door and onto the other side of the road.*

"I'll admit that I wasn't the nicest to him during our senior year, but we've worked through that." Relenting against my grip, I unfold my arms as the tension becomes too much. I jab a finger in the air towards her. "But make no mistake—he and I *worked* through our issues, and unlike some people we know, I never, ever, ever bullied him or left a scar on his body. Not one drop of blood has been shed out of malice. He is part of my world. Always has been." I signal with my head to the door. "Now, fucking leave."

She tosses her hair over her shoulder and storms off as the gentle chords of the next track, "Lucky," fill my warehouse. As Jason Mraz's voice slowly builds in the confines of the room, the erratic beat of my heart begins to slow from its irate pace. I wasn't *lucky* back then, but I sure as shit know my luck now that I have Theo in my life in the right way, and now I've accepted my faults.

Gazing at the clock, I hope that Theo will be here soon. After all, I have a few naughty sketch ideas to create, and why wait until I am on the tram when I can pick at his wicked brain?

Eighteen

The panel shows the broken tree with branches starting to bloom.
TTE

THEO

Firm hammering across the walls sounds as I march across the floor's protective coverings, the thick plastic crinkling under my boots. The latest sketches tap against my thigh with every step as I near the dining area. As I approach Ricardo, who is at the end of the room, the smell of dust and drying paint filters through the area. Another weekly visit, and like the others, it's showing another slow but steady progression, bringing an amalgamation of our ideas into a pretty fantastic fruition. The floorboards are already sanded and polished, ready to be danced on, while the structure has become more restaurant and less old, musty warehouse. The plaster walls are up and freshly painted with their undercoat, while the alcoves carry etchings to mark where the artwork that Ricardo wants there will go later on. A thrill passes across my shoulders as my project visually takes shape. It is no longer just sketches on paper.

Ricardo stands with his phone to his ear, a deep frown lining his face. I study him for a moment, and track his eyes that were focused on a worker in the corner near him. His face tightens as he watches the section of uncovered floor and sharp tools lying nearby. *Rookie mistake.*

I'm still getting used to his mannerisms. Coming from a father who was stoic and impassive, these wayward hand gestures and expressive facial movements all make me take more notice of him. I have caught myself a few times almost mimicking him in childlike fascination, quickly halting my movements to avoid looking like an idiot.

Ricardo's presence in the room is what catches my attention the most. Not his gestures or his voice, but the way in which he stands. It commands attention. He radiates an authority, but for some reason is also able to hold warmth. While he summons his workers to complete their tasks, he values the integrity of the project without demeaning or ridiculing. Sure, he could be a tyrant if there were clusterfucks, but his hard work ethic is really respected. He greets his clients and staff with strong handshakes whilst inquiring how they are.

Not once does he stand behind them and watch them work.

Not once does he demand perfection.

Not once do I feel the need to mimic his gestures to please him.

As the months have passed, I can't bring myself to resent him. I try to keep a distance, but his aura draws me to him. He bulldozed his way in, and there is no way to dig myself out. I am stuck and, surprisingly, content with it.

His hand moves from his pocket, and he clicks his fingers in the direction of the worker while maintaining his phone conversation. Once he gets the guy's attention, he points to the sheet and flicks his finger in a gesture indicating he should cover the corner. The workman shakes his head in shock and quickly covers the area, while Ricardo turns his back to him, all the while continuing his conversation. Without speaking, and after being summed by just a finger, the worker moves faster than I've ever seen. There is no anger—just a silent understanding. Ricardo 's presence is known, but not overbearing. My admiration for the worker's respect shown by quickly resolving the matter to please Ricardo is unlike anything I ever felt for Ko.

Our business relationship has moved into a friendship, and the lines have blurred where client and employee are drawn. I still feel he wants us to be friendlier, but at times I find it awkward to know how to react.

His hand grips my shoulder as we look at plans, his elbow nudging mine to get my attention to something his focus is on—these are all things I'm not used to. I'm not used to the affection that he naturally exudes. But I have mastered not flinching so much when his hand spontaneously gripped my arm in delight.

My firecracker is the only one whose touch never makes me second guess anything, let alone myself. Smiling at our earlier messages, I look forward to delivering lunch to her and spending a little time with her. Even if it isn't to get her bent over her desk. It has been a while since any form of desperate, angry sex was needed to distract us from something shit in our lives. Now, the desperation was replaced with a passionate need. There had been a few close calls. So, from those few near misses, where we stood red-faced and attempted to behave naturally, we cracked smiles at them, wondering if they'd seen my ... *other* crack moments earlier. I groan in frustration.

While I'm meeting Ricardo is not the time to think about Trin and what we get up to. Adjusting the tightness of my slacks behind the sketches while his back is to me gives me little reprieve. *Think of your middle school sports teacher who had the unibrow. Think of that hairy caterpillar... and that, folks, is a quick remedy to deflate alter-egos.* These weekly meetings usually precede my afternoon briefing back at the office. They also gives my boss an excuse to check up on this ritzy project I'm doing. I never was so hands-on with my other projects, yet even though Ricardo had got me here under emotional blackmail, it gave me a chance to get to know him.

"Okay, Johnnie, that sounds on track. Call me if you need anything else," he booms civilly. Turning to face me, his eyes light up as his chin lifts affectionately. I raise my free hand in greeting and walk to the doorway behind him as he finishes his call. The lights illuminate the back room, where the kitchen is destined to go. The polished concrete from the original building gleams under the down lights. It brings a smile to my face as I remember showing Ricardo an image of my own flooring; Elly had described it to him after a recent visit, and he decided to copy it.

Stepping into the room, the shell of the room illuminates to form as sheets of stainless steel lean against the walls, ready to mount later on as benches are installed, giving a faint outline of what the industrial kitchen will look like. A loan espresso machine sits plugged in the corner on a makeshift bench with a water jug beside it, ready to fill it. I smirk at his coffee addiction.

"I imported the fixtures for the sink and bench top." Ricardo's voice breaks into my thoughts. "I don't want cheap shit in my kitchen. It needs to be made to last. I expect it all to be down in three months. No later." He follows my gaze and asks, "You want a coffee?"

"No, I'm fine." I smile. "Once they certify the structure and appliances, I'll bring the latest document over," I add as I look around the room, picturing where the dishwasher and cooktops will go. "No doubt it'll be fine. You'll have enough firepower here to cook for an army." I chuckle as I turn towards him.

"So, a normal Sunday dinner at my place." He smirks. "*Excelente.*"

I hold out the latest sketch, and he grabs it from me and walks over to the bench to take a look at it. He hums softly as he studies the plan for the bar area, which needed a few more tweaks.

"This will hold a lot of wine," he says, as he points to the shelving.

"You did say it was going to be a wine bar, on top of everything else."

"I could throw the dance shoes in there, too," he jokes at the intricate designs above the liquor shelves. I have mapped out where the bottles will go, whilst also keeping with his original idea of a wall of wine. So much for being an architect—now he had me drawing interior ideas as well.

"Too much?" My fingertips tingle, and I want to move the sketch away in uncertainly.

"Never," he muses as his eyes squint at my writing across the page. "Here." He points mid shelf, and I step forward hesitantly, surprised at my sudden shyness. "There should be two rolling ladders, to span the entire wall. Otherwise someone could be waiting while the other has a jolly time. It'll make it easier to grab something from the other side if they have to pass each other."

"Jolly?" I grin, the nerves reducing speed.

He waves his hand at me. "You young people don't understand this term. When I came here over forty years ago, all the Australians said it. So, I *am* a kangaroo too, and I use it." He tilts his head down, so his eyes look above his thick-rimmed glasses at me. "No jolly time for us, today. Just work."

I snort as I grab the pen from my pocket. Quickly drawing an additional ladder, I position it to the side of the other. After a few moments, I turn to find Ricardo staring at me.

"To you, a simple drawing, but to me, it always mystifies me to watch you create something." He smiles, and I feel my collar tighten at the compliment as heat rises along my neck.

"Uh, thanks." I cough to clear my throat. I learnt the hard way to not mention that it was merely a ladder, as the last time I did, he scolded me. "Do you think the circle that Giotto drew for the Pope Boniface was just a fucking circle? No! He knew what simplicity was in that drawing, and perfection stemmed from it." Yep, I got schooled by my new father. The point had been well and truly made.

"Right, so once this is measured up better, we can look at a few manufacturers who can make it."

"*Bien.*" He nods, tapping the sketch twice with his knuckles. "This is"—his nose wrinkles as a smirk lines his lips in affirmation—"going to be brilliant."

I shrug in seeming nonchalance when secretly my insides are about to explode. These compliments are doing my head in. My social ineptitude tells me that silence is the best response, but the look of appreciation across his face pushes me to mutter quietly, "Thank you, Ricardo."

"Come," he commands as he briskly walks past me. "We must review the other areas and check they are up to date."

By now, I know this code is bullshit for spending more time with me, but rather than my steps going to the front door as they had a few months back, they trail eagerly behind him. By the time I leave that day, he has coerced me into dinner at his place the next night, effectively collapsing more of the wall that I had originally built to keep him out.

"So he roped you into dinner tomorrow night?" Elly asks me as I pay for the focaccias and coffees I ordered for Trin and I.

"Geez, I only left the site fifteen minutes ago. Did he message you already?"

"Of course he did." She grins, her green eyes gleaming back at me mischievously. "You didn't say if you were bringing your girlfriend or not. He wanted to double check so Mum caters enough."

I cock my head as an unstoppable grin traces my lips. This is not the first time I've heard of Aria and her cooking skills. Being a chef herself, she had gotten Ricardo's attention at a work function after he complained that the selection of hors d'oeuvres were mediocre. After storming out and confronting him while she was a young apprentice, he took notice of her and pursued her.

Looking into the brown paper bag in my hand that is not only filled with our lunches, but also a slice of cake each, I shake my head. "If she's anything like you, I'm sure there will be more than enough, but sadly, not this time. Once the project is done, I'll introduce her." Reaching for the coffee tray, I gesture with my chin towards it. "Thanks, Elly. You spoilt me yet again when you didn't need to."

"Oh, Theo," she mutters. "When will you realise this is the way we Europeans work? You're going to need to start wearing elastic pants around here. I can't help but want to feed your skinny arse. You're as bad as our little sister."

"Speaking of which, tell her I have a surprise for her. Got one for you, too. I got it a size bigger as I know she hates fitted stuff—fuck knows why."

"Yep, don't get me started. But she'll appreciate it if it's from you."

I shuffle on the spot, using the coffees in my hand as an excuse to get moving. This family and compliments were going to give me a complex.

"Cool, I'll see you tomorrow night." I walk away, eager to get to Trin.

"Wear your trackies as you won't need to eat for a week," she calls out to me, and I chuckle. "She'll probably give you a take-home container too—just saying."

Pushing through the door, I head down the street towards Trin's warehouse, which is in seeing distance. Excitement pools in my stomach as my steps bring me closer, until I notice a group of people standing out front. I pick up my pace as the excitement turns to unease. Two people appear to be facing off towards ... Trin.

As I reach them, Trin stands there with her hands on her hips, glaring at the couple. My footsteps echo loudly across the pavement as the couple's faces turn towards me, and I recognise them both. Brit from high school, with a few body modifications, and her fiancé, Ryder, who also happens to be my agent. Dread fills my stomach. *Oh, what fuckery is this?!*

"For the last time," Trin sneers, "I have asked you to please leave my premises. It's bad enough you felt the need to barge in while I was serving a customer, causing them to leave." Pointing away from her tense body, she continues, "Now leave, before I get more pissed." Her shining eyes hit mine, and I watch the stiffness in her shoulders loosen.

"Everything okay?" I move to protect her and feel the brunt of frustration as my hands are filled with our lunch, preventing me from touching her.

"Just dandy." Her voice tilts sarcastically. "I was telling these souls to move along,"

Brit stands clutching Ryder's elbow, as her eyes meet mine apprehensively. *Yeah, I remember you.* Her grip causes Ryder to turn and cast his eyes down briefly to her hand before turning his head towards me. His head jerks back in recognition, and I step closer to greet him.

"Ryder." I hold up my full hands in apology, "I'd shake your hand, but ..."

"No, no." His red face flinches as he's caught in the crossfire. "That's fine, Theo."

"You *know* this dickwad?" Trin shrieks. "Oh fucking hell," she yells, palming her forehead.

Ryder begins, "Theo is one of my—"

"We've worked together on a few projects." A lump of lead forms in my throat as I struggle to swallow the emissive lie down.

"Well, I hope he was more of a gentleman on the worksite than he has been here today," she snaps as she crosses her arms over her chest. A tendril falls from the back of her hair, and I want to weave it between my fingertips, tugging her closer to me. Pulling her head back towards my lips as she begs for more. When she's fiery like this, she is magnificent in the sack, but now is not the time to plan my next scene with her.

"I believe we asked nicely to have you make Brit's dress and, to be honest, after your revolting display, I hardly think we should have bothered." Ryder's voice cuts through the air as the tension begins to rise again. So much for pleasantries.

"Sorry, I told you guys to get the hell out of my establishment, after you STORMED INTO MY PREMISES DEMANDING MY SERVICES!" She stomps her foot, and I can't help thinking how cute she is. I school my features, as it will most likely end up with a kick in the shin, if she catches wind of it.

"Okay, okay." I stand in between them, more to prevent Trin's volatile behaviour from hightailing towards them in the air. Blowing out a breath, I hope not to lose my current contract by stating, "Look, in respect to the situation, I think it's best we go our separate ways. I believe she isn't interested in being your seamstress. So let's call it a day."

"I did give Brit an option." Trin's hand moves to my shoulder from behind me as Brit flinches.

"Oh?" I pause, watching Brit's face pale. "What was it?"

"Um, it doesn't matter now," Brit quietly says. "I think we've wasted enough time here."

She looks up at Ryder and pulls on his arm to encourage him to step away, but he doesn't move.

"Honey, you raved non-stop about this place." His brow furrows as he stares at her. "You told me you knew the owner, and you couldn't wait to get started. Plus, you made me read all those online reviews."

Brit lowers her gaze to the pavement as he continues, while Trin tightens her grip on me.

"I'd at least like to know what our options are," he says.

"Tell him," Trin urges Brit, stepping to the side of me, releasing her grasp. "You tell him, I'll make your dress. Without question."

I remember all too well how badly those girls hurt Trice all those years ago, and how powerless Trin and Hazel felt watching their friend hide the bruises and cuts from her family. Seeing Trin give Brit a carte blanche makes me pretty fucking proud. It looks like we've both been giving unexpected people potential chances lately.

"I can't," she mutters, chewing on her lip methodically.

"What is it, baby?" Ryder faces her and places his hands softly on her shoulders.

"I ... I was a ...part of something horrible in high school. I'm ashamed to admit it. You'll hate me."

I nudge my elbow at Trin and tilt my head towards the door to move us inside. She nods and opens the door for me to follow her, leaving it open behind us. We stride to the other side, the faint sounds of their voices disappearing as we near the back.

"Whoa, it's intense out there." I place the food and coffee on her front counter and turn towards her. Her shoulders, stiff from whatever transpired before, are soon under my fingertips as I step behind her and massage them deeply.

"They stormed in here"—her voice breaks through the silence, and I knead the knots—"and King Dickhead demanded I speak to them immediately while I was trying to sell one of my formal gowns. I lost a three-hundred-dollar sale as Captain Fuck Face ranted about my disrespect for his beloved fiancée, all the while screaming all sorts of dickheadery around my shop!"

"I'm sorry that happened, Trin. That was a douche move."

"How could you have the patience to work with that piece of shit? I know you have to work with difficult people now and then, but seriously? He takes the cake for being the king of all dicks."

"He was never rude to me, but I guess when it comes to protecting those you love, you'll do stupid shit."

"Yeah, tell me about it." Her head lulls to the side as my fingers crawl up her neck. I lean forward and kiss the side of her face, and she sighs against my lips. Her body softens under my caress as a slow anger builds in my gut. How dare they fucking barge in here? But the tension of the moment is at a standoff, as I can't rip his head off unless I want to find another publisher.

I continue to rub Trin's neck until footsteps from the front grab our attention as Ryder walks in to the shop, alone.

I lean to the side to see if I can see Brit, and find her back to us, her head tilted down. As Ryder draws near, his face is torn in anguish, and I have little doubt that she's told him. He stops a foot away from us, his chest heaving in anger, his fists clenched by his sides.

"I'm a disgraceful idiot," he shakes his head, as he rubs his hands along his thighs. "For that, I am truly sorry. I should have never marched in here like I did, costing you a customer." Reaching into the back of his pants, he continues. "Please tell me the cost of the sale, and I will reimburse you."

"No, no." Trin hurriedly moves forward to him, holding her hands up. "Please, don't. It's fine. Honestly. Many people have admired it, and it'll get snapped up. Not to worry." Her shoulders slump slightly as she asks, "Are you okay?"

He raises his brows in surprise and shakes his head. "After all your friend went through, you're asking if *I'm* okay?" He lowers his gaze to the side. "That shows how blind I was. She is meant to become my wife."

"She still can," Trin attempts to placate him, but his hands move to his pockets as he turns from her slightly.

"I don't know anymore," he murmurs. "If she was hiding this, what else could she be—"

"Look," I cut him off. "This was a pretty shitty thing to hide, but you

178

have to understand why she did it. Not saying it was right, but what you have to learn from this is people *change*. Brit learnt a pretty quick lesson all those years ago."

"She's in social work now," Trin adds, her voice softening. "That's just how much she's changed."

"Why did you want her to tell me?" Ryder turns to Trin, a solemn expression across his face. "Why not keep it a secret?"

"Because my loyalty is to my friend, as hers is to you in its entirety. She can't move forward if freaky bitches like myself need closure. It's not revenge. It's acknowledgement. It's walking into my shop, wanting a service from me when last time we were in the same room, I was watching my friend's wrist bleed. Yes, she was a bystander, but she's not anymore. I promise, I didn't do it to be malicious. I did it as it's something that should never be forgotten and, if anything, I needed to see that she wasn't that girl anymore."

"She's definitely not her," he huffs, as his eyes bore into hers.

"Good." She sighs in relief. "Now, as Theo said, things change. She has, most definitely. If you still want my services, I'll make the dress. But on one condition."

"Oh, what now do you have in store for us?"

"That the next time she sees Virginia, she reminds her to make that waxing appointment so I'm not dealing with Behemoth again."

Ryder bursts into laughter that causes Brit to turn towards us, with visibly tear-streaked cheeks.

"Oh baby." His voice softens as he looks over to her. "I need to go." He begins to walk as he yells over his shoulder, "I'm looking forward to the next edition, Theo. I'll be back at my desk later today."

"Yep, no worries." My heart races as I glance over to Trin. She waves at Ryder, oblivious to what he just said, and looks over to me. He closes the door behind him as the bell jingles. My shoulders loosen in relief.

"That's enough drama for today." Her head tilts to the side. "Lunch, or ..." Her hand reaches for the tie at the side of her top. Pure, unadulterated lust climbs across my skin as I study her face.

Before I can step towards her, the bell chimes, halting our moment.

A seductive smile curves across Trin's lips as she lets go of the tie. "Another time then."

As she turns, I lean forward and whisper, "No use untying—I'd just tear that off you, even if it was double knotted," and relish in her intake of breath as I go and retrieve my sandwich. On her desktop, her little notepad is open to a page entitled "Trice's bridesmaid's dress to fuck with Alex's head" with a few scribbles of underwear. Oh, my little firecracker sure knows how to meddle with people's heads, and not just mine.

"Feel free to add to it," she calls over her shoulder.

This could be interesting. If anything, I have ideas of what to put Trin in to fuck with my own head. Let the games begin.

Nineteen

"This realm might not be mine anymore, but I hope you're making it yours."
Love, Mum.

TRINITY

Trice leans closer to the image with her wine glass in her hand and frowns. Taking a sip, her other hand moves the image closer to her face as her sullen expression turns stricken. Widening her eyes in alarm, she shrieks, "No way! He's gonna flip. Surely these aren't what you want, Hazel?"

Wordlessly, Hazel sips her mineral water to suppress a smile. I'd arrived here while Trice was finishing one of her late afternoon dance classes and had quickly showed Hazel the sketches. Let's just say, there are a lot of corsets and a whole lot of cleavage with intentional nipple slippage and ruffled skirts that rival those on the steam-punk models at Comic Con. There won't be a worry for me to slip a nip. Small boobs meant that I'd have to hold mine up with both my hands to make that happen.

Trice's fingers flick the few pages back and forth erratically, the nervous tension in her brow deepening. "No, this can't be ..." she mutters as her eyes follow the designs. "You've got to be fucking kidding me." I press my lips together to stop laughing as Trice's panicked face continues. "He'll punch someone. He really will. We can't have these, Hazel. Seriously, he's barely able to restrain himself when I'm on stage, and these aren't that far from it. Is it a Burlesque theme? Is that why so much of my leg is hanging out?"

"I don't know why you're worried," Hazel chides. "I can't wear a bra in my dress, the plunge is that low." On top of the bogus bridesmaids' dresses, it was only wise of me to include a faux bridal gown for Hazel. I even redrew them on a fresh page so she wouldn't see my original title. I had intended to give her the Hessian gown look, that ran up to her neck and down to her toes, but since Robbie is going to be arriving soon, I wanted to see his knee-jerk reaction. Operation fuck with Trice's head was working like a charm.

I take a sip of my Corona as Trice continues to fret. There's only so much I can bear without losing my cover. Clenching the beer, I rub the condensation off the label to keep myself busy and not blow our story.

"Honey." Hazel leans forward and places her hand on Trice's leg. "It's a joke, sweetie. We just wanted to see *Alex's* reaction, but yours was superb."

"What?!" She shrieks, "You bitches!"

"Oi!" I wiggle my beer towards Hazel. "I thought we were going to wait for Alex to come home and *then* let them know. Foiled my plan, baby cakes. You could've least waited for Robbie."

"But Trice's reaction was enough. You know how fiery she gets; we're lucky her head didn't explode."

"Screw you, woman!" Trice waves her finger at Hazel, before throwing my notepad at me. "I can't believe I fell for that." She places her hand to her chest. "Honestly, I thought my heart was going to gallop out of my chest!"

"We already took bets on how Alex would show everyone that you were his woman *if* we really did choose these designs." I pick the notepad from my lap and point out the super low-cut corset. "Personally, I was aiming for a burst blood vessel in his forehead with this picture here. Theo suggested I make it even more low-cut, just for special effects."

"Yeah, these boobs could run a ceremony on their own." Trice laughs, pointing to her chest. "Try running in them—they ache like a bitch afterwards."

"Ah, ah!" Hazel holds her hand up, then turns her index finger to her chest. "Don't talk about aching when your boobs are a milking farm that will explode if not emptied regularly. I tried to go for a run with these balloons and was lucky I came home unscathed. I was surprised I didn't have black eyes, let alone a concussion."

"I'm surprised I haven't had a concussion yet." Robbie's laugh sounds as he enters the lounge, with a relaxed Gian, fresh from his bath.

"*Tesoro!*" Hazel scolds, "Not in front of your sister."

"As if she has any right to whine when she and Alex 'move furniture' regularly in their room."

"Dude, we were actually moving furniture the other day," she affirms. "Seriously, go check it out—the bed is at the other wall. Feels like we have more room now." A slow grin picks up at the edge of her lips. "You know, for other activities."

"Ugh, fucking hell!" Robbie groans. "You just had to take it there."

"You started it, you can put up with it!" she teases.

"Tesoro, at least cover his ears when you swear. If his first word is the F-bomb, your nonna will have a heart attack."

"And chase me with the broom ... nah, actually, with her walking frame. She'll just dong me on the head with it. But I could blame Alex. He swears as much as I do—even you do, Trice."

"Not as bad as you guys, but not too far behind either." Trice smirks. *They could probably include me in that, too. I have been known to drop the F-bomb like a comma.*

The doorbell rings and Trice rises from the couch to head over to the front door to answer it. Robbie steps closer to Hazel, and she shifts on the couch to reach out and touch Gian's back, rubbing it tenderly.

"Did you like your bath?" she asks him gently. "I hope you were a good boy for Dadda."

"Of course he was." Robbie turns so Gian's face is peering over his shoulder at Hazel. His little bottom wiggles as he sees her and unleashes a little squeal of delight.

"Oh, I know you're secretly excited to see me!" Josh strolls in, throwing his arms in the air. He swaggers closer to us on the lounge and bends to kiss us on the cheeks, all the while keeping his eyes on Robbie. Standing, he runs a finger down Gian's cheek and sighs. "Hello, beautiful boy. You know, it's really inappropriate for me to be perving on your father while he's holding you."

Robbie rolls his eyes as he shakes his head. "You haven't changed much, have you, mate?" He laughs.

"If you mean, was I hoping you were wood chopping or something out the back so I could see you with your shirt off, then the answer is, 'no.' You're a big boy; you can deal with it, sweet cheeks."

"Josh, we live in a townhouse; there will be no need for wood chopping." Hazel raises her brow coyly at him.

"A man can dream. C'mon! I'm on holidays! I didn't fly in this morning to have my fantasies dry up like an old lady's clacker."

"And, I'll stop you there, too." Hazel points to Gian. "He doesn't need for that to be his first sentence or be part of his first words."

"Where's Alex? He'd chop wood. He has that macho look about him. Maybe he can find something to chop. Like the head of one of Trice's admirers. Keep a stack out the back, does he?"

"He's out to dinner with his sister, Lily. So no chopping for him either."

"Damn it, you're ruining all my fun. I was hoping we could crack open Twister and play 'left hand on right buttock.' "

"On that note, I better get our little man to bed before I head into work." Robbie bends forward so Hazel can sit up to kiss Gian on the face and whisper, "Good night."

He leaves the room, and Hazel rolls her lips between her teeth, staring at the door.

"You okay, hon?" I rub my hand along her foot that's curled up beside me.

"Yeah, I'm fine ... just hate sitting out here when he goes to bed." She twirls her finger around her wayward curl.

"Honey, we'll be fine out here." I shift forward and grab her elbow. "Go and be with him."

"No, it's meant to be like this." She frowns. "I expressed a bottle today, and he's twigged that it's not the same. If he sees me, he won't take to it. Since Robbie's been back full-time, he misses out on a lot, so this is my way of giving him some time before he does his night shift at his club."

After the repairs had been completed on the club, Robbie had slowly opened it again to the public. He'd hired several performing acts for the entertainment while putting in the hard yards to get the bar back up to scratch and as "normal" as he could have it. It hadn't been easy going back to the scene of the crime, where Hazel and Gian's lives were put in jeopardy. But I must admit, he was a trooper for keeping as much of the shit away from Hazel as possible..

"It's great that he's enjoying the club, but I can see how much he misses spending time with Gian. I send photos to him during the day, but I make sure that they have their time." She shifts on the lounge, turning her sad misty-eyed face towards us. "I don't know how many photos I've got of the two of them snuggled up on our bed as he's fallen asleep next to him before putting him in the cot."

"Maybe they could spend every Saturday night together, just the two of them," I suggest, taking a sip of my beer before I continue, knowing that I'm delving into sensitive territory.

"What do you mean? He runs the bar then, like he does most nights."

"Well, maybe it's time to do what you said you would. You came to me saying that you were ready, but you haven't done anything since. It's time to assemble the Emerald Vixens again and perform." The beer feels hot in my hand as I study her face and then turn to Trice who sits on the armchair, nervously biting her lip.

"You want to perform again?" Trice leans forward in her seat, her hands rubbing against each other as she stares at Hazel.

"I do, I just don't know if it is time yet. If Gian could handle having that time without me."

"Of course he can." I wiggle closer to her on the couch. "Has he come out to ask for help, now?"

She shakes her head.

"See? He could stay home, and you could come and have a few hours to yourself where you can be *you.*"

"I do miss it," she admits, as she picks up her mineral water and takes a sip. "You think we're ready to get back together?"

"Sweetheart, of course you are," Josh interjects, waving a hand in the air, up and down her body. "You're looking pretty incredible, too, with those curves. Trinity, you better focus on making them 'pop' in your next costume design."

"On it." I raise my beer towards him and wink. "Already been brainstorming with Hazel and even had Trice in the other week. Let's get this shit started!"

"I'm gonna text the girls." Trice's head is bent towards her phone. "Tell them to make Saturday nights free—we need to get the Emerald Vixens together again!"

"Robbie's got a few acts booked for this month." Hazel begins to bounce on the spot excitedly, her toes tapping the edge of the couch. "I'll check with him, but how about the first Saturday of next month?"

I mentally calculate my appointments off the top of my head and smile. "Yep, I can have them done by then."

Trice's phone beeps as a wide smile flashes across her face. "The girls are in—we just need to work out what we're doing and all that. I'll book a meeting for next week and get the creative juices flowing."

"I have a shitty feeling I might be performing back in Sydney that week." Josh pouts, and he slumps beside me on the couch. "Why the fuck did I say yes?"

"Because you're one of the best dancers I've ever worked with?" Trice asks. "You know I'd love to have you in Melbourne more, but you have people requesting to have you. You're kicking goals, buddy!"

"Flattery will get you nowhere, unless you're a six-foot man with a nine-inch co—"

"Gian's down." Robbie's lowered voice creeps up behind Hazel, her body startling as she jolts in her seat. He chuckles before reaching forward and hugging her from behind. "I'm going to head to work now, *Farfalla*, so I'll see you later tonight." He looks over towards their bedroom for a moment before moving to stand.

"Baby." Hazel holds onto his arm before he pulls away. "What do you think of us getting back on stage and you having Gian to yourself on Saturday nights?"

"I think that's a fucking fantastic idea." He kisses the side of her face. "I'd definitely be up for it. Could switch a few shifts around to make it work."

They stare at each other before Robbie leans in and kisses Hazel softly. My chest tightens, as I miss Theo and wish he were here so I could be all smooch-coo with him.

"I think"—Josh lifts his head to peer behind the couch—"that you'd be up for most things, actually."

"Josh!" I admonish as I slap his arm playfully. "They were having a tender moment, you dickhead."

"I could see that." He waves his hand in front of us. "You can smell the hormones." He flaps his hand more. "Far out, you could light a match and this room would explode. Calm down, you two!"

"Nice to see you, Josh." Robbie runs a hand through his long, curly hair as Hazel smiles at him longingly. He winks at her before he walks past Josh to the front door. "Have a great night, ladies."

"Always a pleasure to see you." Josh lowers his voice. "And your delectable behind."

"Yes, I must agree with that." Hazel nods.

"Right, who wants pizza for takeaway? Or do we want to go Chinese? Let's try to get Josh to carb overload."

"Game on." He sits back on the couch. "You know I couldn't give two shits about that. I'm here with my ladies tonight."

"Glad you came home for a visit." Trice grins at him.

"Oh, don't think I was kidding about Twister. I'm going to kick all of your arses at it later. Mark my words." He rubs his hands in anticipation.

He may be flexible, but I'm little. Less surface area to stumble across. And when all else fails, cheat.

With that, Trice grabs a few takeaway menus from the coffee table and passes them over to us. I was looking forward to the night indeed.

I groan and lean back against the couch, the remnants of a container of satay chicken nestled on my lap. My food coma is fast approaching, but I am planning on round two with dessert. My foot nudges my bag on the floor, and I quickly sit up straighter to check that I haven't accidentally kicked my graphic novel. Yes, it is still covered in plastic, and I swore to myself that I would wait until later tonight to read it. Otherwise, I'll annoy the girls like I normally do. *But Adam and Mila looked so close last edition … I wonder what they're doing now. They could be doing it … eek! Adam better have grown the balls to jump her, or I won't be happy.*

"If you're trying to sneak a peek at the fucking magazine," Trice warns, "I'm going to put it in the cot with Gian."

"Uh … what?" I jolt, as I fold my legs underneath me, almost unbalancing my chicken. "I thought I might've damaged it, but it's all good …" I lean forward. "But I might just check by reading the first few pages, 'cause you never know." I grin back at her as she narrows her eyes at me.

"It's okay." Josh leans in and taps my bag. "I can take it home tonight and inspect it for you. Any hot guys? Or will I need to find my own filler?"

"It has one hot couple who haven't been able to get their shit together, while he's plagued by his past. It's a bit paranormal and fantasy. It's edgy, raw, and full of kick-arse dialogue. Gets me every time." I tuck a tendril of hair behind my ear as I smile sweetly to Josh. "But if you lay a hand on my unread edition, I will bite your freaking face off." I flick my foot out to push my bag closer to me. For precaution's sake.

Josh throws his head back and laughs, not realizing how close to death he is. Kidding. No, seriously.

"How's Theo going with his new family?" Hazel asks, resting her arm along the couch to face me more.

"Not too bad." I sigh. "He seems to be getting along with his father, and his siblings sound cute."

"You still holding off on meeting them?" Trice asks as she starts to clear the containers. She reaches for mine, and I pass it to her.

"Yeah, until the restaurant is done. I want him to have this to himself for now. But come opening night, I'm going to meet them all. Theo says his father is a charmer, so it's going to be interesting."

"As long as Theo is happy, I guess," Hazel adds. "I know what it's like to have a family who couldn't give a shit. For Theo to be so kind and caring goes to show that the good genes from his real father are strong. He didn't let what Ko do to him, ruin the beautiful temperament."

"Just like you, sweets," I add, rubbing her hand as she shrugs.

"So glad you guys finally got your shit together." Trice bites her lip for a moment before continuing, "But I do miss seeing you guys pick on each other. That was kinda hot."

"Oh my God, yes it was," Hazel agrees, wiggling her eyebrows at me. "It was only a matter of time before you both went, 'kaboom.' " She draws her hands in front of her, moving them out like an explosion.

"Oh, they kaboomed." Trice stacks the last container before heading in the direction of the kitchen. "They totally kaboomed."

I take a sip of my beer and chuckle knowingly, even though we didn't 'kaboom.' " today. Our first time was definitely an explosion. Seven years of sexual tension had caused me to have wrist burns that night. *Fun times.* I often think of that time, during nights when I am alone and my fingers want to wander, or when my dreams decide to spice things up a bit. I shift on the couch, trying to stop those thoughts from coming. That's all I need, to call Theo up to relieve me when I haven't seen the girls for a while.

Josh cracks open another beer that he had on the floor next to him and stares at me for a moment. "You know what they say—those who are quiet know how to rock the floorboards. Yeah, I'm guessing from the look on her face that he sure knew how to cause a splinter or two while making good use of his heat-seeking missile—"

The sound of the front door opening distracts us for a moment, until a few sets of footsteps make their way down the hall. With the heavy thumping, it is a wonder Gian is still asleep.

"You know what I like to call a *heat-seeking missile*?" Hazel interrupts, staring back at Josh. "Nipples."

Josh splutters his beer, and we all crack up.

"I swear, Gian could find them in the dark. They're a honing beacon with a hidden GPS."

"Hey," Alex greets as he strolls in with his sister, Lily, behind him. "What did I miss?"

"Hazel's nipples," Josh splutters and clears his throat from his beer cough. Alex shrugs as his movements stop by the bookshelf, his face unaffected. These conversations are just regular for us. Kudos to him for continuing to move on his merry way.

"Hi." Lily's soft voice wavers as she gives us a gentle wave. Her shyness has always been so endearing, and once the fire at Robbie's bar occurred, we began to see her gradually appear at social gatherings to catch up with Alex. They catch up weekly, but their relationship is slightly strained, mainly due to the piece-of-shit wanker Richard that she is dating and living with. None of us like him, but for some reason, she does.

"Where's Bea?" Alex's gaze travels the room, searching for her like a needy puppy. I am surrounded by the love bug and it's contagious. Six months ago, I would've waved that shit away, but now … my chest warms as it tickles the butterflies into a frenzy.

Trice returns carrying a tray of ice cream bowls, and I don't miss her face light up when she sees Alex. "Babe, I thought I heard you come in. You guys want dessert?" She sets the tray down on the coffee table, and he openly checks out her behind.

"I will later tonight." His voice lowers as she turns her head to him and growls.

"Babe! Seriously? Not in front of your sister!" Lily shifts uncomfortably, but shakes her head with a shy smile.

"It's fine. I'm not bothered." Lily says.

"Well, take a bowl, as I brought in extra. Alex might need some to keep his mouth occupied." Trice raises her eyebrows at him as we all reach in.

"I got another visitor at work today," I begin, as I dig my spoon into the creamy chocolate ice cream. I look up at Trice and shrug uncomfortably. "Brit came in again. She wants me to make her dress."

"Oh," Trice mutters, as her head tilts towards her bowl.

My gut tightens, but I continue, "Even after being told to fuck off twice, she came back with her fiancé."

"Who's this?" Alex's gaze travels to Trice's tense shoulders and he moves closer to her.

"She was a friend of Stacey's," Trice adds casually. Alex's demeanour changes, and he puts an arm across Trice's shoulders.

"Babe," he says.

"I'm okay." Her voice brightens as she looks up at him. "Honest." Flicking her eyes to me, she startles when she sees my frown. "I'm honestly okay."

"Well, they demanded that I make her dress, but I told her that it wouldn't happen unless she told Ryder, her fiancé, what she did in high school."

"Oh." Trice's eyes flutter to her wrist. "That was a long time ago."

"It was. She did tell him, though." I tap the spoon against my lip before continuing. "I kinda said I'd make it after she did that. Now I'm not so sure that was the right thing to do."

Trice lowers her bowl and spoon and brushes Alex's hand away to step closer, moving to sit next to me on the couch.

"It's *fine*. Honestly. Yeah, that was a shit time in my life, but I can't dwell on it. She apologised to me all those years ago, and I forgave her. I might never forgive Stacey, but I'd like to think that the karma bus will run her over one day."

"I did it for you. I feel guilty for not being a louder voice when they hurt you." I sigh, the regret tightening my stomach.

"No, never think badly of yourself. They would've found me somewhere else, and often they did. Be grateful it wasn't worse." She rubs her tattoo. "I don't see what they did to me anymore. I've replaced that memory with a better one. I turned an act of hate into an act of love."

Across her left wrist, the letter A, with stars and moons within, covers the shocking scar that Stacey had given her. Alex has the letter B tattooed for his nickname for her, Bea.

"Phew. I almost had a panic attack just then." I hold my chest for a moment.

"It's nice you've forgiven her." Lily smiles at Trice, and I feel a little better. Even she understands the grief her brother went through to get Trice.

"Forgiveness can happen, just so long as it's deserved. We've all got flaws—you've

just gotta try and ignore the crazies. No one is perfect," Trice adds.

"I am." Josh declares, proudly. Holding his beer up.

"Shut up, Josh," I scoff.

"Oh, cue the piano music! I'm feeling sentimental," Josh jokes.

"No!" Hazel panics. "That'll set me off." Grabbing her chest, she whines, "Oh, and my milk builds up when I'm emotional. I'll probably leak."

"Trin, don't stress, hon. You're loyal to a fault. I'm glad you made her sweat a bit before deciding to do her dress. It's great people are talking about you." Trice flicks her long plait over her shoulder as she shifts beside me.

"So ..." Josh raises the Twister board from the ground in his free hand. "Let's make a start, shall we? Now that Alex is here, I can have something to watch. Point that tushy in the air, Alex. Give us all a show. Got that?" He winks at him before setting the game on the floor to unpack.

"On that note ..." Alex thuds his bowl on the table before turning to his sister. "You ready for a lift?"

"No Twister?" Her brow raises, while she stares at Alex.

"Sure, but I'll tap out for this one. You're game?"

"Definitely. I haven't played this for ages."

"I might do some stretches." I stand and raise my arms above my head cockily. "Need to be primed for kicking Josh's arse."

"You know," Josh muses, "if you brought this with you to the club, I bet you'd raise revenue that night easily. Customers would come far and wide to witness the magic that is Robbie's bum. No dry seat left in the house."

"Oh, for fuck's sake, Josh!" Alex groans, holding out his hand. "Just give me the spinner."

"I'll sit out for this one, too, I want to listen out for Gian just in case," Hazel adds, shifting in her seat. "Let's watch them get tangled up." She giggles.

"Still think it'd work better at the club. Even your security guards could get involved. Especially the hot blond one."

"Leon?" Lily asks she timidly kicks her shoes off in the corner. A slight blush lines her cheeks as she pulls her hair back in a ponytail.

"That very one." Josh clicks his tongue against the roof of his mouth. "Jeans were made for that man's body."

I kick my sandals off in the corner but not before I see Lily bite her lip and smile. The few times she came to the club last year, Richard never gave her that blush nor did he give her that faraway look that she has going on now. *Interesting.* I can see a crush is brewing. I bet he has her all in knots inside. Ugh. If only she'd dump the douche.

We assemble around the mat as Alex and Hazel get ready to spin the dial. I stare Josh down, pointing to my face and then his with the *"I'm watching you"* gesture. He flicks his hands back and mouths *"Bring it, bitch,"* as we continue our stare off.

"Let's go!" Hazel calls and I bend slowly, ready to spin a colour.

I'm about to tease Josh again when Alex howls to the side of the coffee table. "What the fuck are these?"

Turning, I find him holding the notepad open to the sketches I've drawn and begin to giggle.

"Oh!" Trice giggles. "Those are my bridesmaid outfit ideas. You like?" She tilts her head, not giving anything away as she smiles sweetly. "I like the one with the frills on the front, personally."

"Better hope there isn't a gust of wind, or you'll might be flashing your morning glory," Josh quips, moving over to Alex to show him the sketches.

"You've got to be shitting me," Alex seethes.

"Mission accomplished!" I throw one hand in the air in victory.

"I'll bring a stage fan," Trice jokes, "to keep me cool."

"You're so easy to annoy. Almost too easy." I tease.

"Say, what?" His glare turns to me, and I laugh.

"Okay, ladies. Enough of the gossip session. Fuck, we're not on daytime TV. Alex, loosen the fuck up, and let's get this started. Now, game on!" Josh stands on the mat and points to Hazel, who flicks the dial to start.

Time to show the mighty Josh how the firecracker does it. First step, tripping him up. Accidentally, of course.

Twenty

The man stands at the edge of the cliff with his arms out, his toes tipped downward to fall into the midst that faces him. "Everything feels as it should be. Unless this is a dream?"
TTE

THEO

Our meeting sails through one hour quickly into the next while we debrief about our current projects. As my workmates discuss the progress on their designs, I notice the time on the clock behind Cole's head and clear my throat to make an excuse to visit the water cooler by the window. Taking a plastic cup, I lean down and fill it, casually turning my head to the side. Like clockwork, Trin's figure comes into view as she sashays around the corner towards the comic bookstore. I don't feel jealous at her infatuation with my novel or the "mystery writer"—just a keen sense of pride. *Here's hoping she still feels it when she discovers it's me and doesn't try to neuter me.*

Her notepad, clasped in hand, makes me almost chuckle at the thought of the potential designs she quizzed me on earlier to make Alex blow a gasket.

Her smooth shoulders catch fragments of the cherry blossoms that are across her skin. My memory automatically pictures every blossom and branch, as her skin is as familiar to me as my own. My fingers twitch, wanting to touch her smooth skin. To make her flesh red with my hands as her head flicks back in ecstasy. She is oblivious to my stare, and part of me is still thrilled by it. The moment is cut short as she skips through the comic store's entrance that leads straight down into the dark stairwell.

I toss my empty cup into the trash to return to the table, lamenting the fact that each Friday I'm not there to see her initial reaction to the novel. This edition is going to be good, too. I tried to capture the intensity of our own kisses in Adam and Mila's, wondering if she has picked up on the secret words in there yet. Part of me knows the second she does, she'll know it was me, but I'm not ready yet. For weeks she's traced the tattoo on my back, with the inscription of, "When the day fades to dark from light, you're the only face I see at night" which are the secret words I had written for her. Instead, her fingers trace the tattoos along my spine, not realising they are the map of us.

I pull out my seat and sit, determined to try not to think about her holding my gift to her. What she has been waiting on. I'd like to be there with her. Our setting is casual, so the guys won't bat an eyelid at my short absence if I decide to "duck out for a minute," but I can't. It is too risky, especially as the clerks in the store know me. So, I do what any self-respecting boyfriend does—I slump in my desk chair. Except flying under the radar isn't always easy, considering Letty knows what I did.

Amongst the guys, we only pay close attention to the drawings and sketches we create. The project discussions, how the clients have given us feedback for what they wanted, and any troubles we find along the way all take our focus. We brainstorm ideas and give each other constructive criticism, all the while keeping it low-key. Cole does his best not to carry on too much, unless the stress makes him a bit of a prat.

Letty, being the only female in the office, notices everything. From Stuart's fascination with wearing ties with roses on them (Letty is convinced it makes him perpetually single), to my preoccupation with the window on Fridays. It hasn't taken long for her to crack me. After all, I absently doodle my character's silhouette on my sketchpad with similar features to Trinity.

Today though, Letty is not preoccupied with watching me by the window with a knowing smile. In fact, over the past few weeks, she hasn't been that interested in *anyone.*

The lack of personal threats to staff has stopped too. If she wasn't threatening to maim you for chewing with your mouth open, then there was something wrong.

"Any other business, before we finish up?" Cole shuffles the papers in front of him in a neat pile as we all shift in our seats.

"Yes." Letty taps the table next to her laptop. "I believe there is still business to conclude."

Cole's face tightens momentarily, before he turns his face away to state,

"Oh, never mind. We can conclude the excess next week. I've already kept you all back over-time, and I'm sure you're eager for the weekend."

"My resignation," Letty seethes.

I flinch, staring at her. *You've got to be kidding me.*

"What about it?" Cole's lips thin as he reluctantly looks back at her.

"You haven't accepted it."

"That's because you're not going." His hands grip the stack of papers tightly.

"I believe I am!" She slams her laptop shut and stares back at him.

"We'll talk about this later."

"You know, I think I've had enough of your *chats,*" she says, rising from her seat to press both hands on the table. "I'm going, whether you like it or not."

What the fuck is going on?

"Look, Leticia ..."

"It's LETTY, YOU TWAT!" Pushing back her chair in haste, she storms over to her desk and snatches her purse. Turning back to Cole, she raises her middle finger and yells, "Have that as your resignation. No reason to keep me now!"

"Stop being ridiculous. You can't leave—"

"Too late, jackhole! Booked my ticket to Toronto. How's *that* for leaving?" She slams the door, and I'm struck numb for a second. *What the fuck is going on?*

"Letty!" I jump up, dumping my things to run after her.

"Theo." Cole's voice drums across the room. "Leave her. Please. Just leave her." He grips the pages in his fists before slamming them hard against the table.

"I'll keep you updated with the clients. I'll compose an email of the latest adjustments to the new office block," my workmate Garry says, looking around the room with a tight brow.

"Thank you." His sombre voice leaves no trace of giving a shit.

"No worries." He replies. Looking at the guys at the table, I make eye movements to the door to get their arses up. I pick up my sketchpad and phone, while they shuffle out of their seats and head to the door.

"I'll leave you to it," I say, and walk out. Putting my phone to my ear, I call Letty. Her voicemail picks up, and I leave a message.

"Letty, what the fuck just happened back there? When you get this message, call me back. Cole is not himself and is actually showing emotion. What the fuck is going on with you two?"

After a few minutes, I get one shitty text.

> **Letty:** I'm sorry, Theo. Can't talk about it. Goodbye.

I try to call her back and get her stupid voicemail. She'll tell me eventually. Until then, I'll just keep trying anyway.

The wrought-iron gates slide across the driveway as I roll in slowly on my bike. The late sun has started to set, but I can still see his place clearly. I can't help the whistle I make as I roll my bike across the driveway. This house is fucking huge. I've never seen grass so well kept, except for in the movies. Living in concrete suburbia has made me forget that there are areas in Melbourne with big gardens.

Pulling my helmet off my head, I pat my hair down before placing the helmet under my arm, while tucking my other thumb under the strap of my backpack. My boots crunch against the asphalt as I walk to the door, marvelling at the neatly landscaped garden. After spending the past hour worrying about Letty and, as predicted, her ignoring my calls, it is time to forget for the night.

The front door opens as my sister Elly stands behind it, a huge smile across her face.

"Hey!" She pulls the door back to step out onto the stair. "I could hear that bike a mile away."

"That's the point." I grin as I shift closer to her. She moves into my chest and hugs me briefly, my right arm hooking around her back for a moment. *Still need to work on this hugging business.*

She shakes her head as though she can read my thoughts and steps to the side. "*Bienvenido.*"

I step into the brightly lit foyer. Smooth floorboards line the corridor while a red-rimmed carpet sits in the centre of the boards as the walkway. I can't help but smile at how similar these boards are to those at our restaurant. I shake my head. *His* restaurant.

My boots halt as I stare at the family portrait that hangs by the doorway. The last portrait I was in was when my mother was alive, and I would have been a toddler. I remember the photo where I sat on my mother's lap, her smile directed at the camera, while Ko sat stiffly beside us.

This portrait is completely different. The family sits in front of a tree and, instead of posing in stiff positions, they are casual. Ricardo looks at the beautiful woman next to him, who I presume is Aria. Her gaze is cast down at her hand, which holds a pink carnation. My sisters, who look a lot younger here, are both staring at each other, laughing.

"Ugh, that picture is so embarrassing. I have the worst haircut. I convinced mum to let me cut it short, and it was horrible. So frizzy." She scrunches her nose before hooking her arm with mine and dragging me down the corridor. "This is the walk of shame. You're not going to stop and examine each one ... no way, *José* `."

I laugh as I tug on her arm, pretending to look at the photos until we are near the doorway, where I see one that makes me pull on her arm abruptly.

Peering closer, I see a graduation ceremony where the presenter is handing out the diploma to ... *me.*

"What?" My voice rises slightly in confusion. "How did you ... not even Ko came ... what the ...?" I falter, adjusting the grip on my helmet as it almost slips through my elbow.

"I was there." Ricardo 's rich voice greets me from the doorway. I turn and find him with a snifter glass in his hand. He takes a sip and studies me for a moment. *"Buenas noches."*

I blink rapidly and turn back to the photo. My neck feels hot as I tug at my collar quickly. The ceremony was only a year ago, but Ricardo and I weren't in proper communication then. Judging from the image itself, he was pretty close to the front.

Pointing to the image, a frown lines my face. "So, you took that photo?"

"I'll explain over dinner. Aria has prepared a delicious paella. I hope you like seafood."

My stomach betrays my confusion by grumbling, but luckily no one hears it. *What was he even doing there? How did he know?*

"Come." He extends his hand and pinches my cheek affectionately. I only flinch a little, but he flattens his palm to touch my face. "Don't look so shell-shocked, Theo." His eyes darken with mischief. "So much to learn still. Lucky we have all night. Now, hurry up and enter our *cocina* before we all starve to death." He winks as his lips curve up, and then he walks ahead of us.

I don't understand his need to grin at me when I'm freaking out.

"Papá¡ Eres insoportable!" Elly scolds as she leans into me. "He's *a pain.* Don't worry, he will explain it later. For now, let's go and eat in the dining room. Just pop your stuff on that small table there." She points to a side table. I drop my helmet on it, but take my bag with me.

I follow her through the wooden doorway into the dining room, with an exposed brick wall. A fireplace flickers behind the dining setting as Ricardo stands by the mantelpiece, his arm relaxed against it. *Cool as a cucumber.* I slide my backpack off and hold it in my hand as the clicking of heels comes quickly from the other side of the house. A short, dark-haired woman wearing a bright red apron over a knee-length dress briskly walks over to me, and I quickly see her resemblance to my sisters. Her dark eyes light up when she reaches me, holding out her arms, and before I can move, she has me in a firm hug. A rich laugh reverberates against my chest, and I'm curious to why she'd let a product of her husband's affair enter her house. For a pixie, she sure knows how to hold on tight.

"Theo." She straightens and holds the sides of both of my arms, taking a long look at me. "It's so good to meet you! I have heard so much about you. Gosh, you look like Ricardo in his younger photos. You are a spitting image! Just a little leaner. With short hair, of course." She grins and squeezes my arms before stepping back. I bite the inside of my cheek to dispel the nerves. Her eyes move to Elly. "Where's your sister?"

"I'm here! Just had to finish my Math Method's revision questions. Why I chose to do that math, I'll never know." Anastasia strolls in and waves to me shyly as she stands by the dining table, her other hand tucked in her back jean pocket. Unlike Elly, who wears a dress and boots, Anastasia has her Avengers Converse with a Spiderman T-shirt. If I were still in high school, I would've hung out with her.

"I was pretty good at methods if you want me to take a look at it?" I offer, understanding the same shyness, but trying to not be an awkward dick tonight. She brushes the hair that covers her face to the side and nods. It's like seeing me ten years ago.

"Come." Aria raises her arm towards the table. "Let's take a seat. Normal people would go sit on the lounge, but Ricardo is an impatient man and likes to eat as close to six o'clock as he can." She turns her wrist and peers at her watch and smiles. "As it's six twenty-five. I'm sure his stomach is protesting and probably trying to eat itself!"

"*Amor.*" His voice rumbles. "I'm old and impatient. You've put up with me for twenty-two years. You should know that by now." He steps over to the table and gestures for us to take a seat. *Twenty-two years?* I'm relieved he never cheated on her with my mother.

I unzip my backpack to bring out two bottles of wine that I had Robbie recommend. Fuck knows if they're any good, but I wanted to make a good impression. Putting my backpack on the side table, I stroll back and hold out the bottles to Ricardo, and he puts his snifter glass down to take them from me.

"You didn't have to bring anything." His voice softens slightly.

"I wanted to." I shrug.

His head lifts, and his eyes reach mine, holding my gaze. "We're just happy that you came. That you're finally here." His voice chokes slightly, and I clear the ball that's suddenly lodged itself in my throat.

"I think the rosé will go well with the paella." I point to the bottle. "At least, I hope it will," I chuckle.

"Excellent choice," he concedes, as we stare at each other.

"Hey, Theo."

I turn, relieved by the distraction of Elly patting the seat next to her, making me move quickly to sit there.

"Eloise." Ricardo chuckles. "Let the man choose for himself."

"I was saving him from your appetite; you might try to eat him." She raises her eyebrows, and I chuckle softly beside her. I haven't been here for even ten minutes, and the warmth isn't only coming from the fireplace. I am enjoying the banter and strangely feeling like joining in, too. But mostly, I want to talk to Ricardo more. Find out about that picture. Work out why Aria is glad to have me here.

Gone is the forceful businessman. Instead, here is the family man who works hard for them. Watching him talk to his daughters kindly, praising Anastasia's work efforts while complimenting the pasta dishes that Elly recently served at her work strikes a chord with me. I can see and feel the sense of pride that he feels for them. Sure, he chastises Anastasia for pouring water with her left hand, but aside from that, he is *interested* in them. Watching Anastasia pour the wine at the table while chatting to Elly and Aria as they walk in with plates in each hand, causes a pang of jealousy in my chest. I never had this from my father. My grandparents tried, I guess, in their own way, but it was slightly strained. *Could my mother have gotten this if she'd left Ko?* My mind wonders for a moment to what it would've been like if I had been part of this family from the start. But the strain of that thought causes a dull pain to thump in my forehead. If that *had* happened, if she had fallen in love with Ricardo and left Ko ... then there'd be no Elly or Anastasia. That thought itself is enough to have me sit up straighter in my chair. Sure, my home life isn't the best, but no fucking way would I substitute it. I would never change a thing if the alternative was losing my sisters.

I tuck my knees under the table as I slide the chair closer. Ricardo watches me with a fascinated look on his face. I tilt my head up to the exposed beams on the roof, and I admire how similar our tastes are. "You have a lovely home."

"Thank you." He grins knowingly. "You're a thinker, and I can see the architect mind has not switched off tonight. You seeing flaws in my structure?"

I shake my head and rub my hands along my legs. "No flaws, but I have a habit of noticing the details about everything." *Especially you. Your smile, the wrinkles around your eyes when you tell a joke ...*

"Those who are observant learn the most."

"Probably,"

Elly reaches out for the bottle of rosé as Aria sets the plate down in front of me.

"I hope you enjoy this," Aria says, grinning as she makes her way to the kitchen for the other plates.

"Should I go help her?" I offer, but Anastasia shakes her head.

"No, not tonight. We're not allowed to get up either. Mum is a proud woman and wants to treat you. So, enjoy. When she's not feeling so showy, she'll get you in the kitchen as her kitchen biatch."

"Hush." Aria narrows her eyes playfully at Anastasia as she sets the last plates down. She takes a seat next to Ricardo as we all sit patiently, and her smile beams at me.

"¡Que aproveche!" Ricardo announces, and I look to Elly. She whispers, "Enjoy your meal," and I smile.

"You'll learn all these phrases soon," Ricardo says, as he lifts his fork. "It's in your blood; I can feel it."

I dig into the paella and feel a change in the room. For once, I'm not trying to fight against it. Instead, I can't help but think, *bring it on.*

The evening continues with more delicious food, including a flan made of baked custard. Trin is going to be super jealous she missed this.

"What did you say?" Elly asks, and I look up at her in confusion. "You said someone would be jealous."

"Oh, I must've been talking aloud. I said that Trinity will be jealous when she finds out what I ate here tonight."

"She could've come, you know."

"She wants to give me a little more time with you all. Besides, I haven't told her *everything*."

"I noticed. Seems that my subtle hints about having a brother who recommended her to my friend didn't work. Mind you, Virginia's antics tend to distract easily."

"Soon. I'll tell her eventually." I spoon the flan, but my stomach quivers. Who knows how she is going to take knowing she's already met my sisters and even read my novel?

"She might already know. Women tend to have a sixth sense about these things," Aria chirps, as she reaches for the wine. I fumble with my spoon while she fills her glass and places the bottle on the table before adding, "The girls talk about you; they told me about her. She sounds delightful."

"She's awesome." Anastasia's eyes light up. "The dress she made me is so cool. I got my shoes this week, so I promised I'd come in and show her what the whole outfit looks like."

"She did a great job. I should get her to make my gala dress." Aria looks thoughtfully as she sips her wine. I groan. All I need is for Ricardo to go in there, and I will have more explaining to do. Considering my sisters have successfully infiltrated my love life, I am on borrowed time until I tell her. Will she be thrilled? Annoyed I kept this to myself as well? The secrets themselves are all beginning to pile on top of each other, and it is only a matter of time until they topple down.

"Anything she can design for me?" Ricardo jokes, as he rubs his chest and pouts his lips. "I'd look beautiful, no?"

Aria grabs her napkin and swats his arm as we laugh. I remember my backpack with the gifts I brought and slide out from the table to retrieve it. I unzip it quickly and put out the shirts that arrived earlier this week. Walking to Anastasia, I throw one at her.

"Here you go, short stack." I smile as she unfolds it, and I toss the other shirt at Elly. "Oh, yeah, you too, I guess." I wink as she laughs and opens it.

Anastasia squeals, and I flinch, surprised that she can be *loud*.

"Theo … oh my God!" she shrills, turning it in her hands. "It's awesome."

"What is it?" Aria's bubbly voice breaks the giggling.

"Give me a second." Anastasia rises from her seat. "I'll be right back."

"This is freaking cool." Elly turns to me. "You did good, Bro."

My chest warms, still getting used to being a brother but enjoying seeing the mirth in her expression.

"Ta da!" Anastasia returns with her hands outstretched, wearing the black T-shirt I had specially designed. On the front, a panel with the tree of life is in the centre, and my headlining couple, Adam and Mila, are in the middle of the tree, their faces turned to each other. I have another guy obscured behind her, though, with only his arms and the top of his face visible. Her left arm is outstretched towards Adam, as the stranger extends his arm to her, not quite touching. His silhouette is faded slightly, his look of anguish capturing every moment of the pain I felt while Trin was sleeping around, before I made her mine. The words *"Shatter Till I Fall by TTE"* sit underneath them in a bold white font. Anastasia turns, showing off the back of the T-shirt, featuring the dark cloud that I use to depict my fear of losing Trinity, painted silver with the phrase *"Another embrace, another headache. When will she see me?"* underneath. I also printed the addresses to my social media profile and website underneath. A living billboard, of sorts.

"I am going to wear this all the time. Gonna sleep in it too!" Anastasia brags, as she does a little twirl, her shoes squeaking against the floorboards. Her eyes meet mine, and she stops abruptly, biting her lip in embarrassment.

"I'm glad you like it," I grin, as Elly holds hers up in the air.

"I might order some and make my staff wear them. We can be your promo girls."

"No, you don't have to do that." I shake my head, feeling a tad embarrassed. "I will be uploading them onto my webpage, but I thought they'd be good for Comic Con."

Elly holds her shirt outstretched and smiles. "You need about eight designs, but I'm going to wear mine around and say, 'This cool dude is my brother, so go out and buy his books.'"

My neck heats as the tickle of embarrassment raises the hair across my skin. I rub the back to cool it down, but it doesn't help. My heart beats erratically against my rib cage as I try to stiffen the nerves. Even when my agent contacted me initially, I still found it hard to take compliments. Architecture work, fine. Doing this—where I hang my heart out to dry, month after month—is different. It still takes a while for me to believe I have actual fans.

"Theo," Ricardo calls out. "Those shirts look excellent. You should be proud of your successes; I know I am."

All the breath that I didn't realise I was holding in leaves my body in a massive *whoosh*. Not *once* has Ko ever said that, even when I excelled at all my piano exams, or got perfect scores on tests, or won a completely paid-for fucking scholarship to do my degree in Melbourne.

Nothing.

"Thank you," my voice pitches, before picking up my backpack and feeling the sudden pressure gripping my chest. *Too much.* "I better go," I hastily add, my heart sinking as the familiar feeling of disappointment shrouds me. *Still I hang on for the moment for Ko to give a shit, even when I have my real father here, really caring.* "Thank you for a delicious meal."

I turn abruptly and head to the front door, grabbing my helmet as I stroll along the rug. I reach the door to hear Ricardo behind me, his breath laboured from following me. "Theo, stay. Talk with me. We still have so much to discuss. I need to explain—"

"I can't." I fumble with the locks until I swing the door open. I chance a look over to him and find his features tightening. *Great, now I'm letting him down too.* "I realised that I need to get some work done. See you at the restaurant next Friday."

I push through the door and whip my backpack over my shoulder before slamming my helmet on. I'm sick of being the weak idiot. Caught between the crossfire of a family so different to what I'm used to, and my adult self, too torn from my past to know how to cope I start my bike quickly and race out of there. Needing the distance. Needing to get to Trin in the hope that she can restore this shell of a man.

Twenty-One

*"Sometimes you have to take that leap, honey.
Are you ready to jump?"*
Love, Mum

TRINITY

As the steady beat of the song plays, my hips sway, my hands moving up and down my sides as I close my eyes to the smooth sound of her voice. The guests have left my dress-up party and now it's only me and ... him under the disco lights in the dimly lit room. Long gone is the belt that was wrapped around my waist, as well as the heels that were on my feet.

Each lyric sends a seductive pulse to my chest as the heat of the intensity trails a single bead of sweat down my chest. I am alone on the dance floor, but I can feel his eyes on me. His gaze might be hidden under the mask of his sunglasses, but his stare causes ripples to cross my skin. I slide my arms upwards along the smooth leather, and it forms a swell of need across my heated body. I move my fingers to the centre of my chest, no longer in hesitation. We have danced our last dance. Now, it's time to tumble.

Slowly, between my thumb and forefinger, I tug the zip down between my breasts, smiling as my chest is bare underneath. My lips curve seductively as my nipples bead under the strain of wanting him.

My nipples have been aching for his touch all night. Waiting for him to stop staring at me and use his hands to do what his eyes have been telling me they want. Lust, heat, passion—I am tired of this dance. I want us to collide. Stumble and fall.

I lower the zipper some more. My eyes remain closed, and I shift my hips to the slow beat of the song. I feel every strum as a caress against my clit as my thighs rub together, the friction causing me to gasp as the cool air from overhead suddenly hits my chest. My frustration heightens as I want to feel his hands dig into my skin and set me alight.

Sudden movement to my side causes my head to turn, as his breath now lingers at my neck. Relief sweeps through me. His lips lower behind my ear as they taste my skin. His hot tongue flicks out, and my clit pulses. My face turns towards his, but his lips go behind my neck, caressing me along the way. "Kiss me," I beg.

One of his hands clasps my hip as the other moves in front of me to draw a line with his finger down the middle of my chest until he reaches the zip. He opens his hand to extend under my suit, sliding underneath the taut fabric, and cups my breast, while his other hand pulls me One of his hands clasps my hip as the other moves in front of me to draw a line with his finger down the middle of my chest until he reaches the zip. He opens his hand to extend under my suit, sliding underneath the taut fabric, and cups my breast, while his other hand pulls me firmly into his body, against his crotch. I feel him against me. Hard. Wanting what I crave. His hand tightens over my breast as his breath increases, and his finger pinches forward across my aching nipple. I gasp and lean back into his touch, my mouth opening in wanton pants.

Holy fuck. What is he doing to me?

He releases my hip and moves across the front of my body to dip within the crevice, his fingers holding my breast. His free hand moves down, his fingers moving to take the zipper with him until it reaches the end. Drawing his other hand away from my breast, he grabs hold of my pantsuit and pulls it down from my shoulders, my skin tingling as the night air kisses along more of my naked skin. The suit moves down my back as his other hand delves below, slipping under my G-string and moving straight down to my clit. His fingers coat my clit in my juices, and he slides them back and forth, teasing me by not focusing on my pussy. I tilt my hips into his touch to hit my clit, but his fingers continue to tease against my needy folds.

His hand darts out from my costume, grabs onto the fabric that still covers me, and yanks it down my body in one swift motion, until I'm standing there in my G-string with a pile of leather at my feet. He taps under my elbow, and I step out, the prickle of nerves beginning to flutter low in my belly. I feel the rustle of clothing behind me, as his heavy jacket hits the floor. I turn my head, and his gaze pierces mine, as he grabs his shirt behind his neck and pulls it over his head, revealing his tattooed arms and chiselled abdomen. It's not as defined as that of the guys in the books I read, but it's still fucking sexy. I flick my gaze up to his, and the intensity of his green eyes has me spellbound. His eyes travel up and down my body, and I twist to face him, watching them darken as they stare at every inch of me. No one has ever looked at me like he does.

He grabs my hand and pulls me with him, walking over to my staircase. He stops at the first step, and we stand transfixed. This is really happening. He swallows, his eyes shine, and I feel my lips part. I want this so badly. My need increases, as he moves us quickly up the stairs before I can change my mind.

Our breathing deepens, and we pass the railing, our hands grasped as the connection intensifies. I move towards my bedroom, but he pulls gently, stopping me from leaving the rail. His hand drops mine, and I feel the loss of the warmth his palm gave me. He drops whatever is in his hand, unfastens his belt, and unzips his pants, while kicking his shoes off to the side. Both hands hook into his waistband, and he stops to watch me, the swirl of passion flicking in his gaze.

He pulls his pants down his legs, showing me that even he spent the night with a little secret of no underwear. My eyes are drawn to his thick, hard cock, and my tongue flicks my labret, eager to get down on my knees and taste him. Stepping out of his pants, he grips his shaft and pulls his hand up and down, his hold tight as the swollen head nestles within his grasp at the start of each long stroke. My eyes meet his stare, his *expression remaining stern, determined, and unforgiving as each stroke is powered with the fierce power of his forearm. His sinews ripple as his grip tightens.*

I move closer to finally get my lips onto his, but he abruptly lets go of his cock to grip my hips and rotate me towards the railing, so I face the showroom. Placing each of my hands on the railing, he moves behind me, his cock jutting against my back. Holding my hands in place, his face brushes against mine, his light stubble sending tingles down my body. "Look out there," his voice whispers against my ear. "Look to the window."

I lift my head to glance where my colourful dressed-up mannequins stand near the transparent curtain. I've left the thick curtains opened. If a car were to go past and shine its lights, we'll be seen. If someone were to walk past and look at those mannequins, they'd see us up above them. I've put up too many party lights to avoid being hidden.

He steps back from my body and walks through to my bedroom until he reaches the window. I tilt my head over my shoulder to take a better look, when I see his arm reach up to the sheer curtain and rip it off the rail.. I startle briefly, sucking in a breath before I slowly exhale, my thighs beginning to rub together back and forth in want. Holy shit. This rush I feel is better than any stunt I've ever done. The heat that climbs under my skin is overdoing any thrill that I've needed to seek before. My body wants him to be that high. I can feel our souls reaching out for each other. I turn to face forward quickly, as his steps sound behind me, butterflies taking flight in my stomach with every step.

Reaching around me, he shows me the long drape in his hands. Leaning into my body, his cock presses into my spine as his breathing deepens. "I want to tie you to this railing and fuck you until you can't stand anymore." Gripping my hip with his other hand, he pushes his cock harder against me. "What do you want me to do?" Holding the material, he tilts his hand back and forth, waiting for my answer.

"Tie me up and fuck me," I pant, desire pooling between my thighs as my folds throb with want. My cunt begs with each pulsating movement, waiting for him to ease the ache..

I feel a grin against my neck before he withdraws his arms and positions my hands to grip the railing shoulder-width apart. The soft material loops around my wrist and around the banister, and my pulse quickens as the movement hypnotically motions me to grip it tighter.

Soon, I am tied to the railing, the excess material looped over the top by my side. I'm immobile. He crouches down and begins to massage my feet and calves, his hands moving around and up my legs, almost tickling me. I squirm as I stand, each hand rising slowly up my legs to rub the sides of my thighs, never once touching between them. His hands then rub up and down my back, and I lean into his touch, each of his hands swirling around and against my cool skin. His fingertips draw patterns across my back, along my tattoos, and down my abdomen before weaving back to caress my shoulders and arms.

My breasts ache for his touch, wanting him to squeeze my nipples. My fingers yearn to touch him, to bring him to release, but my hands can't move. A frustrated growl escapes my lips, and he chuckles before the pressure increases in his touch and his hands move in opposite directions. My breast is warm in his palm, a firm squeeze making my head tilt back until his other hand plunges between my folds, causing me to gasp.

"So ready for me. You want me to fuck you, firecracker?"

"Yes, Theo! Do it now!"

He dips his fingers into my wetness and then draws them out before I hear his lips sucking them into his mouth. Holy shit. That was hot.

He releases my breast, and I whimper as he bends down to fumble with his pants. I can't help but smile, knowing that he had been planning this night.

Once sheathed, he takes hold of my hips to position them. Pushing my shoulders down slightly, he shuffles his legs between mine and draws my body closer to his. Moving his cock to my entrance, he enters me slowly, as my cunt grips him tightly. Hissing, he stops for a moment as my body adjusts, then he pushes in again, and I tilt back, welcoming his cock.

He pulls out and thrusts deeply, sending shockwaves to my core. I scream his name, as the binds pull at my wrists, my nails curling into the wooden beam. He moves his hips faster, thrusting into me until my toes curl to point to the ground, and I lean back into him more. His breath is at *my shoulder for a moment until I feel the indent of his teeth against my hot flesh, my orgasm building as he continues to buzz, buzz ...*

Buzz, buzz.

I wake with a start and stare around my dark bedroom. Damn it! I dreamt about that night again.

Buzz, buzz.

Turning to my bedside table, I see my phone vibrating heavily against the wooden top. My hot skin prickles as I move across my mattress. I pick it up to see *Theo calling* on the screen. Putting it to my ear, I answer, "Hey."

"Hey." His voice is quiet and distant. I sit up in bed as concern whirls in my stomach, my heart still racing from my dream.

"You okay?"

"I'm at the back of your place. Can you let me in?"

"Sure." I move quickly with the phone still connected to my ear. "I'll hit the button so you can get through the gate."

I pass the key hooks and press the button, quickly skipping down the stairs as Theo's bike rolls into my small yard. By the time he's killed the engine, I've flicked on the light, unlocked the back door, and opened it. It's not long before he's standing in front of me, and I close and lock the door. His eyes stare at mine, filled with apprehension. So different from how they were in the dream I just had.

"Theo, what happened?"

"I left Ricardo's ... I've been riding for a few hours ... It got to be too much."

"Did something happen? Were they mean to you?"

"No." His voice breaks. "They treated me like family. They were kind and I ... freaked out."

"Oh, honey." I step forward and wrap my arms around him, his body sinking into mine.

"I'm fucked up, Trin. I can't even cope with them showing kindness. A little was alright, but I just ... I can't explain ..."

I hold him closer to me and kiss his neck. "They'll understand. Try not to be so hard on yourself."

"I don't know how to ... There's still so much I need to tell you, even. Fuck, I don't know where to start."

I lean back and stare at his tortured eyes. "Don't worry about that now. I'm okay, honey. You don't have to tell me anything. Let me help *you*. What do you need?"

His hand reaches up and cups my face, and I lean into his touch. His fingers are cold as ice, but I refuse to shudder. "This. You. I need you."

"You have me," I whisper.

"Your skin is hot," he murmurs. "Are you okay?"

I cringe, wishing I'd left the light off. "Um, no." I bite my lip as a cheeky smile escapes my lips. "I was having a dream."

"Well, it must've been good if your face is so red." His eyes travel down my front. "And your neck. Were you being chased by zombies?"

"No, um, I dreamt about the time, you know, where we ah ..." I take a big breath. "Oh, fuck it. I dreamt about the time you fucked me against the railing. When I had to hide my wrists for a few days, as I had fabric burn."

His eyes widen in surprise before he leans back and laughs. "You have fantasy dreams about ... me?" He points to his chest, as his eyes twinkle.

"Not fantasy, you goof. Reality. It was fucking hot, too. You had just started to thrust inside me after you bit me when you called. I missed my kaboom."

"Your what? Ah ... never mind." He rubs his tongue along his bottom lip, and I lean up and kiss it, my thoughts taking me back to that moment. I need to taste him. His lips move with mine as his tongue delves into my mouth, causing me to groan and hold onto his arms.

We kiss like I wanted to in my dream—hot, wet, and passionate. What he never used to allow me to do. He pulls away from me, taking my hand and leading me out of my workroom, flicking off the light.

Leading me upstairs to my bedroom, he turns on my bedside lamp, and then we strip each other's clothes off quickly. I lie back on the mattress. Theo's hands caress up and down my skin, his lips trailing after them in soft kisses, barely touching me, driving me crazy. He moves down my body, flattening his palms against my stomach and kissing my hips before using his hands to spread my legs.

I watch as he plants gentle kisses further down, the gentle touch of his tongue stroking me. Reaching my folds, his hands part them slightly, and I feel his breath against my clit before his hot tongue swipes against me.

"Yes, baby," I gasp as the sensation of his tongue sweeps deeper into my swollen folds. He picks up speed and licks me deeper, taking time to suck my clit after a few strokes. My chest tightens as I pant, wanting more but wanting him closer to me. He increases the speed, and I tilt my pelvis, needing him desperately. "Theo, baby ..." I gasp. "I need you ... come up here."

"I'm not finished," he murmurs against my clit, sending tingles along my core.

"Yes, you are. I've already had my foreplay. Now, please get up here, I need you."

He chuckles against my skin but obeys, crawling up the bed to put both arms on either side of my face. I lean to kiss him, tasting myself on his lips, and I lick along the seam to move in and caress his tongue with mine.

Shifting my legs to either side of his, he positions himself at my entrance and begins to move inside me, all the while increasing the intensity of our kiss. My arms move up to pull him closer to me, and he thrusts, each stroke sending waves of pleasure down my body. I hold him tightly, each force building a delicious heat that I desperately want.

He leans back slightly, and our kiss is broken, but only so he can stare down at me, a gentle smile playing on his lips. So much emotion lies behind his eyes, which I know mirror mine. Feel me. I want you to feel everything that I am.

His eyes darken as his movements quicken, my hips meeting his, our breathing deepening as the intensity builds. Before I can warn him, my core clutches his cock, and my orgasm soars, my hands bringing his lips to mine in a hard kiss as I moan into his mouth. His thrusts continue until his voice deepens, the shockwaves of his own orgasm chasing after mine.

Slowly, his movements come to a halt, and I release his neck, knowing my nails have probably made a mark again. His hand moves to swipe my hair out of my face, and he stares down at me.

"Trinity," he whispers, emotion surging in his gaze.

"Kaboom," I whisper, too afraid to speak. Too afraid to admit what burns in my heart right now.

He blinks, as a slow smile greets my panting lips. "Kaboom."

Twenty-Two

The panel shows the man standing on the mountaintop, his arms outstretched and a radiant smile on his face. Unbeknownst to him, the land underneath his feet is beginning to crumble away.
TTE

THEO

There's tension at the office. In between Cole still being barely audible and the many secretaries that stroll through our office, who he interviews but never hires, Letty's absence is making things considerably awkward. Her desk has been kept the same, all except her coffee cup which isn't there. I don't remember her taking it. It isn't in the tearoom, or anywhere else that I've checked. Her obsession with soap operas and having Ridge Forrester from *The Bold and the Beautiful* plastered on both sides of her cup was always her way of being a little different. She didn't believe in being conservative, and none of us wanted her to be. Her departure meant that our meetings were kept brief, while the vibe that shrouded us gave us the initiative to keep our heads low and just get on with it.

She did surprise me by sending me a few emails after she arrived in Toronto. The initial one was to congratulate me on my latest novel, which she felt bad for not mentioning sooner. She also threw in a picture of her standing with the CN tower and an awesome skyline behind her, with the caption, "Hope this building makes you wet your pants with excitement. Nerd." It was a pretty cool building, but my thoughts soon turned to Trin, as she'd itch to be able to do the Edgewalk, whereas I'd probably need Valium or bourbon. Possibly both.

I'd responded with, "Definitely. Off to buy my waterproof pants." Since then, we'd exchanged a few emails, with her telling me about her sister's place and the jobs she was scouting for. I got her postal address and managed to fit in a postal stop-off, and sent a T-shirt from the bundle that I'd ordered for her. I could tell that her chipper emails were bullshit. She wasn't herself, so if I could make her smile and carry on, then it was worth it.

Each time she emailed me, I wondered if she had contacted Cole. From his pissy attitude, I didn't think so. But I recognised that look. A man in emotional limbo with that trapped, forlorn expression across his face, while a woman really did fuck with his head. Initially, I'd hoped that, after whatever had happened, he'd be back to his awkward self, but as the days have passed, his mood doesn't appear to be lifting ending anytime soon. Rather than wait for it, I do the one thing that I think could work. Even if the sinking feeling in my stomach is telling me that she is gonna rip my balls off.

"Hey Cole." I wait for him to put his pen down and look up at me from his desk.

"Yeah, mate?" He raises his brow, and I point my finger to the tablet next to me and say, "Just sent you something to check out. Let me know if you want any more help with it."

He nods, and I watch him tap his tablet to access his email. His brow furrows as he reads my message, but the hardened lines loosen in his face as his brows raise in surprise.

Cole,

Below you'll find Letty's address. She's staying with her sister. Think she's having trouble finding a job over there. Also, I've put a link to Webjet. They might happen to have some deals from some airlines for you. You know, just in case.

Theo.

I wait, hoping that I haven't misread that look. He rubs his chin before tapping across his screen a few times. I lower my head to continue sketching the office building that I'm working on when, after a few minutes, my tablet signals a new message.

Theo,

Thanks for that, I'll get right on it. No more assistance required.

Cole

I smile, relieved that I didn't piss off my boss. It doesn't stop me from responding just like I think my little firecracker would in this situation.

Go get 'em, tiger.

He chuckles, and I continue sketching before my mid-morning appointment takes place. I feel a sense of dread beginning to unfurl in my gut, but I keep sketching to clear my mind as best I can. One more hour until I, too, have to grow some balls of my own.

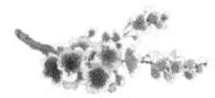

My hand uncurls from the throttle as I glide my bike to a standstill by the warehouse. Outside, it still looks like a construction site, but inside, the restaurant is really taking shape. Considering it's been almost two weeks since I was here last, I had to come and face Ricardo for the project, as initially promised. The guilt for being so pissweak was eating away at me. Rolling in on my bike wasn't anything I normally did, but I had to have something that I could control within my fingertips.

Calling in sick last week had been a cop-out, especially via email. I half expected Elly to march over to my place and rip me a new one, but she didn't. I just got a few messages reading, "Coffee machine misses you. Cups are getting cold." I was just too overwhelmed to face any of them. But enough was enough. I had balls dammit, and it was about time I used them.

Tucking my helmet under my arm and taking my bag off, I walk through the entrance to the building and familiarise myself with the new changes. The bar itself has been built, the wall behind it is almost finished, yet the wine-holder holes look strange with the undercoat. But I know it is going to be pretty cool when completed. Despite the floor's protective covering, I still tap my shoes on the door's step to remove the excess dirt from outside. I no longer took them off, though. Old habits die hard to keep floors clean.

Walking across the flooring, my eyes scan the hall for Ricardo, but I don't see him. Placing my helmet on the bar top, I sign in, then unzip my bag and get my safety vest and hard hat out, followed by the folio as well, to go over the wall designs. I leave the bag next to my helmet. Amongst the sound of drilling and the nails being hammered, workers surround the room, each doing their individual jobs, from painting walls to adjusting lights. I can hear his muffled voice in the distance towards the kitchen. Stepping closer, I see the room is well lit up, and the stainless steel walls and benches have been fitted, showing more distinctly the shape that the kitchen will have.

"Hello, Theo." Ricardo startles me. He stands to the side with a piece of paper in his hand and his phone to his ear.

"Hey." I clear my throat as he continues speaking on his phone, only to cut off the conversation.

"Excuse me, Louis, but my son is here. Yes, the architect. Thank you. I'll pass that on ... Yes, his details are on that business card I gave you. Good. *Adiós.*"

I blink heavily. *My son.* Still feels weird hearing that. *Not going to freak out today. Hopefully.*

"That was my dear friend Louis Owen—"

"From L. Owen constructions," I interject, my mouth drying up. That company owns half of the city. He is one of the big investors. Apparently, he missed out on the casino rights by a sliver. Fuck, this guy is loaded to his eyeballs, and all the architect firms want in on his action.

"He dropped in here last week and liked the look of the place."

"But it's unfinished," I mutter.

"He's a visionary. He can *see* where it will go. So, consider yourself lucky. He's got a new frontier in his back pocket and is probably calling Cole as we speak. Prepare to be very busy. He will work you like a machine. But you can handle it. I have faith in you." Ricardo tucks his phone into his suit jacket and smiles. "Coffee?" His chin lifts towards the machine.

I shake my head. "You didn't need to do that. I don't want it to seem like your friend is giving preference to my work because you're my—"

"Theo." Ricardo turns to face me, stepping forward to place his hand on my shoulder. "Son, you need to give yourself more credit. I didn't need to do anything." Waving his other hand around the place, he continues, "This place speaks for itself. Now, onto more pressing matters."

My gut tightens as he stares at me.

"Do you want that coffee or not?"

I chuckle as my shoulders relax, and I nod. "Yeah, that would be great. Thanks."

He squeezes my shoulder and winks before walking over to the machine to make the coffees.

After they're done, we step back out into the main area as he indicates the changes from last time, not once making me feel guilty for avoiding him. I smile, marvelling at how expressive he is.

"Over here"—he gestures to the side wall—"I want to have portraits of couples dancing. I want them dressed traditionally and put into various poses."

"I could source some dancers and find a costume shop or something ..." I offer, even though it's not my job. But I want to help after running out on him like an idiot. He waves the piece of paper in his hand at me.

"There are at least nine different types of dances. We are not just Flamenco." I nod, taking the paper from him. "I want couples doing the Jota Aragonesa, Muñeira, Zamba Bolero, and of course, the Paso doble."

I look at the sheet. Photos of dresses are printed out onto it.

"You want me to get Trin to sew these?" I hold the images to face him. "She could, but it will have to wait for a month as she's ... busy." I know this project would thrill her, but seeing as her surgery is just a couple of days away, there is a bee's dick of chance that I'll let her see these. She'd try to start, and no way am I letting that happen. She's already teased me about playing nurse for her, so if dressing up in a white dress is what I have to do to make her rest, that's what I'll do.

"Not needed." He shakes his hand. "These dress pictures are of my mother's and a few of my sister's. The girls have some too, but they don't get up and dance like they used to. Eloise is a qualified teacher, who I hope will do a workshop here once a week or fortnight. Maybe a Thursday night."

"My friend Trice teaches dance, I'm sure she'd love to learn. Her old dance partner Aidan would join her too if needed."

"Can she teach, too?" he asks.

"She already has her own classes, and will be back working weekends, but I'll mention it. I'm not sure if she's trained in this style, but it's worth asking. So, do you have a photographer in mind? I could probably suggest who we use for our website. Do you have your models hired?"

"No photos." He shakes his head and gestures to the picture in my hand. "My daughters will be in some of those portraits, but your friend and her partner can be as well."

"That might be expensive, getting in all those models," I explain, but he waves his hand at me.

"No matter. It will be worth it. They will make the pictures feel more real to me."

"Sounds great." I stare at the walls, wondering how big these portraits are going to be, when I realise something. "If you don't want photos, what do you want?"

"Paintings. I want them painted directly onto the wall. Not in frames. I want them part of those walls. They will be our history blended in."

"Sounds fantastic. Have you found an artist? There are a few in town I could locate for you, get them to draw up a few designs to see if it's the style you're after."

"No need. My artist is standing right next to me."

The speed with which my head flicks back makes me wonder how it's still attached. "Huh?"

"Theo, I want you to do it. This is my family, and you're part of it."

A small wave of pride tingles my skin, and I turn back to face the walls. Already, I can see the silhouettes of movement on them. Second to drawing, painting is another interest of mine, and the thought of doing more of it really sends a surge of eagerness within me. I raise my hands, letting the empty coffee cup hang from my finger as I position them into a square in front of me. Yes, I can see what I will do. "I don't know what to say. I'd love to."

I can't wipe the smile off my face, and I hope I won't need to. We walk over to the bar, more ideas beginning to form. "I'll get the girls to dress up," I rush on excitedly, "and get some photos taken to give me an idea. I think they will love it. I'll even find a partner for the girls, if needed."

Ricardo's eyes darken. "So long as they're good boys and I don't need to get my gun license." His brow tightens for a moment before he winks, and I laugh. "Good, the wall is ready. You choose when you're able to do it, after all the other things are finished."

"I can come in after the workers leave and start planning."

"You remind me of your mother, Amaya, when you're happy," Ricardo gently adds, as he puts our cups on the bar top. Our conversation takes a turn into the awkward, but I refuse to close him off this time.

"I only have a few photos of her." I shrug. "Don't remember a lot, to be honest; I was only four."

"What do you remember?" he asks candidly.

"Her laugh and the tight hugs she gave me. Sometimes I remember snippets of when she read to me before bed."

"What do you know about her and I?" He leans against the bar, and my fingers curl into my bag.

"That you met at a conference, and she seduced you to get pregnant and never told you about me."

"That must've been quite a shock," he surmises.

"Yeah, you could say that. Kind of explains why Ko was the way he was with me. Why I resented him so much."

"Why do you call him Ko when he was your father?"

"Because he lost that right when I'd discovered he'd been withholding the truth about you. He never felt like one, so I can't bring myself to call him that anymore."

"Are you still in contact with him?" He tilts his head to the side, studying me.

"Barely." I shrug. "I don't feel the need to make the effort. I answer his calls and have a two-minute polite conversation. That's it, though. I've learnt that I don't need him." I take a moment while the next thought enters my mind, taking me off guard. "I'm surprised that I don't hate him anymore either."

"That's because you have your mother's goodness in you. We did meet at a conference, but it wasn't a sordid affair, like Ko probably suggested. We became friends. Amaya was passionate about living and had a wicked sense of humour. She was serious at work, but had a lust for life. We were both too busy in our lives to have any sort of relationship. Plus, I thought I was too young to settle. I just wanted to have fun. I never knew she was married. That was the only thing that disappointed me—when I found that out. I was sad to leave, as it had been fun, but I never knew the extent of her feelings. I never got the impression it was anything more than a bit of excitement."

"Okay," I grimace.

"I'm sorry that our story isn't romantic, Theo. But I will say that I owe my success to her. She saw in me what I could achieve. We spent hours talking about what Melbourne needed. I wouldn't have this success if she hadn't pushed me towards it. I will be forever grateful to her." He takes a moment, his expression softening. "But my greatest achievement is my family, and that includes you."

I grip the bench to steady myself, to hold it all together. "I'm not used to this type of praise," I say uncomfortably. "My grandparents offered little comfort under the restrained doctrine of my father. They called me half-breed, for fuck's sake. That was how people like me were referred to as. Like it was normal to downcast us. In their attempts at kindness, they always seemed stilted."

"It angers me greatly that you had that life, Theo. It pained me that I couldn't step in and take you away. I was given the impression that it would destroy you. So, I bided my time until I found other measures to assist you, when it was time to be here."

"What do you mean?" I frown.

"You remember your career advisor at school?" He smirks, twirling his coffee cup across the bench slowly.

"Mrs. Parsons? Of course. She was the one who helped me get into college."

"About that." His fingers stop for a moment. "I may have had something to do with that ... as well as your new music building at school."

"What?" My eyes bug out of my head.

"I may have made a sizeable donation to extend the music programme further. I also spoke to the dean at the university you applied to, who was a friend of mine in college, to create ... a scholarship."

My heart sinks. "I thought I got that based on my results, not because I was your son." I grimace, feeling pissed off, gritting my teeth.

"You did, Theo. I wanted to see what my son could do. You aced those tests and earned that scholarship with your own merit. From then, I made sure that you had the best of everything in university. Did you ever wonder why your lecturers were heavily sought out? You had the cream of the crop for your entire degree. That was my condition with Paul, the dean. He made no complaints; he got a sizeable donation, too. You may have seen the new student centre."

"Fuckin' hell," I mutter. "This is crazy."

"No, Theo." Ricardo's voice is stern, and my eyes rise to meet his. "It was all I could do, as a father who missed out on eighteen years of his son's life. If I had known about you from the start, especially after Amaya's death, you would've been welcomed at our house."

"See?" I tap the bar top, with my fingers. "That's what I don't understand. Why was Aria so thrilled to see me? If I calculated correctly, Eloise is just under two years younger than I am. I would've ruined your marriage, coming in later on. Been a dirty secret or something."

"Rubbish!" he snaps. "I met Aria a few months after the last time I saw Amaya. I knew she was the one. Our love was strong and believe me, Theo, she would've welcomed you."

"How could you possibly know that?" I rub my lips together, knowing I'm a step away from telling him to piss off.

"Because she was a foster child and knows what it's like to feel unloved and unwanted. To beg for a family to take her in. When I found out about you, her reaction was to get a suitcase out to help me pack to come and *get* you. She's not a fool, my boy. When you came to our house, she saw what you've been holding in for all these years." He looks around the bar before continuing, "This was all meant to be discussed when you came to dinner that night. I was going to show you family photo albums and discuss my parents and siblings. There are still so many people for you to meet. But that night, we all saw the pain that gripped you." Reaching towards me, his hand clasps mine on the bar as his fingers curl into them. "It's time to let all that go; we're not going anywhere, and you're here where you're meant to be." A sharp intake of breath freezes in my throat. "No more running, Theo. Our family is big, and there are a lot of them who will chase you if you run." He smirks.

"Thank you for the scholarship," I add feebly, not wanting to hold onto any more anger, my thoughts running rapidly in my mind.

Ricardo smiles and nods, watching my face which I am sure is a myriad of emotions. Confusion. Fear. Hope. His hand lets go of mine, and I feel a strange sense of loss, until my shoulder is suddenly grabbed and pushed into his chest. His arms wrap around me, and for a moment I freeze, until the bag I hold loosens from my fingers and drops to the floor. I take a big breath and lift my arms to embrace him, pulling him closer, my head tilting to the side. The rush of emotion pulls me under as my hands shake within his strong hold. I don't let go. This sensation is so foreign to me, but now feels right. I don't care if the builders are watching. Nothing is going to break this moment.

"Now, this is something I've been waiting for." Ricardo 's voice cracks. "Wait until I tell Aria—she is going to tackle you for a hug next time."

A laugh escapes my lips as I add, "After my sisters, though. I think they've been waiting to tackle me."

Ricardo slaps my back before stepping back, his eyes shining with unshed tears. He's unashamed to show emotion. Peaceful. Proud.

"I suggest you brace yourself, as they will make you topple," he jokes.

I smirk as warmth swirls in my chest. So this is what a real family feels like. A family I can call mine. "I will ..." My lips stammer, as I'm about to utter a word that I've never said before. Not even as a kid. "Dad."

His face softens as he smiles, patting my shoulder. "No." He shakes his head, "*Papá*."

"*Papá*."

Twenty-Three

"It's going to hurt, baby, and there's nothing I can do to stop it."
Love, Mum

TRINITY

I glide the steamer over the fabric delicately, making sure I don't get too close to it. The soft chiffon sparkles as the beading reflects under all the natural light. *She's going to look fantastic.* I admire it. Today, Queen Virginia is collecting her dress ,as well as the bridesmaids' dresses. Despite her being a royal pain in the arse and more difficult to deal with than an ingrown hair, I have grown fond of our sessions ... slightly.

Stepping back to clip my steamer on its stand, I check for any creases that I may have missed and position the dress better. It has come a long way from the mock-up that I made months ago. I spent many weeks creating the hand-beaded trim that is now successfully weaved throughout the dress and veil.

In a white satin, the bodice is wrapped tightly with narrow straps that move into a plunging sweetheart neckline. Beneath the breasts, a gentle beaded trim wraps around the front of the torso, which then remains fitted until it reaches the hips. Soft chiffon overlays travel down the skirt in diagonal strips, each giving the gown a weightless appearance and lined individually with a handmade beaded trim. Her back will mostly be bare, giving an alluring look to the shape of her body.

The veil is floor-length, with the same trim from each, to match her dress. Her strappy shoes complement it perfectly, but I know that they are going to kill her feet. For months, she's sworn as she's worn. Trying to follow beauty trends isn't always going to be kind to your toes.

Next to the dress, I arrange the bridesmaids' dresses in individually marked bags for the girls: Eloise, Leah, and Skye. I'm tempted to make pockets to slip in a hip flask in each, as they are sure as shit going to need it.

Her bridesmaids each have a floor-length, pearl pink-coloured, trumpet-shaped gown, where the waistline draws in naturally with a slightly ruched bodice. The gowns have just one strap, with a ruffled detailed vining over it. I had tried to suggest that a different colour would be better suited, but that was another thing Virginia would not shift on. What did I expect from such a princess? Maybe I was the fussy one. Virginia's antics were rubbing off on me. Shit.

They are still pretty, but making these dresses has given me ideas of what *not* to do for Hazel's. Hopefully she'll listen. If we can avoid it, we aren't doing floor-length. As much as I love Hazel, on the off chance that she could become a Bridezilla in a blink of an eye and rise in a whirl of wildfire that will rival Vag's, there is no way I am hightailing arse around with a long dress dragging behind me to be at her beck and call. Nuh-uh. Unless she demands it. *Oh shit.* Fingers crossed.

Unzipping the garment bag, I lie it across the chair next to the dress, ready to start putting it away. The bell from the door jingles, and I turn to the sound of Virginia and her bridesmaids walking in. Behind Eloise another figure appears, and it's not long before I recognise Anastasia strolling in right behind them. The clacking of the ringleader's heels along my wooden floor has me quickly breaking eye contact with Anastasia to focus on her. *Here we go.*

"It's so stuffy in here!" she grumbles, flicking open the buttons on her coat, taking the coat off, and draping it over her arm.

"It's a warehouse; I've got the heater on so I don't freeze, but if you want to die of hypothermia, I'm more than happy to switch it off. They don't call it winter for nothing."

Virginia's eyes travel to the side where my little space heater sits. I could fire up the rest of my heating, but when you're working in just one area, there really isn't a point. Plus, the days were getting warmer, slowly. It is Melbourne after all. It could be a tsunami of sporadic weather. This shit is fact.

Virginia steps closer to the stand, clutching her bag as her eyes roam up and down her dress. We had the final fitting a few days ago, so she has already seen the finished product. As her eyes scan the long material, obviously in search of a hidden insult to try to fling my way, I cross my arms across my chest and wait. I have encountered this look before, when a customer finds an imaginary fault and expects a mass refund. Nope. I'd rather put her dress up on the rack for someone else to buy than put up with that. I am an honest salesperson, for fuck's sake. This is not going to be a moment to open a negotiation. Prices have been established, and there is no way I am going to back down. If anything, this ice princess could leave me a tip for putting up with her fussy arse bull—

"It looks, fine, I suppose," she mumbles, flicking her platinum blonde hair over her shoulder to look to the bridesmaid dresses already in their garment bags.

My jaw tightens at her use of "fine" to describe my designs. I'm not the best in Melbourne, but I also know my value. If she wants to get a rise out of me, she'll be turning me nuclear.

"You can bag that up, as I need to get to an appointment."

I shake my head rather than plough my shoe up her arse and bring the bag over to the table I have set up, and then go to retrieve the dress. Carefully sliding it on top and then adjusting it to move underneath, my fingers feel stiff with agitation. Manners go a long way. I have to keep repeating that mantra. As I tuck in the skirt gently, I can feel tension building until my thoughts go elsewhere. Perhaps I could dedicate her a mannequin display, entitled, "Three Degrees of Constipation of Virginia." Maybe I'll stick her photo on the mannequins' faces to really bring the act to life. Pity they'd look shit though. Pun intended. I chuckle to myself, feeling the tension shift slightly. I glance up to the princess herself. She stands posed and stiff. *Is she holding in a fart?* Part of me wants to make her laugh just to see if she'll let one go.

"I'm glad you think my designs are *fine*. I'm sure I'll have many fine designs to work over with Brit in the next coming weeks," I offer, as the final pieces are tucked safely and neatly.

She blushes slightly, biting her lip before making eye contact. "Thanks for helping my friend." Her pose shifts slightly with unease.

"Next time you pull a stunt of bringing in a bully from my past without warning me, I'll put pins in places you won't be able to retrieve," I pull the zip up and tap the garment bag. "Customer or not, you crossed a line when she threw herself at me in here."

Her shoulders push back defensively, but Leah steps forward and raises her eyebrows at her. "She's right. Especially since she told us about their history. I know you didn't want to make a scene, but still, it was a bit foolish." Looking over at me, her face softens, "I'm surprised you're helping her, but it's nice of you to."

"Let's just say that you can't hold onto grudges forever. You can try, but it'll eat at you. Brit apologised, my friend is fine with us working together, so that's final." Linking my fingers through the coat hanger hook, I lift the dress slightly, and Virginia's chin lifts towards Leah, then towards me. "Nope." I firmly shake my head. "You carry your own dress. They aren't your slaves."

"But I need to pay." She waves her card in the air, and I gesture to my desk.

"Well, let's go and settle that first." Lowering the dress gently, I walk over to my counter and hear a huff as her steps follow sulkily behind me. I process the payment for the dresses, while she nibbles on her bottom lip, waiting for me to hand the card back. "Worried there wasn't going to be enough funds?" I joke, ripping off the paid receipt to hand it to her with her card.

"No, um ... I just wanted to say ..." her lips stammer, and she breathes out slowly, her head shaking a little. "Thank you for your help."

Reaching into her bag, she pulls out a card and plucks a pen off my desk to scribble on it. "When you're free, call this number. It's for *Melbourne Bridal*, and ask for Eva. She is waiting for you to call."

"Um, what?" I take the card she's offering and turn it over in my hands. Holy crap, this is the biggest bridal magazine in Melbourne. I have made appearances in smaller ones, but this is the motherlode.

"She wants to use your designs, not in this edition, but the next, so give her a call soon."

I flick my thumb and forefinger back and forth along the card, tracing the edges, as I openly stare at her, my cheeks tensing, not sure whether to smile or not. "Why did you do this for me?"

"You're great at what you do." She shrugs. "I know you've got a decent amount of exposure, but this will give you more."

"Wow, thank you so much." I smile, flicking the card across my other palm, feeling the need to keep playing with it. A shiver rises along my spine in excitement, and I look at the card again and then decide to safely stow it in the drawer at my counter.

We walk over to the dress, and I hold it up for Virginia to take. She unfolds her jacket from her arm and puts it on before looping her bag over her shoulder. Stepping forward, her manicured fingers hook in the hanger, and she stares at me and smiles. "Besides, once my friends see my designer was in a magazine, they will be all over it. It's not just for you, but ... for me." Her brows raise as she smiles sardonically.

"Oh." I shake my head as I let go of the bag. "You're not so bad for a mutton dressed as a lamb." I smile as she flinches. I hold my arm out to the dresses. "Ladies, here you go, enjoy! It was a pleasure to meet you all." I wink and giggle as Virginia turns awkwardly with her oversized garment bag in her hands. The others retrieve their dresses and give me a wave, except Eloise and Anastasia, who opt to stay. I wave back and wait for the others to leave before the three of us throw back our heads and laugh.

"That was so funny!" Eloise holds her bag in her hand as she clutches her waist to laugh. "She is going to be bitching the whole car ride to drop them home."

"Still can't believe you're friends with her. She's toxic, yet generous. I'm confused how to feel." I muse.

"She is nice, I promise, but she finds it hard to trust people."

"She's just really good at being a bitch," Anastasia pipes up, and we make eye contact and I nod. My eyes drop to her chest, noticing her T-shirt, and I freeze. My mouth gapes as I stare at her.

"Oh my God! Where did you get that? I love that novel!" My voice wavers in awe. Her lips turn up slightly as she looks at Eloise for a moment, before she answers.

"He's my brother." She blushes. "He gave this to me." Looking at her sister, she adds, "She has one too."

"No fucking way!" I shriek. "I'm a huge fan."

"Yeah, I kinda gathered that from when I was here once and you had his novel on your desk," Eloise adds, smiling broadly.

"Why didn't you tell me before?" I lightly tap her arm. "Dude! I would've said to introduce me or something." Her eyes darken for a moment before she wiggles her eyebrows.

"He is a bit shy; you would've scared him," Anastasia throws in. My eyes skim the characters on her shirt, and I feel the giddy rush of happiness flow through my veins.

"Can't believe you're related. You know, I had a massive pseudo crush on him." I laugh. "If I wasn't already taken, I'd be telling you to hook a sister up."

"Well, he's taken too." Eloise tucks a loose strand of hair behind her ear as she grins. "But you should drop in to the café sometime. He likes to come in for coffees most afternoons." Her eyes cut to her sister and they smile, and I wonder what that look that is passing between them means. Maybe he's really weird-looking ... a hunchback or something. Nah. Surely not.

Fuck. Meeting TTE. Wow. This is more exciting than the card in my top drawer.

"I might just do that," I giggle. "He needs to explain why Adam and Mila aren't getting it on. They are on the brink, but he keeps causing rifts."

"He's so good at that," Anastasia grumbles. "I wanted to make him tell me the plot the other week, but he … had to go. Oh, and our mum wants you to make a dress for her for October."

"Oh, sure, cool." My mouth draws in slightly, trying to remember my bookings. "I have a few things going on, but I'll squeeze her in. Tell her to come and visit sometime."

"Sweetie"—Eloise hoists the garment bag over the back of her shoulder—"tell Trin about the formal."

"Oh." Anastasia's voice softens as a soft blush blooms across her cheeks. "I got asked out."

"Yay!" I clap and do a little jig on the spot. "See? I told you that you were gorgeous."

"He's the guy I'm really good friends with, too."

"The lab partner?" I clasp my hands together, eager to know.

"Yep." She grins shyly.

"That's awesome. You must have *great chemistry*." I chuckle as I pretend to beat a drum in the air.

"Nice one," Eloise nods.

"It all happened because I took your advice." She bites her lip. My brows crease as I look from side to side. I struggle to remember what advice I gave, but she soon puts me out of my confusion. "I told those girls that I didn't want to be their friends anymore."

"Yay for you!" I jump and then reach forward to give her a little hug. She stiffens slightly, but accepts my embrace after a little while. "Well done! See? How did they take it?"

"Well, I told them to fuck off, and then Tom came and stepped in. It was really sweet.

They were pointing to my dress and making rude comments, and after I had enough, I felt him grab my hand and lead me to the dance floor. The rest is history."

"Sounds like a top bloke."

"He is." She sighs.

"We need to get going." Eloise looks at her watch. "I took my lunch hour to get this." Her head tilts to the bag on her other shoulder. "But drop in sometime. We're only five minutes away."

I nod as they both begin to walk to the door.

"I definitely will be dropping in now!" I call out.

I hum as they go, happy that Anastasia did what I know a lot of girls wouldn't have had the guts to do. Speaking of guts, I have to get my things organised for my surgery in two days. I'm not looking forward to it, but at least it is a day procedure. He's made up the spare room in his house on the bottom floor, so I can avoid stairs. My heart thuds thinking about how sweet he is and how happy he is making me. Theo has promised me he'll be my maid. I am tempted to whip up a quick frilly apron and make him wear it. *Naked.*

After I tidy up the racks and sort out some stock, I check the time and look around the shop for anything else that needs doing. No one else has come in, so I make a decision on a whim. Grabbing my purse from behind the counter, I quickly stroll out the back and check that the door is locked before getting my keys and flicking the sign to closed before walking out into the street and locking the door. I feel like a coffee, and I know the right place to go.

Walking up the street away from the city, I send a quick hello text to Theo, but no response comes. *He's probably in a meeting or something.* My eyes travel over the other boutiques and cafés, and all the while the traffic keeps driving by.

Eloise's café eventually comes into view on the other side of the road. I smile, admiring how the shopfront is rather quirky and cute. I'm about to watch for traffic before I cross the road, when I notice a familiar-looking figure out the front. A woman dressed in a leather jacket with a vague familiarity stands with her back to me. She's facing a man and drapes one of her arms over his shoulder. He leans forward and kisses the top of her head affectionately, and I freeze. I know that face.

Theo.

Holding another woman.

Theo.

Showing affection.

He *never* shows any affection unless it's … to me. Oh my God. My heart thuds in my chest as pieces of it begin to shatter. The violent rhythmic beat tries to escape my ribs as I clutch my shirt. My breath catches in my throat, and I struggle to breathe for a moment, until it builds up and a pained cry breaks past my lips. Hot tears cascade down my face, each bringing forth a memory of what I had with him. *His kiss, his laughter, his embrace*—all a fucking lie. I look up in desperation to see if it's all a dream to find him brushing her hair behind her ear. *Stop fucking touching her!* I want to scream.

I'm about to step away but his eyes move past her face and clash with mine. A gasp leaves my throat as I turn and run like hell back to my place, not wanting him to follow, but the heavy sound of horns and shouting from motorists roar as I charge down the footpath. My stupid heart wants to turn around to see if he's okay, but I keep running. The sharp pounding of heavy footsteps behind me sounds across the cold concrete, and I know it's him.

"TRINITY!" he bellows, as I continue to zip past people, using them almost as shields as my front door gets closer. I thrust my hands in my bag as I run, clumsily trying to clasp the keys, when I feel his hand on my elbow.

"NO!" I scream, wrenching my elbow from his grasp as though my skin were burnt. Relief swarms me as I'm at my door, and I shove the key in, thrusting the door to get away. His hand pushes against the top of the door as he barges inside, forcing me to keep walking in. Now, though, I'm too angry to run. "GET THE FUCK OUT OF HERE!" I yell, pushing against his chest. I push again, making him stumble back. I want to hurt him like my heart is hurting right now.

"Trin, calm down." He moves out of my way to avoid another push. "You need to let me explain—"

"Like hell I do!" I throw my bag down hard against the floor and ignore the contents that spill from it. I point to the direction of the café and scream, "I saw with my own two fucking eyes, Theo. Did you think I'd never find out? Did you think that you could cheat on me and I'd be sitting here like a lap dog, waiting around for you?"

236

His eyes widen in shock as he steps closer to me.

"Don't you dare come near me. I will rip your fucking balls off and throw them on the tram tracks," I warn.

"You need to let me explain; it's not what you think at all." He tries holding his hands up to protect himself. *Oh you're going to need a force field to protect you if you ever touch me again.*

"See that door? You need to walk right out of it and never come back." My eyes lower to the ground where my pills lie next to my wallet. Anger surges as my foot rises and stomps on the packet, crushing it into my floorboards as I continue to beat it into dust. Rage over every moment that we've ever shared is crushed beneath my shoe. "How dare you fucking lie to me!" I continue to stomp. Ugh.

"Trin! You need to stop! I can explain. I was *never* cheating on you," he pleads.

"Fuck off. Get out of my store," I stomp on the packet one last time as my gaze hits his. "Leave me alone! Now!"

Twenty-Four

The panel shows a man standing on a cliff face, staring out into the sun.
"I'm losing her when I never really had her. Is it too late to leap? What's the point? I'm probably going to lose her forever."
TTE

THEO

"What the fuck?" I bend down and grip my hair. Anguish cripples me as my raging heartbeat thunders against my rib cage. *I've fucked up. I've really, really fucked up.* My legs are restless with every word she throws at me, rapidly constructing a wall in between us. *I can't let that happen again.*

"You need to let me explain, Trin. It is absolutely not what you think. She isn't another woman." My shoulders curl in defeat as her raging eyes continue to stare at me, the love I had seen in there closed off to make way for the hate that emanates from her now.

"I don't give two fucks who she is, Theo. I don't need a name or what the fuck you were doing. All I saw is that you were touching another woman." The sharp sting berates me. "It feels like Claire all over again, and here I am, the idiot who believed in us." She stares at me straight on and delivers her final blow, "I will forget it and forget you."

A hot current burns under my skin as I leap towards her, to hell with the consequences. "Like fuck you will!" I shout. "You need to stop for a minute and let me explain. There are things I haven't told you yet, and now I need to."

"What the fuck? You wait until I sprung you to tell me what these"—she holds her hands up for emphasis—"things are?" She shakes her head. "Unbelievable."

"The girl you saw ..." I say, trying to gather my thoughts as they stumble across my tongue. "She's ..."

Trin holds her hand up and turns her head from me. In an emotionless voice that I've never heard her use before she says, "Please. If you have any respect for me, leave. I can't deal with this, Theo. It feels like you're ripping my heart out, just like you did at Mum's funeral." Her face ticks as she squeezes her eyes shut for a moment, tears rapidly falling down her cheeks. Her blue eyes open to show me the same pain that I saw all those years ago. I want to hold her close so badly, but as I step towards her, she scurries back, like I'm poison. "Please." Her voice fades into a sob. "Go."

"I swear, it's not what you think. I need to tell you, but I want you to calm down." My voice lowers as her face crumbles. "But I'll go. For you. But you can bet that this is not over. I'll give you time to recover, but you're mine, Trinity. Just as I am yours. You're the fire to my ice. Like fuck am I going to let that fade away."

A sob echoes in the room as I walk to her door, each step taking me farther from her. I want to kick myself for being so fucking stupid. All of this could have been prevented if I'd told her.

As I reach the door, I make sure the sign for closed is facing the street, and I flick the lock to stop anyone from coming in. It's the only reprieve I can give her as she breaks apart in front of me, each sob a reminder of what I can't control, ripping a deep hole in my chest.

I begin to walk down the street, no sense of direction or purpose, lamenting over what I've done ... dissolving perfection. Just as Ko believed. I'm about to walk to the park when a gentle hand taps my shoulder, and for a moment I'm relieved, thinking it could be Trin, but it's Anastasia, with Elly beside her.

"Theo, what happened?" Her eyes blink rapidly as she looks at my face.

"She saw me hugging you and thought I was cheating—"

"No, that can't be. Surely, she'd see that we look alike ..." she says, confusion lining her brow.

"She knows I'm not good with affection. Her seeing me hug you sent her off the charts."

"But you were congratulating me on being brave." Her voice pitches. "Oh my God! It's all my fault. What she must think of me to hurt her so."

"I don't know what the fuck she was thinking, as she won't let me talk. She wouldn't even let me tell her who you are. This has gone on long enough!"

"I can go," she offers, rubbing her lips together. "I can tell her who I am, and then she won't be mad."

My eyes dart to her shirt, and I cringe. "Ugh!" I grip my hair in disgust. "That fucking novel is what got me into this shit! It started all the fucking lies!" I turn and face the wall next to me and smack my hands up against it.

"Hey." Anastasia reaches forward and grabs me. "Don't beat yourself up over this. She will calm down, and then you can tell her. Give her a couple of days."

"She's got surgery in two; she won't be in the state to see me. It's not like I can hold

her hostage and make her listen. Unless ..."

"I have an idea." Elly's voice suddenly breaks through my thoughts. Holding up her

Palm, she says, "But I'm going to need your key to copy, and you've got some friends to call before they all want to lynch you. Stat."

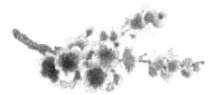

This is nuts. Why did I listen to Elly? This is going to backfire—I can

feel it. Even after explaining myself to Hazel and Trice, I still feel like they're going to slay me. I check my phone for the hundredth time and read the same message from Hazel:

> **Hazel:** She texted to say she was out of recovery and ready to go home, as she ate her lunch. She's in room 202. Good luck.
>
> **Me:** Thanks. I'm going to need it
>
> **Hazel:** You'll be fine. It'll sort itself out.

"Easy for you to say," I grumble, as I step out of Trice's red Barina and press the remote to lock it. This plan is going to go balls up. My lips press together as I stroll to the entrance of the hospital, each step matching the deep pounding in my chest. I tuck the keys in my back pocket and start hoping that Trin's not in the mood to launch at me.

"Her room is just down that corridor to the left," the nurse instructs me, and I make my way down the quiet hall, counting the rooms until I reach hers. The wooden door is ajar, and I hope that some guardian angel is looking over me, or at least putting up a shield around my nuts. Sighing softly, I walk in to the pale-walled room and cringe at how lifeless it feels.

My feet stop as I see Trin sitting on the edge of the bed, with her bag and phone in her hand, her head bent down. I crave to hold her, to make her want me again. I would give anything to have her smile.

I clear my throat to get her attention, and her face lifts, her eyes widening in shock.

"What are you ..." Her voice strains, and I instantly feel pity as exhaustion has reduced my firecracker's frame into a hunched state. I ache, wondering if she is still *mine.*

I quickly begin with the plan I'd formulated with the girls, after I called around there to tell them what had transpired and who my sisters were. Suffice it to say, besides their sympathetic looks, Trice was right in calling me a fucking dickhead for not telling her sooner.

"Hazel called." My words rush out quickly in hopes of stopping her from biting my head off. "Gian has a fever, so she asked me to come and get you. Trice is at class, so I borrowed her car, as I didn't think you'd be able to go on my bike." I push my hands into my pockets and look to the ground. "I know you don't want to see me, but please just let me take you home."

My eyes roam the floor before I have the courage to look back at her. Her hands are clasped around her phone, which sits on her lap as she hunches, her bottom lip moving between her teeth. This is not my Trin. This is the shell of a woman who I've fallen in love with. It is up to me to bring her back, piece by piece.

"Okay." She nods and stands, wincing slightly as she holds her bag and phone. I rush forward. She turns away from me to stop me, but fuck it. I reach out and gently tug her bag out of her grasp and tilt my head to the door, as I know she won't want me to touch her.

We walk in silence, and it's deafening. My pulse thunders between my ears, and I hear every nuance that surrounds us in the corridors. Monitors beeping, the shuffling of feet, coughing patients ... all are part of a wall that keeps us separate and silent.

After the paperwork is signed, we go to the car, I unlock the doors and climb in, knowing that if I try to help her, she might refuse to enter the car. She steps in awkwardly, and I have to hold my tongue to stop from asking how she's feeling. I don't want to push her, and, besides, she will flip her shit at me soon enough.

We drive in silence as she rests her head against the headrest, facing away from me. Songs play on the radio station, and I begin to think she's sleeping until she asks, "Why are we on this side of the freeway?"

I shuffle in my seat, my legs too long for this Barbie mobile, and I respond, "I'm taking you home." I attempt to dissuade her questioning, but she's not sleepy enough. Can't fool her.

"I can't believe this," she mutters, as we take the turn off and head to my place. As the minutes pass slowly, I wait for her to snap, to call me every name under the sun, but she doesn't. We pull up in front of my warehouse, and I hit the button to open the roller door, but I don't drive in. I leave the car parked on the street.

"Why can't you take me to Hazel's? I can't stay there."

"It's a full house and harder now with Gian being sick. Plus, they don't have any room."

She grumbles in her seat and turns to face me for the first time. "Well, just take me home then."

"I can't. You have stairs. Plus, you're not supposed to be alone for the first twenty-four hours."

She thuds her head back against the headrest and groans. "This feels like a trap. I don't want to be here."

"Look." I turn to face her. "You have to rest for the first few days, and I have another project at work that will take up my time, so I will barely be here." Her eyes slide to mine, but her body remains tense. Her chest rises and falls. "You will hardly see me. I will be upstairs when I'm home, I promise."

She groans in frustration and grabs the door handle. "Let's get this over and done with. The sooner I'm here the sooner, I can go home."

We dismount from the car, and I lock it, carrying her bag. I then activate the doors to close, and they pull down, leaving us to stand in the darkness. I can hear her heavy breathing and, although I want to touch her, the sharp intake of her breath isn't a welcomed one. It's laced with fear, panicked. I haven't even touched her. My heart sinks.

I move my arm, and the motion sensors kick in to light the space up slightly. I quickly distance myself from her to move towards the kitchen. Flicking the other switches, I head to the back room that only a few weeks ago we had joked about being the maid's den. The melancholic feeling of this room no longer holds the jokes from before.

Turning on the light, I step to the side to allow her to enter the space. She moves to the side of the room, so I take the opportunity to quickly walk to the table to put her bag on it. I turn back and find her staring straight at me, causing a lightning bolt to surge in my chest. There is no emotion in her eyes, just a vacant stare.

"This is your room." I gesture stupidly, waving my arm around. "If you need anything, just ring that bell."

She blinks to break her stare and glances around the room until she sees the bell on her nightstand.

I point over to the cupboard and add, "In there you'll find some clothes that Trice got for you. I'm going to cook something for dinner, and I'll bring it down to you—"

"Not hungry." Her voice hardens as she opens the cupboard door. "I'll just go to bed, seeing as all my *friends* have all my *stuff prearranged* to do so." She huffs, sliding her outfits across the rail harshly.

"She just dropped them off." I flinch at her tone but know that she isn't fooled.

"Whatever, Theo. Knowing they're in on this shit, puts them on my shit list. The sooner you leave, the sooner I can get to bed."

Reluctantly, I exit and close the door behind me. I go to the kitchen to give her some space, and eventually I start dinner. *Would she be talking to me now, if I told her the truth in the car? Her vacant eyes tell me differently.* The nurses warned me that she might not be up for much, so I make a sandwich and pour a glass of apple juice, hoping she'll eat something. Carrying her food on a tray, I go to her room and balance the tray over one arm, as I tap on her closed door. Silence. I keep balancing the tray to open the door, and I find her fast asleep in bed. Using the light from the kitchen, I walk in and place the tray on the side table, careful to not make any sound.

The light shows just enough of her to see her huddled in a ball on the bed, and my fingers itch to touch her, to brush the hair from her face so I can see her. But I don't. Instead, I take in her soft features, hoping that she soon lets me tell her. I *need* to tell her. My eyes roam her face some more as the artist in my mind takes flight.

"Mila, you need to turn towards me. Let me show you ..." Adam begs.,

"No." Her shoulders are stiff, tortured. "Leave me be."

I blink and shake my head, banishing those scenes. If I can't get my characters to make sense, what the fuck are my chances of restoring us? She is so goddamn stubborn. All it would've taken was a minute to explain and she didn't give me the chance. Fuck, I've had a million chances and I've wasted every single one. Maybe she'll be better in the morning, after she sleeps. Maybe she'll let me speak without throwing a chair at my head. *Screw it. The moment she isn't hurting, I'm fucking busting down that door.*

I spend the night tossing and turning, just missing her. Her warmth, scent, and my throbbing cock can't take her being downstairs and away from me. I miss her.

I get ready quickly after my alarm sounds and spend some time in the kitchen organising a few things for her, so she'll be taken care of while I am out. I look at the time on the microwave and grimace. I only have an hour left to be out of here and get to work.

I stack a plate with toast and pour some juice, wondering if she's missed me too. I knock on her door, hear a faint shuffling, and groan, wishing I was beside her to wake her up like I normally do. *Not now. You need to fix this.*

"What?" Her tired voice lingers, and I turn the door handle while balancing the tray.

She's coiled up in bed with the covers drawn to her chest. Her eyes squint in pain as her legs point away from her body, which I guess is to avoid touching her stomach. I didn't notice if she did this last night. My head was too far up my own arse.

"Have you taken your pain meds?" I put the tray down on the side table and look at her.

She puffs some breaths as discomfort scrunches her face. Even in her pain, she is the most beautiful woman I know, and the stubbornest. "I don't need any," she says through clenched teeth. "I'm fine."

"Trin, you need to take them if you're sore. Where did you put them?"

"I don't need your help." She scowls, her face pinching as she shifts on the bed. "This isn't some fucking Stockholm Syndrome. When I can move, I'm breaking out of this Alcatraz. We're done."

Fuck this shit right off.

"Not talking about this shit now." I ignore her jab, as the protective instinct rises in me. I need to make her feel better. Seeing her hurt is doing my head in. "Where did you put them?"

"Leave me. I can manage without you. I forgot to bloody take them. I don't need you," she hisses, and it pushes me to the brink. I growl and lean forward, planting my hands on either side of her body. I move closer, and she flinches, but I persevere. "Give me your fire, your anger—give it all to me. You're allowed to hurt, but if there's relief, then I will find it for you. Even if I have to walk to the edges of the earth, I will."

She stares back at me, her nose wrinkling as she holds back tears. "I don't want you to see me like this," she sobs. "As weak. I want you to let me be."

"There is beauty in pain. In you, I see your strength through it. It shines through you. Don't push me away. Let me see you. All of you. It's me, Trin. Please, let me help you."

She reaches a breaking point as her eyes well with tears, and she closes them firmly in a feeble attempt to stop crying. A lone tear rolls down her cheek, and I want to wipe it away.

"They're in my bag," she whispers, defeated. My pulse quickens as I know my firecracker is still in there, and I just need to find a way to bring her back out.

I quickly rise from the bed and get her pills, watching her eagerly take them. Her tray from last night sits empty, and a part of me is thrilled that she is letting me in, in little crumbs.

"Don't think this is the way for you to get back with me," she mumbles, as she grabs a piece of toast from the table and tentatively takes a bite. "You're not wearing your suit." She chews as her hand waves up and down my body. I look down at my jeans and jumper. "Doesn't mean you can take the day off and babysit me. That's not gonna happen. I don't give a fuck what the nurses think."

"I'm not staying here today. I have another project."

Trin flinches, and I catch a flicker of disappointment. *Yes. She does still care.* I push my hand in my pocket, frustrated that I can't just march over there and kiss her to shut her up.

"I'm no fool." She squints at me in disapproval. "Once I'm better, I'm gone. You broke my trust. I can't get over that." She throws the crust on the table, as I grab the empty tray next to her and tap my hand with it, staring at her grimace. Her mouth twinges as her face tightens in pain, but I have to let that slide.

"That day in front of the café," I begin,

"Theo. Don't." Her legs shift from the bed to the floor. "I will leave here if you mention it again."

Is this what it is going to be for us? Always fighting to build something and then crashing it down?

I don't break eye contact, but the hope that I stupidly felt starts to fade. If I tell her and she forgives me, will it only be a matter of time before we try to sabotage ourselves again? When will it all stop?

I love her. God, do I love her. Every pulse in my body beats for her. But in all this mess, I'm starting to wonder if fighting for her is worth it. I'm tired of being torn down in life. Loving her and putting up with the mental merry-go-rounds is doing my head in. Yes, I fucked up. But not listening to me for a second is bullshit. This is not a situation where I can bind her hands and fuck her senseless against my bedhead to show reason or gain control. She took that from me a long time ago. This is *us,* and I am tired. So very fucking tired. I refuse to be silent anymore.

"She's my sister," I blurt, watching her face spark in surprise as her hand flies to her chest. Moving to the door, I leave her with the final straw. "I know I owe you an explanation. If fact, I owe you a dozen or so, but right now, you need to think about us and remember how fucking hard we've worked to get to this point. I can't do this anymore. I won't lose you again, Trin. Brace yourself. If it's love and war you want, it's love and war you'll get."

Twenty-Five

"When your heart gets broken, use the right tape
to put it back together."
Love, Mum

TRINITY

Oh my God.

His sister. That was his *sister*. Who I said I'd wait to meet. I didn't even see what she looked like, just saw that he'd touched her. Oh fuck.

My hand curls into the mattress edge as I groan. *What a complete fuck up.* My stomach rolls, as a light degree of nausea rolls through me. Oh, I want these drugs to start working soon. I feel like shit. I spent most of the night in agony, as I was being a petulant shithead and didn't want Theo to hear me shuffling around and come to help. He'd already left me some sandwiches, which my stomach had a moment of not wanting to upchuck, so I ate them greedily.

I look down at the bed and sigh. *"I can't do this anymore,"* he said. My hand smooths down the covers as a deep sense of longing blends with the unease I feel. I missed him last night and the night before. He almost sounds as if he's stopped missing me. My heart tightens at the thought, as I rub my sore shoulder in defeat.

I was so angry with him that day. I spent the first night in a fit of tears, reading all the letters that I'd opened from my mother while searching for a theme scribbled on the front to resonate. I'd found it.

Break-ups

My baby girl,

There's going to be a time in your life when you're going to experience a dreaded break-up. You know, like you've probably seen in movies— where the girl cries her eyes out—her makeup doesn't run, by the way, as it's the movies—and she thinks her life is over. She wails, howls, and loses her damn mind.

You're going to feel that ache one day, and I'm not going to sugarcoat it. It's going to sting. It's going to burn, and you will feel that life is really, really crap. It's going to hurt, baby, there's nothing I can do to stop it. You know, if I could, I'd egg his car or something.

But this is what you're going to do.

You're going to get your girls, your real posse, and you're going to get a tub of your favourite ice cream, and you'll eat from the tub. None of this unnecessary bowl washing. Just a spoon and a box of tissues. By the time that tub is empty, you'll have kick-started the healing process. I promise. No break-up is worth ruining yourself over. You are strong and fearless, and you can do this.

When your heart gets broken, use the right tape to put it back together. The best man will make sure that you never need tape at all. No man is perfect, but he'll damn well try.

Love you,
Mum.

I hadn't taken her advice to get the girls over. I'd kept silent. I hadn't been able to bring myself to talk about him and what I had seen. Instead, I'd wallowed. I'd turned into a ball of pity and remembered all our time together, like a morose reel of memories, stemming all the way from high school. Our first class together, the day I'd realised butterflies were tickling my insides every time he smiled at me. I was hopelessly and utterly in love, overcome with loss from losing him, the betrayal etching itself so close to my heart that I wondered if there were any pieces left.

Instead of calling my friends, I'd found some old red skirts that I'd sewn and some white material. I'd done what I could to process. To alleviate the ache. I'd created. I'd designed. Until the early hours of the morning, the erratic punching of the sewing machine needle through the cotton had threaded the details of my ideas into a blunt array of colour.

As I'd used my scissors to slice through the final fabric, tears were held back; pressed my lips together to keep my emotion in check. I'd been determined to prove that I could do this. That I could move on. Even if it had barely been twenty-four hours.

Grabbing what I'd needed from my makeup bag and shoving it into my back pocket, I grabbed the cutouts and marched upstairs to my kitchen to retrieve my lighter. At the sink, with the window open, I'd lit the frayed edges and burnt them. Not entirely, but enough. I'd then gathered them, raced downstairs to get the designs, tore the old display off my mannequins, and began to dress them.

The Queen of Hearts had stood in her various forms. The first was haggard, with torn clothing, and I'd called her "Holding on by a Thread." The second, "Tearing at the Seams," was an improvement over the last, but still dishevelled, with fewer tears than the final mannequin, which I aptly named "Fake it Till You Unravel." That had appeared to be well-put. Simple gold ribbon crowns had been wrapped around the tops of their heads, and I'd plucked the red lipstick from my back pocket and wrote, "Love is a myth" across their faces and chests. I'd stood back and stared at them all in a moment and bent down, grabbing the burnt pieces of cut-out hearts and scattering them around by the mannequins' feet. "You can do this," I'd said, brokenly.

Now, I'm sitting here like a fucking idiot, because I realise that I should have listened. Who does that? Not give a person a chance to explain? It isn't freaking daytime TV. Instead, I'd been reduced to my troubled self, choosing an escape route for heartache that meant literally pushing him away. *"I can*'t do this anymore." Yes, you can, Theo. Please come back to me.

I stand slowly and collect a few things to have a shower. I remember a tiny bathroom being down here, which is what he started with when he first built this place. It is tucked in behind my room. I didn't notice until now that even my toiletry bag was in there. He's thought of everything.

Sighing, I turn on the water to heat it up and begin to strip slowly, making sure my dressings are completely sealed. Testing the water, I step in gingerly and hope as I lather up my skin that I can work out a way to apologise that is sincere and genuine. Yes, he should've told me, but fuck, I should've listened. What a fucking mess.

I leave the shower feeling refreshed, but only on the outside. Inside, I'm a tumultuous wave. I take my clothes to my room and see my phone lying on the bedside table. I want to text him, to make him come over, but he's at work. I've done enough damage, and I don't need him to get into trouble because I'm desperate to listen. As I gently tie my hair back, conscious of the wounds on my abdomen, I hear the rise of the roller door. My heart skips as I finish my hair and check out my appearance. *He's here. He's come back.*

I try not to run out so I don't pop a stitch, but it takes a lot of willpower. I stroll out to the main area only to find it's not Theo, but Eloise. My head flinches slightly, wondering why she is standing there.

"Um, what are you doing here?" My legs are stilted, as I stand awkwardly to stare back at her. She strolls in confidently, holding a green canvas grocery bag, without the normal cheeky grin on her face. Instead, she is expressionless, almost militant.

"I'll explain in a minute. For now"—she gestures to the chaise lounge in front of me—"sit."

"But ..." I put my hands on my hips, not liking the vibe she's giving me. "I want to know why you're here." Fatigue weathers against my spine as my energy depletes slightly. It's tough work being pissy.

"Trinity." Eloise's voice is stern, unforgiving. "Can you sit your butt down on the damn couch. I don't have time for this, and I think it's past the time for *you* to be demanding things. Now, sit."

I narrow my eyes at her but move to the couch. Whatever this is, it's preventing me from working out a strategy to get Theo back.

I can't cross my arms across my chest, as the aftereffects have me aching too much, so I sit petulantly with both hands by my sides, staring back at her.

"Now ..." Her face relaxes slightly. "I'm going to tell you a story."

I roll my eyes. *What's the point of this?* I'd ask her, but the drill sergeant seems to have a stick up her arse today. "Do I get milk and cookies?" I smile sweetly, titling my head.

"No, but you might need something stronger afterwards."

I stiffen in my seat as my lips pull into a grimace. "Okay," I drawl.

"You see ..." She stands at the coffee table and places the bag on top. "There was once a guy who was a very talented artist. He had a busy mind, and the only way he could decipher things was to create his own little world. Things that didn't make sense or work out in his real one worked out there." She reaches into the bag and retrieves the latest edition of the TTE series.

"Why am I learning about your brother?" I frown. "What the fuck does that have to do with why you're here?"

She looks at me disapprovingly and shakes her head. "Looks like this is going to take longer than I thought," she mutters, before retrieving the next novel. "This guy was lost, despondent. He chose to keep people at a distance, as he didn't like affection—it made him feel displaced, alone. So, as he picked up his marker, he began to draw the things that mattered to him. He drew how his thoughts constantly battled with him, while also responding to what his heart wanted." She continues to pull out novel after novel, gently stacking them. "There was one person he could show emotion to, however. One that he decided to immortalise by giving her a character in his text—Mila. She was the one he cherished and loved more deeply than anyone else in his life."

"He sounds lovesick." I shift in my seat, watching each novel stack in a pile and remembering the scenes from each and how deeply they'd affected me. "Did his family help him?"

"See ..." She stops stacking for a moment. "He's never really had a family until now. That in itself has been a real challenge. He's had to cope with new identities wanting a piece of him, while he battles the demons of his past. He can barely handle his sisters cuddling him."

My chest thuds. The prickling sensation covers my skin in a mad rush, spreading tingles that force my body to squirm. *Surely not? These points are so close to—*

"I've even got to meet her," she continues. "Sure, she's loud and feisty, and a complete contrast to him, but when he talks about her, his face is peaceful." She frowns. "Not many people do that for him. My brother is a clever guy, and he still didn't realise what a hopeless romantic he was." She reaches into the bag and retrieves the first edition of the magazine that I ever bought, the one I saw for the first time here. At Theo's place. I turn in my seat towards the bookshelf and see the same novels, which doesn't surprise me. But my eyes begin to trace the books that are stacked around it.

Art books, design tip manuals, Magna advice texts ... all about techniques on how to draw. Normally, this wouldn't give me pause, as Theo's always been an artist, but the pricking along the back of my neck is telling me otherwise. It's telling me to really look and really see him. Just like Adam asked Mila to do for all these months.

"Oh my God." I gasp as I turn sharply to the front, a ripple of pain tearing in my abdomen. "Oh fuck," I groan, breathing quickly as I continue to ache.

"Honey," Eloise says, "take it easy. He'll kill me if you get hurt."

I pant, the tears stinging my eyes as I gaze at her, picking up on subtle resemblances between her and Theo that I should've seen earlier.

"You're ..." my voice falters.

"My brother calls me Elly. You can call me that, if you'd like."

I nod, still stinging from the impact of the turn of events. "But how..."

"Shh," she coos as she reaches into her bag and retrieves a pen and notepad. "I can see those cogs in your brain turning, but there's something you need to know." Placing the materials next to me on the couch, she moves the pile of novels closer. "He knew he struggled with revealing his feelings and knowing how to reach out to the woman he loves." She bends and picks up the novel.

My mind is playing the words "woman he loves" on a loop.

"He thought if there was a chance that she'd notice him, that she would find that it's been there in front of her all this time." Elly flicks open the first novel and skips to the final page. She points to the bottom crevices and puts it under my nose to see. "Do you see it?" She holds it closer.

I stare at the images and frown. "What am I looking for?" I grab it from her, and my eyes roam along the page. Her long slender finger moves across the page to the left panel, to where I now see the word.

"When," I whisper.

"There's more." Her head shifts to the stack to the side of her. "I suggest you get the piece of paper and pen ready." She walks past me to the kitchen, but I don't follow her. I shift closer to the table, without affecting my stomach too much. I reach for the second edition and eagerly flick to the last page, finding the next hidden word: "the." My pulse pricks up as I carry on through the pile, flicking through the coloured pages, past all the memories I had of Adam and Mila's journey as the throb continues to beat in my throat. I swallow thickly, desperate to write all the words down, knowing deep, deep down that I already know where this is leading. By the last novel, I don't need to look for the word, as I already know what it'll say.

"Night." I gasp. My hand covers my mouth in a soft sob. My fingers travel across the words on the page as tears prickle my eyes.

"When the day fades to dark from light, you're the only face I see at night."

"I can't believe this." I blink rapidly as tears fall down my cheeks. I've traced those words many times over the past few months. Reading every letter, blending my finger with them, hoping that his latest tattoo had something to do with me. Yet afraid to ask. On his back, he has a giant tree of life with a heart in its trunk that those words circulate. "Oh my God!" I grab the latest edition and flick to the centre and freeze. The tree that captured my attention after the many times we shared our bodies faces me. "How did I not notice this?"

I sit bewildered. Mila and Adam stand facing each other, and my eyes drift to Mila's shoulders, where faint tracings of indecipherable ink are weaved across her skin.

"That's you, by the way," Elly says from over my shoulder.

"But, Adam's eyes are covered," I notice.

"That's because he isn't seen. He's hidden."

"Oh my God." My hand covers my mouth as a laugh escapes. "Trice said to me once that she thought the girl looked like me. This is just so ..."

"Romantic? Tortured?" Elly offers, as she munches on an apple.

"Theo." I wipe my eyes and stand slowly. Straightening my T-shirt, I clasp her free hand. "Please, take me to him," I beg.

"You're not supposed to leave his place, unless I feed you. I have strict orders." She smiles mid chew.

"What did he say about you telling me all this?" I gesture with my other hand towards the novels. "I guess I frightened him too much for him to tell me." I shrug.

"Oh no, he doesn't know I'm revealing his big secret. I told him that I would bring you some soup. Oops." She fakes a gasp. "I forgot it, but I know a great café near a soon-to-be open restaurant that we could go to."

"Yes." I step around her to get my bag, and I realise I don't need it. "Let's go." I step towards the front of his place, turning abruptly while holding my side. I look at Elly as my lip trembles. "I'm sorry if that was you who was hugging him the other day,"

"It was Anastasia, and don't sweat. She's not upset with you. More worried about her big bro, like I am."

"Oh fuck." I shake my head. "Poor girl. Now she must think I'm a fucking bitch."

"Nope, not at all." Elly twirls her apple in her hand as she strolls towards me, her eyes narrowing slightly. "Provided you get your shit together and go kiss and make up."

"I hope Theo gives me a chance to beg for forgiveness." My tongue flicks my labret as my mouth pulls in at the side.

"Of course he will." She grins. "Didn't he chase you at first? But seeing as you're standing there ready to aim and fire, let's go. You're making it your turn to hunt him down. Hope you have your running shoes on."

"If only I could bolt there. I can't even walk for long, but I want to see him. Let's go."

"Be my guest." She waves her arm in front of her, holding a novel. "Maybe you can grab his signature while you're at it," she sniggers.

I snatch the magazine from her and smile. "I told my friends once that I'd do TTE like a dinner if I ever found out who he was." A giggle tickles my lips as I run my hand across the first edition cover.

"Ew, that's my brother. I don't want to hear anymore."

"Too bad." I wink at her. "You're taking me there now, so buckle up, sunshine."

We walk out the front. My heart overflows with the hope that he'll be at the restaurant to catch me when I need him the most

Twenty-Six

*The panel shows the tree of life with its branches outstretched, the
heart within bursting through the trunk. "I will fight for you,
even if you don't fight for yourself." The shadow of Mila
stands to the side, waiting.*
TTE

THEO

The strong drumming of the Foo Fighters' "Best of You" plays in my ears as I wipe down the brick wall, cleaning off the excess dust before I begin to sketch. I'm looking forward to getting the enamel paint on there, as it will give it an alfresco feel, but with a shimmery twist. I sense someone approach, and I pull out one of my ear buds.

"I thought you were going to get some photos done this week." Papá's voice trails beside me.

"I will later on, but I wanted to see the surface again during our normal appointment time and get a feel for what would look good," I say, as I wipe the edges closest to the ground. I want this to be perfect.

"Well, you're certainly doing that," he laughs. "It's good to see you aren't afraid to get your hands dirty, either," he adds, as I look down at my dusty fingers.

"Hard to keep clean when you're working with these materials." I tilt my head to face him and hold my hands up. "This is nothing compared to what you'll see when I actually start painting."

"I look forward to it," he muses, as he steps away. "You want an espresso?"

"No, *gracias*," I respond, enjoying the look of his eyes widening in surprise while he walks backwards. His arms move in front of him, waving around simultaneously. I know he's about to speak from the way his mouth twitches, so I raise my finger. "If you're about to rattle off something in Spanish, I won't understand. I'm just learning a few expressions at the moment. Thanks to *Google* and *Faulty Towers*."

He nods proudly and smiles, bending down to grab my shoulder. "I will teach you." He squeezes my shoulder. "It is in your blood, and it is one of the languages of love, so it might be helpful with your lady, no?" He raises his eyebrow and smirks. No doubt my sisters have clued him in on my latest kerfuffle.

I shake my head as I grab the cloth from the floor. "She's not interested these days," I shrug. "She's being difficult, and I'm not sure if it will even work out. I think I'll need a lot more than speaking Spanish."

"You could start by taking off your shirt," a very distinctive and feminine voice orders. I turn to find Trin standing there with Elly, biting her lip.

I dump the cloth and get up straight away, taking the few paces I need to stand in front of her.

"What are you doing out of bed?" My voice is laced with concern. "I'll go grab you a chair." I step to the side, but she holds her hand up to stop me.

"I'm fine," she snaps. "Now, take off your shirt." Her eyes are cautious, yet hopeful.

I look around the warehouse, where many other guys are completing odd jobs here and there. Has she gone a bit *loco?*

"I'm at work." I hold out my hand. "I can't take my shirt off."

My jaw sets, confused as to why she is even standing here. Her eyes flick over my shoulder, as she raises her eyebrows at my dad.

"Is it alright with you? I need to check something." She tilts her head to the side and smiles, batting her lashes innocently at him.

"Oh, I think I know who this is," he laughs. "I have no problem."

"See?" She turns back to me. "He has no problem. Now strip."

I wince as I feel all eyes on me, and I shake my head. "This isn't the place. I don't know what you're trying to do." I want to add that my family doesn't know about all my tattoos. I stare back at her, trying to gauge her thoughts.

"Take. Your. Top. Off," she commands, before raising her brow. "Or are you chicken?"

I straighten as my discomfort is instantly squashed when her eyes pierce into mine. I put my hand to the back of my neck and curve my shoulders to reach and tear off my long-sleeved T-shirt. I hold it out and swing it around my hand until a whistle sounds to my side, making me stop while Elly gushes.

"Bro has a dragon! That's awesome!"

I grab Trin's hand and bring her behind the middle wall, away from the attention, away from everyone else.

"It's not all that he has," Trin calls out as she steps up to me, putting her hand on my side. "Now turn around." Her fingers turn me towards her. I comply, but begin to stiffen when I realise what she's looking for. Now I get why Elly wanted my keys. What I don't understand is why Trin is being so flirty. Surely she's about to skin me alive for not telling her?

"Trin." My throat dries as her name becomes stuck in my mouth. Soft, warm fingers begin to trace along my back, and I've missed her touch like an addiction. I can't help but flinch as she lightens the feel against my skin. "It tickles." My head jerks to the side, but her fingers then press farther. I know what she is tracing, and my heart pounds dangerously.

"I found your note," she says, "with some help from a little birdie."

She moves her fingers deeper, nudging me, as she must feel the increased pounding of my heart under her fingertips. Her hands move down the shape of the tree of life on my back. "The roots here are broken." She traces. "There's a heart encased, and it's bursting." Her fingers move to my shoulder blades. "But as I shift up here, the tree is whole. Why?"

I forget who could be near us. To be honest, I just don't care. She's touching me. That's all that matters right now. "It's symbolic," I husk, as her fingers continue to torture my skin.

"Tell me," she coos, and I feel her step closer, her body a hairsbreadth away.

"Of us. Our journey."

"Tell me."

"How we've both experienced horrible circumstances and now we're together, we're whole."

"What does this symbol mean?" She traces the individual Japanese character on my right.

"Harmony," I add, closing my eyes as her fingers rhythmically entrance me.

"You only had this tree finished recently. How did you know it would be us?" Her voice catches. By now, I have to stop her touch before I push her against the wall. My body is responding to hers, and I know this can't happen. *Yet.* Turning sharply, I grab her hand as she startles, placing it quickly on my heart, and staring down at her.

My chest rises with every beat as my gaze rakes over her features. Searching for any sign of anger at her revelation, I don't see one. Relieved, I continue. "You are the map on my skin, and the journey that I want to take for the rest of my life." I squeeze her hand in mine, as she blinks rapidly. I raise my other hand and place it against her soft cheek, feeling the tension ease from my spine as she leans into my touch. Her blue eyes shine into mine. "I'm sorry I didn't tell you about any of this." My voice lowers. "I was still getting used to having a legitimate family, and half that time, it took me a while to even let them show kindness."

"I understand now," she murmurs against my hand.

But I'm not done. "It's hard to admit something that you've felt for so long, since you were twelve years old. I never really understood, until now, the depth of how I feel." I half expect her to frown at me, at the lunacy of my mind, but she grins instead.

"What does TTE mean?" Her brow furrows as her hand cups mine against her face.

"Trinity. Theo. Eternal. Our trifecta." Her lips part, as her eyes brighten. "I started drawing it shortly after Harmony's funeral, when I thought I'd fucked up. Those few months that we didn't talk, I didn't know how else to reach you, so I put my thoughts into drawings, and the rest is history."

"Wow," she gushes, straightening out of my grip to face me better. "So every time I went to get my own copy ..."

"I watched from my office across the laneway."

"No way!" she shrieks. "I used to have a dodgy feeling that someone was looking at me, like a sixth sense or something."

"Yeah, it was me, hoping to get a glimpse of your excitement. I used some of your outfits in my storylines too. Always leaving breadcrumbs for you to stumble across. None of which worked." I shrug.

"They worked in a different way." She places her other hand on the side of my neck and stares up at me. The hairs at the back of my neck prickle, as I don't see the coldness in her eyes. I don't see her vacant expression. My firecracker is back.

"You got under my skin, Theo Eien."

"Is that so?" Her lips smile, and hope builds in my chest. "In what way?"

"In every part of me, you exist too." Her face sobers slightly. "I'm so sorry for not listening to you. I was stubborn and heartless." Play the card, I want to tell her. You can have all the aces. You will not run again. "I know I used my insecurities from the past to push you away. I can't do that anymore. It's not fair to us. There's too much at stake."

"Such as?"

"I want a future with you. Everything. Adventures, babies, all of it." She frowns slightly.

"What's wrong?" I stroke her face.

"What if I can't have babies? If even after the surgery, there's still no chance?"

"Then you'll have me." My thumb rubs her cheek. "You are who I want. Everything else is a bonus."

"I'm in love with you." Her lips tremble. "So fucking in love with you."

"Well, thank fuck for that." I laugh as my mouth moves closer to hers. "I'm in love with you, too." Before she can respond, I pull her face closer, crushing her lips to mine. We kiss like no one is watching, but we also kiss like everyone is. She's mine, and I'm claiming her back. Her hands run up my sides, but I feel her tense underneath my touch, as her breath hitches.

"I'm a little sore," she breathes against my lips. "I need to sit down."

"Oh shit." I release her instantly and dash to the chair by the side wall, bringing it back to her. "Here, sit. Can I get you anything?"

"Yeah," she holds onto my arm to bring me closer so she can kiss me on the cheek. "Can you grab Elly for me?"

"Coming!" Elly's voice chirps from behind the wall. "I was waiting on you both to quit being so *Nietzsche*." She skips in playfully. "So much suffering for silly reasons. Now you're better!"

"Okay." I look at her incredulously, wondering if our father has suddenly started stocking booze behind the bar.

"Can I get that book you have, Elly?" Trin reaches towards her, and Elly's face lights up as she registers what my girl wants, digging into her bag. Pulling it out, she hands it to me, and I laugh.

"My novel." I shake my head. "What? You haven't read it enough yet?"

"Yes, but there's something else." Trin reaches over, and Elly hands her a pen. "Can I please have your autograph?"

I throw back my head and laugh, leaning down towards her to grab her face for a kiss. She leans back slightly to avoid my lips. "No, I'm serious, I want one." She chuckles. "Make it a goodie."

"Oh, I'll make it a goodie." I wiggle my eyebrows as my lips reach hers. Won't I ever. *You ain't seen nothing yet.* I'm about to get a taste when we're rudely interrupted.

"Oi!" my dad yells. "Can I meet her yet, or are you two going to hide there all day?"

She giggles against my lips as we break apart to look around, but Elly is nowhere in sight. "Well, I did try to strip you straight up, so I better go

262

and erase that first impression."

"Indeed." I stand and hold out my hand. "You okay to walk?"

She nods as she grabs my hand and stands.

"Well, come and meet my dad."

Her smile beams across her face as she shrills, "I can't wait!"

I lean back on the bed beside her, as she rolls to her side to face me. My boss, aka

Papá, didn't mind me taking the rest of the day off to spend with her. She'd gone straight to bed, but not without whining for me to stay with her. Her body was riddled with fatigue, and as she drifted to sleep, I soon followed.

Now, it's approaching dinner time, and my stomach is gurgling.

"Go cook, chef!" She gently touches my chest. "Feed your woman."

I raise my hand to the side of my face and salute before giving her a kiss on the forehead. "Thanks for coming back to me," I whisper against her skin.

Her hand grabs my arm and squeezes. "Thanks for letting me come near you again, after I threatened to remove a certain appendage," she quips.

I chuckle and roll back, enjoying the carefree vibe that's returned. "Feel like steak?"

"Sounds great. It's kinda the only *meat* I can have for a few weeks anyway," she jokes.

"I'm not worried." I tap her nose with my forefinger. "You need to rest, and I'm more than happy to wait. Besides, the time is going to fly."

"I hope so." Her bottom lip drops. "We won't be able to have make-up sex."

"Just save it up, you know, like credit or something." I roll off the bed and stand.

"I'll just fill out an IOU," she says, as she rolls onto her back. "It'll gain a tonne of interest by then." She taps the bed beside her. "Might even accumulate to proportions never seen by mankind."

"Get up, grumpy pants, and I'll cook your dinner. I might be able to put a smile on that dial of yours."

"Ease up. I'll get there." She slowly moves to sit and then rubs her eyes. "You go, and I'll use the bathroom."

I make my way to the kitchen and gather all the ingredients. As I line them up on the bench, an idea comes to me. I jog back through my place and up the stairs to my study, where I grab four of my sketchpads, along with my other one that I hope she wants to see. Racing down, I put them on my small kitchen table, along with a pen.

Once Trin is out, she makes her way to the table and smiles. "Are these what I think they are?"

"Sure are, but this one is what I've wanted you to have for a while." I open the cover and watch her eyes widen in surprise.

"My mum." Her voice softens. Her fingers reach out to gently touch the face I'd sketched. Harmony's face is the only part I've sketched in this image, but from the angle of the pose, with the sun beaming down on her cheeks, it feels warm. Trin's fingers lift the next page, which leads into a series of images where Harmony is drawn laughing, drinking her tea, or admiring her sunflowers. I've only sketched ten pieces or so, but from the brightness in Trin's eyes, you would think I'd just handed her the world.

"These are amazing." Her head tilts up to look at me. "I feel her through these pages. I can almost hear her laughing or telling me something quirky."

"I'm glad you like them." I kiss her shoulder as she tilts her head for me to kiss her there again.

"I *love* them." Her eyes look up at me. "You are bringing me the world today, aren't you?" Her lips lift in a gentle smile.

"Not yet, but hoping to." I wink as she closes the pad and reverently places it to the side. "Now let's bring you more into *our* world." Reaching over, I pick up the pen as she opens the first sketchpad.

"Wow, it's like a movie," she sighs. "Where did you sketch all these?"

"In my study, next to my bedroom."

"And to think I used to walk past that room thinking there was something strange about it."

"Disappointed it wasn't my sex pad or something?" I tease.

"Nope. You have enough of that in that box in your room; I'm just astounded it took a sledge hammer to my face for me to notice. I see it everywhere here now."

"Take a look." I lift my chin, eager to have her go through my ideas, no longer afraid.

She peruses the pages, and I stand and admire her gentle features.

"I love everything about it." She flicks through them. My heart does a back flip as her smile continues to radiate.

"There's just one thing," I say, as she continues to read little sections and admire the sketches.

"Hmm?"

"I haven't worked out the ending yet." Picking up the last pad, I flip to the most recent part and hold out a pen to her.

"So maybe while I'm cooking dinner, you could think of one for me?"

Her mouth gapes as her body wiggles on the chair. "Yes!" she squeals, grabbing the pen. "I wanna have a go!"

"I'll leave you to it," I say, smiling as I walk back into her bedroom with another idea. "I hope I can give you some inspiration," I call over my shoulder.

"Sure," she responds vaguely, and I know she's too busy trying to draw. For us artists, there is a sense of completeness when we have a pen in hand. She'll be distracted while I get ready.

I walk to the other cupboard, pull out the outfit that I found a few weeks ago, and start to strip. As each piece of clothing drops to the ground, I listen carefully for any movement so my plan isn't ruined.

Tying the apron around my waist as the bitter winter chill makes its way across my skin, I shiver before securing the cap to the top of my head. Picking up the feather duster, I walk out, holding it in my hand.

I expect Trin to look up, but she's too absorbed. Instead, I walk back over to the kitchen and begin preparing our dinner, waiting for her to notice that there's a full moon tonight, in more ways than one.

It's not until I'm serving up our dishes, a long time later, that she taps the page and gushes, "There. I think I got the ending figured out. What the fuc—"

I look up from the bench and try to keep my face passive as her eyes rove up and down my skin.

"You really are taking this nursemaid gig seriously," she giggles. "Although I never mentioned being naked. I'm not complaining, though. It's your job and all."

"Absolutely." I wiggle my chest to make the apron move. "One must always have a maid at hand."

Lifting the plates, I take them over to the table that I had even set without her noticing, and smile. "You like?" I turn to the side and give her my best pout.

"Where did you find that?" She points to my crotch. "It's barely covering you!"

"I got it at the toy section in Kmart. Best eight bucks I've spent in ages!"

"It's so revealing." A slow grin appears across her lips. "I bet I could make the flap lift completely."

I turn away and cover my crotch. That's all I need—to get hard when we're about to eat and not be able to do anything about it.

"I was feeling a little cheeky." I shrug as I sit opposite her. Lifting my cutlery, I gesture for her to start. She shifts the notepads to the side and picks up her fork to eat her vegetables.

"I could totally make that apron lift." She stabs a piece of carrot on her plate. "Wouldn't even need to look at it."

"Careful, firecracker," I warn. "I won't be broken to being seduced, but if you try, I have a wide selection of fun things upstairs that I won't hesitate to use in"—I lift my bare wrist and pretend to calculate— "twenty-one days, four hours, and thirty-five minutes."

"I can't wait," she crunches down on a carrot and gives me a wink.

266

"Did you work out our happily ever after?" I lift my carrot onto my fork and take a bite.

"Yep." Her seductive grin vanishes and is replaced by a jovial smile. "I have it all mapped out."

"Good. I'll have a look. I'll then get my people onto your people to get back to you," I wink.

"I look forward to a proper consultation." She wiggles her eyebrows as she cuts into her steak. Cheeky minx.

"I'm sure it'll be very thorough," I add, suggestively. "You'll find we'll have all the resources to make it work."

"I'm sure you do." She runs her tongue across the bottom of her lip, and I groan, feeling my cock thicken.

"Careful, or your interest rates will be through the roof," I grit through my teeth.

"Told you I could get you to lift that apron." She wiggles in her seat in a happy dance. "I win!"

Well, at least there's that smile I've been looking for.

"For now, my little firecracker. We still have four weeks to go, and we know that payback is going to be awesome. Time is going to fly."

Twenty-Seven

"You found him when you were twelve, but if you've changed your mind since, the new bloke better be a decent guy."
Love, Mum

TRINITY

Recently, I've discovered that I have been right about two things. One—my mum did in fact believe that Theo and I belonged together. She saw a stillness, a connection that we didn't see while we were caught within it. Even Theo was oblivious. She thought we were tethered together, and she made it pretty clear that she was thrilled about it. The fondness she felt for him was obviously mutual, with her name tattooed on his back.

The second thing I've discovered is that four weeks is a seriously fucking long time. It hasn't flown past at all. Nope, it has strolled, like the cocky fucker it is. As much as at first I ached from the surgery, once my body felt less like a pincushion, I got my mojo back. With brutal force. Theo, however, has been fine. He's travelled along, like he doesn't have a care in the world. No longing looks, no hugs leading to sex—nothing. When my doctor gave me the all clear, Theo decided he wanted to wait a little longer, just in case.

I continue having showers with him and have resorted to shamelessly pulling all the awkward sexy poses I know, including bending down, once my stomach could handle it. Rubbing soap up and down my legs, I've lathered my skin while looking over my shoulder at him, scrubbing between my toes. I don't think my feet have received so much special treatment—ever. Washing my hair has become a performance, too, as I push my chest out while I shampoo, my little hands moving in big circles to really try and get some type of jiggle going. But nothing. He probably thinks I just liked the smell of soap. There's no way I could act in a daytime TV soap opera. Even the old biddies would think I was doing a crappy job.

If he doesn't hop back on it soon, I am going to break out the vibrator and use it in front of him. My blue bean is about to send out an S.O.S. of the orgasm variety. So, if I'm going to beat it ... he's going to join me. I just need to devise a plan. A plan of mass seduction. If it doesn't work, then all our dilemma could possibly be is that he's suddenly broken his penis and has been too ashamed to tell me.

Theo is my rush. My thrill. If something doesn't happen soon, I am going to jump out of a plane.

I grab my phone and called Trice, eager to brainstorm.

"He-y scee-ds—" her muffled voice answers as I hear an incessant buzzing in my ear.

"What is that noise? Is that your vibrator?" I hold the phone from my face for a moment, and cringe. Everyone is fucking doing it, even while answering the phone.

"H-g on." A gush of water sounds with something being tapped against it. "I was just brushing my teeth. Not using my vibrator, you idiot."

"Sorry, I heard the buzzing ..."

"Why the fuck would I stick it in my mouth?" She laughs. "You alright over there?"

"I have vibrator on the brain. Can't seem to get Theo to have sex with me. We have been given the 'all clear' and everything."

"Oh honey, that would be a killer. He's probably worried he'll hurt you or something."

"I wouldn't mind if he did, I'm that bent up," I whine. I'm two steps away from asking the builders at his father's construction site to make me a Saint Andrew's Cross. I could make the padding. Easily. I could fit it in my spare room. Absolutely.

"Maybe he needs to see that you're okay," she suggests., "Walk around naked or something."

"Done. I went to get clothes from the laundry and it did nothing."

"Shower touching?"

"Nope. Didn't work."

"Did you get a fresh wax?"

"Yesterday, and he didn't pay attention to it." I sigh.

"Fuck. Alex would've jumped me the second my top was off … He's a hard customer. You busy today to keep you distracted at least?"

"Not really, no appointments, but tomorrow is pretty full. Thursdays are usually quiet. I might get some customers in the afternoon, but it's slow in the mornings."

"So you're bored and horny?" she teases. "Your poor bean."

"Shut up biatch. If you were in this position, you'd be clawing the walls."

"Absolutely. I'd tear those bitches down, too." She laughs.

"Ugh," I groan, my skin feeling tight. "I think I'm losing my touch or something."

"Oh, hell no. He looks at you like you're his whole world. You just need to up your game as he's protecting you. Maybe go out and get something cute to wear and some killer heels … Take charge."

"That's it!" I squeal. "You've just given me the best idea."

"What are you going to do?" Her voice pitches, and there's a pause at her end.

"Take charge." I look around the warehouse, and my enthusiasm deflates. "Damn it. I can't leave." My mouth twitches as I shift the phone against my cheek. "Trice …"

"I'll be there in twenty," she says. "I did a pretty good job while you had time off, so I think I can handle an hour or two break."

"An hour, tops."

"I'll chuck a nicer tunic on and come over."

"Thanks so much, honey—"

"Please," she cuts me off. "We all know what you're like minus your fun times. I'm doing this to preserve humanity."

"I'm giving you the finger through the phone," I growl. "He won't know what hit him."

"Go get 'em, tiger. But you can't, until I get there!" She laughs.

"Oh I will," I purr. "Later babe."

We hang up, and I scan the area for any little things I need to do. I have a few more dresses to steam, but I can do that later. I send a quick text to Theo to say that dinner will be here tonight, and he replies, "Great, see you then. Love you."

My heart warms every time he tells me that, as I feel it unequivocally. Excitement builds low in my belly as I roll forward on my toes and back to my heels, doing a quick search on my phone for the store I want. Satisfied when I've found it, I grab my keys and bag and wait for Trice to come.

Later that night, my plan begins to take shape. The mist rises as I rub the lotion into my legs, lathering it up and down, caressing my soft skin. I continue to massage the lotion evenly, taking the time to cover every inch of my skin and leaving my body warm and relaxed. I spritz some perfume on the pulse of my neck and my wrists, and I turn my long hair into a twist at the top of my head to keep it out of my way.

I leave the warmth of the bathroom in a fluffy blue robe, keeping my skin warm as my slippers shuffle along the floor. I bend down and begin to flick on the battery-operated tea candles that I picked up today, and I begin to illuminate the landing leading to my bedroom, while the rest of the warehouse is plunged in darkness. As I reach my bedroom, I turn on soft music and begin to fold down the comforter on my bed, rubbing my hands along the sheet, feeling its softness. I neatly fold it at the bottom of the mattress.

Disrobing, I place my gown on the chair by the window and grab the black piece of satin that I sewed before and tie it to the bedframe's right bolster. Moving to the other side, I tie the other piece of fabric, and then decide to start the party on my own.

Opening my top drawer, I smile at my selection and marvel at a few new purchases that I picked up for future sessions. Tonight is going to run a bit differently, though, with a slice of mischief as well.

I retrieve my new cards and a few other things, place them on the bedside table, and then pull my beloved and under-loved Lelo, which I'd charged earlier, from my drawer.

I turn to my bed and move to the centre, adjusting the pillows to sit comfortably behind my neck. Lying down, I turn the button on, adjust the settings to a gentle hum, and rub it up and down my chest, slowly running around the curve of my breasts. Closing my eyes, my toes begin to curl as the tip traces my nipple and I trail the other with my finger. Running my free hand up and down my chest, I slowly massage my skin, feeling its softness. The peaks of my nipples respond.

I continue to rub down my stomach as my other hand follows, sending soft pulsations to my abdomen. My fingers walk across my skin and down to the apex of my thighs, but they don't touch. Instead, they begin to rub circles across the skin of my thighs, my legs parting as my back arches in response. As one hand massages, the other flicks the switch to increase the vibration speed, circling it across my skin and weaving a tapestry of patterns, as my pulse begins to quicken in need.

One hand squeezes my right thigh as the other teases along the edge of my inner left thigh, getting closer to my vagina. I reach across and grab my lube, uncap it, and squeeze a small amount into my hand. I flick the lid closed and move my hand back down my body, opening and closing it to coat my fingertips in the cold, creamy texture.

Tracing the edges of my vagina in the lube, I run my finger around my needy folds while my other hand moves up my body, tracing the tips of my breasts as the gentle tremors send goosebumps down my skin. My finger circles around my clit, pressing down slightly, and my mouth opens, my feet shifting as one knee moves out to welcome my hand.

I lower the vibrator to my core and adjust the pulsations to move in a beating thrum. Each throb, a tap against my clit, tightens my insides with need. I gasp for more. My Lelo turns and traces the edges of my folds as my other hand rubs my clit in slow circles, pressing with every turn, my breathing deepening as I point my toy to my entrance and push it in slowly. The vivacious rhythm beats against my walls as I press in and draw it out, my knees bending as my back arches.

My tongue runs along the bottom of my lip as I press hard on my clit and plunge my Lelo deeply, my shoulders curving off the bed as I begin to move it in and out, my intake of breath intensifying while my finger flicks my clit back and forth. The movements of both my hands increase, the need so raw that my body hungers to chase it down. I can feel it approaching. I want it.

But my mind is telling me to slow, to wait. I pace my movements and bite my lip in frustration as I remove my Lelo and flatten my fingers across my core, keeping the orgasm from erupting.

"Why did you stop?" Theo's voice breaks through my thoughts, and I open my eyes to find him seated on a chair at the end of the bed, watching me.

"I didn't hear you come in," I pant.

"I know. But don't let me stop you."

"I only meant to play a little, but I got carried away." My voice wavers as my breathing begins to slow.

"Tell me what you want," he demands.

"You."

He bends his head forward, his mouth tightening, as a hard look appears across his face. "Are you sure you're ready to—"

I narrow my eyes and hold my Lelo in the air while staring at him. I flick it to the most intense setting and say, "It's either you or him." I flick the vibrator along my hand to rotate, pointing down. "Strip or watch," I demand.

His eyes darken as he stands, staring at me.

"I'll just ..." I move my hand back to my body, "... keep doing what I'm doing, while you make up your mind."

My other hand glides to my clit as I lower my Lelo to my core, watching his hungry eyes follow my fingers. He tears at the collar of his shirt, pulling his tie off and tossing it on the ground, untucking his shirt from his trousers. He unbuttons his cuffs as I trace my folds, biting my lip, watching him loosen a few top buttons before his hand reaches behind him to pull his shirt off quickly.

"Eager, are we?" I tease, as I dip inside my body, loving the look of need on his face. He frantically kicks his shoes off while his eager hands unfasten his belt and tear off his pants. He kneels on the bed, and I continue to tease myself, my lip pressed between my teeth as I'm so fucking turned on.

"Bedside table," I pant. "Pick a card."

His hand grabs his cock, and he stares at me for a beat before he moves to grab the position cards. He reads the title for a moment and chuckles before pulling the lid off the box and tossing it on the ground. Reaching in, he nabs a card from the deck and smiles. "Lock and load," he says, and flips the card over to show me the picture. "You can stay right there."

"Lock that cock, baby," I tease. "I want you to lock that cock."

"I'm about to." He tosses the deck on the floor and shifts between my legs. Shuffling to my core, he moves my hand and takes hold of the vibrator. "But I just want to play for a bit."

His mouth moves to my entrance and he licks up and down my folds while tracing my clit with my Lelo. *Holy shit.* I squirm under his touch as his tongue plunges inside of me, tasting me, ravishing me.

"I'm close," I pant. "So, so close."

He gives me a final long lick before he shifts to grab my legs and push them upwards, my hands resting at my sides until his thighs reach mine. My ankles rest on either side of his neck, while my knees are bent. He looks down at our bodies to guide his cock inside. His strong arms lean on the bed on either side of my face as he supports his weight and begins to thrust slowly, his cock plunging deeply, every sensation felt and intensified. I grip the back of his thighs to bring him in even farther. I want all of him. Every single inch. I want it as deep as he can go.

"Fill me," I moan, my lips panting as the thrusts quicken. "I want to feel you drip down my thighs."

He leans forward, penetrating me farther, and I smile, watching his face tighten, knowing that he's close as his cock continues to fuck me senseless.

"I'm going to come," he pants as I feel his balls slap against my arse, my core tightening, as I'm close too.

"I need you," I say, the heat surging through my pussy as my orgasm rises and pulsates through my body, my back arching as I scream into the room. His movements are jerky as he comes, his thrusts continuing to send shockwaves through my clit as he shouts with each thrust.

My legs lower down his sides as I feel him pulsate inside me, his face moving closer to mine to capture my lips in a passionate kiss. His tongue thrusts into my mouth as his hips push into me more, and we both relish in the afterglow.

Theo strokes the side of my face and smiles, his kisses moving around my cheeks as he sits up to stare at me. "I love you," he whispers, smiling down at me.

My heart explodes with emotion as I rub his chest. "I love you, too."

We kiss some more before I lift my leg to shift him over, rolling him onto his back, breaking our connection. I kiss him quickly before moving off him. "Stay there, I just need to clean myself up."

He smiles and grabs a tissue from the bedside table, and I rush out to the bathroom, squeezing my legs together. I'm not so keen on having it drip down anymore.

I clean up quickly and redo my tangled hair, letting it hang loosely down my back before I begin the next part of my plan. Behind the door, I grab the garment that I prepared earlier and begin to dress, rolling on my thigh-high tights and unzipping my outfit, while keeping an ear out for any movement.

Looking into the mirror, I apply my deep red lipstick and fasten the lace mask over my eyes. *This is going to be epic.* I grab the rest of my outfit and shoes to hold in my hand as I open the door and check to see if he's out. When the coast is clear, I quickly run on my tippy-toes to the kitchen to grab my last item and a spoon. Slipping on my new and very high stilettos, I walk to my room and march straight in. Theo sits in bed with the covers over his waist, and his head jerks towards the door when he sees me walk in.

"Holy fuck." His voice breaks as he swallows deeply. He straightens in bed, his fingers clutching the sheet as his eyes roam freely over my body. "You look unbelievable, Trin. What's going on?" He smiles, looking at what I am holding in each hand.

"Thank you. I wasn't finished with you." I walk closer to the bedside table to place the contents down slowly before walking around to the other side of the bed. He watches me for a moment as my hand lifts to gesture for his hand. He moves it into mine, tilting his head to stare closer at the satin he noticed in my other hand. "For tonight ..." my voice hardens, commanding him, "you will call me *Mistress.*"

I loop the material around one of his wrists and begin to fasten it, grateful for the time I spent researching knots on the Internet today. I walk around to the other side and tie his other hand, before grabbing my first prop from the table and asking, "Are you ready?"

"Yes, Mistress." He smirks, his eyes darkening as I flick the whip in my hand and smile. Dressed in a black corset, thigh-high tights, and crotchless underwear, I wanted to have some fun while keeping him under control for once.

"If you're a good boy ..." My voice lowers slightly, seduction deliberately hovering in my undertone. I flick my eyes over to the other prop, the jar of Nutella. I continue, "... you might even get a Nutella blow job."

"Whatever you say, *Mistress.*" He squirms under the binds. The covers lift as now he's thickening underneath.

"Right." I flick the whip in my hand. "Let's see how much of a good boy you've been today, shall we?"

I run the tip of the whip up his leg and smile at the way he trembles under my touch. *Oh, this is going to be so good.*

Twenty-Eight

The panel shows Mila and Adam in an embrace, her shoulder on his, her smile beaming. "I've always seen you."
TTE

THEO

Holding a couple of beers and a scotch and coke between my hands, I leave a tip on the bar. Lifting my chin to Robbie before weaving through the crowd, I make my way over to the booth where the rest of the gang are situated. Alex, Ty, Aidan, Trin, and I are here to see Trice and Hazel, alongside their band, performing tonight at the Emerald Vixen. After being absent for more than eight months, they are finally making a comeback. The repairs were done a few months back, and I haven't been back since I inspected the finished product. Robbie's parents have driven down to babysit Gian, so he can be here for support. Now, with a lively crowd, a full house of staff, and entertainment, the Emerald Vixen has been beautifully restored. I'm happy to see that Robbie is being his normal self, back in the bar.

As I bring the drinks back to our booth, the vibrant murmur of the crowd creates a buzz of excitement. The headlining act, the EVs, consists of Hazel, Trice, Maxi, Roni, and Jules—the group that was extremely popular here last year.

I place the beers down on the table and pass Trin the mixer. I shift to sit next to her on the leather bench seat. She moves across slightly, but her mouth pulls in a slight twinge, her movements delicate as she shuffles slowly along the seat.

My mouth moves closer to her face and I whisper, "You okay?"

A secret smile spreads across her lips as she tilts her face towards mine. Our eyes clash. "Definitely. I'm just a little tender from before." She squirms a little in her seat as she turns the bottle in her hand, pretending to pick at the label. "*Someone* was very enthusiastic earlier."

"I'd normally apologise but, you know ..." I raise my eyebrows at her and wiggle them.

"You smug bastard." She smacks me lightly on the arm.

I take a sip of my beer to hide my grin as she laughs next to me. My free hand goes under the table, and I rest it on her thigh, giving her a playful squeeze.

"I had a thought the other day." Ty, Alex and Robbie's mate from high school, reaches for his beer, and he brings it closer to him.

"Only one?" Trin asks innocently as she tilts her head at him. "This is going to be good," she teases.

"I was at Alex's place," he continues, ignoring her jibe. "All those books Trice has on her shelf? I could do that."

"Do what exactly?" Alex leans back in the booth, his arm casually draped along the back, his beer hanging from his fingers.

"I was impressed with all the lady porn on the shelf. You know, I like to think up new porno scenarios, so maybe instead of whacking off, I should write my thoughts down."

Trin jolts beside me, and I turn to find her wiping her chin with her hand from her spilt drink.

Ty takes a sip of his beer, oblivious to the coughing and spluttering happening beside me. "I'd make a killing."

"You're not serious?" Alex shakes his head. "Part of me wants to ask what you'd write about but ... never mind." He chuckles.

"I could write about my experiences, like some *man of the night*." His voice dramatically deepens.

"Manwhore Adventures?" Trin offers. "Or Tales of your Todger?"

"I like that." I nod, clearly impressed. "My girl has a way with words." I rub her knee affectionately.

"I honestly reckon I could do it." He looks around enthusiastically. "I could fill it with all sorts of tales. Like the time I tried pegging. I realised I couldn't take it rough. That'd be a best-seller."

"Dude, a filter. Please," Alex pleads. "Get a motherfucking filter."

"I'm sure it's already been done," Aidan, who used to be Trice's dance partner, adds, tapping the tabletop as he laughs. "But now that you mention it, my mum has a pretty extensive stack of novels that she reads." His face tightens. "I don't want to think about that, anymore." He slumps in his seat. "But give it a crack, pardon the pun." He smiles, and I raise my beer towards him.

"Touché," I say, and we clink glasses.

"Hope the girls are out soon," he says. "I haven't seen much of Jules today."

"Trice mentioned that you went to visit her family, down mid-west," Alex discloses, as he puts his beer on the table.

"Yeah, that was fun ..." Aidan growls. "I got to meet her burly father and three brothers.

The three farmer boys spent most of the weekend asking me to twinkle my toes and shit.

They're stuck in the ice ages, thinking that any man who can dance is a 'poof.'"

"That is bullshit, man." Ty's voice hardens. I look over at him, and his fist curls on top of the table. "My twin came out to me last year, and I was pissed he hadn't done it sooner."

"Sam?" Trin grins. "That's awesome. I know a heap of single men if he's looking for love."

Ty's eyes soften as he grins. "I'll let him know, but he's up in Sydney now, and I think he's seeing someone. It's all hush-hush, though. Still shit that people generalise."

"It doesn't matter," Aidan muses, as he twirls the beer between his fingers. "Turns out the quickest way to emasculate a country boy is to kick his arse in footy."

"That's awesome," Alex muses. Trin grins beside me, tapping my hand with hers.

"They brought out a football after lunch, being all cocky and speaking to me like I was slow or something. But once we started playing, I soon showed them who was fucking boss. Those fat bastards might've been tall, but I was stronger and faster. I showed them who could twinkle their toes."

We begin to laugh, but our laughter is cut short by the dimming of the house lights. The hush of the crowd descends as they wait for the show to start, the only sound that of quiet murmurs here and there.

The stage is dark until a small droplight turns on, pinpointing Hazel sitting on a stool at centre stage, with Maxi sitting on another beside her, holding her acoustic guitar. The two of them smile at each other, and once Hazel nods, Maxi starts to play a different rendition of the song "I Wanna Dance With Somebody," and the room instantly silences.

Hazel's voice summons the attention of the entire audience, and I glance back to find Robbie standing at the bar, admiring his fiancée knocking it out of the park. As the song reaches the chorus, the figures of the rest of the band step into their places. Jules hops on the drums to jump into the song, and she plays an upbeat tempo with Roni beside her. Trice is to the side on the other microphone, singing back-up, and I sense Alex shifting in his seat next to Trin.

"There's my girl," Alex boasts softly. "Fuck." His voice changes into a low growl, laced with possession.

"Easy, now, dude." Trin's voice is laced with humour. "They're only costumes."

"She looks sexy as fuck," his voice lowers.

As their first performance continues, I take a moment to see what has Alex in a spin. My firecracker made some pretty awesome costumes. Trice and Hazel wear tight-fitting emerald corsets. Trin showed me how she'd hand-sewn some black feathers into the cleavage of the bodices, outlining their chests, while also making some shiny short skirts. Even the band is decked out in EV tight-fitted emerald shirts, suspenders, and ties to go with their black pants.

Trin's first goal had been to make Alex unsettled, and it had worked. Alex's jaw remained locked for the rest of the performance, and he glared at any wanker who chose to try to play Russian roulette with his life by ogling Alex's woman. I won't be surprised if he gets up and heads over to the rowdy guys whistling in the front who just started to perve at the girls. Trice is his life, and he protects her as if she were made of glass.

"Where's Lily?" Ty utters, as his voice breaks through the tension that surrounds Alex.

"She has reports to write, so she decided to stay home. Plus, *Richard* doesn't like her coming here as it's an unsavoury establishment, apparently."

"Ugh," Aidan groans. "She still with that douche?"

"Yep," Alex responds. "No idea why. He's a complete and utter fuckwit."

"Sounds like she needs to upgrade," Trin muses. I look at her, and her chin points over to the side of the bar; I turn to see the security guy, Leon.

Alex picks up on Trin's gesture and shakes his head. "He'd eat her alive."

"You say that like it's a bad thing." Trin raises one of her brows at him. "I think you'll find he might be just what she needs."

"If only she'd give him the time of day," Alex concedes.

"Leave it with me," Trin winks. "I'll get the girls on it."

"Go for it." He looks over at Trin, a small smile on his face. "I'm all for anything that makes my big sis happy." A knowing look passes across both of their faces, and I rub Trin's leg in support.

We continue watching the song, and Maxi breaks out into an instrumental. Ty shifts, focusing his full attention on her. Normally his eyes are on the waitresses when we're out, but he's transfixed.

"She's pretty good." He moves his head to the side of the patron walking past to see better. "Totally smashing that riff."

"She is multi-talented," Trin agrees.

We watch the girls blitz through their pieces, each one really packing a punch. Alex leans forward from the bench seat and places his hands on the table. "Did she just wink at me?"

I look at him, and he rubs his chin.

"No idea." Trin's voice wavers with mirth.

"She just did it again." His voice pitches. "Are her hips going crazy, or is it just me?"

"I think she's being a cheeky minx," Aidan laughs. "You've got yourself a handful there, mate."

"You're so alpha, Alex," Trin jokes. "Trice thinks it's hilarious that you get all pent up. And for me, half the fun in making the costumes."

"I bet. She just winked again, the tease." He shakes his head with a knowing smile.

The current song ends, and we applaud as they bow. The house lights come on, and the girls move to take a break out the back for intermission.

"I'm just going to the bathroom," Alex says, and we shuffle along to allow him to get out of the booth. His eyes are transfixed on the stage. He walks towards Trice, but we know he'll be stopping at the door just before it.

"And look—there goes Robbie, while Deacon the bartender is left being the head bar bitch. Everyone avoid going near the dressing rooms." Ty gives Robbie a whistle as he weaves through the crowd, but he ignores it.

"Yep." Trin holds up her drink, about to take another sip. "Last time I strolled in there, I copped an eyeful of Robbie's arse. They lock the door now." She shudders, and I'm surprised we can't feel the walls shatter, thanks to what's going on in there right now.

A short time later, while ordering more drinks, Robbie returns with a lovesick expression on his face. I give him a knowing look, and he shrugs, without a care in the world. Unlike Alex and his constant pissing contests over Trice, Robbie is hardly possessive at all. Instead of threatening the nearest guys with a court martial for staring at his fiancée, he'll choose to wink at her or raise a glass, thrilled that it is *his* woman on stage, wowing the crowd. He doesn't give a flying fuck who is watching because *he* gets to take her home. If anything, it is visual foreplay for them both. Robbie's messy hair and a smile the size of a planet are dead giveaways of their backstage activities.

I nod at Robbie and return to the booth just as the lights descend for the second act. Trin snuggles into me with her hand on my leg, her head against my shoulder, as we both watch the stage. This time, Trice is seated at the piano alone, and she begins to play an instrumental version of "Colours of the Wind." The music affects me more than I'd expected. I shift in my seat, and Trin moves her head to look at me.

"Do you miss playing?" she asks, loud enough for only me to hear.

"I shouldn't"—I look down—"given how I was taught. But I can still appreciate beautiful playing. Just weird to feel a loss for it."

"It's not weird; you would've loved playing at some stage. Some part of you wanted to be a pianist. Just sad that the joy you're supposed to have was taken away from you."

"I could never measure up to his standards, though."

She shifts next to me to sit up more and grabs my face. "You are not defined by his expectations, which were unrealistic. You are defined by yours. Never forget that. If you want to play again someday, then play. I'd love to hear something on a rainy Sunday or a Friday evening ... anything. It doesn't matter."

I rub my nose against hers, admiring how the soft glow from the stage light touches her face. I marvel at how this beautiful, strong woman is finally mine. "Thank you, my little firecracker. I needed to hear that."

"Now, all I have to do is convince you to jump out of a plane, and we're set."

"That I won't do ... and before you ask, not base jumping either."

She laughs, and we turn to the stage, my arm around her shoulders, holding her close as we watch the EVs perform. A year ago, we could barely sit near each other without teasing, wanting a reaction to get contact. Now, I can hold her all I want. And I'll do just that.

Epilogue

"I might not be there with you, but know that wherever you go, you carry me in your heart, just as I carried you in mine.
"Your next adventure is around the corner. So, what are you waiting for? Live it!"
Mum

TRINITY
Six months later

My **Converse scamper across the brick-covered laneway as** my heart picks up speed. This feeling usually intensifies the closer I get to my destination, but this time, my heartbeat is even more forceful, like an erratic drum, eager and impatient. I quicken my pace as my hips twist to weave between the crowds gathered around. *Maybe I need one of those yuppie scooters with a drink holder; I'd zip past these peeps in no time.*

I just had my last appointment for the day, which happened to be Brit. The fitting went well, though I still kept my guard up. It is a hard habit to break, but I am working on it.

My hand clutches my side strap as it awkwardly flaps against my hip, the movement causing me to pull it against my neck. My toe catches in an uneven part of the path, and I almost trip, panicking slightly as I worry about the precious goods that I'm carrying.

I round the corner to find Theo standing by the entrance, his hand in his suit pocket as he talks on his phone. Dressed in a suit, he is sex personified—mysterious, gorgeous, and with those green eyes contrasting with his suit. He turns at the sound of my little wolf whistle and smiles, quickly disconnecting his call to come to me. *He can wear that suit all day, every day, but I want the tie.*

"Hey," he greets me with open arms, welcoming me in his embrace. I go eagerly, wrapping my hands around his waist and raising my lips to his.

"Hey, hottie." I smile as his lips meet mine. We kiss softly on the footpath for a moment as my pulse flickers like a dragonfly. I pull away as the excitement causes me to move from one foot to the other. "You ready? Let's go!"

He steps back and looks at my shirt, and smiles. I have his latest design, *Shatter Till I Fall*, which I had specially ordered to read "I'm with Adam" on the back under Theo's social media links. I'd wanted "I inspired your comic porn addiction," but he hadn't let me. Killjoy.

He takes my hand, and we head towards the stairs. I swing his arm, turning to look up at his building. Since I found out that he was my TTE, I've taken pleasure in looking up at him when I visit to collect my own edition of the comic. He doesn't like me paying for the novels, but I'm not going to let him pay for it. I am too used to my monthly tradition of coming here, and now that I know it is Theo's, I feel proud to go into the comic store and see his work there. Bragging rights are at an all-time high. Today is the first time he is coming to experience it with me.

"How's work?" I look to his face and smile, trying to stow my excitement a little to hear about his day.

"Not too busy today, as we're just finishing up a few quotes. Cole is a bit chirpier, too." He stops at the stairs and looks up at the building. "Letty still pretends to be annoyed at him, but I know she's not."

"I guess you would have experience with broody females," I tease, squeezing his hand.

"Fuck dating tame ones; I like to live on the edge."

I take a step closer to the store's entrance and tug his hand. "Let's go live on the wild side, *mi amor.*" I bat my eyelashes and smile sweetly, remembering the many times I've used that phrase with him.

"Right behind you, *florecita.*" His voice warms my insides, triggering the butterflies in my stomach to take flight. The informal Spanish lessons he's had with Ricardo over coffee or a family dinner are going great. Sometimes I join them, but mostly I want him to have that special time to himself. Theo has learnt a few phrases and can work out bits and pieces, but the first time he called me a *little flower* was swoon-worthy. When he puts on that delicious accent, it's like he is sending a tap straight to my clit. It is a wonder we resurfaced from home as he often tries it on me. *Don't think about that now.*

We walk hand in hand down the stairs, and I restrain myself from quickly dragging him, as I am eager to see the latest edition. I've been patient each month, not asking him about the storyline, and just waiting. It takes everything not to slip it into conversation, or when he works in his study not to offer to make another cup of coffee or give him a blow job for a panel. We still joke about the happily-ever-after that I'd sketched, which had Adam on one knee, shouting, "MILA, YOU ARE ALWAYS RIGHT." I had been being a mega smart arse. Nothing new.

We reach the landing and smile at each other briefly before we stroll over to his section. I become more eager with each step. As the shelf with Theo's novels comes into view, I squeeze his hand excitedly and let go of it to move forward and retrieve his latest copy. I rub my hand over it in fascination, the tree of life no longer dull and raw. Instead, the heart within is vibrant and the branches are in bloom. Just like how I am feeling these days.

I walk to the register and am about to pay, but Theo stops me. "I hate you paying for this." He frowns as he grabs his wallet.

"Just let me. I won't allow you to," I say, pushing down his wallet. "It's part of the tradition." I wink and pull out my note when the cashier pipes up.

"Dude, be lucky you can even touch that thing. She's protective over it." He laughs.

"Damn straight I am." I nod and pay, ignoring Theo's grumbling next to me about "more orgasms" or something. Not like I'd complain about that. My bean will be more than happy.

I clutch his novel in my hands and go to move when I feel a hole in the plastic behind it. "Oh no," I whine as I turn it over in my hands, "It's ripped."

"Oh shit," Theo says, "but maybe it's not damaged. Peel it off and take a look."

"Yeah, if it is, I'll give you a new one," the clerk says, and I nod, too shaken to respond. I've become such a precious idiot over these, but now knowing they are Theo's, I have to make even more sure they are okay. Peeling off the plastic carefully, I place it on the counter and turn the comic around in my hands, not noticing any damage.

"I think it's okay." My eyes carefully zoom over the edges.

"Take a look inside," Theo urges. "We don't want to get home and find a page was damaged or something."

Without blinking, I press my thumb across the pages and flip each one, carefully looking at every page while trying not to absorb any of the beautiful story that I'm getting glimpses of. But it's useless. I'm in the sweetest torture, being tempted to fall into my usual habit of just sitting down on the floor and reading. I can only be tempted by so much.

As I turn the final page, I sigh. I can't help it. "Okay." I resign myself to just one peek. "I need to see if you've written me a secret note, and that's it. I'll even cover the page with ... this." I grab a pamphlet from the desk and unfold it quickly.

"You can do whatever you like." Theo rubs my cheek. "It's your novel."

His eyes sparkle, and I watch him for a second as his smirk twitches. *That's strange.* Shaking it off, I slip the pamphlet into the back and open the page fully, sliding it up slightly to only see the edging of the panel. As the store is dimly lit, I walk closer to the droplight near the counter and search for a message. My eyes spot it straight away, and I laugh.

Stop looking for a message when all I want to say is written on this page.

"What?" My head darts up to look at Theo. He doesn't say anything, but he gently tugs at the pamphlet to loosen it from the page, uncovering a series of panels. "But I don't want to read anything just yet." I poke my bottom lip out.

He taps my lip playfully and says, "Just this once?" Tilting his head, he gives me puppy eyes. "For me?"

I narrow my eyes at him but smile, as I secretly want to read some. I start in the corner and see two young people sitting side by side at a table, looking at each other, with a caption above them saying, *It all started here.* My breath catches as I notice the familiar pincushion in the boy's hand. *Aw, it's us!*

I look over to the next panel to find the characters older and in an art class, their beaming faces closer together, sharing earphones. The caption above says, *I tolerated your music to be close to you.*

"You secretly loved it. Venga Boys all the way, baby!" I nudge him in the side with my elbow.

I chuckle as the panels continue, showing different moments of us from teenagers through to adulthood. As the drawings progress, the mood transforms from childhood innocence to adult understanding. A series of moments are flickered together, showing us staring at each other in our costumes at my housewarming party, and then us riding on the back of his bike. Each drawing grows in intensity. Even our argument is depicted with the splatters of reds and blacks that highlight how broken we felt, followed by us standing by a wall, reunited. I reach the second-to-last one of us, which has us facing each other, with the caption, *Now, you see me.* Shivers tickle behind my shoulders, and I squirm. I feel like my heart is about to overflow. My cheeks feel damp as small, unexpected tears trail down my face. I look up to see him smiling at me.

"You still have one more panel." Theo gestures to the one that my hand is covering unintentionally. I take a deep breath, pull my fingers away, and gasp. *Holy moly.* The panel shows me standing on the mountain with the sun behind me, and Theo kneeling at my feet, a ring box in his hand. The caption reads, *Trinity, will you be my forever, not just in here but in real life?*

"Oh, Theo." My hand clutches my collar, and I turn to face him, but he's no longer standing beside me. Instead, he's kneeling, just like he is in the drawing, holding a ring box open to me. My fingers touch the box as he clears his throat.

"What do you say? Will you marry me?" His eyes hold unshed tears, and I shriek.

"Yes! Of course I will." My eyes sting as I sniff, trying to hold the tears at bay as his sentiment fills my chest with love.

"Suppose I better give you this, then?" He stands and takes the ring from the box and slides it onto my finger. I stare at it for a moment, my hand shaking as I gaze at it, dumbfounded. It's beautiful. Spectacular and so me. A round amethyst sits in the middle of a white-gold band with a diamond on either side.

"This is so me, with a splash of colour." My voice trembles.

"It's like I knew." Theo smirks as he touches my hair, the newly dyed deep purple ends and chocolate base colour rubbing between his fingertips. My eyes connect with his, and his smile becomes slightly strained as a lone tear cascades down his face, causing my tears to fall again, my jubilant smile trembling from all the joy. Stepping forward, I reach my hands up to his face.

"It's beautiful. I love you." I bring his lips closer to mine, and his breath shudders.

"You're my forever girl," he says, before kissing me. Our lips tremble at first, until I wrap my arms around his shoulders and kiss him as hard as I can, trying not to cry.

An instant eruption of applause from the customers in the store surrounds us, making us stop abruptly. I quickly turn from him to see all the smiling faces, and I wink before yelling, "My fiancé writes the best happily-ever-afters EVER!"

Theo chuckles next to me, before saying, "But living it will be even better," then pulling me back for another kiss that I don't stop until we're ready to.

Later that evening, once we arrive at the restaurant, the nervous energy trickles down my spine. I spent some time this afternoon calling my dad and the girls, who were all beyond thrilled. They weren't able to make the opening tonight, as Robbie's working while Hazel's parents and Trice is teaching her dance classes, but we've scheduled some girl time before their performance tomorrow night. Theo has stolen the limelight today, but there is a part of me that will shine a bit brighter tonight. For him.

My dress is a fitted black peplum dress, with a lace overlay that covers my back. I went to my favourite fabric shop to source the right lace, as tonight is a special occasion. The ends of my hair are curled, and my makeup a little bolder than usual, with my deep red lipstick that pops. My chandelier earrings sparkle under the lights, and my legs look like they go for days with my new stilettos. Theo wears a black suit, with a black shirt that he's teamed with a deep purple tie. I've even put my hand against it, and the stone matched. Him and his secret plans. It is my turn sometime soon. Just have to find the right moment.

As we enter through the glass doors, Theo's eyes drift down to my ring as we smile secretly, knowing that his family will all be here.

Looking around, my eyes are drawn to everything. The restaurant is abuzz with staff serving at tables and the bar, while the chatter of patrons is heard. A piano plays in the distance, and I take a farther step in.

"Whoa," I gasp, as my heels click across the deep hardwood floor. To my left, there is a lengthy mahogany bar that shines under the droplights. What floors me, though, is instead of shelves for bottles, the wall itself is a dark metal grey with cutout holes that each contains a bottle that is lying down. Two metal ladders run on a horizontal rail on little wheels that can be pulled out to climb and pushed in to store. That is freaking cool.

"Spirits are under the bar." Theo's lips are near my face, and I nod before turning to check out the rest of the place. A grand chandelier hangs from the centre of the room while other droplights illuminate the area. The restaurant itself is lined with grey tablecloths, classic silverware, and crystal wine glasses. Theo's finger rises, pointing to the back. "The kitchen is located over there, but we won't go into it tonight as they'll be stress heads." He waves his arm across to the other side of the room. "Bathrooms are down there, and over here is my side project that you saw me start that day."

"Oh, when I stripped you?" I tease

"Yes, in front of my dad, too. Cheers for that."

"Anytime." I wink.

His hand lowers on my back as he leads me over to the brick wall that has been completely transformed. The wall has been divided into sections with hand-painted portraits of dancing couples. Each section holds a different pose and costume, but the figures are all different. Even the detail to their hands is realistic. I remember learning in art class how hard the hands are to draw, and Theo has made it look easy.

"They look like they're bursting out of the brick." I step forward and look at the black and red dress at the end, and my mouth drops open. "Is that Elly?"

"Sure is."

Walking closer, I see Elly looking over her shoulder, her back bare in a deep plunge, wearing a long black dress with frilled trim and red ribbon running along the edges. A man in black pants and a tight black shirt is positioned against her, with one arm above her and the other to the side.

"Is that Aidan?"

"Yeah, he's the partner in all of them. All the girls are different."

"Trice would've loved to have been chosen to be part of this."

"She did," Theo says, and I gasp, watching his finger point along the wall as he continues, "Here is Anastasia, Trice, and Hazel."

I gaze at all their portraits in wonder at the intricate detail of their faces and body shapes. I turn slightly. The figures continue down to the other wall that leads back to the entrance, and I chuckle at how I did not notice them before. *My friends are here!*

"This is incredible." I grab Theo's arm. "They look real."

"He's done a great job." Ricardo 's voice sounds behind us, and I turn to find him, Aria, and Theo's sisters, who are dressed in traditional Spanish dresses.

"I thought the dancing was going to be on Thursday nights."

"Yes, but we wanted to look the part tonight," Anastasia responds, holding her dress out slightly. "Plus, it's fun to dress up now and then."

"It sure is." I beam at her, as most of her legs are showing under the various frills at the hem. "Nice pins." I wink and watch her face deepen in a crimson blush. She's just adorable, and her shyness reminds me of Theo at that age. I was blind to have missed it at the start. I push my hair behind my shoulder and hear a gasp.

"No way!" Elly marches forward and yanks on my hand before turning to Theo. "Are you engaged?"

Anastasia races forward excitedly, and they both examine my hand as I wiggle my fingers under their faces.

"He proposed this afternoon, and even wrote it in his novel!" I boast proudly.

"Oh, so that's why you didn't want me to read it until tomorrow." Anastasia points at her brother. "You sneaky, sneaky man."

Aria and Ricardo come closer, with grand smiles on their faces, and Ricardo takes Theo's shoulder and pulls him into a hug. I hear muffled words of congratulations.

Aria holds my hand for a moment before leaning in to give me a cuddle. "So happy for you," she beams, "Perfect match."

I squeeze her back, knowing that as corny as it sounds, she is totally right.

We spend the evening enjoying the company of Theo's family. The tiny similarities that he has with his father do not escape me, especially when Theo listens to people speak. His mouth quirks in the same way and his eyes brighten when he is happy or excited, just like Ricardo's. Even the girls look similar in their characteristics with Theo. There is a gentle ease to him now. Theo knows he belongs, is welcome, and can be relaxed with them while being himself. His strain with using emotion has loosened, making him more carefree to give and receive affection, not just with me, but with everyone here.

Once dessert is served, Theo excuses himself to go to the bathroom, and I chat with Aria about her next fitting, as I have been making her a dress for an annual fundraiser that she organises. As we chat, her eyes run along my body a few times, and I glance down to see what she is looking at.

"You've got the glow." She beams as she looks at me.

"Oh, I think it's just the wine." I pretend to touch my face, knowing that my skin still feels the same.

"You haven't touched any wine tonight." Her brow raises.

My eyes dart to the side as I nervously bite my lip and shrug. She leans in to speak, but her gaze darts over my shoulder, where she indicates for me to turn around.

Across the room, where the band will eventually play, is a piano. Right now, seated at the piano is Theo. *My fiancé.*

We make eye contact, and his shoulders move as he takes a deep breath. I don't want his tortured gaze to return, so I nod enthusiastically and smile, hoping that my proud expression is encouraging him. His arms shift as he raises his hands to the keys and begins to play. I expect him to play a classical music piece, but, instead, the opening chords of "What A Wonderful World" play. My eyes brim with tears, remembering how much my mother loved playing Eva Cassidy at home and how even though this was her funeral song, it does not remind me of her death. It reminds me of her vibrant life and the beautiful letters she's left for me. I smile, remembering an envelope entitled, *So you're getting married,* and my hips wiggle with excitement.

I watch the man I love serenade me using his darkest fear. Using the love we share to give him the confidence to make it his grandest performance. All his exams are nothing compared to this. A cleansing. A rebirth into the man he is now. I watch the man I love play with such beauty that I am compelled to rise from my seat. And I do. Without taking my eyes off him, I weave between the patrons and staff, dodging the children that run around, all to get to him. To be with him. And he plays with such pride that I feel my chest will burst. I move around the piano and place my hand on his back, marvelling that there is no tension there, just loose muscles under my touch. I begin humming the lyrics while I stand behind him, the heat of his back that warms beneath my fingers.

When the final chords play, a polite clap from the restaurant is heard, but I take no notice of it. Theo turns to face me and draws me into his body, his head sitting against my chest as I stroke the back of his head and neck, curling my fingers into the ends of his hair. "I want to hear you again and again."

"Then you shall." He cuddles into me.

"You going to teach our children how to play one day?"

"Yes." He shifts his head against me. "But I will make it fun. Fill our house with music, and they can choose to learn it if they want."

"So, I guess our place is going to be a bit noisy in about seven months then," I continue to stroke his hair.

I bite my lip when he jerks under my touch. His hands grip my hips as he leans back and stares straight up at me. "We're having a baby?"

"Yes." I touch his face, watching as his eyes brighten with awe.

"How far are you?" His hand moves to my belly, warming my stomach.

I shift his fingers lower. "Bub is there. I'm eight weeks. Kind of explains why I was feeling off a few weeks ago."

He watches his hand as he rubs gentle circles around my stomach. "So this is what it feels like," he murmurs.

"What, honey?" I run my fingers around his ears and across his cheek.

"To be loved before even being born. The feeling my mother wanted so desperately." His lips kiss my belly, and my tears threaten to fall as he whispers, "I feel what she did." Looking up at me, his eyes widen as he says earnestly, "I'm so glad she fought for me."

"Me too, my love." I sniff as the tears tumble, no longer able to keep them at bay. "Amaya fought with everything she had, just like my mum."

His head tilts to my tummy as he speaks. "You are loved, baby. You are so unbelievably loved." He gives my belly one more kiss before standing and taking my face in his. "You, my fiancée, are my heart and my soul. You are my tree of life."

I gasp as his strong hands wrap around us, his lips meeting mine in a passionate and reverent kiss.

My mother was right about him. Not only is she carried in my heart, but our children will go on to carry her in theirs, just as they will Amaya. My heart soars with a stronger charge of adrenaline than any stunt or ride I've had in the past. I'm here, with the man that I love and our child. Our future is going to be full of adventure. There will be no greater high than with them.

Acknowledgements

It astonishes me that I'm here once again, yet I'm thrilled to be. I am so incredibly grateful for this journey and especially for the support from family and friends who have stuck beside me. I owe a lot to these wonderful people, and like always, I apologise if I have forgotten anyone.

Firstly, **my husband** for his endless support, encouragement and his colossal fear of reading one of my many naughty scenes. That fear is a keen motivator to take it up a notch. Thank you for distracting our kids with endless Netflix shows and catering to my chocolate needs. I love you to the moon and back.

To our adorable **munchkins** who remind me everyday that dreams can happen. Strive for your own dreams and soar. Also, don't read mamma's novels until you're at least 16. I mean, 27.

To my **parents** and **siblings** for your support and encouragement while I chatted about plot twists and scenes that you pretended to be interested in.

To my amazing editor **Lauren McKellar**, who continues to push me to become a better writer and encouraging me to be the best that I can possibly be. You're awesome! Editing is not so painful with your cute little comments.

To **Hang Le** for understanding my characters for who they are and representing them in yet another stunning cover. I am mystified by your ability. Thank you for adjusting to my needs and being so incredibly nice about my constant changes. I can't wait to see what my future covers will be like with you.

To **Max Henry** for your fabulous formatting. Thank you for making Fractures look pretty schmick.

To **Faye Gemmellaro** for being an incredible proofer. Thank you for your friendship and your support has been a breath of fresh air along this journey. I look forward to the day we meet to give you that huge hug, I've been promising.

To **Tamara Roach** for joining me on my beta team. Our chats about scene positioning, character development and our friendship has meant the world to me during this process. Thank you for kicking me up the butt when I needed it and supporting me. You're awesome!

To **Junis Cariello** for your wisdom, insight and critique in the development of Trin and Theo. Thank you for making me give Theo the grit he needed to face off against Trin. You are a beautiful, sweet and kind friend.

To **Karen Mandeville-Steer** for reading over sections of my novel and telling me to 'get on with it' when I needed to. This was a crappy year for our family and I'm so glad that you pushed me to keep going when life itself tried to get in the way. Thank you for your friendship, chickie.

Eva Lenoir, you are an amazing writer and friend. I'm so glad we stumbled across each other and I can't wait to see where the future will bring us. Thank you for your critique with Fractures. I look forward to future projects with you.

Krissy Reid, Ebony Markham, Deon Blaby, Rebecca Paget, Stacey Lawn, Maree Jones, Eddie Nielsen, Malisa Rodriguez, Rose H, Jennifer Grieger, Joseph Mascaro and **Irene Reed** for helping me write the intricacies necessary to bring Fractures to life. From Theo's identity, the structure of his apartment, to the ways in which a bridal gown is made; you all helped my characters be as authentic as possible.

I would like to extend my sincere appreciation for **Shameless Book Club's *Dear Mistress*** for her delectable intuition with the dynamics of Theo and Trinity's relationship. They lit up the page, all thanks to you.

To **Penny Rudge, Angela Palamara, Julie Hartnett, Lila Rose, Lisa Sleiman, Tania Cooper, Bex Williams** and **Sarah Burns**, thank you for your support throughout the year. This author world can be a tough place, and I'm glad I have you guys here with me. I love your faces. Bring on cocktails soon!

Thank you to **Kylie McDermott** and **Give Me Books** for yet again, another awesome release week. Thank you so much for helping to launch my book baby to the world. You rock!

Special mention to the countless bloggers, authors, family, friends and fans who shared my blitz and wrote reviews. Thank you doesn't seem enough. You rock my world, repeatedly.

A special shout out to the members of my reader group. *Left of Field*. Bring on the wine and pics of BT. All day. Everyday. Thanks for your encouragement and I look forward to future shenanigans with you.

About the Author

M R Field is an author from Rural Victoria and has completed a Bachelor's degree with Honours from Latrobe University, Melbourne.

After growing up with the river at her front door, she returned back to her hometown after many years of living in the city. She now lives a tranquil lifestyle with her husband and two young children.

M R Field has always held a love for writing, filling journals as a child which progressed to more eloquent pieces as an adult.

After ten years of creative instruction, she decided to turn these ideas into manuscripts. She adores creating new story lines and is a big fan of a happily ever after, but believes strongly in making her characters work for it.

She loves to hear from readers, you can find her online at:

Bookbub:
www.bookbub.com/authors/m-r-field

Website:
www.mrfieldauthor.com

Twitter:
https://twitter.com/Mezmfield

Pinterest:
www.pinterest.com/mrfield80/

(Continued over page.)

www.ingramcontent.com/pod-product-compliance
Lightning Source LLC
Chambersburg PA
CBHW060950030726
47503CB00003B/814